CW01622276

ELEVEN DAYS

by Malcolm Havard

PRELUDE

FRANCE
NOVEMBER 1916

It was obvious we were in trouble when the other chaps started to pull away from us.

At first the motor just wouldn't give full revs, then it coughed, and missed, popping and banging like a wet log on a fire. Whether it was dirty petrol, that we'd been hit or it was just a dud I don't know and, to be honest, it didn't matter. All that mattered was it was failing.

Brown was doing what a good observer should – which was why I had chosen him – scanning the sky in the direction I could not see, behind, kneeling on his seat facing me and looking back over me and the engine, so I got to see his fear. Muffled as he was against the frigid November afternoon, I could see it in his eyes, I knew what he was thinking: we were as good as dead.

Time was when a lone FE was fine, even a lame duck like ours. In the Summer, we had been birds of prey, not eagles perhaps, we were too big and slow, but maybe a lessor raptor like a buzzard, with talons and beaks that could bloody the crows that flew against us. Now though, there are hawks: faster, more nimble, deadly. They may be called Albatros but hawks they are nonetheless. They are not solitary birds either, they hunt in flocks.

Suddenly the sky was no longer a safe haven. It was threatening.

We welcomed the towering cloud castles on the way in. They may have soaked the poor infantry beneath, whether they be grey, khaki or blue, but they gave us cover to sneak around as we crossed the lines on the way to our target. Now the Gods of weather showed their fickleness; the clouds both hid our plight from our comrades and offered our hunters perfect cover for stalking and ambush.

The misfire grew worse. I believe both Brown and I were praying to God and Beardmore to keep it running and us safe. I do not believe our prayers to either maker were heard. We were still some miles from the line when Brown yelled, his words lost in the gale, the whistle of wind through the wires and the death rattle of the motor but I did not need to hear, I knew. I put the nose down, sacrificing height for speed as Brown stood to grasp the rear gun, his feet just below the coming of the cockpit, his gauntlets grasping the spade grip, his thumbs over the trigger.

I glanced over my shoulder. It was worse than I thought. A gaggle of them; the leader, pennants streaming from his interplane struts, ahead of the rest, firing.

Brown fired too, half a drum. He's a good sort, Brown, he didn't flinch as the first burst from the Spandaus hit us, ripping through the centre section, splintering a cabane strut and puncturing the radiator.

The Hun was a good shot, his next burst hit me in the boot. It was like being struck by a sledgehammer, my whole leg went numb and I must have involuntarily kicked the rudder bar or pulled the stick back because suddenly we were spinning. I don't know how Brown stuck with us but hold on he did. It took a huge effort to get out of it, to straighten up, using my good foot to work both sides of the rudder bar and head back to the lines. We had lost so much of our precious height that we were down in rifle range and the chatter of machine guns told me we had not lost our pursuer; he had clearly followed us down to make sure of his kill.

Perhaps he was overconfident, perhaps he misjudged our speed, thought that Brown was out of the fight. Whatever, as we crossed the German front line, his last attack, the one that finally stopped our engine, took him past us in a skidding bank.

Time seemed to slow. For a moment he just hung in the air so I could admire the Albatros's sleek lines, shark like, ruthless and efficient. It was such a soft, honey blonde colour though, the finish of the fabric-covered wings contrasting with the smooth ply of the body. I saw the pilot, the setting sun glinting on his goggles, the brown leather of his flying helmet and his coat; a silk scarf, yellow, streaming in the airflow.

Then Brown gave him the other half of the drum. The honey fuselage was suddenly streaked black with oil and the Albatross nose dropped. I knew we had got him just as I knew, we too were down as part of our top wing folded up.

We seemed to hit the ground almost immediately. I had not realised how low we were. We had a fair bit of speed so it must have been a spectacular prang to watch. In a cacophony of splinters and cracks we shed wheels and wings and prop in a shower of mud and stones. I saw Brown leave the ship without permission which I thought was dash bad form but then we vaulted one shell hole before splashing down in the next.

And then things went blank for a while.

I woke in pain with a soundtrack of machine guns and mortar rounds. Someone was fiddling with my shot up ankle which smarted somewhat.

'Get off, Brown. What do you think you're doing man?' I said, kicking him away.

But it was not Brown. The man who had taken off my flying boot and was gingerly peeling down my blood soaked sock was tall, blonde and familiar. He glanced up and smiled at me.

'Percy,' he said. 'I seem to have made a bit of a mess of your leg.'

I looked down at the bloody wreckage and had to agree with him.

'So you have, Siggi.'

'But then you did shoot me down,' he said, taking off his lemon coloured silk scarf and binding my ankle and foot. 'Or rather your man there did.' He nodded over to the other side of the shell hole. For the first time I saw that Brown was huddled there, glowering at Siggi and clutching the bayonet he always carried with him for occasions just like this. There looked to be something odd about the way he was lying which Siggi confirmed.

'Both of his legs are broken. I dragged him here but he woke up and then he would not let me touch him.'

'He's a bloody Hun, sir. A bloody filthy Hun.'

I sighed. 'Brown, I was at school with Siggi. I've known him most of my life.'

Brown looked shocked.

'But he's the enemy, Sir. '

'Only temporarily, Brown, only temporarily,' I said. 'In fact, Siggi here is actually family. Please let me introduce Siegfried Otto von Leitner, my brother-in-law. Siggi this is Sergeant Brown.'

'Pleasure. Oh yes, Alice asked to be remembered to you if I saw you,' said Siggi. 'Though I never expected that I would.'

He held his hand out to Brown who shrank away whilst looking at me with some degree of suspicion. 'I'm not shaking hands with a Boche,' he muttered.

'Don't be silly, man,' I said. 'And let Siggi look at you. He's a doctor.'

'No, that is not accurate,' said Siggi in his precise way. 'I would have qualified if this present affair had not started. But I am the best there is here, old chap, so please let me look at you.'

Old chap, I thought. Germans educated in our system often turn out more English than we do and Siggi is a case in point. Whatever, Brown relented and let him tend to him. For all his limitations he's a stout-hearted soul because his legs were in a hell of a state but he suffered our ministrations in silence. Siggi splinted his legs with some spruce from the wreck of the FE that I had crawled across to and retrieved. He did his best to keep Brown's spirits up, but I could tell from Siggi's face that all was not well.

'He will do for now, but we need to get him some proper medical attention,' he murmured to me so Brown could not hear.

'It will be dark soon,' I replied, edging my head cautiously above the rim of the shell hole. Both our boys and the Boche had shelled the wrecks of our kites but in a rather half-hearted way. The Somme campaign had been long, both sides were exhausted and no one seemed to have any enthusiasm for such things. Whatever, things had now quietened down somewhat.

'We are nearest to your lines,' I observed.

Siggi nodded. 'I know. It would not be proper though. There are two of you and just one of me. It would not be fair to have you both become prisoners.'

I knew what he meant. I was in no state to get Brown back on my own, what with my game leg, and yet I could not allow Siggi to take him into captivity, whatever the reason, whilst I made for the British lines. It was just not honourable. But it was also not honourable for Siggi to take advantage of our wounds. "Play up and play the game", that was what he had been taught. As I said, Siggi was more British than the British.

So, without further discussion it was decided. Once it was properly dark, we headed west, for the British lines, dragging poor Brown between us.

It was a foul night. The clouds had gathered whilst we waited and dumped their contents on us, soaking us and chilling us further. Still the rain had the benefit of discouraging the snipers, hiding us from view. It also had the blessing of hiding the worst of the nightmares we crawled through. The stench, and the squealing of the fat rats whose eyes showed red in the occasional brilliant white lights of flares sent up into the night, told their own tale of what surrounded us. The classic image of Hell is of somewhere rather hotter, but nothing can persuade me that this was not the very mouth of Hades itself. The pain of my own wound was almost unbearable, so how Brown stoically endured our ordeal with barely a groan said much about the man's character. I pitied us but I pitied the poor bloody infantry who had to endure this day after day far more.

To some war is a noble enterprise made up of a series of individual gallant actions. Those of us who have experienced it, however, know that war merely provides the rationale for inexplicable acts of unspeakable cruelty, that the perpetrators must live with for the remainder of their lives. Fundamentally, we were all the same: German, French, British, Australian, whatever, Siggi reminded me only too well of that fact. We were all brothers, yet we were made to kill each other because our countries, our duty, said that we must.

Duty comes before humanity. If it didn't this would all stop. It was Siggi who was out of step with the world. We were not yet ready to be human again. The evidence of that fact was all around us, we experienced it every day.

Duty comes first. That was my conclusion.

With the necessity of halting frequently so as not to attract attention when no-man's-land was illuminated, it took us over an hour to reach the edge of the British wire by which time Brown was largely insensible. Siggi indicated to me that we should retreat a little way, back to the nearest cover. I knew what he was going to say.

'This is as far as I can go,' he said. 'I have no desire either to spend the rest of the war in a camp nor to view the detailed disposition of the British wire and front line. You and your man will now be able to get help. I hope you understand?'

'I do Siggi. Thank you,' I said. Reaching out into the darkness I grasped his hand. For a moment we were boys again, sharing in the triumph of the first eleven, comrades; brothers. With my left hand I took out my service revolver.

The shot alerted the sentries as to our presence but it still took some effort on my part to convince the Tommies as to our bonafides and still more that we needed them to come and get us. I could not blame them, for the report had also stirred up a hornet's nest amongst the Jerries who loosed off a volley of rounds as well as lobbing over trench mortars, though none fell really close to us.

The CO of the party that came for us saw the body in the light of a distant flare. It lay on its back, eyes open with its fair hair plastered over its forehead, partly covering the neat red hole from which a trickle of blood ran.

I could see that there were powder burns around the wound.

'Who's that?' said the CO.

'Oh just some filthy Hun,' I said without a backwards glance.

PART ONE

CHAPTER ONE

England, Monday 8th January, 1917

'Netheravon.'

Second Lieutenant Edward Greville had been dozing so, for a moment, he was not sure whether he had really heard the conductor's call or just imagined it. The train had certainly stopped but none of his travelling companions had made any sort of move to leave, indeed all of them seemed to be sleeping, hardly surprising given how early it was.

Eddie leant across the vicar sat next to him and rubbed the condensation from the carriage window. Outside he could see that it was misty, and it took him some time to make out the station name. He had just decided that it was indeed Netheravon when he heard the Station Master whistle and call 'All aboard.'

He tumbled onto the platform from the moving train whilst still apologising to his companions, having stood on the foot of the vicar, and jabbed the lady opposite with the corner of his case in his haste to leave, but at least he had made it. Was this the right place? Now the mist was beginning to lift it appeared they were in the middle of nowhere.

Looking up and down the platform he could see that six others had alighted from the train. To his relief, they all looked to be like him; young, perhaps no older than 20, all in uniform, all holding suitcases or bags of some kind and with the same where-do-I-go-from-here look that he strongly suspected that he, himself had.

He had seen this look a lot over the past few months, ever since he had joined His Majesty's armed forces, in fact. Soldiers and sailors not sure where they were, where they should be or what they were supposed to do once they got there seemed the normal state of affairs.

Eddie walked down the platform to the pair nearest to him. They were contrasting sizes: one short the other tall and so thin that his army greatcoat looked like it could wrap round him two or three times. They were facing away from him and the smaller of the two held a piece of paper that Eddie guessed was their orders. Checking his own orders might be useful, but he had mislaid them the previous day. He suspected he might have packed them away amongst his writing kit, though he had a sinking feeling he may have accidently posted them to his mother.

'Excuse me, chaps,' he began but then the shorter one turned around and Eddie stopped in surprise.

'Bunny!'

'Eddie! Is it really you, old man?'

'Of course it is, Bunny,' said Eddie hugging his friend. 'What the blazes are you doing here? You joined the RFC?'

'I certainly did.'

'I never knew you were interested in flying.'

'Oh I'm not really. It was Mater's idea. Didn't like the idea of her little boy slogging it out in the mud with all the common boys and the Huns being all beastly with big bits of lead. Bent Pater's ear about it and he pulled a few strings and here I am. Oh where are my manners? You've not met Bean have you.' Bunny grabbed hold of the tall youth next to him and dragged him forward. 'Bean, this is Eddie. Edward Grenville, we were at Sedbergh together. Eddie this is Hector Monroe, Bean to his friends. We went through basic together. Bean's from some wild backwoods place north of the border but he's not such a bad old egg for all that.'

'Heriot's School, Edinburgh,' said Bean, holding his hand out which Eddie took and shook. 'Actually, I think we might have met. Are you a runner?' Bean's accent was crystal clear Home Counties with only the slightest edge of a burr that hinted at Caledonian roots.

'Yes, a quarter miler. Wait, you're a miler, aren't you? Scottish Schools against English Schools. You were damned quick.'

'Oh I was lucky old boy, damned lucky.'

'Excuse me, sorry to break up this reunion but have any of you chaps any idea where we are supposed to go?' They had been joined by the other three lost souls, all of whom were looking hopefully at Eddie.

'No idea, Timpson,' said Bunny.

Eddie decided to take the lead.

'Perhaps there's someone waiting for us outside the station,' he said.

There was. A truck was parked next to the station gates, two privates leant against it, cigarettes in hand.

'I say, are you our transport?' said Bean.

'Oh aye, sir, that's us,' said one. 'Best luxury charabanc to your holiday camp.'

The other sniggered.

'I'll thank you to keep a civil tongue in your head and remember who your betters are,' said Timpson.

'Oh yes, sir, I will that sir,' said the first private without the slightest hint of genuinely being bothered. 'Now get in,' he added. 'Please. Sir.'

'Who'll take our bags?' said Timpson but the privates were already climbing up into the cab. 'Bloody cheek,' he muttered but got in the back, as did the others. With a jerk and a crash of gears, the truck set off.

Bunny was sat next to Eddie on the bench seat.

'How did you persuade your old man to let you join the Flying Corp,' he said. 'I thought they'd have wanted you in the Guards like your uncle.'

'That is just what they did want. And if it wasn't for my maiden aunt popping her clogs and leaving me a small legacy, that's where I'd be.'

'I don't follow.'

'I heard that the RFC never turn down a qualified pilot. I used the legacy to pay for my ticket at Hendon. As soon as I went solo I asked for a transfer.'

'So your folks don't know?'

'No fear. I'll only break it to them when they can't do anything about it.'

'Good idea. And good thinking about taking flying lessons.'

'Well I can thank my brother for that. He told me.'

'Good old Percy. But if you are already a pilot what are you doing here?'

Eddie sighed. 'Apparently I have to learn the correct military way of doing things. Everything by the book and all that.'

'Tough luck, old chap. At least you will have a head start on the rest of us. I haven't got a clue to be honest.'

'Oh I'm sure you'll catch on pretty quickly, old thing. And I'm sure we will be flying some more up-to-date crates than I did at Hendon. I did my ticket on an ancient Farman.'

Their conversation was interrupted by their arrival at the airfield.

'All change,' called the driver, who clearly considered himself a bit of a wag. The neophyte airmen, despite the early hour and the cold, fell over themselves, laughing and elbowing each other as they clambered out of the lorry.

'Attention!' The word was barked in true sergeant-major fashion and so Eddie was not surprised to find it originated from one. 'Officer on parade!'

Any thoughts of giving the NCO backchat and reminding him of his rank was forgotten as the group saw that they were being given a particularly black look by an immaculately dressed officer. They formed themselves into a reasonable approximation of a parade line. The officer scowled, sighed, then strode along their ranks.

Eddie heard him mutter 'God help us,' under his breath. At the end of the line he turned, then walked in front of them and turned again to face them.

'This is not a good start, gentlemen, not a good start at all. I'm going to expect better from you, is that understood?'

There were a few muttered murmurs of assent.

'I can't hear you, gentlemen.'

'Yes sir.' they all chorused.

'That's better. Right, I'm Major Anderson. I am in charge of this station and that makes me in charge of you. I run a tight outfit here, I expect you to behave, like British soldiers and British gentlemen. You may be here to learn to fly but you are still in the King's army, never forget that, however irregular the activity you are undertaking. I expect you to do your absolute best, obey your instructors but, above all, I expect you to follow the dress code at all times. Is that understood?'

We have a right one here, thought Eddie, but chorused 'Yes sir!' with the rest.

'Good. There will be a briefing at ten hundred hours in the main hangar. Sergeant-Major Jones here will see to your hut allocation. Go and put your kit away. The stores will be open from Oh Nine Hundred to draw any flying gear that you require. Do you have any questions?'

'No sir.'

'Good. Sergeant, take over.'

The officer marched smartly away.

The sergeant-major watched him go. Eddie saw him noticeably relax when Anderson went inside a nearby building.

'Right, at-ease young sirs,' he said in a remarkably friendly tone. 'Don't mind the major, his bark's worse than his bite. Old cavalry type, I think he misses the horses. Just keep yourself smart and in uniform at all times and he'll let you be. Come on, I'll show you to your huts.'

Netheravon Airfield proved to be a former cavalry base. The parade ground and stable blocks were still there but behind them was a wide, largely level grass field with hangars. Mechanics in brown overalls could be seen pushing an Avro out of one of the hangars. Near the stables a series of huts had been built. These looked new but rather spartan, which did indeed prove to be the case. The huts each had a common dormitory with five beds on each side and a washroom at one end.

Eddie, Bunny, Bean and Timpson found they had all been allocated beds in Hut 2. There was only one other occupant of the hut. Sat on one of the beds was a pale-faced, mousy-haired young man. He sprang to his feet when the four came in through the door.

'Who are you? What do you want?' he said. He looked alarmed and flustered.

'Steady on, old boy, we're just moving in,' said Bunny. 'I say, you're a bit on edge, aren't you?'

'What if I am? What is it to you?'

'Nothing at all, old man, nothing at all,' said Bunny, putting his bag down on one of the beds. He caught Eddie's eye and raised his eyebrows. 'Is this bunk free?'

'Yes, they're all free. Can't you see that for yourself?' snapped the young man.

'We should introduce ourselves,' said Eddie, feeling the need to calm the situation. 'I'm Grenville. These chaps are Cavendish, Monroe and Timpson.' He held out his hand to the young man, who just looked at it before, eventually taking it. He gave a little smile and suddenly relaxed.

'I'm Prentice,' he said. 'Philip Prentice. Pip to my friends.'

They all shook hands with Pip in turn.

'How long have you been here, Pip?' said Monroe.

'A few days.'

'On your own? That must have been a bit of a sickener?'

'No. I wasn't on my own. Not at first anyway.' Pip sat down on the bed and returned to staring at the far wall.

'Oh, where are the other chaps then?' said Bunny.

'Gone,' said Pip.

'Gone where? To the front?'

Prentice didn't answer.

'We should put our gear away,' said Eddie to end the awkward silence. 'What are the instructors like? Do they teach you well?'

'Teach you?' Prentice was still staring at the wall.

Eddie shared a puzzled glance with Bean. They clearly had the same thought; what was wrong with this chap?

'I suppose we had better go and draw our...'

'It depends on who you get,' said Pip. 'Mine doesn't say anything. I've no idea what I'm supposed to be doing.'

'Oh, surely you can't be serious,' said Bunny. 'They must teach you. That's the point of us being here.'

'Well they bloody well don't!' yelled Pip, leaping to his feet and rushing at Bunny.

'Hey, steady on old chap,' said Eddie, stepping between them. 'No need to lose our rags, is there? Old Bunny here didn't mean anything, did you Bun?' He looked at his friend, encouraging him to back him up.

'No, no, not at all,' said Bunny. 'I was just surprised that's all.'

'Well just don't go shooting your mouth off about things you don't know anything about,' shouted Prentice.

'We won't, we promise, don't we chaps?' said Eddie. The others all made noises of agreement. 'Now come on, Pip, you're obviously an old hand around here. Why don't you show us the way to the stores? We're supposed to report there. How does that sound to you?'

Prentice nodded. 'Yes, yes, I can do that. Come with me.

Prentice led them out of the hut. Bunny and Eddie were the last of the group out of the door.

'What do you reckon all that was about?' murmured Bunny.

'No idea. Odd that he's on his own here, don't you think?'

'Oh, I don't know. Perhaps they've done it deliberately. Because he's a bit, you know, unbalanced?'

'Maybe,' said Eddie. 'We'll have to see.'

CHAPTER TWO

England, Tuesday 9th January, 1917

The next morning, Eddie was up early. He found they were not due to commence flight training until 10am, so went for a walk rather than go straight to breakfast.

He did not achieve much, other than to discover just how cold Wiltshire could be in February and to find the hangars. Here he discovered both a hive of activity and a rude shock. The hangar was full of riggers and fitters, fogging the air with their breath as they toiled, just as he would expect from a military base. What they were working on was the shock.

At Hendon he had done his ticket, little more than a take-off and a landing and a figure of eight circuit in between, on an archaic Maurice Farman pusher. He assumed that when he joined the flying corps that he would be flying up-to-date military types. To be fair, there were some BE2s and an Avro, but the majority of the aircraft were more of the same type he'd learned on with one difference: these looked even more worn. In fact the term 'knackered' sprang to Eddie's mind. The machines were patched, stained and dripping oil, looking unloved, mistreated and, to be frank, downright dangerous.

Somewhat shaken, Eddie decided he needed breakfast after all so he headed for the mess.

None of his fellow newcomers were there, either they had been and gone or they had taken advantage of the leisurely start to catch up with some sleep. Eddie had the choice of either sitting with a group of officers that he was sure were the instructors, Prentice, the strange young man they had met the previous night or another cadet he did not know, who was reading a paper. He did not fancy trying to make the effort to try and get some conversation going with Prentice, one of the instructors had glared at him when he stepped towards the table, so he chose the third option.

'Morning,' he said. 'Mind if I join you?'

'Not at all, old man, feel free,' said the young man, lowering the corner of his newspaper. 'I take it you're one of the new batch?'

'Yes, I am. I'm Grenville, Edward,' said Eddie holding out his hand. 'Eddie for short.'

'Bramwell,' said the other in return, shaking it.

Eddie's eyes were caught by a photograph in Bramwell's paper.

'I say, is that Ball in your paper?' he said.

Bramwell looked down, 'Oh yes, he's been made an honorary freeman of Nottingham. Had a big ceremony.'

'He's quite a chap, isn't he? Wonder if he's going to go back to the front soon?'

'Apparently he is. Well, that's what he said in his speech. I can let you read it afterwards if you like?'

'Oh yes please. I've got a scrapbook full of articles on him. Wouldn't it be wonderful to get posted to his squadron?'

Bramwell shrugged. 'Chances are we'll end up in a two-seater outfit. That's where the need is.'

Eddie's face fell. 'Oh, what reconnaissance?'

Bramwell nodded. 'We can't all be scout pilots, I'm afraid. That's where I came from. I did three months as an observer last year. Jumped at the chance to retrain as a pilot.'

A white jacketed mess orderly came and took Eddie's order. By the look and age of the man, Eddie guessed that he dated back to the time when this was a cavalry base.

'So you're an old hand?' said Eddie. 'Been here a while?'

'Oh yes, at least two weeks,' said Bramwell with a smile. 'Around here that makes me a survivor.'

Before Eddie could ask him what he meant by this, Prentice caused a commotion by dropping his tea cup into his saucer. The orderlies hurried over to clear up the mess and Eddie noticed the instructor who had glared at him earlier, give Prentice a look that could easily have killed.

'He's a bit of an odd sort,' murmured Eddie.

'Who, Prentice?'

'Yes.'

'Oh he's all right is old Pip, been through a lot. Well, I say old but between me, you and the gatepost although he claims to be 18, word is that he is a damn sight younger than that.'

'Really?'

'Yes well he came here with his older brother and *he* was 18, so stands to reason that Pip's younger.'

'Was?'

'Pardon?'

'Sorry, I just thought I caught the past tense when you were talking about his brother.'

'Oh yes, I was. Terrible prang. Came down in the middle of the field first day he was here. Flamer. Burnt to a crisp, him and his instructor, right in front of old Pip there.' Bramwell took a thoughtful sip of his tea. 'Rather knocks a chap for six, something like that.'

'Gosh, yes, I can see that,' said Eddie, now seeing Prentice through more sympathetic eyes. 'I don't like to think what I would be like if anything happened to my brother.' He shuddered. He needed to change the subject. 'I've just been across to the hangars. We don't fly those Farmans do we?'

'The old Rumpeties? Oh yes, we do, at least at first. Nothing wrong with the old Rumpety. Good steady old crate.'

'Old is the word.'

'Just well run in, like an old pair of shoes.'

'Really?' said Eddie. He looked across at the instructors as his scrambled egg on toast arrived. 'What are they like? Know their stuff? Friendly?'

'Yes,' said Bramwell. 'And no.'

Eddie was confused. 'Well, which is it?'

'It's both, I'm afraid. The ones that know their stuff are not friendly. The ones that don't, are.'

Bramwell must have seen the puzzled look on Eddie's face so explained.

'The older looking ones, like the one that glared at you, that's Captain Francis, by the way, they are the ones who have been over in France.'

'Well they should know what they are about.'

'Oh they do, old chap, they do. The trouble is they don't want to be here. When they finished over there, they thought they'd escaped but they got posted here. This is no cushy number, this is bloody dangerous, maybe more so than facing Johnny Hun over Flanders. They call us Huns too you know.'

'Why?'

'Because we kill more of them than the Jastas do. As a result they are hardly too keen on doing more than the bare minimum. All they care about is staying alive and who can bloody well blame them?

'The others, the young ones that look that they are barely out of flying school? The ones that are sitting to one side only speaking when they are spoken to?'

'Yes,' said Eddie, taking a casual glance at the instructor's table.

'Well they look that way because they are. Some have no more than ten hours solo. They've done their training and got posted here. They know bugger all - but they are friendly. It's Hobson's choice who you get.'

'Great,' said Eddie. 'I can hardly wait to find out.'

*

Eddie got one of the latter kind.

He came over to the new recruits clutching a piece of paper. Eddie could see his hand was shaking.

'Right,' said the instructor, trying to give the impression of being brisk and efficient. 'I'm Lieutenant Ashburner. I'll be your instructor whilst you're here at Netheravon. Hopefully I've got a Grenville and a Nash here.'

'That's us,' said Eddie.

'Good, come with me.'

He turned and set off across the frost covered grass towards one of the Farmans.

'Sir?' said Nash. 'Can I ask you a question?'

'Certainly...Grenville?'

'Nash sir.'

'Yes indeed, of course, Nash What is it?'

'How long have you been an instructor, sir?'

Eddie was obviously not the only one who'd heard the gossip. Ashburner visibly reddened.

'That's none of your damn business, Nash,' he said.

'But how many hours have you done?'

'I'll have none of your insolence, thank you. Remember I am a senior officer.' By one pip, thought Eddie but said nothing. 'Any more of that lip and you will be on a charge.'

'Yes sir,' said Nash sullenly.

'Good. Now have either of you been up in an aircraft before.'

'No sir,' said Nash.

'Yes,' said Eddie. 'In fact I've...'

'Good well you can come up with me first, Nash. Grenville, there's a brazier in that hangar. Go in there and keep warm for now and I will come and get you in about half an hour. Nash, get in.' He pointed at the Farman.

Eddie was not upset to be given the chance to keep warm. Even in his flying gear the chill seeped in.

He arrived at the hangar just in time to see Captain Francis grab hold of Prentice by the lapels of his coat and thrust him against the wall of the hangar.

'Don't give me that rubbish. Just get in that bloody kite and get on with it. You understand?'

Prentice at this moment could have passed for twelve let alone sixteen. Tears streamed down his face, he was shaking. He nodded.

'Good. About bloody time.' He dragged Prentice away from the hangar and threw him in the direction of the Farman. Francis glared at Eddie. 'What the hell are you looking at?'

'Nothing, sir,' said Eddie. He hurried off to find the brazier. Bunny and Bramwell were already there warming themselves.

'What was that all about?' said Bunny.

'It's that bastard Francis,' said Bramwell before Eddie could answer. 'He's making poor Pip go solo.'

'Is that so bad?' said Bunny.

'Poor kid has only done a couple of hours and even then he says that Francis never lets him do anything himself. I don't think he's ever actually done a landing on his own.'

In the distance they heard the erk echo Prentice's instruction from the cockpit. 'Switches on! Contact!' and then swing the prop. The already warm rotary roared into life.

Captain Francis had not stayed to watch. He marched into the hangar straight to the brazier. The three trainee pilots quietly made room for him. Francis turned and hitched up the back of his flying coat and thrust his backside against the heat.

'You man,' he yelled at a passing fitter. 'Get me a mug of tea. A fresh, hot one mind, with plenty of sugar. And jump to it!'

'Yes sir!' said the fitter.

The Farman in the meantime had set off and was now bouncing from wheel to wheel across the frozen grass. Eddie winced as one of the wingtips brushed the ground but then Prentice levelled up and the aircraft wobbled into the air.

'Bloody brass monkeys this morning, eh lads?' said Francis rubbing his hands together.

'Yes sir,' said Bramwell and Bunny.

Eddie was concentrating on Prentice. 'More speed,' he muttered under his breath. 'Don't turn until you've got more speed.'

Eddie was not clairvoyant but could predict what was about to happen. Prentice would worry about flying away from the airfield, about losing sight of it, getting lost and not being able to find his way back. He would want to turn as soon as he could, even whilst he was still climbing. When he did, the nose would drop alarmingly and the instinct would be to pull back on the stick. Eddie knew that he would want to do all of this because it had happened to him and it had nearly killed him. It hadn't because, unlike Prentice, Eddie had his instructor behind him, who had rapped Eddie firmly over the head and taken control.

Eddie was vaguely aware of the young fitter returning.

'Your tea, sir.'

Francis took it, blew into it loudly then took a sip. He winced. 'Have you stirred it?'

'Yes sir.'

'Well go and put some more bloody sugar in it.'

'Yes sir.'

In the meantime the Farman had begun to turn.

'Oh my God,' said Eddie.

It happened in slow motion. Halfway through the turn the nose rose. The speed bled off. The right wing dropped abruptly, the turn sharpened and rapidly became a spin.

Eddie found himself outside and running, running towards the inevitable point of impact. He was not alone.

About a hundred feet up there was a sharp crack and the wings folded back on themselves. The engine stopped and, spinning like a sycamore key, the wreckage completed its journey to the ground.

Eddie felt the impact first, then heard the sickening crunch.

Probably the best runner on the base, other than Monroe, he got there first.

The aircraft had impacted nose first. The frozen earth was as unyielding as concrete and the heavy engine had carried on its line of travel to embed itself into the ground, crushing everything in its way, cockpit, instruments, fabric, spruce - and Prentice. Eddie caught sight of what was left and jerked away, retching.

He was aware of hands on him, leading him away.

'Leave it to us, sir, we will deal with him it's our job.'

It was the chief mechanic, a rough, weather-beaten character with a face as wrinkled as a walnut.

'Go on, sir, you can't do anything now. Go and get a nice cup of tea, eh?'

Eddie nodded and stumbled back to the hangar.

He was halfway there when the bodies of Nash and Ashburner landed not 20 yards from him whilst their plane continued, inverted but flying perfectly straight and level, towards the nearby village.

CHAPTER THREE

England, Thursday 11th January, 1917

'All rise.'

The occupants of the courtroom, bar one, got to their feet as Justice Souter, bewigged, scarlet robed and sour faced made his stately progress from the robing room to his seat of honour.

The person who had not risen was sat on the back row of the public benches. It was a cold day outside so it was perhaps understandable why this man wore a dark, thick overcoat yet having the collar of this turned up was less justifiable given he was indoors.

That this partially hid the man's face gave a better reason as to why he wore it in this way, as did his choice of seat, tucked away at the end of the row behind a rather large couple sat on the row in front of him. The man wanted to see but not be seen.

Once the judge had taken his seat, the court, with a shuffling and clumping of boots and shoes on the old floorboards settled down into their seats again. There was a chorus of coughs as the populace took the opportunity to clear throats and chests whilst they were still able, like an audience before the start of a concert or a play. This commotion allowed the man in the overcoat to look around him without attracting undue attention.

His gaze fell on the press benches, the place where he, Frank Holloman, would, under other circumstances normally sit. He could not help but smile.

The benches would normally be packed with reporters jostling for elbow space but today there were only two and Holloman recognised neither of them. He guessed that they were either freelance or from the suburban papers sent up to the city by their editors. He saw them look nervously at each other and then at the gaps next to them. He knew what they were thinking; what did the others know that they did not?

Holloman knew.

Someone less astute might have thought that a high-profile defamation action such as this would have attracted newspaper men in their droves, falling over themselves to report on the demise of their hated adversary and rival. He knew differently though and so did the other editors and proprietors. They were far too smart to fall into the trap. The fall might happen but not here, not yet. Fitzroy's highly paid counsel would humiliate the defendant. Reporters also risked facing the treatment themselves as their pieces and editorials would be pored over by Fitzroy's legal team for even the slightest error or implied critical slant. With a powerful, rich bully like Fitzroy, quick to rush to the law at the least slight it was not worth being bold. They would bide their time for a better opportunity.

So they sent no one, left the story unreported except by these two rather naïve members of the fourth estate who were now realising their error and were clearly wishing they had left whilst they had the chance.

'Are you ready to proceed, Mr Headley?' said the Judge, peering over his half-moon reading glasses.

'Yes, M'lord,' said Headley, counsel for the prosecution, getting to his feet. 'I wish to call the plaintiff, Mr Maxwell Fitzroy.'

'Very well,' said the Judge, his voice cool.

The court usher bowed to his lordship and made his way to the side door to the courtroom. There was a murmur of conversation in the public gallery, a clear sense of expectation.

Maxwell Fitzroy did not disappoint.

He swept into court like an oriental potentate entering his throne room. Fitzroy was a big man, tall and wide, just edging towards uncontrolled plumpness resulting from the richest of living. He was sleek though, his dark hair slicked back, his beard immaculately trimmed. His chin was held defiantly high, his face determined, in all his bearing the perfect manifestation of a man whose honour had been cruelly slighted and sought an apology.

Punitive damages and humiliation of his opponent would be an incidental, but welcome, bonus.

This thought made Holloman smile and distracted him enough to almost reveal himself. Fitzroy had reached the witness box, stepped inside and had looked around the court. Just in time Holloman ducked down as if retrieving something that he had dropped on the floor. He peered round the bulk of the man in front of him to see that Fitzroy's gaze had moved on. He was staring at the two reporters on the press bench with a cold disdain. Holloman saw the men visibly flinch under the assault. Mixed with contempt for their stupidity he also felt considerable sympathy for them.

Frank Holloman listened to the evidence for an hour before slipping out during a brief recess.

*

'Nice of you to drop by.'

Holloman gave his young colleague a glare.

'I'd thank you to remember I am the senior reporter and you are the junior. I'd also remind you not to be so damned impertinent, Price, I'm not beyond boxing your ears,' he said.

King and Country magazine's only other full-time employee, Frederick Price, sat alone behind a pile of paper in what the editor and proprietor (who were one and the same person) grandly, and without the slightest trace of irony, called the newsroom. The fact that the staff consisted only of Holloman and Price was overlooked by the man who always grandly presented the publication as if it was of equal standing, prestige and history to a Times or a Daily Telegraph. The truth was King and Country had been founded only in 1915 and was rather a sensationalist rag of dubious parentage and doubtful financial stability, always being chased by its printers for payment whilst barely making it to the newsstands every month.

Holloman cursed the day he had accepted the job.

He sat down at his desk and leafed through his in-tray. There was little of interest in it.

Price peered up at Holloman through the thick glasses that betrayed his poor eyesight. This and his delicate physique had limited his employment opportunities but had the benefit of keeping him out of the trenches. Though he had limited ability as either reporter or sub-editor he had had one quality their proprietor favoured over all others. He was very cheap.

'Where have you been all morning?' he asked.

'None of your business,' said Holloman.

'You're just lucky Herr Neuhaus wasn't in,' said Price.

Holloman glared at him. 'I would be very careful if I were you, young man. Don't call him that, even in jest. For all his bonhomie he has a limited sense of humour but unlimited vindictiveness.'

'Perhaps poor old Jones had a case after all then. That that chap Lindemann really did know him in Danzig like he said. And if he is a Kraut then that would explain his lack of humour.'

'Ambitious bastards don't need nationalities,' muttered Holloman more to himself than to Price.

'Pardon?'

'Forget it. And if I were you I'd forget those rumours too. What are you working on?'

Price sighed and tossed the paper he was holding onto his desk.

'I'm editing a piece by that old windbag Percival on munition production.'

'What's it like.'

'Utter rubbish, like everything else that comes out of this newsroom.' The booming voice came from the doorway. Price and Holloman looked up. It was the proprietor-cum-editor. Maxwell Fitzroy.

'Good afternoon, sir,' said Price and Holloman together.

'Holloman, forget the pleasantries, I want a word with you, now,' Fitzroy strode across the newsroom and into his office.

His cheeks pink, Holloman followed, ignoring Price's smirk. Once inside he shut the door and turned angrily to his boss.

'Sir, I'd thank you not to...'

'Shut up, Holloman. I was told when I employed you that you were a first class newsman.'

'I am...'

'I have yet to see anything of the quality I expect to see from you.'

'That's not true, sir and you know it. I have been delivering...'

'Delivering? What have you been delivering? Are you talking about this re-heated hash you've been giving me? I wouldn't wipe my backside with it.' He screwed up Holloman's latest copy and threw it at him.

'But...'

'No buts, Holloman. Our readers – this country – are in desperate need of real tales of derring do to inspire them. From the reports that Buchan, Gibbs, Thomas and Russell send back, everyone would think that we'll be in Berlin by Easter. It's all rot and the people are getting wise to it all. They're starting to listen to those damned socialist agitators. We have to counter the naysayers, keep spirits up, don't you see that?'

'Yes sir but...'

'We have to do everything we can to help win this war, Holloman. Our Empire - our very way of life - is at stake. Our job is to inspire people, get men to put their backs into producing that extra ton of steel, or for the women to put in extra hours in the munitions factory and still be home to get tea on their tables for their men folk.'

Holloman knew there was no point interrupting. The editor was well into character now, he was giving his hustings performance, as if practicing for the next election, which, on reflection, he probably was. Once started, there was no stopping him.

'We want stories that will make mothers proud of their sons at the front and will be willing to send more of her boys whenasked.'

'Yes sir,' Holloman said, now just playing the role expected of him; an audience.

'And above all Holloman we want stories that achieve one other vital thing.'

'What is that, sir?' even though he knew the answer.

'I need stories that sell my publication. I want the great British public to buy it and not the Sketch, or the News of the World or the Mail or the Express. That will make me happy and if I am happy so will you be, Holloman.'

'Yes sir.'

'You understand the type of story I want?'

'You want stories of heroism, sir.'

'Exactly, Holloman. This country needs heroes and it is up to us to give them to them.'

'Sir, I know that but there is the problem of finding them. The War Office...'

'I said I didn't want excuses, Holloman. Just give me the damn stories.'

'But how...'

'I don't care. You have an imagination don't you?'

Holloman stared at Fitzroy. 'Are you serious? You want me to make up stories?'

'Why not? Is there a problem?'

'Well, yes there is. There's my reputation for one thing. What happens if people find out?'

Fitzroy folded his arms and regarded Holloman over his generous belly.

'Holloman, you've just said the War Office control everything. If you can't get information in the first place how then is anyone going to check the facts? Who would know?'

'I would,' said Holloman quietly.

'And why would that matter? You're a washed up has been who's got rather too fond of the bottle. None of the heavyweights will look at you anymore. If you're worried about your reputation, don't be. You haven't got one to lose.'

'That's not…' Holloman began but then his voice trailed off.

'That's not what, Holloman? True? You know it is. Fair? Who cares about fairness?'

Holloman said nothing.

'Holloman, my patience is not limitless. If you cannot deliver what is required you should perhaps seek alternative employment. You and I know that you will struggle to find anything worthwhile as it is but believe me, I will make it impossible for you to work in London ever again if you leave here. I hope I make myself clear?'

'Yes,' said Holloman through gritted teeth.

'Then go and damn well do what I want.'

Flushed with anger, Holloman stalked out of Fitzroy's office. He walked straight out of the newsroom, being careful not to catch Price's eye.

He was desperately in need of both a drink and inspiration.

CHAPTER FOUR

England, Wednesday 31st January, 1917

Holloman sat in the public bar of the Red Lion trying to be patient. He took a sip of the rough whisky, the best that the Red Lion offered; the sour bite fitted his mood. This was his last chance. If this didn't work he'd be finished. This lead had to pay off.

He had tried to talk to troops returning from France and had been rewarded with being threatened with arrest by the military police. How serious this threat had been he was not sure, but it was a sobering experience. The War Office were close to paranoia over controlling what was written and what was said. The chances of finding a really great story were limited.

Yet Holloman knew he needed one or he would be looking for a new position. At his age, 47, this was not going to be easy, at least in London. There were jobs in the provinces, but he did not want to spend the rest of his life writing about the Women's Institute Beetle Drive and the results of the local horticultural society show. No, he was a Fleet Street reporter and wanted to stay that way.

He did consider doing what he knew others had done; use his imagination and make it all up. After all, who would know? If no one had sources to provide stories, then how could they use those same sources to check the veracity of a sensational tale? After all the Angel of Mons had passed from imaginative fiction to folklore many now believed was the gospel truth.

It was tempting but Holloman could not bring himself to do it. He was too old-fashioned for that.

He had almost been in despair but then, out of the blue, he'd got a break.

Like all good reporters he had a tendency to always half-listen to other people's' conversations. In this case it was the gossip of women from the building's post room; one had a husband in the trenches who had just sent a letter home and she was telling her friend about a pilot who had carried his badly hurt observer back to the British lines even though he himself was wounded. Holloman soon had his notebook out and was getting as much as he could from her, though there was little more than he had overheard. He might have left it there – it was an interesting enough story but hardly unique – but for a number of odd facts that piqued his journalistic curiosity. Even then, individually, they did not amount to much but together...well, it certainly was enough to justify taking time to look into it further.

The first odd thing was the men had apparently been pursued across no man's land by a German pilot. Although Holloman was sure that Fitzroy would have just explained it away as a typical Hunnish way to behave he was not convinced. What had caused the man to be so determined to prevent his quarries reaching safety?

The second thing that had really interested Holloman was the name of the British pilot as reported in the letter to the soldier's wife; Captain Grenville.

Holloman happened to know there was a big wheel in the City called Sir Arthur Grenville, and that Arthur's brother was a General on Haig's staff. He also knew that Sir Arthur's son was a Captain in the Royal Flying Corp, he had seen them at a war bond garden party he had attended the previous year. Could this pilot be one and the same person? If so this would make the story huge.

But that led to the third odd fact: The letter was sent at Christmas but referred to the incident having happened in November. It was now February, yet there had been no mention of anything in any of their rival papers – Holloman had personally checked the back issues in the British Library - nor had there been any notification of a gallantry award in the London Gazette.

This made him doubt the story – or maybe not the story but that the Grenville mentioned was one from this prominent family. With those family connections the army would surely not hesitate to make an award. All the papers would want to report it. So was this a different Captain Grenville? Or had the event not happened?

There was no point asking the family directly. It would be beneath them to talk to anyone as low as a press man. Even so, he had tried but had received a cold "Sir Arthur and Lady Grenville are not receiving visitors" from a footman and had found the door slammed in his face.

Which was why he was here, working on a last long shot, on something he had heard from chatting to some pilots on leave at the RAC club.

Actually it was not that much of a long shot. The private aero club that the Central Flying School had taken over in 1914 was on the edge of the village, this was the only pub. Young RFC personnel on such a primitive base would be almost certain to gravitate here.

On the previous night two officers had been in, Holloman had taken them to be instructors. He had been momentarily puzzled when he heard one say: 'At least there aren't any Huns in here tonight' but then remembered he'd been told that this was what instructors often called their charges; graveyard humour given that the trainees often took almost as great a toll on RFC flyers as the enemy did. Holloman kept quiet; it confirmed what he thought and he did not want to forewarn his quarry about his presence.

It was worth waiting, even if Fitzroy had sent telegrams asking where he was and when he might be submitting his story.

Tonight his patience was rewarded, for with a noisy thump the lounge door burst open and three young men, laughing like schoolboys freed by the bell, almost fell into the pub.

Holloman suddenly felt old. The newcomers looked closer to their schooldays than manhood, he suspected one of them might not even be shaving he was so pink-cheeked whilst the tallest had the gawky angularity and acne of adolescence. Only the uniforms they wore, the fresh wings with the initials RFC above showed that their country felt they were old enough to die for their King.

Holloman was not the only one to take notice of the group; the landlord came through from the tap room, cleaning a pint glass with a tea towel, and glared at them.

'Now, now, if you please, Gentlemen,' he said. 'I thought I made myself clear to your lot. This is a quiet establishment, we don't want you lot disturbing the locals.'

Holloman could not help but give a little smile. The current population of the pub consisted of himself and two old gents playing cribbage by the fire in the other room. The flyers obviously thought the same thing and the pink-cheeked one raised his eyebrows and sighed in exasperation at the gawky one but the third, almost as young looking as the others but with the air of a natural leader stepped forward apologetically.

'Sorry, mine host, we got a bit carried away. We'll be quiet as little mice, won't we boys?'

'Yes, Eddie, of course we will,' said pink cheeks. 'Won't we

Bean, old chap?'

The gawky one nodded eagerly, 'Oh yes, of course. Sorry.'

'That may be so,' said the landlord. 'But we had trouble last week, don't know if you were told. I had a mind to bar you lot...not your officers, mind but the rest of you. '

'Excuse me,' interrupted Holloman, getting up from his seat. The landlord and the three flyers turned to look at him, the latter with some suspicion, Holloman guessed that they expected him to object to their interrupting his quiet drink.

'Yes sir?' said the landlord.

'I just wanted to say that I, for one, am not the least disturbed by these fine young men. In fact...' he went on, talking over the landlord who seemed about to object...'in fact, I would like to stand them a drink. They are serving King and country, risking their lives in those flimsy contraptions of theirs after all.'

'Well...' said the Landlord, clearly doubtful.

'I'm sure these Gentlemen will be on their absolute best behaviour, particularly if they sit with me.'

The three nodded eagerly and looked expectantly at the landlord.

'Oh alright then,' he said. 'On your head be it,' he added in a low mutter in the direction of Holloman.

'So what will it be, then, gentlemen?' said Holloman.

'I think we should be buying you one, old chap,' said Eddie quietly. 'Thought we were in a sticky spot there.'

'No, I insist. I'm too old to serve so I feel it really is the least I can do,' said Holloman. 'Now what can I get you?'

'Well that's dash good of you, beers all round?' Eddie asked his companions.

'Shandy for me,' said the gawky one.

'You lightweight, Bean,' laughed Eddie. 'That will be two beers and a shandy please then Mr... er'

'Johnson, Charles Johnson,' said Holloman, nodding at the landlord. 'And the same again for me, please landlord.'

'Nice to meet you Mr. Johnson. These reprobates are 2nd Lieutenants Cavendish and Monroe, or Bunny and Bean to their friends. And I'm Grenville, Edward Grenville.'

Holloman almost punched the air in triumph but said and did nothing until they had sat down at a table.

'I've met a Grenville. A banker, as far as I recall,' he said.

'That would probably be my father,' said Eddie. Holloman noticed that he gave a little sigh as he said it. 'I hope he was generous.'

'He was...business-like.'

Eddie smiled. 'That certainly sounds like pater. I take it you are in commerce?'

'I'm in the paper business,' which, Holloman thought, was broadly true at least. 'Your health, gentlemen,' he said raising his glass, to which the others did the same in response. 'So you young chaps are flyers I take it?'

'That's right, well, we're in training anyway,' said Eddie. 'Got to get through that first, not sure if our instructors think we are the right material to face the best of the Kaiser's mob.'

'Your instructors are hard taskmasters then?'

Eddie gave a wry grin. 'Hardly, well not all of them anyway. We have some keen ones though who seem intent on showing us the error of our ways.'

'Yes,' said Bunny with a hollow-eyed stare. 'Captain Hollinghurst. He's a bit beastly to us.'

'Och, he's not so bad,' said Bean. 'He knows his stuff, been over in France. And he's only tough because he cares enough to actually bother teaching us properly.'

'It's alright for you, Bean, you've got a natural bent for these things,' said Bunny. 'And as for caring, all the Captain seems to bother about is his motorbike.'

'He's had me cleaning it too, Bunny,' said Bean.

'And me,' said Eddie. 'It's his standard punishment, you know that. We'll get it properly filthy, mark my words.'

Bean seemed to notice Holloman's puzzlement.

'Captain Hollinghurst has a motto, if the bike is clean -'

'Your flying is shit,' chorused the other two.

Holloman saw the landlord look across at the pilots and frown. This was no good, the conversation was putting them at ease but he needed to get them back on track and the last thing he needed was to have them all thrown out before he got what he needed out of Grenville.

'I bet you can't wait to get it over with though, go and have a crack at the Huns,' he said.

The three pilots nodded eagerly in agreement.

'Particularly you, Lieutenant Grenville, if I may be so bold, with your family connections.'

The atmosphere went distinctly cooler.

'You have me at a disadvantage. I don't know you but you seem to know my family rather well, Mr. Johnson,' said Eddie.

'My apologies,' said Holloman. 'Didn't mean to cause offence.

I was just aware that Sir Arthur's brother was on the General Staff and obviously thought that would make you particularly keen to serve.'

'No more than any of the other chaps,' said Eddie coldly.

'I say, Eddie, steady down a bit,' said Cavendish. 'You really can't go around falling out with a chap who got us in here and bought us drinks now can you?'

'I suppose not,' said Eddie quietly. 'Sorry Johnson, my family are a touchy subject with me.'

'They wanted old Eddie here to join the cavalry,' said Bunny. 'A far more acceptable crowd than us ruffians!'

'I prefer my horsepower to come from petrol not hay and my mount to backfire rather than fart,' said Eddie. They all laughed. 'The days of the cavalry are over. They are about as much use as long-bows and pikes in this war. Anyway, I want to be like Ball.'

'Albert Ball? The air ace?'

'Yes that's him.'

Holloman smiled. 'He's quite an odd little chap you know.'

Eddie looked at Holloman in surprise. 'You've met Ball, Mr Johnson? Gosh, you meet a lot of people don't you?'

Holloman cursed inwardly, he was making Grenville suspicious, sounding like a reporter and not a businessman. The lie came easily though: 'Yes, I met him at a War Bonds dinner. He's actually quite a shy boy, very quiet.'

'You're so lucky. I wish I could meet him. He's one of the main reasons that I wanted to become a pilot.'

'Still, it must have been hard to get your family to accept your joining the RFC?'

'It was. Luckily my brother had trail blazed for me. After the first born and heir had thrown in the silver breastplate and sabre for the wings and taken the buckshot for it, the family weren't so bothered about me.'

'Your brother is a pilot as well? At the front?'

'Yes, or rather he *was* at the front. He copped a blighty a few months ago.'

Calm yourself, old man, Holloman told himself, you're nearly there.

'A blighty?' he said, though he knew exactly what Eddie meant.

'A wound,' said Cavendish. 'Bad enough to get one sent home.'

'Oh dear, nothing life threatening I hope?'

'No. A bit of a leg wound but I understand he's on the mend.'

'Ah. So what happened?'

'I don't know much in the way of detail,' said Eddie. 'From what we can gather he was caught on the far side of the lines with a dud engine, got ambushed by a Hun squadron and crashed in no man's land.'

That fitted exactly with what he had heard. He had a story. Now Holloman could dig for more details.

'You lads are so brave even to go up in those contraptions,' he said. 'Let alone facing the Huns. So was he on his own?'

'No, at least I don't think so. He flew Fees.'

'Fees?'

'Sorry, FE2s, two-seater pushers. He'll have had an observer with him.'

'Oh, so did he get back too?'

Eddie shrugged. 'No idea. We really don't know much in the way of detail. We didn't even know Percy was wounded and in hospital in France. Mother moved hell and high water to get him back to a British hospital. Didn't want any foreign doctors touching him.'

'Understandable. So he's back here now?'

'Yes, he's kicking his heels in a sanatorium down in Ascot. I'm hoping to get leave to see him.' Eddie sipped his beer, for all their bravado none of the young men seemed to have had much drinking practice. In his excitement, Holloman realised that he had finished his whisky.

'You must have been thirsty. Fancy another one?' said the tall one.

Holloman was tempted but his eyes were drawn to the clock above the bar. It was just after half-past seven. There was a train into London at five past the hour. If he left now he could be at his desk at half-past nine and the story on Fitzroy's desk first thing tomorrow morning. He'd got enough.

'Gentlemen, my apologies, please excuse me. I quite forgot I have to catch a train. It was most pleasant to meet you, my best wishes for the rest of your training.'

And with that he was gone, out into the chilly February evening heading for the village station.

*

Two hours later, the three pilots staggered through the gates of the airfield. The guard appeared from inside his hut. He looked cross, though whether this was from having drawn guard duty on such a frigid night or from being dragged out into it from the relative warmth of his shelter to challenge them, or a combination of all three was hard to determine.

'Halt!' he called. 'Advance and be recognised.'

'Oh for heaven's sake, Strachan,' said Eddie. 'You know us, let us in. I'm in desperate need of a pee.'

'Me too,' said Bunny. 'I'm busting for one.'

'Orders is orders, sir. Papers.' The guard thrust out his hand.

'What if I say no?' said Eddie.

'You can't.'

'Yes but what if I do? What happens then?'

'Please don't be awkward, Lieutenant Grenville,' said the guard.

'No don't, please,' said Bunny. 'Or I'm going to need a clean pair of trousers.'

'Ah, but you see he does know me,' Eddie persisted. 'So why does he need to see my papers?'

'Everyone knows you, Eddie,' said Bean, grabbing hold of Eddie. He unfastened Eddies coat and extracted the papers out of his pocket, showing them to the guard. 'They just need to keep reminding themselves that the army actually let you in.'

'Pass sirs,' said the guard with clear relief that it was all over. 'Get to bed quietly now, don't want the major getting all het up about noise after dark again, do we sirs?'

Eddie was about to start arguing again but Bean thrust his papers back at him and pushed him through the gate.

'He was only doing his job,' he muttered.

'Well it's a bloody stupid job,' said Eddie. 'And what's that guff about noise? We're not noisy, are we?'

'Will you shut up?' said Bunny. 'You'll have the guards out and I can't wait much longer.'

'Well, so do I,' said Eddie, squinting into the darkness. 'And I know just the place , come on.'

He strode off towards the officer's quarters.

'Where are you going? Oh no, you're not...' said Bean.

Eddie was stood by Captain Hollinghurst's motorbike.

'Oh but I am,' he said, unbuttoning his fly. 'It needs another wash, don't you think?' He unleashed a stream of pee and directed it at the bike.

Bunny giggled, 'I do believe that I think you're right, Eddie old thing,' he said and stepped up to add his own golden arc onto the machine.

'Will you two stop it,' said Bean. 'Someone will see.'

'No they won't,' said Eddie, shaking the last drops off. 'Anyway, it's dark, how would they know it was us? Come on, let's get inside. I could murder some toast.'

As they walked back to their hut, Bean looked back over his shoulder. He could not be sure, but he thought he saw a curtain drop back into place on one of the windows.

He decided not to say anything to the other two.

CHAPTER FIVE

England, Thursday 1st February, 1917

'Rise and shine, sir. Brought you a nice cup of tea.'

Eddie opened his eyes and immediately wished he hadn't. It was still dark. The hut was filled with the unmistakable aroma of paraffin from a Tilley lamp. Although not that bright the light hurt his eyes and the pressurised hiss of the lamp made his head throb.

'Smith, what on earth do think you are doing man? It's the middle of the night.'

'Captain Hollinghurst's orders, sir, he wants you and Lieutenants Monroe and Cavendish to report to Hangar One at 6.15 sharp in full flying gear. Sir…wake up sir'

Smith was shaking Bunny's shoulder.

'Six-fifteen? Six? It's not light 'til gone seven.'

'Maybe so, sir, but that's the Captain's orders. Lieutenant…it's time to get up.'

Bunny muttered somthing and rolled over.

'It will be because of last night,' said Bean, swinging his legs out of his bed. One of the advantages he had over the rest of them by drinking no more than shandy was that he tended to be more alert in a morning. 'I told you both to keep it down but you wouldn't listen.'

Eddie screwed his eyes up against the light and tried to focus on the hands of his watch. 'Old Hollinghurst isn't that vindictive. He isn't one to bear a grudge. Smith, it's 5 am! Why are you getting us up at this time?'

'Captain's orders, sir. He was most particular about getting you up at this time, Sir. Lieutenant…'

Smith was still trying to rouse Bunny with little sign of success.

'Well whatever, I still say he is taking his revenge. Hold fast there Broadhurst, I'll get him up for you,' said Bean.

There was a full pitcher of ice-cold water they kept by the basin for shaving. Bean picked it up and emptied it over Bunny's head.

This had the desired effect.

*

The three of them stood miserably in the hangar.

'What time is it?' said Bean.

'Ten to seven,' said Eddie. Despite having his full winter flying gear on he was shivering. Bunny in the meantime was swaying like a small tree in a stiff breeze.

'I think I'm going to die,' he muttered. 'Bury me by the oak tree. It's tried to kill me enough times on take-off. That's where I belong.'

Two of the mechanics preparing the BE2 next to them exchanged knowing glances and grinned. Eddie knew Bean was right; this did look like revenge.

He saw Captain Hollinghurst leaving the officers' mess and heading in their direction. Now they'd find out for sure.

'Look out,' said Eddie. They shuffled to an approximation of attention.

Hollinghurst walked slowly down their line. He was the shortest of the four of them, barely five foot three and probably only two or three years older but he could have passed for forty. There were grey flecks in his hair and, although his face was unlined, his eyes were those of someone who had experienced enough for a complete lifetime. Eddie knew that Hollinghurst had served a full year at the front before being posted to the training squadron; there were rumours he had run up against the German ace Boelke and had barely escaped with his life.

He reached the end of the line and then walked slowly back again, looking into each of their faces. Still he said nothing.

Eddie would have much preferred it if he had chosen to shout and scream.

At last Hollinghurst turned to face them.

'At ease,' he said and they all exhaled and relaxed.

'So here you are, my three best students.'

'That's nice of you to say, sir,' said Bean.

Hollinghurst walked up to Bean and stared up at him from a distance of about three inches. Eddie suddenly had an image of a Jack Russell trying to dominate an Irish Wolfhound – and succeeding. He had to bite his lip to stop himself laughing, he knew it would only make things worse.

'Monroe, did I give you permission to speak?'

'Sorry, sir, no sir.'

'Have you perhaps heard of sarcasm, Monroe?'

'Yes sir, I have, sir.'

'So when I called you my best students what do you think I meant, Monroe?'

'I don't know, sir.'

Eddie allowed a snort of laughter to escape. Within moments Hollinghurst was in front of him. Eddie rigidly stared ahead of him and tried not to look into the face of his instructor.

'What rank are you, Grenville?'

'Second Lieutenant, sir.'

'Well if you want to live to be a full Lieutenant, I suggest you stop spending your time getting drunk and coming back to the field at all hours and start paying more attention to what we are trying to teach you. Do I make myself clear?'

'Yes sir.'

To Eddie's relief, the Captain backed off. 'And that goes for all of you.'

'Yes sir,' chorused Bean and Bunny.

'Right, well let's see if we can teach you something to keep you alive for a day or two over in France. We are going to spend this morning practicing formation flying, out to Beachy Head and then back along the coast.'

Eddie sighed, then realised he had done it loud enough for Hollinghurst to hear for the Captain was immediately back under his nose again.

'You have a problem with that, Grenville?'

'No sir, but…'

'But? But what, Grenville.'

'Well, it is a bit…well, boring, sir.'

For a moment Eddie thought that Hollinghurst was going to explode.

'Boring? Boring, is it now? I tell you what, Grenville, you will find it really boring when you get separated from your formation over the lines and some Hun drills you and your poor bloody observer full of lead. Your mother will find it really boring when she gets the telegram saying her little boy is intimately interred with a heap of doped linen, spruce and iron ten feet down in the mud of Flanders. Your observer's widow will find it really boring explaining to her children that their father isn't coming home. And they would all find it particularly boring to discover it all came about because some wet behind the ears young pilot could not be bothered to learn the discipline of formation flying.'

Hollinghurst paused, and took a deep breath. He was a little more composed when he spoke again.

'I'm just trying to help you stay alive, Grenville, that's all. You may think this is all a game then home to the mess for crumpets, but it's not, it's a bloody serious deadly game. Grow up, Grenville. All of you, in fact. Do I make myself clear?'

This time all three of them chorused; 'Yes sir.'

'Right, I'm going to take the Avro. Cavendish, you are with me in the front seat, please try not to kill me. You two take a BE each.'

'Yes sir.'

'I want a tight formation. Watch for my signals. Keep with me in the turns. If you mess this up we will be doing this every morning at this time until you get it right or one or all of us dies, and having seen some of your flying, I'm not sure which is the best bet. Any questions?'

'No sir,' they said together.

After all this the flight itself was largely incidental.

Apart from Bunny throwing up in a turn and covering the captain in the cockpit behind with a combination of stale beer and milky tea.

CHAPTER SIX

England, Sunday 4th March, 1917

It was cold, very cold. It was, after all, England in early-March. It was a beautiful day, crisp and still but the gathering clouds amidst the eggshell-blue promised rain later, perhaps even snow.

It was even colder because Eddie was so high up. He did not absolutely trust his altimeter but it read 9,000 feet and that seemed about right. Eddie did not care that it was cold, or that it might rain later because he was in the throws of falling in love. He knew that he was falling in love twice over: with the machine he was piloting and the sheer, exhilarating joy of flying.

The machine, although old and well-worn, was light and agile. It was so unlike the archaic Farmans and the trundling BE2s that he had flown so far in his training. This felt entirely different, a thoroughbred, coltish, light and responsive, almost like an extension of himself. It climbed like a monkey and danced between the clouds, so precise he could choose how far to brush the wing-tips through the whisks of water vapour.

Above all though it was special because of what it was and who had flown a machine just like this one. It was French, a Nieuport 17, one like Ball had flown in his last tour before returning to England as a hero late the previous year. Although he knew it was unlikely, Eddie wondered if Ball himself had flown this very machine, perhaps even ferried it back over the channel when he had come home. It was armed too, and Eddie could not resist squinting down the sights and letting his gloved finger caress the trigger lightly, being careful not to depress it, imagining an enemy aircraft in his sights, seeing his rounds go home, it starting to burn and spin down out of control.

He smiled, and took his finger off the trigger. This was no game, he knew that, but, for the first time, he felt that he was getting close to actually doing what his heroes did, Ball and Hawker.

Oh and Percy, he could not forget him, he was a hero too, all the pilots were.

Still he had to get back. He had been told by Captain Hollinghurst to take the Nieuport up just to get a feel for it, it was a treat. Hollinghurst must have seen the way Eddie looked at it every time he came into the hangar but then all of the fledgling pilots had been the same. Despite this, he had only asked Eddie whether he would like to try it. Eddie knew it was an honour and he did not want to blot his copybook by taking it for too long or, even worse, smashing it up.

His approach was even more careful than ever, he blipped the throttle of the unfamiliar rotary as he crossed the threshold of the field and set the little scout down in an almost perfect three point landing, probably better than any other he had managed at his training. The machine trundled up to the waiting mechanics, Eddie switching off as they reached him. Slowly, unwilling to give up the machine so quickly, he undid his belts and climbed out. He couldn't help but smile.

'It's rather special, isn't it?'

Eddie turned and saluted Hollinghurst but the captain waved that away and put his arm through Eddie's. 'Let's walk a while, Grenville.'

'Sir.'

'I was watching the way you handled the Nieuport, Grenville.'

Eddie's heart sank. He was about to be told off. What had he done wrong? He thought he had done pretty well.

'Yes sir?'

'To me it looked like flying a scout came pretty naturally to you.'

Eddie almost yelled in relief, but said, 'Thank you, sir.'

'There is another squadron I could send you to, once you graduate from here. They are just forming up, they are going to be flying Pups, excellent machines, very like the Nieuport but even nicer to fly.'

'That sounds fantastic, sir.'

'It would mean more training. They're only just getting their machines and have only got a handful of pilots so far. They probably won't be over in France for a few months, maybe not until the Autumn.'

Eddie thought about the implications of this. 'Oh right,' he said. 'What about Bean and Bunny, er, I mean Cavendish and Monroe?'

Hollinghurst shook his head. 'I can't recommend them for this, Grenville. Monroe is a sound pilot but he's just not bold enough. As for Cavendish, well...Anyway, the brass are crying out for more two seater pilots over in France. I was only allowed to look for a select few.'

Eddie could not help but feel the pride rise inside of him. He was being singled out, just him. Yet it would mean leaving his friends. And prevent him getting to France for quite a while. That wouldn't be so bad but, well, he knew that Bunny looked to him as a leader, almost a big brother. Could he leave him in the lurch like that?

'Oh right. Well, I'm not sure...'

Hollinghurst smiled. 'Look, I understand about not wanting to be split up from your friends. Chances are you would be anyway, it's unlikely that you'd all end up at the same squadron. Anyway, I believe you have some leave coming up?'

'Yes, I was hoping to go and see my brother. He's in hospital you know?'

'Yes I knew. Well, use the time to think it over. This is quite an opportunity, Eddie.'

It was only after the captain had gone that Eddie realised he had called him by his Christian name. It filled him with almost as much pride as being asked to be a scout pilot.

CHAPTER SEVEN

England, Wednesday 7th March 1917

'Excuse me?'

Eddie had been engrossed in his Sherlock Holmes so had not been paying attention to the comings and goings in the train compartment. He looked up into the brown eyes of a young woman. He quickly got to his feet, trying to take his uniform's cap off. In his haste he dislodged it and sent it spinning to the floor.

The newcomer smiled. 'I suppose I should be flattered. I don't usually have that much of an effect on people.'

'Sorry,' said Eddie, picking up his cap and dusting it down.

'I was asking whether this seat was taken?'

'Oh no, it's not. Feel free.'

'Thank you.'

The young woman sat down on the opposite bench whilst Eddie resumed his. Even though he knew it was rude, whilst she was sorting through her bag he took the opportunity to look her over as he pretended to read his book. He couldn't help himself. She was dressed in a long, light coloured coat and a dark hat with a narrow brim, both wet from the rain that lashed against the train window. Her hair was short, dark and wavy with hints of auburn whilst her features were small and neat, indeed there was something almost oriental about her.

'What a foul night it is,' she said, checking her face in a compact, brushing drops of water from the strands of hair that peeked out from under her hat. He was no expert on the opposite sex but guessed that she perhaps a few years older than him. It didn't matter, she was very attractive.

'Yes, it looks pretty beastly,' agreed Eddie, trying desperately to think of something to say.

She closed her compact and looked at Eddie, tilting her head a little to one side. 'You look quite familiar,' she said. 'Have we met?'

'I don't think so,' said Eddie, certain that he would have remembered her.

'Oh. Perhaps you remind me of someone.'

Eddie waited, hoping she would carry on talking but, instead, she sat back and looked out of the window, seemingly more interested in the driving rain and the village they were now passing through than continuing.

How did you talk to a woman? An attractive one? There had to be a way.

'I'm a pilot,' he blurted out.

She turned to look at him. He saw her eyes flick to the wings and RFC badge on his uniform.

'I'd worked that out,' she said.

'Oh, right, yes, of course.' He felt himself blush.

'Have you been over in France?'

'No, not yet. I'm in training.'

'Oh, right,' she said, her voice dull.

Eddie felt himself flush even deeper. 'I've nearly finished. Hope to get a squadron posting soon and get over to France.'

To Eddie's eye, she remained unimpressed.

'I wouldn't be in too much of a hurry to do that,' she murmured.

'I'm quite ready face the Boche,' said Eddie. He inwardly cursed his voice which had risen higher than he would have liked and his tone which he knew to be harsh. This was not going at all how he wanted it to go.'

'I'm sure you are.' Her voice was gentle and therefore somewhat eased the suspected condescension.

They travelled in silence for a few minutes, with Eddie trying to concentrate on his Conan Doyle but finding his gaze drawn to the nurse. He tried not to stare but, for all the difficulty of their conversation, was entranced by the curve of her high, pale cheekbones and their contrast with the curl of the hair that peeked out from beneath her hat. He thought his examination of her was quite discrete but then realised that she could see him in the reflection of the carriage window. As he quickly looked away he thought he saw her lips twitch into a slight smile.

'I'm sorry,' she said. 'I shouldn't tease.' He turned back to find she was looking straight at him. She held her hand out. 'I'm Annie Ross.'

Eddie took it. 'Grenville. Edward. Eddie.'

'Ah, that's why you look familiar. You're related to Captain

Grenville?'

'You know Percy? He's my brother.'

She nodded. 'I'm a nurse. He's one of my patients.'

'Oh right. That's good. Thank you.'

She shrugged. 'It's just my job.'

She went back to looking out into the darkness, leaving Eddie wondering how to keep her talking. She was simply, suddenly the most wonderful person he'd ever met. Should he ask her to dinner? What about Percy? He was going to see him. Oh, and he hadn't asked how he was. What would she think about him?

'You're following your brother's path then.' Her voice brought his thoughts into the moment.

'Yes. Well I'm trying to at least. My family aren't too happy about it but what he has been doing is so exciting.'

'Exciting?' She puffed out her cheeks and gave a long drawn out exhalation. 'You could call it that. I wouldn't.'

Eddie was so taken aback that it took him a few seconds to reply.

'I beg your pardon? What on earth did you mean by that?'

'I've seen what it's done to people like your brother.'

'Percy? What do you mean? Is he badly wounded?'

'You don't know?'

'Know, know what? What's happened to him?'

'Oh no,' Annie said. 'I'm sorry, I didn't mean to alarm you. I was just surprised you didn't know his condition. He's not that bad – Not physically anyway.'

'He's not been in touch with the family. We've only just found out where he was.'

Annie nodded. 'Ah, I see. Yes, that would fit.'

'Fit? What do you mean? And what do you mean. "he's not physically that bad"?'

'I...' Annie sighed. 'Look I shouldn't say. You should see him for yourself.'

All thoughts about getting to know Annie better had now been driven away.

'No. You can't leave it like that. Tell me. What's wrong with him?'

Annie looked at him for a few moments, Eddie realised that she was weighing up what to say.

'He's...difficult,' she said at last.

'Difficult?'

She nodded. 'Withdrawn, remote, at least most of the time.'

'And the rest?'

'Then he's bad tempered and very angry.'

'Angry? Who with?'

'Everyone but, I think, with himself more than anyone.'

'Himself? You can't be talking about Percy. He's the mildest mannered, polite chap, always been known for it. He'd leave a room rather than have an argument. He's the best brother a chap could ever have. I won't hear a word against him, and I'd ask you to take it back.'

Annie pulled a face and shook her head. 'I'm not criticizing him. I'm just telling you how he is.'

'It sounded like criticism.'

Annie stared at Eddie, a thoughtful expression on her face.

'When did you last see your brother?' she said at last.

'Not for some time. He's been in France for a year. I was away at school until last summer. I even missed seeing him when he was last on leave.'

Annie nodded slowly.

'That would explain things,' she said.

'What things? I certainly think you need to explain yourself.' Eddie found his temper rising. Annie did not seem to notice.

'You'll find that war changes people. Often radically,' she said.

'Not Percy.'

Annie shook her head and sighed.

'I'm sorry. I'm tired,' she said. 'I've been doing long shifts. Yesterday was my first day off in weeks. I'm not trying to upset you but I'm not telling you anything that isn't true. I've perhaps been less discreet than I should have been.'

'Yes, you have. What right do you have to talk like that?'

'You're right I don't have any right. But I have been nursing men back from the front for more than a year now. If you'd seen what I have then...'

Her voice tailed off and she turned to stare out of the carriage window again. It was a few seconds before she spoke.

'It's been rewarding but it has also been hard. The physical wounds can be horrific but there are other things as well, hidden things, things that people do not talk about but might actually be far worse.'

'Are you saying that Percy is crazy? If you are then...'

'Please,' said Annie turning back to face Eddie. 'I really don't want to make you angry. I'm certainly not saying he's crazy but not all wounds can be seen. It is just, from what you have said, you must be ready for a change in your brother and make allowances. '

Eddie sat back, not knowing quite what to make of this conversation. It had come completely out of the blue. He'd badly wanted to get this woman talking but, now he had, it had gone in a very unexpected direction.

'I'm sorry,' she said again. 'We really have got off on the wrong foot, haven't we? What must you think of me? Are you coming down to see your brother?'

'Yes, that was the idea. I thought it was the best use of my leave to come and see him tonight.'

'You have a long leave?'

'No, it's basically just tonight. I was only able to get a 24-hour pass.'

'Oh.'

'What? What is it?'

'You'll have missed the visiting times for today,' she murmured, biting her lip in thought. 'They end at six-thirty.'

Eddie put his head in his hands.

'It's past seven now! I only have this evening. I have to be back with my squadron tomorrow morning.'

Annie put her hand on his knee. I tell you what, what if you come with me to the hospital and I will have a word with matron, explain the situation, how does that sound?'

'It sounds better,' said Eddie, surprised at what a jolt he felt deep inside when Annie smiled at him. The train started to slow.

'This is our station,' said Annie. 'Keep your fingers crossed I can swing something for you.'

CHAPTER EIGHT

England, Wednesday 7th March 1917

Eddie hated waiting.

He was not the most patient of people anyway but particularly disliked hospitals, so having to wait in the entrance hall of one was doubly bad.

He had bitter memories of being dragged to one as a child, the family visiting his grandfather, to watch the old man, a skeletal shell of his former hearty self, cough the last of his life away.

He found the silence oppressive, the echoing surfaces cold and unwelcoming and the smell of carbolic masking a hint of stale urine sickening. He wondered if it was just the memory of death or that hospitals also reminded him too much of school; another cold, austere, loveless institution with an autocratic regime.

Somewhere in the distance, someone screamed. A man, although the sound was almost inhuman, a primeval howl that sent shivers up Eddie's spine. The screaming went on for a full minute before it became intermittent. Someone else could be heard talking, he could not make out the words but the voice was lower, calming yet still firm. Soon silence was restored.

Footsteps started, echoing off the hard surfaces, accompanied by the squeak of an unlubricated wheel. The half-glazed doors to the entrance hall were pushed open by a nurse as she backed through them. She seemed to be struggling, the doors had closed on the wheelchair she was pulling. Eddie sprang to his feet to hold one of the doors open whilst she disentangled herself.

'Thanks,' she said.

'Don't mention it,' said Eddie and glanced down.

In the wheelchair was a man, or at least the remains of one; he had no arms or legs, he was just a trunk. His face white and waxy, his eyes staring at a point some distance away as if he did not want to focus on what lay below.

The nurse swung the chair around and headed across the hall, leaving Eddie standing, shocked. What would life be like for someone like that? No wonder he looked out of things, Eddie was sure he would be the same.

'Would you mind doing the honours?'

Eddie realised that the nurse had spoken.

'Pardon?'

'The door?' she said, nodding in the direction she was travelling where there was a matching pair of double doors to the one she had just come through.

'Oh yes of course, sorry,' said Eddie and hurried over to hold the door open.

The nurse smiled her thanks. Eddie found it easier to keep eye contact with her than look down again.

He found he was trembling as he sat down to wait again.

It was less than a minute before Annie came back from the back office.

'You're in luck,' she said. 'Matron is in a reasonable mood. She says that under the circumstances you can see your brother but only for 20 minutes. Sorry, that's the best I could manage.'

'It's better than nothing,' said Eddie.

'That's the spirit. Come on then, he's down here,' said Annie, leading the way.

'Annie?'

'Yes.'

'Thanks. I really do appreciate this.'

Annie gave a little ghost of a smile which gave Eddie another jolt.

'I'll take you up there, then go and get changed for my shift. Then I'll have to come and get you again.'

'And see me off the premises?'

'And see you off the premises, yes. Matron was most insistent about that.' Annie took them up a set of stairs. 'He's in the small room at the end. He's on his own at the moment.'

Eddie walked on but then realised that Annie had stopped at the end of the corridor.

'Aren't you coming in?' he said.

'No. I...your brother and I...you've not seen him for ages. I'll... go and get changed.'

Annie turned and hurried off before Eddie could reply.

Bemused he knocked softly on the door of his brother's room and stepped inside.

The room was in darkness, the only light coming from the corridor. Eddie stood at the door and peered into the gloom. There were three beds arranged in a line along the far wall but only one was occupied. This surprised Eddie; the hospital had struck him as being busy, it was odd that they would have unused beds.

Eddie edged towards the bed, his eyes adjusting to the lack of illumination. He could see that Percy was laid on his back but his face was turned away from the door.

'Percy? Percy, old chap?' said Eddie softly.

'What do you want?' Percy had not moved.

'Percy, it's me, Eddie.

'Eddie?'

'That's hardly a friendly way to greet your little brother.'

'I know. I...I...just don't want people fussing around me.'

'Well I'm not one to fuss, am I?'

'No.' There was a sigh from the bed. 'All right. Put the light on would you. The switch is by the door.'

Eddie did as he was told.

He could now see Percy properly. His brother was pale and frailer than he remembered. His face was pinched, his lips thin. He looked much older. The blanket over his legs was lifted off the mattress by some kind of frame. Eddie was about to ask Percy about it but his brother spoke first.

'Oh God, Eddie, the RFC? What on earth possessed you?'

Eddie looked down at his uniform.

'What's wrong? I thought you'd be pleased.'

'Pleased? Why the hell would I be pleased?'

'Well because...you...'

'Why didn't you join the navy? You would be a damn sight safer there.'

'Safer? I don't care about being safe. Anyway, I hate boats. I love flying and I want my chance to have a crack at the Hun.'

'A crack at the Hun? What the hell do you know about that?'

'But...'

'Be quiet Eddie and listen for once, it might just save your life. Flying at the front is not a game. Things have changed; we were on top but we're not now. The Jerries have much better aircraft than us. It's no jaunt up in the clouds anymore, it's deadly, a killing ground. You'd last five minutes. It's not a place for a boy.'

'Boy? I'm not a boy any more. When did you get so defeatist? I didn't put you down for someone who would buy all that Pemberton-Billing guff.'

'Guff it may be but I know what I've seen. I've buried far too many friends.'

'Ball and his like hold their own and more.'

'Ball's a freak of nature. And he's lucky. It's only a matter of time before he buys it flying the way he does.'

Eddie opened his mouth to say something but then shut it again. He shook his head.

'What are you saying? That we're losing? Why have you got the wind up?'

'Don't talk about what you have no idea about Eddie. And don't you dare question my courage.'

'I wasn't. I wouldn't do that.'

'It sounded very much like you were.'

'Well I didn't mean it to. I was only answering you, it's you who is acting and talking strangely. I'm just surprised at you. I've not seen you for a year and the first thing you do is have a go at me, just because I've done my duty and signed up. I expected you to support me. I didn't expect you to be so negative.'

'Well perhaps I have grown up.'

Eddie stared at his brother. He considered leaving but then remembered what Annie had said. He would be patient. He did, after all, have something to tell Percy. He pulled up a chair and turned it to face his brother's bed and sat down.

'Let's not fall out,' he said. 'We never have done before.'

'I know. I'm sorry. It's just...' Percy's voice trailed away.

'That's okay. Anyway, it's not like the Jerries have had it all their own way,' he said.

'What do you mean?'

This was going to be difficult. 'Siggi...' he began.

'I know,' said Percy quickly turning his face away from Eddie.

Eddie sighed in relief.

'How did you find out he was dead?' Percy whispered.

'Alice wrote to mother. She had just heard the news that he was missing. She was distraught.'

'Missing,' murmured Percy.

'Yes. Sorry, we were not sure whether you knew. We knew how close you were. Apparently, he was last seen following one of our planes over the lines.'

'Poor Alice,' Percy muttered.

Something was bothering Eddie. Something Percy had said... What was it? Then he got it. 'Dead?' he said.

'Pardon?'

'You said dead, not missing. How did you know?'

'Oh leave it will you?' yelled Percy. 'It's just a nicety. Dead, missing, shot to bits, burnt to a crisp, what does it matter? It all means the same bloody thing. Dead, gone forever. Some mother grieving, some wife or sweetheart weeping for their lost love. It's all the bloody same.'

'Percy...'

'Just sod off, Eddie. Sod off back to mother and father, sod off back to your squadron and just leave me alone. All of you.'

'Percy. You're upset. You don't mean that.'

'I do mean it. I want you all to go away and stay away.'

Percy had turned his head away. Eddie waited, thinking that it would all blow over, that Percy was upset by the news about Siggi - they had always been close - and his thinking impaired by pain. Eventually he realised that his brother was in earnest and intent on ignoring him.

'Oh dash it, be that way then,' he said, getting to his feet. 'Be like that if you must. I *am* going back to Netheravon and I *will* stay in the Flying Corp. There's a war to be won, in case you hadn't noticed and I'm going to do my bit.'

He should leave, he knew that. He had said his piece and Percy had said his. There was no point in staying. Something stopped him though, though what it was he did not know. Somehow, Eddie just knew that something between them had remained unsaid.

Despite this feeling he almost gave up, was on the point of turning, walking to the door, when he heard Percy doing something that he'd never seen him do before: crying.

It was more than tears. Percy was sobbing.

Eddie started towards his brother, then hesitated. What did one do with a crying man? He was not even sure that Percy knew that he was still there, he would surely be embarrassed if he knew? Should he say something, cough, let his brother know he was still there? Or just leave?

'Eddie, Eddie,' Percy whispered. 'Where are you?'

Eddie stepped closer. 'I'm here, old chap. There's no need for all this, is there? Stop it, eh, Percy. Please.'

But Percy didn't stop, if anything he sobbed harder.

Eddie wondered if he should call someone, a nurse, Annie? Yes, Annie, at least he knew her. But would that make Percy feel worse.

Percy was still facing away from him, awkwardly half-rolled

over in the bed. Eddie guessed that whatever was wrong with his leg restricted his movements. He sat on the bed next to his brother and, rather limply, patted Percy on the shoulder. 'Easy there, old man, I don't know what's wrong but is there any need to -'

Abruptly, Percy rolled back and, to his great alarm, threw his arms around him and pushed his head against Eddie's chest. He could feel the wetness of Percy's tears soaking through his shirt.

'Percy...' he began, but then stopped, realising that he had no idea what to say. He wanted to push him away, tell him to pull himself together, to start being his big brother again, but he knew he could not say any of these things. But what did you do with a crying man? A crying brother, someone who had always protected you? He put his own arms around Percy.

He really hoped that Annie would not choose this moment to come back.

'Percy,' he said again.

'Siggi,' Percy said, his voice muffled by being pressed against Eddie. 'Siggi, Siggi, I'm so sorry.'

'We're all sorry about Siggi,' said Eddie. 'He was a nice chap. We all will miss him. It must be dreadful for Alice -'

'Don't say that! Oh, don't say that!' Percy's sobs, which had died down, now redoubled.

'I'm sorry, I was just saying.'

Percy suddenly jerked upright, letting go of Eddie, who could not help but give a sigh of relief. Perhaps this was all going to be over, his brother was going to pull himself together, get back to normal.

'I killed him Eddie,' Percy said.

Eddie just stared at him. 'Pardon?'

'I killed him. I killed Siggi.'

Eddie's mouth dropped open. 'You shot him down? How do you...'

Percy had stopped crying, but his eyes were red and rimmed with the dark circles of someone who found sleep difficult.

'Eddie, I have to tell you,' he said. 'I have to tell you what I've done.'

CHAPTER NINE

England, Wednesday 7th March 1917

Eddie slammed the door so hard that the panes of glass in the skylight above rattled. He ran down the corridor and down the stairs; He needed to get out, he needed air.

Which way to go? He had not been paying attention on the way in. Where was the exit? He tried one set of doors and found himself on a long corridor that looked familiar but, on following it, arrived at a ward full of amputees. A pair of nurses were lifting a legless man into bed, struggling under his weight. One of them stared at Eddie.

'What on earth are you doing? You shouldn't be in here.'

'Sorry,' said Eddie, and turned back the way he had come. It occurred to him that he could have asked the way out but he just wanted to get away, he did not want anyone looking at him. He went through door after door, getting more and more lost.

'Eddie, Eddie. What are you doing?'

The call came from behind him. He turned to find Annie hurrying along the corridor.

'Eddie, where have you been?' she said. 'I came to get you and found you'd gone. If the matron finds you she'll skin you and me alive.'

'How do I get out of here?' Eddie yelled. 'Let me out!'

'Eddie, what's wrong?' Annie put her hand on his arm. 'Calm yourself. What happened?'

'I...I can't tell you. Please, just let me get away from this place.'

'Alright, alright.' He found Annie's voice calming. She must have to use this way of talking a lot with her patients, whatever he found it was working. 'Come on, it's back this way.'

She led him back along the corridor down which he had dashed. His temper cooling, meekly, he let her guide him.

'Here we are,' she said at last, as they entered the entrance hall.

'Thanks,' he said. 'I'm really sorry for running around like that.'

'That's all right, no harm done,' she said. She was staring at him, concern in her eyes. 'Did your brother...' Her voice trailed off.

'That's between me and him.'

'Of course.' said Annie. 'I'm sorry. I did warn you that he was difficult.'

'Well you were right, weren't you? No need to rub it in.'

'I wasn't rubbing it in. Really.'

Eddie took a deep breath. 'I'm sorry. It's not your fault. It's his.'

Annie frowned. 'Don't be so hard on him. War affects people. Don't judge him because of that. He needs his family.'

Eddie shook his head. 'No he doesn't. He doesn't need anyone. In fact he should be locked up.'

'You don't mean that.'

'I do. Believe me, I do. I want nothing to do with him ever again.' Eddie sighed, shook his head. 'I should go,' he said. 'Thank you for all you have done.'

He turned and walked to the door.

'Eddie wait.'

He swung around.

'What time is your train?'

He thought for a moment. 'I don't know. I suppose it will be first thing in the morning now.'

'Where are you going to stay?'

He shrugged. 'I don't know. I suppose I will just walk to the station, find a bench to sleep on.'

Annie frowned. 'It's freezing out there, and raining.'

'I don't have a choice, do I?'

Annie looked up and down the hall. There was no one around. She put her hand in her pocket. She took his hand and pressed a key into it. 'Go to the nurses lodge. It's the white building by the entrance. My room is number two on the ground floor. There should be no one around at this time of night. Go and let yourself in, but for goodness sake make sure no one sees you. My shift ends at two. I'll see you then.'

'But...'

'No buts,' she said. 'You've had an upset. I don't like the thought of you wandering the streets of Eastbourne in the state you are in. Go on, quickly!'

She pushed him towards the door, her touch giving him a jolt like the one he had had on the train when she had smiled at him.

'Thank you,' he said, and headed out into the night.

The rain hit him like a slap in the face. It was perhaps what he needed, it woke him up, helped him to think. What was he doing? He was heading to a woman's room, why was he doing that? What kind of girl was she to suggest this? Didn't she care about her reputation? He should leave, go to the station. He should get away, away from that...that...*thing* that looked like his brother, but which had done such an unspeakable, disgusting thing.

How could he do that to Siggi, to Alice?

Why?

Why had he done it?

The night was cold, the rain was coming on harder. He was getting wet. He realised that he had left his coat in Percy's room. Well he wasn't going to go back and get it.

He had reached the lodge. There did not seem to be anyone about. He might as well go inside and leave the key in there otherwise she might not be able to find it. She seemed a kind person, she had been helpful, he did not like the idea of her coming off her shift tired and unable to find her key to get to bed.

Inside, the hall was lit by a gas light turned low. She was right: there was no one around. Room two was on the left-hand side. Eddie unlocked it and went quietly inside, leaving the door open a crack whilst he put the light on, then closing it to as softly as he could.

The room was small, with only a tiny window, the curtains of which he quickly drew. There was a bed, a small armchair, a dark wooden wardrobe and a dressing table which had seen better days. On it were two picture frames: a studio portrait of an older couple, him moustachioed, sitting whilst the lady stood slightly behind, her hand resting lightly on the shoulder of the man. Although there was the customary stiff formality in the portrait there was somehow no coldness between the pair, and there was enough of a resemblance to each of them to make it obvious that this was Annie's parents.

The second picture was smaller. A young man, dark haired, with a trim moustache. He was in uniform, Eddie recognised the cap badge as that of the Royal Engineers, but face did not look soldierly. There was a softness in the eyes and the man's mouth hinted at humour, like he was going to break into a smile as soon as the shutter had been pressed.

Who was he? Brother? No, he looked nothing like Annie or her parents. So an intended, a betrothed, a husband? Probably.

Eddie put the photograph down. What was he doing here? He should go.

The rain splashed against the window. It sounded like a filthy night out there. It wouldn't hurt to wait until it had stopped. Eddie sat down in the armchair. Although it was small and worn it was surprisingly comfortable.

His thoughts were filled with Percy. Percy and Siggi - and Alice too. The three of them were almost inseparable, Eddie, as the younger brother, always felt like an outsider when they were together. Siggi and Alice. It always seemed so right, so natural that they would be married. Their wedding, in the church in the village had been so memorable. Siggi's family, over from Germany, so open and friendly, so unlike Eddie's own parents and their generation.

Four years ago now. That was so hard to believe. Four years.

So much had changed. The big world had gone mad since, and so now, apparently, had their little world.

Percy. Why had he done it?

CHAPTER TEN

England, Thursday 8th March 1917

'Eddie.'

He woke with a start. Someone was knocking, softly but urgently. Where was he? Who was it?

'What, what is it?'

'Shh, keep your voice down.'

Annie's voice, little more than a whisper. Of course, he was in her room. He'd locked her out.

Quickly he got up and unlatched the door. She stepped inside and shut it behind her.

'I'm sorry,' he said. 'What time is it?'

'It's after two,' she said. 'I've just come off shift.' She straightened up and unfastened her coat. She was carrying another. 'You left this in your brother's room. I brought it over for you.' She put it on a chair.

'Thanks,' he said.

'He was very upset,' she said, hanging her own coat on the hook behind the door.

'I don't care,' Eddie said, getting to his feet and picking up his coat. 'I'd better be going.'

'Don't be so silly,' she said. 'You look as tired as I feel and the weather's foul. Sit down for goodness sake.'

'I'm fine.'

'Yes of course you are.' Annie sighed, and sat down on the bed. Eddie could see the tiredness in her face. There was also something else, something he had seen in her eyes on the train. A dullness, a sadness? 'Please sit, Eddie. I was just worried about you. About you and Percy in fact. He *is* my patient.'

Eddie paused, his coat half on.

'I'll light the fire, make some tea. Then you can go if you wish. How does that sound?'

It did sound good, Eddie had to admit. 'Alright,' he said. 'That sounds nice, thank you. I'll help you with the fire.'

'If you must,' she said, getting to her feet and going to the fireplace. 'Whatever you do though, please do it quietly. These walls are thick but I know from experience that the male voice carries through them.'

'Oh. Do some of the others have their husbands stay over then?' Eddie took his coat off again and joined her at the fireplace, helping to break sticks to make kindling.

He noticed her smile.

'You are quite an innocent, aren't you Eddie?'

'I'm sorry?'

'Nothing,' she said. 'There is some old newspaper over by the door. Get it would you?'

*

They sat drinking their tea on Annie's bed. She had offered condensed milk, but Eddie had refused it, preferring to take it black rather than have it sweet. He found sitting in such proximity to her quite awkward, he was conscious of her warmth, of her scent, a mixture of cologne and carbolic soap. For something to say he nodded at the photographs.

'Are they your parents?' he said.

'Yes.'

'Where are you from?'

'Nottingham.'

'Oh right, that's where Ball's from. His father is the mayor or something.'

'Ball?'

'The pilot? Albert Ball? He's the top scoring British ace. He's a spiffing chap.'

'Oh, all right. Yes, now you mention it, I think I've heard of him.'

They lapsed into silence. Eddie could not help but glance at the other photograph.

'That's David, my husband,' said Annie without prompting.

'Oh, right,' said Eddie.

'He was killed nearly a year ago.'

'I'm sorry.'

Annie continued to stare at the photograph. 'So many people have lost someone. Husbands, fathers, friends.' She turned her head to look at Eddie. 'And brothers,' she added.

Eddie turned away. 'I don't want to talk about him,' he said.

She sighed. 'Eddie, one of my biggest regrets with David is what I didn't get to say to him. There was so much that I wanted to share with him, what I wanted to tell him. The moment never seemed to be right, there was always going to be another time. And then there wasn't.

'You have to make allowances for what he has been through, Eddie. It's an awful strain being over there. I know.'

She was silent for a few moments.

'I didn't get to see David after he was posted to the front. He was due leave but he was killed before he could take it. There was a change in him though, in his letters. You can tell, you know, how people are from a letter. Not in what they say but how they say it. It was dreadful to see, I could only guess what he was going through.'

Annie put her hand on Eddie's. Despite his emotions, despite his hostility, her touch made his whole body tingle. He let it lie there for a few seconds but then jerked his hand away. He did not want his emotions to be so conflicted.

'No one should be changed like Percy. It's no excuse. He's become a monster.'

'No, he's not. He's been at war. People do terrible things in a war.'

Eddie looked at her for a few moments. Did that mean what he thought it meant?

'You knew?' he said.

'Yes,' she said. 'He told me.'

'He told you?'

'Yes, a few days after he came in. I think he needed someone to confess to.'

'Yet you've done nothing?'

Annie shrugged. 'What was there to do?'

'Tell the authorities.'

'Tell them what? That he did his duty?'

'His duty?' Eddie shook his head. 'How could that be duty?'

'Our troops kill hundreds every day. Is this really different?'

'Of course it's different. It was murder.'

Annie nodded. 'Yes, it was.'

'You didn't tell me. You should have done.'

'It wasn't my place to. You're his family.'

'I'm not. Not anymore. I can never have anything to do with him again.'

Annie shook her head. 'Percy needs you.'

Eddie looked at her in astonishment. 'Percy? Are you mad?

You want me to have sympathy for that monster?'

'Shh, keep your voice down,' she whispered urgently. 'People will hear.'

'I don't care.'

'Well I do. I'd like to keep my reputation, if you don't mind.'

'Reputation? What reputation? It was you who invited me into your room.'

She abruptly stood and walked to the fireplace. Eddie's head slumped, that was uncalled for, his anger had made him go too far. He got up and went over to her.

'Annie, I'm sorry,' he whispered. 'I didn't mean anything by that. I was upset.'

To his surprise, she turned and put her arms around him, pressing her head against his chest. Hesitatingly, he put his own arms around her.

He heard her whisper. 'You look so much like...'

'Like who?' he said.

To his surprise, she pulled away from him.

'I'm sorry, I think you'd better go,' she said.

Eddie stared at her in confusion for a few moments. 'Oh right, of course,' he said at last. He picked up his coat and put it on. He saw that she had sat down on the bed and was staring at the photographs again.

'I'll see myself out,' he whispered and turned to go.

His hand was on the door handle when he heard the rustle of her clothes and felt her hand grab his arm. She turned to face her. He could see that her eyes were red.

'Forgive me,' she whispered. 'I didn't mean to do that to you. I'm just quite...lonely.'

'I understand,' he said, though he knew in his heart that he didn't. 'Can I write to you?' he surprised himself by saying.

She smiled very briefly, then nodded. 'Yes, I'd like that.'

Eddie gave a little smile back, then let himself out.

CHAPTER ELEVEN

France, Thursday 29th March 1917

Eddie sighed, pen hovering over the paper upon which he had written just a couple of lines. What now?

He had got this far before. On the floor next to him was a wastepaper basket so full of screwed up pieces of paper that it had started to overflow onto the floor. They had all started the same way, with his address ('Somewhere in France' in deference to the censor), the date (March 29th, 1917) and the same salutation ('Dear Annie'). It was from this point forward that things started to go awry.

Everything he had written either sounded trite, or juvenile, or banal and boring. In some versions he had managed to achieve all three.

This one was rapidly heading the same way. Eddie threw his pen on the desk and, for a bit of variety, tore his latest effort into shreds.

Bean, lying on his bed, put down the book he had been reading and said: 'Affair of the heart, old chap?'

'No!' said Eddie. 'Well, not really anyway.'

'Ah, even worse then.'

'What do you mean, worse?'

Bean smiled. 'A want-to-be affair of the heart.'

'What would you know,' said Eddie.

'All the signs are there, Eddie old chap. The moping, the sighing, the big puppy dog eyes, the whining. I've seen it all before.'

'You have? When?'

'Pater's old gun dog. Had a thing for the bishop's spaniel. You've got just the same look.'

'No I haven't,' said Eddie, feeling himself flush red. 'Have I?'

'Well apart from the cold wet nose and waggy tail, yes you have. Now why don't you tell your old Uncle Bean all about it?'

'Old? I'm three months older than you.'

'Yes but you're certainly not wiser. Anyway I'm bored and nosy and you'll feel better for getting it off your chest. Who is she?'

Eddie got up from the desk and went to lie on his own bed.

'She's a nurse,' he said.

'A nurse, eh? You sly devil. When did you meet her? You've been with us night and day for the last four months. Except when you went down to see your brother...ah. He's in a hospital isn't he?'

'Sanatorium.'

'Same difference. But, my word, you act quickly don't you? You only had a 24 hour pass.'

'It wasn't like that. She had been nursing Percy, yes. When I saw him there were some...things about him that I needed to ask her about so...I walked her back to her rooms.'

'Great excuse, old chap, I never had you down as that quick witted.'

Eddie shook his head in exasperation. 'I wasn't thinking that way, truly I wasn't but, yeah maybe she did. I don't know, I really just wanted to know about Percy.'

Bean nodded sagely. 'Ah, disappointed the lady did you?'

'No. Well maybe, yes, I'm not sure. She hugged me and then... well she seemed to change her mind.'

'Bit of a tease, eh?'

'No,' said Eddie, thinking things through in his own mind for perhaps the hundredth time. 'No, I don't think so. She is older than me, 25, 26 maybe, you know how hard it is to tell?'

'Gosh, a full seven years older than you, Eddie. Married?'

'A widow. Husband was killed in fifteen.'

'I see,' said Bean, doing the sage nodding again.

'What? What do you see? And how would you know?' Eddie found himself getting angry.

'I have four older sisters, remember,' said Bean with a rueful smile. 'I have seen the workings of the female heart at close quarters.'

'And? What does this great experience tell you?'

'I think perhaps you reminded her of her lost love, albeit fleetingly. But then she remembered him and felt guilty. And then she remembered what you are.'

'What do you mean by that?' Eddie swung his legs off the bed and crossed his arms. 'That I'm just a boy, a foolish young lad?'

'No, not at all, Eddie.' Bean's voice was calm, cool and steady. He sat up himself and leaned across the gap between the beds. 'I didn't mean that at all. I was talking about those.' He ran his fingers over the wings on Eddie's RFC badge. The touch was so soft as to almost be a caress. Bean's face was serious, his eyes, first fixed on the crest, then moved up to look into Eddie's. He smiled. 'She remembered you were a pilot. She has already lost one person and will have seen shattered young men like Percy and other pilots pass through her hands, what would be the point of spending time with another? Let's face it old chap, we aren't exactly in a secure occupation, are we?'

Eddie nodded.

'Yes, I know but...' he began but Bean had got to his feet.

'Just forget her, Eddie. You need a clear head where we are going otherwise the beastly Hun will be celebrating you as another victory and will be carving another notch in their bedposts, or whatever it is they do. Let's go and have a few beers and put your Flora or Victoria or whatever her name is out of your head.

'Her name is Annie,' said Eddie, also getting to his feet. 'But how come it's okay to get a fuzzy head from drinking but not to be thinking about a woman?'

'Because it just is, and that's an end to it. Now get your tie fastened and let's get to the mess before some other sod drinks it all.'

But before they had time to time to do this, Bunny burst into the room.

'Eddie! I think we've got a posting!'

'What? All of us?'

'No, just you and me,' said Bunny. 'Sorry Bean.'

'You said "Think",' said Bean.

'What?'

'You said think. Why don't you know for certain?'

'Ah yes, well you see, I bumped into Charleston...'

'Oh no, not him.'

'Yes, well, he was over at the Old Man's office trying to get a travel warrant. I told him he didn't have a chance, but he wasn't having any of it. You see he met this girl in Boulogne and...'

'Bunny! Never mind about that, what did he say?' said Eddie.

'Oh yes, right, well he said that a new batch of orders have come through. They've just been put up on the board. Charleston says our names are there.'

Bean shook his head. 'If Charleston says anything then I tend to believe the opposite. I don't actually think he was posted here, he just took off from Kent one day and got lost. He's wrong. He's got to be wrong. It's never us.'

But despite Bean's doubts, it did, indeed, prove to be true. Amidst all of the other, badly typed, flimsy pieces of paper pinned to the board were two of special interest to Eddie and Bunny. They both said the same thing with only the names being different:

2nd Lieutenant E.M.Grenville, RFC Transport Depot St Omer to 159 Squadron, Acq 1200 hours 02/04/17

'See?' said Bunny, bouncing on his feet like his animal namesake. 'Isn't this just absolutely top notch?'

Bean, who was busily scanning the rest of the board, just grunted a reply.

'Oh! Sorry Bean, you poor old thing. It's a bad show you've not got a posting, of course,' said Bunny.

'I'm sure yours will come through soon, Hector,' said Eddie, putting his hand on Bean's shoulder and giving it a squeeze.

Bean did not say anything, he just nodded. Eddie suspected that he was choking up a little.

'It's absolutely fantastic that we're staying together,' said Bunny, still bouncing.

'Yes,' said Eddie, wishing that Bunny would, for once, learn to shut up . 'Where the hell is Acq?' he added. 'Sounds more like a bad cough than a place.'

'Near Arras,' muttered a passing pilot. From his castor oil stained leather flying-jacket, tattered and cracked sheepskin-topped boots, lined face and world-weary shuffle, Eddie put him down as a ferry pilot whose combat days were behind him.

'Excuse me, you know it?' said Eddie, adding a 'Sir,' when he caught sight of the airman's rank as he opened his coat to take out his cigarette case. The ferry pilot was a captain.

'Yup,' he said. 'You were right about it sounding like some disease. You got the wrong end though.' The pilot lit his cigarette.

'Sorry, sir?'

'It's more like piles than a cough,' Eddie could not help but notice the pilot did not offer the smokes around. 'It's a fleapit. Small field, trees all around it, everyone sleeps in old cowsheds. The mess is alright though.'

'Small field, trees,' muttered Bunny, more to himself than the others. Eddie noticed that his enthusiasm had faded somewhat.

'I'm sure you'll have other things to worry about whilst you are there boys,' said the Captain, taking one of the flimsies from the board and strolling unhurriedly towards the exit. 'Best of British.

You'll need it,' he added.

'Wonder what he meant by that?' murmured Eddie.

'Well, there you go, chaps. A plum posting by the sound of it,' said Bean, who had perked up as much as Bunny's mood had darkened. 'I definitely will have to stand you a drink to celebrate.'

'Trees,' muttered Bunny, staring glassy eyed at the paper.

'Arras?' said Eddie. 'How on earth are we going to get there?'

PART TWO

Eleven Days

DAY 1

APRIL 2, 1917

Although Eddie had been hoping to fly to Acq by ferrying a replacement machine to the airfield, they were ordered to travel there by train.

The journey was interminable. There were constant, unexplained halts. The train was shunted into sidings, twice it reversed for several miles back up the line they had just travelled down. The carriages were crowded with troops. It was not too bad at first as Eddie and Bunny were able to travel with the officers of an infantry brigade fresh from England but, in some drab, anonymous town, they decamped and were replaced by others.

The two cohorts could not have been more different. Their original fellow travellers had been young, fresh faced and eager. Their replacements were unshaven and grubby. They clambered wearily into the carriage and, to a man, slumped down heavily into any available seat and, when they were full, onto the floor. The stench of the unwashed bodies was so strong that Eddie could not help but pull a face.

'Aww, poor little fly-boy,' said the nearest of the soldiers, a private. 'We a bit strong for your delicate little nose, are we?'

Before Eddie had time to answer, Bunny pitched in: 'I'll mind you to keep a civil tongue in your head. Remember that you're talking to an officer.'

'And what exactly are you going to do about it, little boy?' said the private, rising to his feet. Eddie was not sure whether it was because he, himself was sitting down, but the soldier seemed around seven feet tall and broad in proportion.

'Now then, Bunny,' he said, trying to keep his voice calm. 'These men have clearly had a hard time and none of us want trouble, do we?'

'That's by-the-by,' said Bunny. 'Their own officers should control them.'

Eddie sighed inwardly, making a mental note to have a word with Bunny later whilst keeping eye contact with the huge man looming over him. For a moment he thought he was going to get a thumping but then the giant's resolve seemed to evaporate and he sat back down.

'It's all right for your lot. You've got it cushy you have,' he muttered.

Bunny looked like he was going to chip in again but Eddie silenced him with a glare and said; 'Yes, I suppose we have.'

'Na' then Jonesy, don't need to take it out on the young sirs,' said the small soldier who was jammed in at the end of the row. He was sharp in features, tanned and bright eyed with the build of a bantamweight boxer. 'It wasn't them that sent us up the line was it?'

He just got a grunt in reply from the giant, who closed his eyes and settled down to sleep.

'Don't mind him, sir,' whispered the bantamweight, leaning forward. 'Private John Roberts, at your service,' he added, giving a near approximation of a salute, or the best he could manage given the cramped surroundings.

Eddie introduced himself and Bunny who offered Roberts a cigarette.

'You're a real gent, sir,' he said, taking a light. 'Sorry about these lads, sir. You ain't goin' to report them, are you? Had it tough, we have.'

'No we aren't going to report you, Roberts,' said Eddie.

'Where are your officers?' said Bunny.

'Dead. Well most of them. I think we've got a couple of sergeants and a lieutenant but he's a bit knocked around. So you're flyers?'

'That's right,' said Eddie. 'Just posted to our squadron.'

Roberts puffed out his cheeks and shook his head. 'Wouldn't get me up in one of them things. Don't like heights. Before the war me and the missus went up Blackpool Tower for a laugh but I don't mind tellin' you, I was ruddy terrified. How can you stand being so high up?'

Eddie shrugged. 'It doesn't seem so high in an aeroplane somehow,' he said. 'It feels safe.' A vision of the smashed body of

Prentice came into his head and would not leave. He tried to ignore it.

'Well you're all ruddy heroes to me,' said Roberts. He frowned. 'Beggin' your pardon, sir, what did you say your name was again?'

'Grenville.'

'Grenville,' Roberts repeated thoughtfully. 'I was reading about one of you boys in King and Country. Have you read it, sir?'

'King and Country?' Eddie said, raising a weary eyebrow at Bunny. 'I'm more of a Hare and Hounds sort of chap I'm afraid.'

'Oh you should read it, sir. Very stirring it is. Tells things like they really are.'

'If you say so, Roberts,' sighed Eddie, reaching for his book in the hope that Roberts might take the hint.

'I do sir. And there was a Captain Grenville in the last edition, I'm sure there was.'

'What?' said Eddie, staring at Roberts.

'Is that your brother?' said Bunny.

'I don't know,' said Eddie.

'If it is, sir, I'm bloody honoured, sir. Ruddy marvelous what he did, should get the VC for it, he should.'

'What? What did he do?' said Bunny. 'Have you got it still, Roberts?'

'Oh yes, sir. Always keep it with me. Never know when you might need paper, if you know what I mean, sir?'

'What? Oh, quite,' said Bunny, cottoning on.

'It's in me pack, sir, hold on, I'll get it.'

Whilst Roberts was rummaging in his knapsack, Bunny nudged Eddie.

'This is amazing if it's him,' he said. 'Why didn't you say anything? You saw him last week, didn't you? What did he say?'

Eddie did not reply.

'Here it is, sirs,' said Roberts, handing them a much creased, slightly grubby copy of 'King and Country'.

The story was on the front page. Under the banner headline of 'Saved by the Bulldog Breed' was a rather lurid drawing of a British officer, wounded but standing heroically, revolver raised, in front of another British soldier prostrate on the ground, whilst a German, a snarling caricature with square jaw and cropped hair, crept towards them.

Quickly Eddie turned the page to the story itself. He was not surprised to find the prose it was written in was well-matched to the picture.

'King and Country can reveal the name of Great Britain's latest hero in this country's battle with the dastardly legions of the Kaiser; Captain Percival Grenville of the Royal Flying Corps.

Although himself badly wounded, this selfless hero carried his injured gunner back to the British lines after their aircraft was downed in no-man's-land. This would have been noble enough but Captain Grenville not only had to do this under enemy fire but also fought off one of the Kaiser's rabid dogs who, with the scent of blood in his nostrils and the desire to kill in his black heart, pursued the plucky pair back to the British trenches. He would have succeeded but for the fortitude of this brave officer, who, with his companion insensible by his side, used the last of his strength to shoot the Hun dead with his service revolver.

King and Country Says:

It was only through the efforts of this publication that this story can be told. This hero kept the tale completely to himself, it was only when we heard the reports through those who had witnessed it that we investigated and uncovered the truth.

This modesty is so typical of the natives of this great island nation - and typical of his class. Captain Grenville is a credit to his breeding and his country. He himself was selfless, he did not seek any praise or honour, he just did the right thing. But this does not mean that his heroics should not be rewarded.

***King and Country** urge His Majesty's Government to make an immediate award of the highest recognition of gallantry that this country can bestow; the Victoria Cross.*

We humbly ask all our readers to write to their MP to support our demand.

'Good grief,' said Bunny. 'Is that Percy?'

Eddie was still staring at the paper. He could not risk using his voice, he just nodded.

'What? That's your brother?' said Roberts.

Eddie said nothing.

'Yes, it is,' said Bunny. 'Good heavens, Eddie old boy, why didn't you say something? Didn't you know?'

'I didn't know *this* story,' was all Eddie could manage.

'It would be a great honour to shake the hand of the brother of a true hero,' said Roberts, holding out his hand. Eddie just stared at it.

'Eddie...where are your manners?' said Bunny.

Eddie took Robert's' hand.
The face he saw looking back at him was Siggi's.

*

The train creaked and clanked as it slowly drew out of the station. The coaches that had brought Eddie, Bunny and the troops into Arras, bore away a full load of weary and wounded soldiers. The new troops were quickly drilled into ranks and marched away. The two pilots, meanwhile, seemed the only ones on the transport who had no idea as to where to go and kept getting in the way of those who did.

'Let's get outside and see if anyone is waiting for us,' said Bunny, smiling an apology at a Sergeant-Major who was trying to march his troop away from the station. He got an exasperated glare in return.

'Good idea,' said Eddie.

Outside the station it was clear just how hard a war Arras had had. Most of the buildings were damaged, some no more than piles of rubble. Although there were some civilians on the street, the majority were in uniform, and mainly British ones at that.

'Gosh,' said Bunny, looking around the battered square. 'This really brings it home doesn't it? Squint and this could be good old Horsham.'

Eddie nodded.

'You're still very quiet, old boy,' said Bunny gently. 'Anything you want to talk about?'

'No,' said Eddie quickly. 'I was just trying to work out whether all this is from air raids or...' He was interrupted by a whistling sound. Everyone around them dropped to their knees or tried to take shelter. Before Eddie or Bunny had time to do the same there was a sharp crack, the rumble of falling masonry and the sound of small stones impacting the street. They swung around to see the gable walls of a house about a hundred yards away, collapsing.

'Well, there's my answer,' said Eddie. 'We're in artillery range.'

'Great,' said Bunny. 'That's a really comforting thought. Where's our bloody transport?'

As if in answer, a battered car tore into the square. The driver had to brake hard, blowing its horn as an old woman, dressed in black and carrying a loaf of bread, crossed the street. Her pace did not change but she stared at the car as it passed by her and muttered something under her breath. The car, a Crossley, set off again but then drew up alongside the two airmen. The sole occupant, a weary looking man in a tatty cricket jumper worn over his uniform looked them up and down.

'You our new chaps?' he said.

'Are you from 159?' said Eddie. 'We were expecting -'

'Well, what are you waiting for? Chuck your bags in the back,' the newcomer said, pointedly revving the engine.

Eddie and Bunny exchanged glances but did as they had been bid.

'Is there anywhere I can buy some new razor-blades, old chap,' said Bunny. 'I meant to pick some up before we left but there wasn't time.'

'I'm not here to run you around on bloody shopping trips. Get in.'

'Friendly,' murmured Eddie.

The car set off as they got in the Crossley and they landed, rather than sat in their seats. Eddie was alongside the driver and had a chance to study him as he drove. He was struck by two contrasting features of the man's face. His skin was lined, weather-beaten, signs of strain written across it, yet the eyes were young. His first impression outside the station, was of a man in his mid to late thirties at best, yet now Eddie could see that he was much younger, probably not too much older than Eddie himself.

'How many hours have you done?' said the driver abruptly.

'Ten and a half,' said Bunny from the back. 'I say, can we slow down a bit?'

'Ten? Bloody hell, I hope I don't get you,' muttered the driver ignoring Bunny's plea. 'You the same?'

'Twenty-two,' said Eddie. 'I did my ticket privately.'

'Not bad,' said the driver, violently swerving to avoid a cow crossing the road. 'You've got a chance. I'm Hastings, acting leader of A Flight.' Hastings took one hand off the wheel and held it out to Eddie. Eddie took it quickly, hoping that Hastings would take it back and use it for steering again.

'Grenville,' said Eddie.

'I'm Cavendish,' said Bunny eagerly from the back seat, leaning over and offering his own hand. Hastings ignored him.

'Twenty-two,' said Hastings again, nodding. 'I'll have a word with the old man and see if I can get you in my flight.'

'Good, thanks,' said Eddie. 'What do we fly, by the way?'

'Quirks,' said Hastings.

'Quirks?' said Bunny.

'BE2s.'

'Oh, right. Good,' said Bunny.

'Good?' snorted Hastings. 'There's nothing good about the Quirk. Museum pieces. Useless heaps of junk that should have been pensioned off years ago.'

'I rather liked them when we were training,' said Bunny. 'Nice stable things.'

'Exactly,' said Hastings. 'They're death traps.'

'That's a cheerful thought,' said Eddie, gripping the door of the car and wishing he'd put his goggles on against the dust from the road.

'Just telling things how they are,' said Hastings. 'The rumour is that we are getting RE8s any day but I'll believe that when I see it.'

'They're supposed to be a lot better, aren't they?'

'Yup. Lots more power, anyway. They're a fair bit faster than the old Quirk which is good. Fixed gun too, and the observer's got another in the rear. Okay, you can't see where you're going in it, and if you look at it funny it will spin you into the ground but that's a reasonable trade-off in my book. That's what I've heard anyway.'

'Spin?' said Bunny. Eddie noticed he had gone white.

'Yes, apparently they are really tricky bastards,' said Hastings. 'But it will sort the men out from the boys.'

'Tricky?' repeated Bunny. 'I don't think I like the sound of them.'

'Ah don't worry about it,' said Hastings. Eddie noticed he was smiling. 'I'm sure that you won't have to bother about mastering it.'

'Why not?' said Bunny.

'You'll be dead long before you get chance to fly one,' said Hastings, winking at Eddie. 'Here we are, Acq in all its glory.

Hastings had swung the car through the gates of what, to Eddie, looked like a farm. He soon found that his first impression was right, the airfield had been built around the battered remains of one, either commandeered from the occupants or, more likely, occupied as an expediency after it had been abandoned.

It was in the classic French form, a quadrangle of stone built buildings set around a central yard. Beyond the farmyard was a large barn where Eddie could see BE2s being worked on by the mechanics. Next to the barn where two of the canvas hangars that the RFC took with them wherever they operated. In front of the barn was the airfield itself. Although the countryside around them was not hilly, the field was far from flat and did indeed have trees, poplars in the main, on all its perimeters. It did look very small after the wide-open spaces of Salisbury Plain that they were used to.

'The mess and admin are in the farmhouse,' said Hastings, braking abruptly and bringing the car to a slithering halt. 'We have billets in the cowsheds,' adding, with a wink at Eddie. 'They took the cows and the shit out first. Well, most of it. Come on, you can drop your things off before you report to the CO.'

Hastings got out of the car and set off towards the buildings to the left of the farmhouse. They dragged their bags from the car and trailed behind. He led them through an opening in the side of the barn that had been weatherproofed with a large tarpaulin. A brazier with a pile of wood alongside it was burning against the chill of the Spring day. The pair gratefully dropped their bags onto the cob stone floor, whilst Hastings leaned through a doorway and peered into the gloom.

'Evans!' he called, 'Taff, where are you?' He looked at Eddie. 'Evans runs the place. It's bloody marvelous what he can get, believe me, though it does get a bit tedious seeing his ugly mug at 5 am. At least his tea is a half decent brew. Evans, where...ah, there you are.'

Corporal Evans was short, dark and slight and could have been aged anywhere between his mid-thirties and mid-fifties, though Eddie suspected it might be closer to the latter. He gave the approximation of a salute, more by instinct than duty.

'Yes sir,' he said. 'What can I do for you today?' Eddie had expected a Welsh accent but there was a distinct Northern burr to Evan's voice.

'Taff, this is Grenville and, er...' he waved his hand vaguely in Bunny's direction.

'Cavendish,' said Bunny.

'That's right, Cavendish, yes. Taffy can you find billets for the lieutenants here, then point them in the direction of the CO? You do have space for them?'

'Oh yes sir, there are always spaces these days,' said Evans, sadly.

'Right, well I'll leave you in the capable hands of Taff here, I'd better see if I'm wanted,' said Hastings. 'You'll find that we don't stand on ceremony much here, by the way, not really the need, don't you know.'

After Hastings had left, Evan smiled at the pair. 'Now then, sirs, if you'll come with me, I'll get you settled in.'

Evans showed them to one of the billets, explaining who they were in with, but Eddie didn't really pay attention. He was pleased that they were staying together.

'You can unpack after you have drawn your flying kit. The stores are on the other side of the entrance, one of my lads is in there all the time. Now I had better get you to see the CO, Major Reeves.'

Obediently, Eddie and Bunny followed Evans back outside and they walked across the yard towards the main farmhouse.

'You'll find the officers mess on the left as you come in, cook uses the old farmhouse kitchen. There's also a bar of sorts in the old parlour, very nice it is, sir. The Major's office is upstairs. Orders are on the notice board in the hall,' said Evans, leading them inside and up the stairs. A bespectacled, balding captain was sat at a small desk on the landing. He glanced up at Evans and the two airmen.

'Ah our new recruits, eh?' he said, standing up. 'Thank you, sergeant, I'll take over.'

Evans saluted the captain then turned to Eddie and Bunny.

'I'll be somewhere around the stores if you need me, sirs,' he said and headed back down the stairs.

The captain gave a grim little smile. 'So you must be 2nd Lieutenants Grenville...' he looked up inquiringly.

'Sir,' said Eddie, coming to attention.

'At ease, son,' said the captain, 'Which must make you Cavendish? Right well, I'm the squadron adjutant, Captain Marsh, although everyone calls me Pops, can't think why. Good to see you chaps, now...'

'Marsh?' came a call from the room behind and to the right of the adjutant's desk. 'Is that the new pilots?'

'Yes sir.'

'Well I haven't got all day, get them in here.'

Marsh gave a patient smile. 'That's Major Reeves. You'd better go in,' he said, giving a little nod towards the office.

Reeves was sat at his desk, pen in hand, reading through some documents. He did not look up as the two airmen walked in, came to attention and saluted. He was dark haired, and looked fairly short, stocky and powerful in build, reminding Eddie of a bullterrier. Reeves made a few notes on the document, flicked through the next few pages then tossed it onto the desk in front of them, before looking at the pair.

'At ease,' he muttered. 'You can forget that parade ground stuff here. Right, so you will be...' he started rifling through his in-tray. 'Cavendish and Grenville.'

'Yes sir.'

'Straight from training?'

'Yes sir.'

'God give me strength,' muttered Reeves. 'Well I suppose you'll just have to do.' He shook his head and ran his fingers through his hair. 'There's no time to settle you in, I'm afraid. You'll have to go straight onto jobs. There's a big flap on, you see, we've been given jobs to do that we have to do, no excuses, at whatever cost.' There was a splatter of rain against the window. Reeves glanced across at it. 'Bloody awful weather too, that doesn't help,' he said, though Eddie that this was more to himself than the pair.

'We don't fly in this, surely sir?' said Bunny.

Reeves turned sharply to look at him.

'Of course we, do Grenville,' he snapped.

'Cavendish, sir,' corrected Bunny.

'Cavendish, whatever your name is.'

'But...sir...it's blowing a gale!'

'You'll fly when you are bloody well told to, boy,' said Reeves. 'This isn't prep school. You can't get a note from your mother just because it's not very nice out. This is war, Cavendish. A brutal, bloody war and we have a brutal, bloody, vital job to do, understand?'

'Yes sir,' said Bunny.

'And you?' said Reeves, turning to stare at Eddie. 'You understand that as well?'

'Yes sir, I do,' said Eddie.

'Good,' said Reeves. He sighed and sat back. Eddie saw his face soften. 'I'm sorry, boys,' he said, 'Didn't mean to snap. I know it's hard coming from training. I'll put you on with our most experienced flight commanders for your first few missions. Grenville, Hastings has already been up to see me, he wants you in A flight. Cavendish, you're with Captain Milne in B flight. They'll give you orders from now on. That's all. Dismissed.'

The pair came to attention, and saluted. Reeves had already gone back to his paperwork before they had left the office.

Outside, they found Marsh's desk empty.

'That was a friendly welcome, I must say,' said Eddie.

'Yes. I wonder what Milne is like. Nicer than that Hastings, I hope,' said Bunny. Eddie could see the worry on his friend's face.

'Perhaps he's in the Officer's Mess. I say old chap, there's something I forgot to ask the old man. Why don't you nip down there and see if you can find him and I'll join you in a second?'

'Oh, it's all right. I don't mind waiting.'

'No, on you go, it's personal, you understand?' said Eddie, feeling himself start to blush. 'Might take a few minutes.'

'Ah. Your young lady. Right, well, I'll see you in a while then.'

Bunny gave Eddie his little half-smile and headed downstairs. Eddie waited until he was sure that he had gone out of earshot then knocked on the door of the CO's office.

'Come,' Major Reeves looked up in surprise. 'Cavendish? Was there something else?'

'It's Grenville, sir.'

'Grenville, of course. What is it? Can't you see I'm busy?'

'Yes sir, but it's about Bunny...er, Cavendish, sir.'

Reeves looked puzzled. 'Yes, well what is it?'

'It's about what you said, sir, about us going straight on to missions.'

'Yes, that's right. What of it?'

'Well, it's like this, sir. I've known Cavendish since school. He's a good chap, one of the best but, well, he's not the most confident, sir, never has been. He'd hate me if he knew I was doing this, sir, but I've seen it in training too. When he gets nervous, he freezes. He's fine once he gets a bit of confidence though, sir.'

Reeves leant back in his chair, a frown on his face.

'What are you saying, Grenville? Not have him fly?'

'Yes, sir. If you just give him a couple of days to settle in -'

'Give him a couple of days?' said Reeves, rising and leaning over the desk. 'Are you a bloody imbecile, Grenville?'

'No, sir but...'

'Then are you trying to tell me how to do my job?'

'I wasn't, sir, I...'

'I told you what our orders are, to photograph the lines. Not to try to, not to do our best but to do it, understand?' Reeves thumped the desk with both fists. Eddie had a memory come unbidden into his head, of seeing a gorilla at London Zoo, of it pounding the ground with its mighty hands in impotent frustration at its incarceration. Reeves looked just like the beast had.

'We've no room for passengers. Not you, not Cavendish. Everyone pulls their weight, everyone. It's that or a court martial, do I make myself clear, Grenville?'

'Yes, sir, sorry sir.'

'Not a good start, Grenville. Get out of my sight.'

Eddie saluted, his face red. He hurriedly left the office and shut the door behind him.

He found he was face-to-face with the adjutant. Marsh raised his eyebrows at him. Flustered Eddie stared at him for a moment, then remembered that he was a senior officer and saluted. Marsh smiled then shook his head.

'Come on,' he said quietly. 'Walk with me'

'Yes sir,' said Eddie, following.

'Call me Pops, I said.'

'Yes Pops.'

Pops led Eddie into hall at the bottom of the stairs.

'That was a noble thing you tried to do there,' he said, his voice low. 'Stupid, but noble.'

'You heard then?'

'Most of the airfield heard. Well, the last bit anyway.'

Eddie's shoulders slumped further. 'I've made an awful mess of this haven't I?'

Pops gave Eddie's shoulder a reassuring squeeze. 'Most people wouldn't have even tried, Grenville. Look, don't judge the Major. He's got the worst job of all. He knows how bad things are but isn't given a choice. Trenchard has made it clear, the job must be done. What makes it worse is that he is not allowed to fly himself, HQ have banned Squadron Commanders from it, they were losing too many so he just has to sit and send boys like you and Cavendish out day after day, then write the letters to their mothers and fathers when they don't come back. We all have our way of coping with that. The Major's way is by shouting. Don't worry, his bark is worse than his bite. Do a good job and he will soon forget, believe me.'

'Right,' nodded Eddie. 'Thank-you, Pops.'

'And I will have a quiet word with Milne, see if he is willing to give Cavendish a chance to find his feet a bit first. Can't promise anything though.'

Eddie found himself slightly choked, so just gave a little nod of gratitude.

'Right, let's get you and your pal some flying gear from the stores. You'll be needing it soon enough.'

Eddie followed Pops out as they went in search of Bunny.

*

After they had got their kit, Eddie and Bunny killed time unpacking, exploring the airfield and reading the week-old newspapers scattered around the messroom.

There were relatively few pilots and observers around. Hastings was laying on his bed, reading, whilst a couple of others were playing cards. None of them seemed to be interested in making their acquaintance or, indeed, welcoming them at all. It reminded Eddie of his first day at school with the older boys members of a club that the newcomers were not yet a part of.

Tiring of this, Eddie left Bunny reading and braved the elements crossing to the hangar where the mechanics were working on the aircraft not out on missions.

As he had first observed, the squadron seemed to be flying BE2Es, though there were a couple of examples of the older C types around, one of which was being cannibalised, presumably to keep the rest flying. The mechanics nodded to him, a few saluted, but generally they kept to their tasks. He was not surprised; even in the hangar the conditions were cold and miserable, the bitter wind whipping the canvas flaps into a frenzy. He had a small motorbike at home, much to his mother's disapproval, which he had worked out his mechanical curiosity on, so was used to the skinned knuckles and exquisite pain of handling metal tools and trying to shift stubborn nuts in the cold. It was better to keep busy, keep moving, rather than bother with any interruptions.

Whilst he was out, the first of the aircraft came back in. Conditions were clearly marginal, even the normally stable BEs were wobbling on approach as the wind gusted and veered. At the first sound of the engines there were mechanics at the hangar entrance, clearly ready to spring into action.

First one landed, then two more in quick succession. All three bumped upon landing, then ran smoothly to a halt, swinging around and taxiing towards the hangars. Before they had stopped moving, the ground crew had swarmed around them, taking hold of the wings and tail and wheeling the machines away. The observer of one had his hands full of cases which he handed to a waiting Lieutenant. He in turn hurried off towards the squadron offices, carrying the cases as if they were treasure. Eddie realised that they probably were for these were the fruits of the mission, its very purpose, the exposed plates off to be developed.

In the meantime, the aircrew were clambering out. This wasn't easy, given that the garb they were wearing against the bitter cold: gauntlets and inner gloves, fur outer boots over flying boots, long, thick leather coats, flying helmets and goggles with scarves wrapped around both neck and face. The pilot of the nearest aircraft stretched, easing out the tension from his arms and shoulders whilst his observer stripped his gloves off and started dismounting his Lewis gun from the Strange mount. Alongside him, a pair of mechanics were unhitching the large camera mounted on the fuselage side pointing vertically down.

'Chiefy,' the pilot had pulled off his helmet and goggles revealing a shock of blonde hair, sweaty despite the cold and sticking up in all directions.

One of the mechanics overseeing the work saluted, 'Yes sir?'

'We got a few rounds through the upper plane and tail; it will need checking. The oil pressure is a bit low too.'

'I'll get it checked over straight away, Captain Milne.'

'Good. Is Summers back yet? He had to turn back about an hour ago with a dud engine.'

'No sir, you're the first.'

Milne pulled a face. 'Right, well hopefully he'll have put down somewhere. Ah, Pops, have we heard anything from Summers?'

Captain Marsh had joined the party in front of the hangar, bundled up against the cold in a long overcoat.

'No David, not a thing. I'll call around the other airfields, see if anyone has seen him.'

'Thanks, Pops.'

'How was it?'

Milne shrugged. 'About what you'd expect. The weather was foul but at least it kept most of the Huns away. We just had a close shave with a two-seater who was scrapping for a fight. We managed to scare him off, though God knows how. Oh, a new face?' The captain's gaze had fallen on Eddie.

'Yes, sir, Grenville, sir,' said Eddie, coming to attention.

'Take it easy, Grenville,' said Milne. 'No need for any of that formal stuff. Good to meet you, David Milne.' He held out his hand and Eddie shook it.

'Edward,' he said. 'But everyone calls me Eddie.'

'You're not related to Percy Grenville, are you?'

'He's my brother,' said Eddie, rather flatly.

Milne seemed not to notice Eddie's tone. 'He's a good man. I did my training with him. Excellent pilot. Sorry to hear about his prang. How is he now?'

'He's... on the mend.'

'Good, good. Well it's good to have you on board though this is a bloody awful time for you to join. Come on, let's get inside and let the chaps get on with their work.' Milne and Pops started walking towards the mess. 'I presume the CO has given you chapter and verse?'

'It's all hands to the pump, isn't it?'

'I'm afraid so. I don't like throwing you new bods straight into the action, but we have not been given a choice. Summers for one, he's only been with us for a couple of days. Hopefully he's just lost and will turn up in a few hours with his tail between his legs but these days...'

They had reached the farmhouse. They went inside and stood in the hallway.

'It's tough out there then?'

'Oh it's always tough but the last few months...' Milne's voice trailed off. 'We need new aircraft. The Quirk is a tough old bird but it was past its best this time last year. And we are getting short of air-crew.' Eddie saw that Milne was frowning, clearly thinking deeply about things. He looked at Eddie and smiled. 'Let's not dwell. Are you the only new arrival?'

'No, I arrived with a chum of mine. Cavendish. He's in the mess.'

'Right, then, Let's go and say hello then I will have to go and check whether there are any other jobs for us to do today.'

'I would appreciate a quick word, too,' said Pops, with a quick glance at Eddie. Eddie realised that Marsh was going to talk to Edwards about Bunny. He felt a stab of concern; was it right to have spoken to anyone about it? Was he undermining his friend, demeaning him in the eyes of his peers. He could kick himself, what he had done was stupid, he shouldn't have done it. Still, it was too late now. What was done, was done, there was no changing it now.

With some uncertainty, Eddie followed Milne and Pops into the mess.

*

In the end, the weather closed in and got so bad that flying was scrubbed for the day.

After a very reasonable dinner of chicken in a white sauce, Milne explained that their cook had been a chef at a large hotel in Manchester before joining up, the wine started to flow, a piano was dragged out into the middle of the mess upon which tunes were, literally, pounded out amid enthusiastic singing.

One of the songs, sung as a mock psalm by Daley in his best

church tenor voice, was one Eddie had heard before:

> *The B.E.2 is my bus; therefore I shall want.*
> *He maketh me come down in green pastures.*
> *He leadeth me where I wish not to go.*
> *He maketh me sick: he leadeth me astray on all cross-country flights.*
> *Yea, though I fly o'er No-man's Land where mine enemies would compass me about, I fear much evil, for thou art with me: thy joystick and thy prop discomfort me.*
> *Thou prepareth a crash for me in the presence of mine enemies; thy R.A.F. anointeth my hair with oil, thy tank leaketh badly.*
> *Surely to goodness thou shalt not follow me all the days of my life, else I shall dwell in the House of Colney Hatch for ever.*

'Amen,' chorused everyone.

Eddie did not find the words very reassuring.

Although Milne did his best to include Eddie and Bunny in everything and to introduce them to the other officers, Eddie still felt like he did not belong and was sure that Bunny felt the same.

They found themselves sitting together on the edge of the group, getting quietly drunk whilst the party went on around them. Some of the games reminded Eddie of school, particularly the pillow fights that involved, the smallest men in the Squadron being hoisted onto the shoulders of the largest with the object of knocking the 'jockey' off. Eddie and Bunny had quickly been eliminated, leaving the final round to be a pilot called Armstrong and his observer, Kerr, and two of the other officer observers, Collier and Palmer. Collier was a stocky, bull of a man, so much so that Eddie wondered how on earth he managed to squeeze into the front cockpit of a BE2, let alone manoeuvre camera and machine-gun whilst he was there. As he was looking for a new pilot, he had offered his services to both Eddie and Bunny. As Bunny was smaller and lighter, Eddie was pleased when Bunny had taken up the offer. He did not want the handicap of additional ballast when he went over the line.

Just as Kerr, with the aid of a trip by Armstrong, managed to unseat Palmer and send him crashing into a pile of old dining chairs, Pop Marsh came into the mess carrying a typed page. He went straight to Milne who waved Hastings across. Hastings read it and smiled.

Milne walked into the centre of the room, both his hands up and shouted over the bedlam.

'Quiet QUIET. Settle down now. Listen to this. Collier, put Armstrong down and pay attention,'

The roar of young voices died away.

'As you know, the RFC reconnaissance squadrons are to be gradually re-equipped with the new RE8 which will give the service more chance of defending itself against the Hun.'

'Yes, well that would be rather nice, I must say,' said Armstrong. 'But when are we getting this beast? It's been as mythical as the unicorn so far.'

'That's the news, Pop has just heard from HQ,' said Milne. 'We have just been told that 159 is the next in line to re-equip. We start changing over tomorrow morning.'

There was a stunned silence.

'Are we being taken out of the line?' said a pilot whose name Eddie had not caught.

'No and there's the snag,' said Hastings. 'We still have to keep up the job.'

There was a chorus of objections.

'How can we do that?'

'That's bloody impossible. We can't learn a new machine and still patrol.'

'It's madness.'

Milne held his hands up for silence. Gradually things quietened down. Eddie was impressed how much respect Milne was shown. Eddie wasn't sure he'd ever have the nerve to command. He had no idea how Percy did it.

Percy. Eddie was annoyed with himself. Percy was the last person he wanted to think about and certainly not as a model to follow.

'We *can* do it.' The babble of objections threatened to start up again. 'Yes, we can. Yes, there is the push coming up and, yes, we are under pressure. But there is a way.'

The room had gone quiet again.

'What the CO has suggested, and I think it's a great idea, is that one of the flights ferries our old machines over to the depot tomorrow morning and picks up the new kites whilst the other covers anything that HQ sends us. Then, over the next few days, when the flight that has got the new machines has got used to them, we can do the same in reverse.'

There was general silence for a few moments.

'Well, all right,' said Collier. 'But which flight is going to get what?'

'Yes, which one?'

The wine-fuelled chorus started up again.

'There's only one fair way,' said Hastings, getting to his feet and thrusting his hands into his pockets. He pulled out a silver franc. 'Whoever wins gets the new machines first. David, heads or tails?'

'Heads.'

Hastings tossed the coin into the air, caught it and slapped it on the back of his other hand. He held turned to Eddie and said, 'Call it, new boy,' and lifted his hand up.

'It's tails,' said Eddie.

Half the room cheered, the other groaned.

'A Flight it is then,' said Hastings, grinning. 'Hard lines, David.'

Milne gave a resigned shrug. 'Right you are then, B Flight, you'd better pack it in for the night, we will be on at first light, and you'll need a clear head.'

There were several grumbles but everyone in the flight, Bunny included, got to their feet.

'I'd better try to sleep. Gosh, now it's come down to it...well, you know,' said Bunny.

Eddie was trying to think of something to say to cheer his friend up but before he could, Milne called across.

'Actually, Cavendish, I wouldn't mind seeing how Grenville flies. Trained with his brother you know. Would you mind him switching with you, just for tomorrow?'

'Er, no. Not at all,' said Bunny, although he looked a little puzzled. 'If you don't mind, Eddie?'

'No, not at all.'

'That's all right, isn't it, Clive?'

Hastings shrugged. 'Sure, I don't mind. It would help for Grenville to get a bit of experience before he flies with me.'

'Sorry, Grenville,' smiled Milne. 'That means an early night for you, I'm afraid.'

'That's fine,' said Eddie, himself getting to his feet. 'See you all in the morning.'

'Not all of us, old boy,' Hastings grinned. 'Not at the time you'll be seeing old Taff anyway.'

DAY 2

APRIL 3, 1917

Eddie woke to a spotlight being shone into his eyes.

'What, what time is it?' He squinted, trying to see who it was. At first, he thought it must be Bunny coming back from the mess after the party and crashing about in the middle of the night, but then he saw the cot opposite him was occupied.

'It's 5 am, sir. And here's a nice cup of tea for you, sir.'

There was the clunk of china on wood. Eddie's eyes began to adjust, his brain started to function. It was Evans, the spotlight was just an oil-lamp.

'Evans? 5 am? Really?' Eddie remembered to keep his voice down so as not to wake Bunny. The third occupant of the room, Daley was already starting to get dressed and was splashing water on his face.

'Yes, sir. You're off at first light. I've got a bowl of water coming for you, sir, so you can wash and shave. There's breakfast in the mess, sir, then a briefing in Hangar two at oh six hundred hours.'

'Breakfast?' Eddie groaned.

'It's best to have something,' Daley said. 'Never know when you're going to get fed again.'

Somehow Eddie managed to swallow some of the overly-sweet tea without retching and to wash and shave without slitting his own throat, though his hands were shaking. Whether it was from fear or tiredness, or a combination of both, he wasn't sure. Certainly, he had found getting to sleep difficult and had woken several times in the night.

He did not feel like he was at all ready to go to war.

Nor did he feel much like breakfast but did manage to force down some eggs and greasy sausages. He wasn't sure whether they were going to stay down.

There was little conversation in the mess. Everyone seemed l-ost in their own personal world, contemplating what lay ahead, Eddie included.

But because it was so quiet, the sound of raised voices from the hallway outside carried quite easily. One of the voices, reasonably calm but clearly irritated, was Milne's.

'Smith, that's the rota. You *will* fly with him.'

'Begging your pardon, sir, but I won't. It's not on. I've got a wife and two nippers at home that I'd rather come back to, if you don't mind. Sir.'

'We are at war, Smith. It's a dangerous business in case you hadn't noticed.'

Eddie found this conversation odd. It was Milne talking to an observer. As the observer wasn't in the mess that meant he was one of the other ranks, probably an NCO. Although the RFC lacked the regularity of the ground forces, he always assumed that following orders was still sacrosanct, so why was this man Smith refusing them?

Then the context of the conversation became clear.

'I know that, sir,' said Smith. 'I'll fly with anyone else sir, but not with a new chap. It's just not safe, sir. You know the odds. You can't make me do it, Sir. Please.'

Eddie flushed. They were talking about him. All of the mess knew it, everyone's eyes were now turned on him.

'I've nothing against the young gentlemen personally, sir, but I'm just not doing it.'

Milne muttered something that Eddie could not catch and then said, 'Yes, right, well this will go on your record, Smith, be in no doubt of that. You can stand down.'

'But sir, I can...'

'I said stand down, Smith. Go back to your billet. I'll deal with you later.'

Eddie had heard enough. He pushed his half-eaten breakfast away and rose from the table.

Outside it was still dark. The wind was gusty, a splatter of rain came abruptly, wetting his face. Eddie found it more comforting than annoying, like a slap on his cheek, a wake-up call from God to chase away the last of his drowsiness.

Over at the hangars the storm lamps were burning. The mechanics were busying themselves around the machines. One was being fuelled, cans of petrol being passed up from the ground to the cockpit area, another had the cowling off whilst the engine was being worked on: obviously some last minute problem, perhaps an oil-leak, had developed.

Eddie gave a little prayer that his machine was going to be sound and headed back to his billet to get his flying gear.

There was no sign of Daley, but Bunny was still sleeping, just the top of his fair hair sticking out from under the blankets.

Eddie was transported back to school: in the dorm, Bunny was always the last to rise, naturally reluctant to give up the warmth for the less appealing joys of the cross-country run, or the school chapel on a Sunday which always seemed cold even as spring turned to glorious early summer days of June.

Eddie turned away and busied himself with layering up for the cold. Next June seemed too far off to even contemplate. He put on his warmest jumper, his old school cricket sweater, pulled on his flying boots, wrapped his scarf around his neck and picked his coat up to put on at the last minute in the hangar. He was starting to sweat already but knew well that at 10,000 feet he would be bitterly cold even under his layers.

He was about to leave when Bunny stirred, pulling the blankets off his head and blinking in the light of the lamp at Eddie.

'You off, old chap?' he muttered, his voice still thick with sleep.

'Yes. Sorry to wake you.'

'Don't be silly. Good luck, Eddie,' said Bunny. 'You are going to come back, aren't you.'

'Of course I am, ' said Eddie, surprising himself with how confident his voice sounded. 'I'll be fine. Bring back some good machines from the depot, won't you.'

Before Bunny could reply, Milne appeared in the doorway.

'Ah, there you are Grenville. I was looking for you. Change of plan. You're flying with Collier as your observer. He's an experienced chap, should keep you out of trouble. You alright with that?'

'Yes sir, thank you sir,' said Eddie.

'Good. Are you ready for the briefing?'

'Yes sir, just coming.' Eddie headed for the door.

'Hold your horses,' said Milne, nodding at Eddie's bed. 'Won't you be needing those.'

Eddie saw that he had left his sheepskin gauntlets on the

blanket.

'Oh yes, sorry,' he said, blushing and snatching them up.

'Calm down, Grenville,' Milne said gently. 'You'll do fine. I know it. Come on, lad, let's go.'

As he left, Eddie glanced back at Bunny. He had put his head under the blankets again.

On the field, all of the aircraft were now back together. The riggers and fitters were grouped around, around ten to each machine. Some rested their hands on fabric or strut, almost as if grooms calming a highly-strung racehorse. But there the analogy broke down, for the steeds they seemed so reluctant to give up, were not sleek thoroughbreds, powerful and muscled with the threat of violence just under the skin, but frail-looking, patched beasts, more asinine than equine. They were patched, worn-out, outdated. To Eddie's eyes they looked terribly vulnerable.

Yet these were the very machines he was going to be trusting his - and Collier's - life to.

Eddie felt his stomach churn. He hoped he was not going to disgrace himself by being sick.

Collier smiled at Eddie and nodded in welcome. Eddie returned the nod.

'Gather round, men,' said Milne. 'Today's first job is important. We are to photograph the enemy positions around Athies. Intelligence believe that new guns have been brought up in the last few days and so it's vital we get good, clear images of the area.'

The aircrew did not say anything, but Eddie noticed them shift uncomfortably from foot to foot. Clearly Milne noticed it too.

'Yes, Athies is a long way over the lines, and Johnny Hun will know that we'll be snooping. That doesn't change anything, we have to do it. The big push takes precedent over our safety. That's why we are going in numbers.

'Armstrong, Kerr, you are the prime photographic aircraft. Warburton and Daley, you're the back-up but the primary mission of the other aircraft is as escort, understand?'

There were a few mumbled 'Yes sirs'.

'Do we have a fighter escort?' said Kerr.

Eddie saw Milne glance outside the hangar. The weather was still blustery.

'The DH5s of 41 will try to cover us,' he said.

'Try? Right,' said Kerr nodding. 'We're on our own then.'

Milne nodded. 'There's is a good chance that the scouts will scrub. Given the weather the Huns might stay in their beds too.

Right, any questions? Good. Let's get going.'

The aircrew saluted and headed for their aircraft which the ground crew, taking the cue from Milne's lead, had started to wheel out onto the field itself. Milne walked across to Eddie. 'Just stick close to my side and follow my lead. Collier will keep an eye out for you, you just concentrate on keeping station with me. I've instructed the ground crew just to mount Collier's gun, give you less to worry about. Collier has also got the map. He'll show you where you are. Alright, Grenville?'

Eddie just nodded though he felt himself start to redden. Did Milne do this for everyone, or had he determined that Eddie was not up to it, and needed special help?

'Good man,' said Milne and gave Eddie a pat on the shoulder before heading off to his own machine.

'It's Eddie, isn't it?' said Collier when they got to their own aircraft. 'My name's John. As the skipper said, I'll look out for us in the air. You just get us there and back in one piece, deal?'

'Deal,' said Eddie.

He waited whilst Collier eased his bulky frame into the front cockpit, then took the Lewis gun from the fitter and fixed it to the Strange Mount, before Eddie, fastening his coat and putting on his helmet, stepped into the pilot's cockpit.

Over to his left and right, the engines of the other aircraft were already running. Eddie looked to the left of Collier to see the fitter waiting at the prop for his signal. Eddie pumped the fuel tank handle to pressurise it, then gave a nod to the mechanic.

'Switches on,' the mechanic called.

'Switches on,' Eddie repeated, toggling the magneto switch.

'Contact.'

'Contact,' Eddie replied.

The mechanic gave the prop a hefty heave, the RAF V8 coughed, hesitated then roared into life. Eddie quickly came off the magneto and set the throttle for a fast idle. He checked the rev counter, all looked fine. He glanced to his right; Milne was watching him. Eddie gave him a thumbs up. Milne looked away, tapping Palmer on the shoulder. The latter raised a Very Pistol and fired, a green flare shot into the air.

Milne's aircraft started to move across the grass, the ground crew running alongside, holding the wingtips until the BE was safely underway. The other machines started to move. Eddie realised he had quite forgotten his training, he had not checked his controls to see if they were working properly. It was too late now, anyway, how could he see in this half-light? He nodded to the ground crew and opened the throttle.

His heart was thumping in his chest, racing almost as much as his aircraft's engine was revving, as his aircraft bumped over an old set of ruts and onto the field proper.

His senses were heightened, he could distinguish the aroma of the oil lubricating the pistons from the lighter grade from the Lewis gun. He could smell petrol from where a careless splash had been made on the wicker seat he sat on as the fitter had filled the main tank beneath him. He could pick up the flapping of a wire against fabric, probably the untrimmed end of a bracing wire, he could hear the swish of the wet grass against the wheels.

The field seemed to be reluctant to let the machine go. Eddie felt the resistance, the machine hesitate slightly as it ran through a patch of longer grass. The tail was up now and he momentarily feared that the BE would nose over, that the prop ahead of him would splinter, that his first ever mission would end in ignominy and embarrassment, but then it gathered pace, hit a larger bump and bounced into the air.

The sun was just coming up into the cloud ridden April sky.

It took at least a minute for Eddies racing heart to slow. Collier looked back at him and gave a thumbs up. Eddie could not see his face from under his goggles and scarf but he was sure he was being given an encouraging smile. He raised his own thumbs up in return.

Eddie looked around, searching for Milne's aircraft. For a moment he panicked, he couldn't see anyone but then picked them up, in front and slightly higher, just at the point when Collier pointed his arm in their direction and gave an exaggerated gesture forward, telling Eddie where they were and that they should catch up.

'I know, I know, I see them,' muttered Eddie.

Speech was pointless over the roar of engine and the slipstream but he felt better having said it. The throttle which he eased back after take-off was advanced again as he closed the gap to the others.

He had a notion that he could sense Milne's irritation by the way his aircraft was flying, that he would be cursing Eddie's inexperience. He told himself that this was silly, that Milne had been the model of patience, far better than he suspected Hastings was going to be, but he still wanted desperately to be as good as he could be, not to let the side down and disappoint Milne.

Eddie found himself cursing Collier's bulk for holding them

back. His weight was bad enough, but he also stuck out into the airstream and added drag. Eddie was now thankful that Milne had told the mechanics to leave off the second Lewis gun. He had felt vulnerable, deprived, slightly inept and not trusted by the decision but now could see the sense. It made them lighter.

It was with great relief that Eddie at last drew up to the three other machines. He took his allocated position. He saw Milne look across and back at him and raise his arm. Eddie waved back. Milne then looked ahead.

The four aircraft were climbing. Eddie glanced at his compass, they were flying virtually due North-West, parallel with the front and away from Athies.

Eddie guessed that they would try to go over the lines as high as they could get, which for a BE2 was around 10,000 feet. To get that high would take at least half-an-hour, no, he thought, longer because that was in training machines. Although often abused, older machines, pensioned off from service in France, and this was an E, the latest model with the better wings, but in training there was no war equipment, no Lewis gun so the trainers were lighter and flew better.

Eddie realised with a start that he had drifted away from the formation. He swore at himself, increased the engine revs and within a few minutes was back on Milne's quarter again. He saw Milne give an exaggerated shake of the head. He must have taken both his hands off the stick for he held his gloved palms up for Eddie to see and brought them closer together three or four times. Keep up, keep closer. The signal was clear.

Eddie felt stupid, ashamed. Why wasn't he doing better? Why hadn't he listened to his instructor, Captain Hollinghurst more? He had to concentrate, try harder.

Milne waggled the wings of his aircraft to get everyone's attention, then started a turn to the right. Everyone, Eddie included, followed. Still they climbed, the details on the ground beneath them, whilst becoming clearer as the sun rose higher also grew smaller as they clawed ever higher.

Eddie was doing better in keeping his place. Collier seemed to see it too, he turned and gave another gesture of encouragement.

But he was tensing, gripping the stick so hard that he was sure that his knuckles must be white under his gauntlets and gloves. His shoulders and back felt like he had been hauling a load of wood. He tried to relax, loosening his grip, rolling his shoulders to ease the tension. How long had they been up? His eyes found the clock on the instrument panel: 6.55. Twenty minutes, only twenty. They could be out two hours or more. He was exhausted already. How was he going to keep this up?

Milne executed another turn, they were flying almost due south now. Eddie glanced at his altimeter, over 9000 feet. He could have judged that with his eyes closed for, even with his layers, he was bitterly cold. His fingers were stiff on the column, he had to swap hands from right to left to allow himself to wriggle his fingers and restore some feeling to them. When the feeling did come back, he regretted it for it was intensely painful.

Just to the left of the BE2s nose was a village, beyond that was a town - or more accurately a city, for we he could see the shell of a cathedral. That had to be Arras, he decided. Collier must have read his thoughts because he leant over from the front, map board in hand. He jabbed his finger down at the village that they were now coming level with, then at the map. Etrun, Eddie read. He nodded, then again when Collier jabbed his finger at Arras on the map, then at the city below.

Eddie looked to his left. The day was improving, the cloud cover was about three-tenths and he could see many miles in all directions. And the view to that side was dominated by one thing, a long, dark stain, dark brown against the verdant greens of spring, stretching away north and south as far as the eye could see. That had to be the front line, no-man's-land. Just out of sight, to the south, that would be the Somme where last year's vicious battles had taken place. Where Percy had been based.

And, apparently, Siggi too.

Percy. Why did he bother about him? Why waste the effort?

Collier was waving, what did he want? Eddie brought himself back into the present with a start. Collier was pointing at Milne. He was signalling, another turn, off to the east this time. Of course, time to cross the lines.

Eddie signalled his acknowledgement, and executed the turn with reasonable accuracy, closing up to keep his allocated station. How stupid was he? What was Milne going to think of him? That he was a daydreamer? He must keep his mind on the job.

Milne signalled again, that they should circle. All four machines started to do this. Eddie frowned, why were they doing this? Collier seemed to be looking for something too, what was it? They were still well over the British side of the lines.

He caught Collier's eye, and tried to get over his question with a hand gesture: why? Collier leant forward, Eddie realised that he was scribbling something on his pad in pencil. He held it up so that Eddie could see. The pad had one word on it: Escort. Eddie nodded in understanding; Milne was waiting for their escort to appear. He continued to hold station.

He was immediately puzzled by a strange phenomenon that he had not encountered before, white clouds that magically appeared close-by over to the right then just hung in the sky as they passed. He saw Collier look, then look back at him and shake his fist in mock anger and understood. It was Archie, and not just any Archie but British Archie. That did not feel right, his first experience of war and it was his own side that was shooting at him.

Milne was pointing off to the east, then turned, putting the nose of his aircraft down slightly, allowing the speed to build. Eddie understood, Milne was hoping this was enough to put the gunners off their aim and height calculations.

Whether this was the case or because the gunners had realised that they were shooting at their own side, the puffs of white, so innocent looking but deadly, were left behind them.

It was obvious they were no longer waiting for their escort, they were going over without. They were over trenches, although still well back from the front. Thin, jagged lines led forward towards the front itself, like the veins in a leaf, though these fed men rather than sap.

All food for where it was needed, thought Eddie, shuddering at the analogy.

Collier was now more active, scanning the sky all around them, twisting around, looking back over Eddie's head, to each rear quarter, down and then forwards, then repeating the process, time-after-time, the same. Eddie felt his throat go dry; this was it, he was at war, he was a serving, war-service pilot. This was no longer training, this was the real thing, down there, that was the front line, the place where so many men had faced each other for two and a half long years, had fought and died.

Were still fighting.

He did not feel ready.

He desperately wanted a drink. All his instincts told him to turn back, to swing the BE around, point the nose down, run away as fast as he could. But he could not do that. He had to do what was expected of him. He stayed close to Milne, trying to keep station, keep an eye on Milne's hand signals but also trying to look out himself, both to find landmarks so he could find his way back on his own if he needed to and also to help Collier out.

So why were they going without an escort? Why not wait? Eddie thought this over. Of course, it was because of the Archie bursts. It would have been obvious to anyone who was looking that there were aircraft around, the shell bursts was like a finger pointing them out. Observers on the ground or up in the Drachens would be telephoning back to the airfields. Any fighters up early would have seen the signs and have turned towards them. Eddie cursed the gunners even more, damn them, why could they not have looked more closely and held their fire?

They were over the front now. The patchwork of fields had given way to a churned up mass of browns and greys, interspersed with the zig-zag lines of trenches, most running almost exactly north-south but the saps and communication trenches pointing due east, towards the German lines. Eddie could not imagine what it was like living and fighting down there, crawling like rats in the mud.

As they crossed over the British front line, a section of ground just behind erupted, mushrooming up towards him, immediately followed by another and another. Shellfire, a battery was targeting the lines, lobbing death and destruction from several miles away, possibly even from Athies, where they were heading. This was why they were there, to give the British batteries chance to fight back, to protect the troops. To do that they needed to know where to target, they needed eyes in the sky, photographs, observation.

They needed people like Eddie.

He squared his shoulders, his resolve, which had wavered, was restored.

It was timely for they were now well into no-man's-land.

Below was a landscape pockmarked with innumerable shell holes, some filled with water, glistening in the April sun penetrating the scattered cloud. It actually looked quite beautiful, a ribbon of tiny lakes stretching up to the higher land that he knew to be Vimy Ridge to the north-east, but Eddie did not want to imagine the horrors that lurked beneath the tranquillity of their surface.

The clouds were definitely thinning now. Milne had lead them down to the cloud base, Eddie knew that he was using them as cover, hiding them from any German scouts that might be patrolling the front. The trouble was that hiding places worked both ways, they were as useful to the hunter as to prey.

The German lines, neater and more ordered than the British, appeared and rapidly fell beneath. Eddie glanced down at his airspeed indicator, then away. It was meaningless; there was clearly a strong tailwind blowing them into enemy territory, the ASI would not show that. Eddie no longer felt cold but the thought of what the tailwind meant chilled his soul. They were being rapidly delivered to the Germans but, once there, escape would be much harder. They would be virtually crawling back.

A sharp crack to his right made his heart thump. The aircraft lurched and wallowed, then settled. A series of black puffballs hung in the air, more appearing, silently this time, further away but most definitely at their height.

So this was it, he was under fire again but by the enemy this time, by people who really wanted him dead and smashed to pieces. This did feel different, there was more intent, more threat.

Something was wrong, the aircraft was wobbling, weaving. What was it? Were they hit? Eddie checked the wings, the struts, the ailerons, craned his head around to see the elevators. Nothing seemed amiss.

Then he realised the problem: it was him. He was shaking, his whole body was trembling, his feet almost dancing on the rudder bar, his hand jumping on the stick. Collier paused in his scanning of the sky and looked back at Eddie. It was obvious he was wondering what was going on.

Eddie pushed down with both feet onto the rudder bar. He was scared that he might break it but he had to stop his legs shaking. He also brought his left hand over and grasped his right on the stick, holding it still. The machine steadied, so did Eddie. Collier looked away. Eddie breathed again and checked his position with Milne. He had drifted away slightly, he closed the gap again. Milne looked across and gave him an encouraging thumbs up.

They were clear of the Archie for now. The patchwork of fields underneath them was back. On the other side of the lines these had seemed friendly, reassuring, showing that life, for all the present madness, went on. Here they seemed ominous, threatening. This was still France but it was occupied France. They were over an alien world.

Milne signalled again. This time it was not for him but for Armstrong and Kerr. Their aircraft pulled away slightly, Milne and Warburton falling back slightly and climbing. Eddie stayed with Milne, slightly behind and to his right.

Eddie could see Kerr busy with the camera mounted on the side of the BE, sliding an unexposed plate into the top. Armstrong was peering forward. Eddie had done this in training, lining up the machine on a target, concentrating on keeping the wings steady, on allowing the observer to take a clear picture. His results had been mixed, in fact it had become a bit of a joke to kick the rudder as the observer was pressing the shutter. They had all laughed at the results when they had been developed. He and the others had been berated for their attitude, they had scoffed at the photographic instructors for their fussiness but now it came clear why they were the way they were. This was no jolly jape, the photographic aircraft was flying slowly, steadily, on a dead straight course, an easy target for scout or Archie, in fact, they all were, the escort too. The joke of upsetting the photographer's framing, of blurring the image no seemed to Eddie as what it was, a puerile one, a stupid schoolboy prank. This took nerve. Eddie was not sure that he hard the courage to do what Armstrong was doing.

Yet one day, very soon, he would have to.

On cue, Archie started again. The Germans clearly did not welcome the intrusion and this time they definitely meant business. The black clouds blossomed around all four aircraft, close enough to hear over the engine, which Eddie had throttled back to keep pace with his companions who themselves had slowed to keep Armstrong's aircraft in front and below them. Eddie's aircraft was twice rocked and buffeted by the concussion of shell bursts close by his wing tip.

Milne's aircraft was drifting higher, Eddie spotted this immediately and followed suit. Soon they were at the level of the broken cloud. He realised that Milne was probably looking for its cover.

He could feel water dripping off his hair under his helmet and knew that, despite the cold, he was sweating.

The aircraft was shaking again, bobbling, rising and falling, though he could not be sure whether the cause was the turbulence from the clouds or from the bursts of Archie. Whatever, he found it increasingly hard to keep station, and had drifted a little way away from Milne's aircraft as they droned on through the cloud mottled sky. But then he worked it out, he knew what it was, it was something that he had been prone to in training. Once it had been pointed out to him that he was doing it he had had to work hard to correct the fault over the next few flights. He was over-correcting, not anticipating but reacting to changes and overdoing it, the corrections getting more and more abrupt as he chased and lost smooth flying.

Under stress he had fallen back into bad habits. Pleased with himself for working out the problem, he concentrated just on flying. The machine steadied. Good, he told himself, well done. If he could still think and reason under pressure, then he could do this.

The BE flew straight and level into a thicker patch of cloud. Eddie relaxed his pressure on stick and rudder bar, keeping everything central, making only the slightest of adjustments. They flew out of the other side, the wings perfectly level.

He was just congratulating himself on this when he realised that Collier, who had been keeping up his scanning of the sky, was waving at Eddie. For a long moment, Eddie could not understand why he was so animated but then saw exactly what the problem was: they were alone in the sky.

Eddie cursed himself. Where had the others gone? He twisted in his seat, to and fro, trying to spot them. They must have turned, he'd missed them doing it, where the hell where they? He banked the BE around, turning in a tight circle to scan the sky but only then remembering he was throttled back and had not checked his airspeed.

It was too late. The BE abruptly stalled, the horizon started to rapidly revolve around them.

Eddie felt a moment of panic, bitter acid rising in his throat, his unwanted breakfast threatening to return, before he got a grip of himself and remembered his spin recovery technique.

He tried to forget the gut-wrenching fear that he had gone through in training in taking the terrifying step of actually inducing a spin in the first place - like stepping onto the top platform of a diving board, he had described it - and replayed the words of Captain Hollinghurst: 'Let the nose fall, centralise the controls, opposite rudder to the direction of spin, fly the recovery - and don't pull the wings off.' He did this and, almost magically, it worked, though he did see the long upper-wing extensions flap alarmingly as he pulled up out of the dive.

Collier was gripping the sides of the cockpit, he let go and stared back at Eddie who could only imagine the choice words that his observer was muttering right now, and with some justification. What a fool he had been! First losing sight of the formation then succeeding in stalling and spinning a Quirk, an aircraft almost infamous for its stability. Three novice errors in a few moments. Stupid.

He started to search the sky for Milne and the others. They had lost a lot of height in the spin and recovery, at least 2000 feet, maybe more. It would take several minutes to recover that. Eddie increased the revs and started to climb but, immediately, Collier waved his hand, clearly indicating that he disagreed.

He wrote another single word on his pad and held it up for Eddie to see: HOME, then pointed to the west.

Eddie tried to swallow but his throat was too dry. He had messed everything up, he had let everyone down, not only that he had put Collier and himself into even more danger, they were alone now, they had lost much of their precious height, that made them even easier meat for any predator lurking in the clouds above them. Ashamed, he levelled out and swung the nose around.

His first mission and he was running for home with his tail between his legs.

Collier was up in his cockpit, scanning the sky all around, but particularly behind and above them. Eddie tried not to make eye contact with him. Would any observer fly with him again after this debacle?

He tried to concentrate on his course and his flying, to at least do that well from now on. He looked down at the ground, he was shocked at how little progress west they were making, they were hardly moving. He scanned around beneath him and soon found what he was looking for, something burning, perhaps a wreck of a building hit by shellfire in the night or the previous day. The smoke plume was long and close to the ground and virtually exactly from the direction that they were flying in. The wind had indeed got up since they had taken off and now they were flying, crawling in fact, straight into it. Eddie estimated their ground speed to be no more than 40 knots, maybe a lot less.

The lines seemed a long way away.

The fear that had subsided in Eddie came back. He felt his legs start to shake on the rudder bar again. He tried to control them, to get control of himself, to avoid further shame but it was not at all easy.

Collier obviously was feeling the same anxiety, worse possibly because he had to place his trust in someone else for he ceased scanning the sky for a moment to write another word: FASTER?

The question mark at the end of the word served to remind Eddie of his responsibility. He was flying, it was up to him to get them back. He had to pull himself together and get on with it.

His shaking subsided. He nodded at Collier and put the nose down a little to increase the speed. They would run the risk of being exposed to ground fire as they passed over the lines but the risk had to be worth taking.

Black puffs opened out just above them, just about where they would have been in fact if Eddie had not reduced height.

Eddie could imagine the gunners on the ground cursing him, they had calculated the height and his drift almost perfectly, it was only by a fluke that they had missed.

But then perhaps the fluke was an omen, that they were destined to get through this. Eddie asked himself; did this feel like the day that fate determined was going to be his last? Oddly, it didn't. They were going to get through this, he wasn't going to die, this wasn't his time.

His resolve stiffened, he shifted the stick a little to the right, flew for a few seconds on the new course, then repeated the manoeuvre to the left. No point letting fate do all the work, he decided, a little helping hand could not hurt. The next Archie bursts were at a more comfortable distance.

He repeated this for the next ten minutes, being careful not to be too predictable about the duration of each zig and zag. They were at the German rear lines now. He could see grey-uniformed figures below. Even from the height they were at, around two and a half thousand feet, he could see some raise rifles to their shoulders and fire at them. He felt safe though, they were unlikely to be hit at this range. Now, in his head, he was rehearsing what he would say to Milne when they got back, how he would apologise, how he would ask for a second chance.

It was some moments before he realised that the Archie had stopped. Was that it, were they clear? Collier clearly thought not, he was now kneeling on his seat, his hand on the Lewis gun, staring intently at the sky above Eddie's head. Eddie saw him lean forward, staring at a patch of the sky above and to the left. Then he thumped Eddie on the shoulder, pointed upwards, leant backwards, his finger on the trigger of the Lewis, his eye lined up on the sights.

Eddie looked back over his shoulder. Two dots had appeared against the clouds. German scouts, they had to be.

Was this fate mocking him, teasing him? Letting him think that he had escaped only to take him after all? He pushed the nose of the BE down, desperate to get more speed. It would bring them into the range of small arm fire from the ground but so be it. Despite doing this, the ground stubbornly refused to move more quickly underneath them, if anything the strong westerly breeze was blowing harder lower down.

Eddie looked over his shoulder. The two dots were getting much larger, resolving into aircraft, biplanes. Flashes appeared at the nose of one, it was firing, from a distance admittedly, but shooting nevertheless. Collier pressed the trigger of the Lewis gun, firing back over Eddie's shoulder. The report of the weapon, so close to him, even over the roar of the racing engine, was like a hammer blow inside his head.

He was momentarily confused, unsure as to what to do, should he manoeuvre or fly straight, allow Collier a decent shot?

Packa, packa, packa

The machine gun fire from the German aircraft, clearly audible over everything else followed by the splintering of wood and the ping of a bullet ricocheting off something metal, made him decide but more by instinct than rational thought. He heaved the stick over, kicked the rudder, anything to get away. The BE reacted typically slowly, banking lazily. Eddie saw the two German fighters, sleek, streamlined Albatros, overshoot and then to turn back towards him. Eddie levelled the wings, then repeated the turn in the opposite direction, aiming his machine at the lines again.

The Albatross had given themselves more space, they were turning in front of the BE, one of them climbing. The pair were painted gaudily in blues and yellows, they reminded Eddie of birds and his own aircraft, dowdy in its drab greens and brown, as a tired old moth, caught in the daylight, desperate to avoid their sharp beaks but unable to do more than slowly turn this way and that whilst the lithe predators could go where they wanted.

Collier was waving at them, trying to tell Eddie something, whilst swinging the gun around. Too late he realised what his observer was saying, that the Albatros were getting in his blind spot, in front and above, where he could not bring the gun to bear. Eddie pulled the stick to the side, started to turn.

It seemed to happen in slow motion, yet, at the same time, in an unstoppable instant.

A cacophony of noise: packa, packa, packa, the zip of bullets whizzing by him, one tugging at the shoulder of his coat, his windscreen shattering, the tearing and splintering of fabric and wood, the physical thump of steel clad lead against the cast iron of the engine that seemed to cause the BE to hesitate in the air.

And Collier's goggles flying off, his flying helmet bulging strangely.

Something wet and dark splashed over Eddie's own goggles, blinding him.

The engine stopped. The only sound now was the wind through the wires. There was a strong smell of petrol mingled with something else, something Eddie could not recognise but was vaguely familiar.

He snatched his goggles off, wiping his eyes, and blinked in the slipstream. He expected to see the black of engine oil but everywhere was red, red flecked with grey and white.

'John, we're hit,' he said and looked for his observer.

A cold hand seemed to grip Eddie's chest.

Collier was still kneeling, his hand gripping the Lewis gun but the right quarter of the top of his head from his right eye socket to his ear was gone. Blood was still fountaining out of the ragged hole, but with decreasing strength as Collier's frightened heart beat its last. His left eye was open and it stared blankly, unseeing, back at Eddie.

Eddie vomited into his scarf.

*

He had entered into a state of acceptance. The world still existed but was going on without him.

His world was quiet, confined to the few square feet of cockpit around him, even the noise of the air rushing past and whistling through the bracing wires had gone. Was this death? If so it was very peaceful, inviting. He was so tempted to accept it.

The rattle of machine guns and the tearing of fabric brought him back to reality. He started, almost like he had been in a deep sleep, yet one where he woke to a nightmare rather than from one.

His strength, anger, will to live returned. He was going to fight, to cling on to life. He had to believe that there were better days ahead, ones to live for.

Instinctively he kicked the rudder bar of the BE, slewing it to one side. One of the Albatross shot by, his aim put off by Eddie's manoeuvre. Eddie saw the helmeted head turn to look at him, for a moment he was sure he saw pity in the man's eyes.

Eddie looked down. He was over the middle of no-man's-land, quite low, possibly only 300 feet up. The BE was gliding smoothly, Eddie was now thankful for its stability, it had looked after him whilst he had gone elsewhere. With a dead engine and a stopped prop though, he knew his flight was only going to go on a few seconds more. Could he reach the British lines? For a moment he was hopeful but then realised that this was a pipedream. The lines were quite wide apart here, he would be well short.

At least the Albatross seemed to realise he was down, they had backed off a little way, were back behind him, higher, over the German front line probably.

How bad would the crash be? The ground was churned up, pockmarked. It would not be good, and, given the strong smell of petrol, the tank had to have been holed, the machine was sure to catch fire. If he was trapped in the cockpit he would burn alive.

A thought struck him. The tank was holed, it was the main pressurised tank beneath his seat. Was that why the engine had stopped? Cursing his stupidity, Eddie reached forward and turned on the gravity tank. Why hadn't he thought of this before? He held his breath, waiting a few seconds. He looked down, less than a hundred feet. He switched on the magnetos.

The engine coughed, the prop turned. He tried again. The engine caught and roared into life. The machine rose slightly.

Eddie did not climb, his one aim now was to get over the lines, to get down and get out of this hell.

He looked back over his shoulder. Sure enough, the Albatross had seen him, were banking towards him. He could imagine their anger, the pity that he had seen - or imagined - was long gone, now they would want to kill him.

Suddenly though, he had friends again. He was less than a hundred yards from the British lines, over the piles of barbed wire in front, and could see rifles being fired, not at him but past him, protecting him. As he crossed the line, still only barely 50 feet up, he saw the cheering troops, saw a machine gun crew elevate a Vickers gun, saw the tracer shoot up at the aircraft behind him. He risked a glance over his shoulder, the Germans had turned away, it was clearly too hot for them this low down.

Eddie quickly left the front line behind him. He was following the line of a sap. He saw alarmed faces look up at him, he could understand their fear, this far back they would not have seen his drama unfold. He could be a trench straffer or bomber. The friends could become enemies again.

He crossed the second line. The ground was still pock-marked with shell holes but it was less intense, more normal.

Should he try to find an airfield? No, he decided, he was still sitting in petrol, indeed his trousers were wet and his shins starting to hurt which must be from the spirit burning his skin. He wasn't going to risk a fire, he just wanted to be down, out of the cockpit. He did not want to look at that thing any more.

The thing that used to be Collier.

'My name is John.'

That's what he had said.

Someone's son. Someone's love. Not a thing with that jagged mess of a head.

His name is John.

John.

Eddie saw a road ahead. It looked reasonably flat and, although there were men on it, he was pretty sure that they would work out what he was doing and get out of the way.

He cut the engine.

The wheels touched, bumped. The aircraft slowed, then stopped, bumping onto the verge.

Even before it had, Eddie had undone his belts and was out.

He tried to run away but something was wrong, his legs seemed to be out of his control, unable to bear his weight. Eddie stumbled, then fell heavily, rolling onto the road.

He tasted blood, the grit in his mouth.

Was it his blood? Or Colliers?

Abruptly all went black.

*

He heard voices. Someone was turning him over. Where was he? In bed? In a dream? No, it was cold, it was wet; rain. He was outside.

'Get his coat undone.'

There was a massive thump. The ground shook.

'Get off, get off me,' Eddie pushed away the hands that were fumbling with the buttons of his coat.

'Just trying to look you over, mate, see where you're hurt.'

A strange accent. Not English.

'C'mon cobber, give a bloke a chance.'

Another thumping crump, the ground seem to rise to hit him in the back.

Suddenly Eddie knew where he was.

'I'm all right,' he said, pushing the hands away and sitting up. 'Really, I'm all right. I'm not hurt.'

He found himself looking into the concerned eyes of a khaki-clad pair of soldiers, one in a slouch hat, the other with a standard issue British helmet. The buttons on their tunics read 'Australian Military Forces' around a map of their country. That explained the strange accent.

'But you keeled over like a shot dingo, mate. And you're covered in blood.'

'It's not from 'im,' came a voice from further away. 'It's 'is mucker. Not a pretty sight.'

'Ah, sorry about that, mate,' said one of the soldiers. 'Your observer -'

'I know,' said Eddie. 'He's dead.'

And it's all my fault, he wanted to add, but couldn't bring himself to say the words. He pushed the men away and got to his feet. He was still shaky but at least his legs held him upright now. He was careful not to look directly at his aircraft but was aware that there were more of the Australians around the front cockpit. 'Where am I?'

'Near Christchurch, mate.'

'What?'

The nearest soldier grinned. 'It's a cave, mate. The Kiwi's named it, stupid sods, just the kind of lame name those drongos would give it. Just south of Arras. I'm McAllister.'

There was another huge thump, making the pebbles on the road jump and the puddles in it to ripple.

'We're from the artillery battery in the next field. Saw you coming down. Cap told us to go and see if you were alright. You'd better come and see him.'

Eddie now glanced over at his aircraft. The soldiers were, with some difficulty, pulling Collier's body from the cockpit.

'I should...' he began.

'Nah, mate, c'mon with me,' said McAllister quite gently. 'They'll see to 'im, don't worry. The Cap'll be wanting to speak to you.'

Eddie allowed McAllister to lead him away from the BE in the direction of the guns.

*

It turned out that the battery commander, Captain Henry, was busy with his three huge guns to give much time to Eddie when he reported to him.

Henry received McAllister's report, asked about Eddie's general health, then said, 'Sorry, I'll come and have a word with you later but I'll get someone to call your squadron, tell them you're alright. You look a bit of a mess. You can use my tent to get yourself cleaned up. McAllister, show him where to go.'

Eddie tried to protest, tried to persuade Henry to get him some transport back to Acq but knew the Captain wasn't going to listen. He had a job to do, and Eddie's arrival was an inconvenience. He allowed McAllister to take him to the Captain's tent, and there did the best job he could of cleaning himself up. He was shocked how much the blood had soaked him and got under his helmet and into his hair, it was sickening to wash it off. The leather of his helmet and coat were another thing, the blood had left a dark stain on both.

Eddie could not get the idea out of his head that this was appropriate. Collier's death was always going to be a stain, whatever he wore, wherever he went.

It was then he remembered the pain in his legs from the petrol burns. He hesitated, somehow it didn't seem right to be stripping off at the front, in someone else's tent but then told himself that he was being silly and pulled off his boots and trousers. The petrol had sloshed down his boots and worked its way up his thighs. His skin was reddened but had not blistered. He used the water in his wash bowl to rinse his legs down and then to wash the spirit out of his trousers.

He was just wondering where one hung out your washing at the front when Captain Henry walked into the tent. The Captain looked in surprise at the trouser less pilot, Eddie wondered what the protocol was at moments like this, he was not sure what King's regulations said about saluting a senior officer when partly undressed. Luckily, the Australian seemed to take it in his stride.

'Had a bit of an accident, Lieutenant?' he said, squatting down at the end of his camp bed and opening the travelling case that rested there.

'Yes...oh, not like that, it was petrol. My tank was holed. Not the...er...other thing.'

Henry gave him a grim smile. 'You wouldn't be the first or the last to soil himself around here, believe me,' he said. 'I'll get one of the lads to get you some spare kit, save your blushes at least.' Henry had taken a bottle of brandy out of the case. He poured big slugs into two tin mugs and offered one to Eddie.

'It's a bit early for me,' he began to say but was interrupted by the long whistling sound of an incoming shell. Involuntarily he ducked down. The explosion that followed made the brandy jump in the mug and rattled the canvas of the tent.

'Get it down you, you've had a shock, you're still shaking,' said Henry, ignoring the shell burst and thrusting the mug at Eddie.

Eddie took it this time. He noticed for the first time that his hand was, indeed, trembling. Steeling himself, he took a big gulp. The spirit burned his throat, he managed not to choke and cough. He felt it warm him, felt his nerves start to calm.

'Thanks, sir.' he said.

'No problem,' said Henry, sitting down on the bed. He waved his hand at the chair. 'And don't bother with the "sir", we don't go in for that much around here. You been out here long?'

Eddie sat down, cradling his mug.

'No,' said Eddie. 'A week in France, two days with my squadron. This was my first mission.'

'God,' said Henry, shaking his head. 'You poor young sod.'

Eddie's head dropped. 'It was my fault,' he said. 'I messed it all up. Lost touch with my formation.'

Henry pulled a face. 'Don't be so hard on yourself. This is war is full of people doing their best but making mistakes. Bloody hell, the whole thing is a mistake, believe me, so don't beat yourself up about it.'

'But a man died, because of me.'

Henry stared into the distance and gave a brief, mirthless smile. 'Lots of people die because of you and because of me every day. That's what we do. You spot them, we shell them.' There was another whistle of an incoming shell, followed by its detonation. 'And they shell us,' Henry continued. 'Seriously, lad, don't dwell on it. You can't otherwise you'd quickly lose your senses. And get that down you.' He nodded at the mug of brandy in Eddie's hand. Eddie took another swig. He had to admit it did help.

'We've called your squadron. They're sending some mechanics to look at your machine, see if they can get it airworthy again and to get you back.'

Another shell arrived, slightly closer this time. Henry did not flinch but did screw up his face. 'Don't count on them being here soon though. Not with this counter-barrage going on. If they have any sense they will keep away until it's died down. Now drink up, you'll be needing a couple more of those, believe me.'

*

Over the course of the next few hours, Eddie did indeed have several more of the Australian Captain's brandies. He was thankful for them, they helped to get him through the stress of rest of the morning and the afternoon as the shells whistled all around them.

'They've no idea where we are,' sneered McAlister. 'They know we're around here somewhere but they haven't pinpointed us. They're just taking pot-shots. That's thanks to blokes like you, mate, keeping their kites and balloons down.' He gave Eddie a hefty thump of thanks on the shoulder that made him stagger.

Pot-shots or not, Eddie found being under shellfire nerve wracking. The notion of huge cylinders of death being lobbed in his general direction from 5-6 miles away, well aimed or not was not reassuring. He tried not to dwell on the thoughts that, at any moment, they could get lucky, that he would not hear the explosion that followed the whistling because he would be in it. He had no understanding of how people stood this day after day.

After lunch the battery had received new orders so were busied in swinging the howitzers, 8-inch field guns, McAllister told him, round so their barrels pointed at a new target. Eddie could do nothing but watch. He saw Henry get messages from his headquarters, he guessed that these were originally from people doing jobs like he would do, artillery spotters radioing something they had spotted by Morse.

He was fascinated with all the activity at first, the trajectory and wind-driftage calculations appealed to Eddie's mechanical bent. But, when the battery started firing and the realisation of what the huge shells being loaded into the breaches of the howitzers would be delivering at the other end of their flight hit him, he had to get away.

He went back to his aircraft. He half expected he would find it smashed, that a shell had reduced it to a pile of splintered wood and canvas. He wondered whether his speculation was a wish, that he wanted it to be destroyed so he would not have to go up in the damned thing again - but that was cowardice, it wouldn't do, he told himself. If everyone else had to face it then so must he.

Secretly though, he knew that he really did want the machine gone.

It wasn't. It was still just where he had left it.

It looked lost, out of place but, other than being splattered with mud from passing carts and trucks, it seemed to have not been damaged any further. The only thing Eddie noticed was that the machine kept lifting up and shifting in the stiff breeze. He knew that there was a risk that it could tip over and still be wrecked.

For a moment he was tempted to leave it, to plead ignorance as to its fate but he told himself to grow up.

Hunting around, he found some old sandbags stacked by the side of the road. Staggering slightly under their weight, he lifted half a dozen up onto the wings to help hold them down, then added more onto the tail. He then chocked the wheels fore and aft with some stones.

Satisfied it was now as secure as it could be, he inspected the damage. He counted 14 bullet holes in the machine, two of which had gouged long scores in the engine block, one having passed right through the petrol tank under Eddie's seat. This seemed to be the only thing that prevented the machine from flying, though he would want someone to look it over properly before he took it up. And for the petrol which still dripped onto the cockpit floor, that would need mopping up.

The petrol that mingled with Collier's blood.

A match. That was all it would take. Fanned by the strong breeze, with all the doped fabric and spruce it would be gone in a few moments. A funeral pyre for a lost hero. Eddie had matches in his pocket.

He stepped down from the cockpit and walked swiftly away, pausing only to see if he could see any sign of Collier.

There was nothing. He wondered whether he'd been taken somewhere for burial.

Would he ever know where?

*

The afternoon dragged on. The battery was sending shell after shell somewhere off towards the North-East. Eddie's head was throbbing, though whether this was from the howitzer or the Cognac that Henry kept plying him with, he wasn't sure. Still no one came from the airfield.

Was a blessing or a curse? On one hand, the longer no one came the more that getting back in the cockpit could be put off.

On the other, he now started to wonder whether he was neglecting his duty, shirking, that he should leave his aircraft and try and get back to Acq some other way. But then would he be on a charge for abandoning his machine? He was surely in enough bother as it was. He had tried to ask Henry as what he should do but the Australian, busy with his own duties, just shrugged and told Eddie that it was up to him.

Eddie wondered if the squadron had abandoned him as a bad job.

The mechanics turned up at about 5pm, a sergeant and two privates.

'Sorry, sir. we had 'ell of a job getting away and then when we tried to get round Arras the road was blocked,' said the Sergeant, though Eddie could not help but notice red wine stains on the man's overalls. He did not say much but walked with them to the machine and waited whilst they looked it over.

'It'll be a couple of hours, I'm afraid,' reported the Sergeant at last. 'Got to patch the tank and there's a bit of damage to the spar on the top plane that we'll need to splice. Won't be done before nightfall. Look's like we're all here for the night.'

'Right.' sighed Eddie. 'I'll go and organise some tents for us all.'

'Great,' said the sergeant with no enthusiasm. He looked back at the aircraft. 'Don't know why you didn't put a match to the damned thing. Heap of junk it is. It'll be off back to the depot this week anyway. Anyway, now we're 'ere suppose we'll have to mend it.'

Eddie just stared at him.

*

The repairs were not completed until after 9pm.

Eddie, was, by this time, feeling no pain whatsoever. He was sat with Captain Henry and the battery's junior officer around a brazier drinking Cognac, then moved onto something that one of the Lieutenants had acquired on leave in Normandy the previous week. At first Eddie found it hard to keep up with the seasoned, hard-drinking Aussies, the unfamiliar spirit burning his throat, and he was content to listen to their tales drawn from more than three years of war, from the burning shores of the Dardanelles to the mud of Belgium. In the end he caught up with them and his tongue loosened. He talked about his own training, of the Rumpeties, of Prentice and the half a dozen others who had failed to even make it to France.

And he talked about the patrol, of his spin, of the Albatross, of how helpless he felt when they were cutting the BE to pieces around him.

In the end he talked about Bunny. How it should have been him on the patrol, not Eddie.

'I left the little blighter sleeping,' he said, staring into his drink.

'I hope he appreciates what you did for him,' said the Australian. 'He owes you a drink. Speaking of which...'

He reached over and topped up Eddie's mug with a generous slug.

DAY 3

APRIL 4, 1917

Eddie awoke thinking his head was being assaulted by a hammer.

All around him was noise, thumping reports. It was the heavy guns, dozens of them, the smell of cordite sour in his nostrils. He was confused, not knowing what was happening. It was dark, where was he? It took a few panicked moments to remember. He was on the floor of Captain Henry's tent, still fully dressed and just covered in a blanket, his coat rolled up under his head.

Stiff and cold, his head throbbing and stomach churning, he got up. The flashes from outside the canvas showed Eddie that the Captain was already up and gone. Gradually he worked out what was going on; they were not being shelled, this was the battery in action. This was not like the relatively leisurely barrage of yesterday, this was intense, relentless. And he knew that it could not just be this battery alone, there had to be more, the noise was too deeply layered to be anything different.

He put his head outside the tent flap to reveal a vision of hell. The sky was rent by flashes for as far as the eye could see, the ground shook, time after time as shell after shell were launched on their deadly journey. There were answered by the report of detonations, four, five or six miles away, perhaps more.

Eddie shuddered. If it were hellish here it was beyond comprehension what it was like at the other end.

He retreated into the tent and sought out his boots and coat. He found that someone had brought Eddie a cup of milky tea. Even the smell of the brew was enough to make him feel queasy. He pushed it away and went in search of the Australian captain.

Henry was stood by his guns.

'Morning. As you see, the barrage has started.'

Every few seconds huge gouts of flame and red-hot gasses shot from the barrels, accompanied by an ear-splitting report. The crew opened the breech, the shell case was yanked out and tossed onto a growing pile of brass behind the battery. Even before the old case had stopped rolling a new shell was rammed home, the breech shut and locked and a gunner turned away and yanked a lanyard to fire. It was like a carefully choreographed dance, a waltz of death.

'How long will it go on for?' asked Eddie.

Henry gave him a look that told Eddie that he should not have been so stupid even to ask.

'Your men have gone down to your machine already so you can be off at first light. The cooks will have breakfast on if you want to grab a bite before you go.'

Eddie shook his head, then wished that he hadn't.

'No, it's fine,' he said. 'I'd better be getting back.' He started to button his coat.

'So be it,' said Henry. He came over and offered his hand to Eddie who took it. 'Good luck, Grenville, I think you're going to need it. And don't be so hard on yourself.'

'No sir.'

Henry smiled, a grim smile, then returned to his men and his guns. Eddie wondered if he should say something more but could not think what, so went back to the tent and picked up his goggles and flying helmet.

The first sign of dawn breaking was showing in the eastern sky. He shivered. It was cold, windy and was raining.

He found the Sergeant and the two mechanics stood by his machine, smoking and looking rather miserable. They quickly discarded their cigarettes, flicking them into the mud.

'All ready to go, sir,' said the Sergeant. having to shout over the roar of the guns. 'We've had her running, she's as sweet as a nut. The road looks clear and it's pointing pretty much into the wind. You should be fine.'

Eddie knew what had been unsaid; Please, just get off so we can get out of this hellhole

'Thanks, he said, climbing up into the cockpit. He tried to ignore the empty space in front of him but found that he couldn't. 'I've got a spare seat,' he said. 'I could give one of you a lift back to the airfield if you like.'

'No thanks, sir, you're alright. We'll make our own way back. Let's get you on your way.'

Eddie flushed. For all their wanting to be gone, they either did not trust him or their own repairs. Either way it was not exactly reassuring.

The Sergeant was stood by the propeller, waiting to swing it. There was no going back now. He gave the signal to start.

The roar of the engine immediately transported him back to the previous day. Eddie found himself holding his breath, he needed to calm himself. His hands were shaking again, he told himself it was the cold, though he had his now dark-stained flying gear on. He willed the shaking to stop but concentrating on it just seemed to make it worse. The mechanics were watching him, holding on to the wing tip struts. He simply had to pull himself together and go. Eddie signalled that he was going to throttle up, he did so and the machine began to roll.

The take-off run along the road was quite short and, oddly, the action seemed to distract his sub-conscience for his shaking subsided. This was a good job as the found that the wind was far from exactly on the nose as promised and the machine swung alarmingly towards a shattered, denuded tree as soon as he got twenty or thirty feet into the air. For a moment he was sure that he must hit it but his wing tip passed no more than a yard away.

Eddie climbed rapidly, turning away from the line of guns. The last thing he wanted was either to meet one of the huge projectiles coming the other way or to spook any anti-aircraft gunners protecting the batteries. The machine felt lithe and lively, far better than any other BE2 that he had ever flown. Briefly, he rediscovered the simple joy of flying but then remembered why the aircraft was so light.

He had no observer.

Sobered, and finding that he was clear of the gun flashes, he set his course for Acq, hoping that he could at least find his way back.

He used Arras itself as the first marker, flying right over the shattered city, the shell of the cathedral looking ghostly in the rain and low cloud. He saw aircraft, some singletons, some formations, all heading towards the east. It struck him that there was a lot more activity than he had seen the day before at this time but then that might just have been down to his lack of awareness. He had, after all, had a lot on his mind then.

Yesterday. It was only yesterday, just 24 hours ago that he had made the flight in the opposite direction. It seemed so long ago now. Was this what it was going to be like. You would age quickly here. It was no wonder Percy looked so much older.

Crossing out of the city to the north he was briefly lost, it was so murky that he could not even see the front. He reached for the map, large parts of which were stained red, and dropped lower to find a landmark. At last he recognised the road pattern of the village that Collier had pointed out to him; Etrun.

'Thanks, John,' he muttered and turned in the direction of Acq.

Even with the marker, he nearly missed it. The wind must have blown him to the East because it was only seeing movement to his left, a glint of weak sun on doped fabric as a shaft of light briefly broke through the clouds, that he saw the aircraft taking off from the field, He turned, battling against the wind. It seemed to take an age to even reach the airfield but, at last, the familiar pattern of the hangars set against the quadrangle of the farm buildings came into view.

Eddie made a reasonable landing straight into the wind, then taxied up to the hangars. As he approached a group of mechanics dashed out from the cover and grabbed the wing tips as he cut the engine. He undid his belts and climbed down. Chiefy was waiting for him.

'Welcome back, sir,' he said. 'There's coffee in the mess. And Captain Marsh asked if you'd go and see him straight afterwards.'

'Thanks, Chiefy,' Eddie said.

He trudged disconsolately toward the farm buildings. Well that was it, he was being called in for his dressing down. Perhaps it would be more than a dressing down, perhaps he would be sent away in disgrace for incompetence. Well, he deserved it.

Bunny would laugh, that was the kind of thing he would do. Well damn him, he should know. In fact, Eddie decided, Pops and coffee could wait, he was going to see Bunny.

But then it wasn't Bunny's fault, was it? Not really. Eddie had decided for him. You couldn't stay angry with old Bunny for long.

He'd be worried about Eddie though. He would see him first.

Eddie turned and went into the stable block rather than continue into the mess. He walked straight to their dorm, pulling the blanket out of the way.

No one was there. And whilst Daley's bed looked to have been recently vacated and his things were by it and on the table next to it, Bunny's bed was neatly made, and his side of the room empty of any personal belongings.

Eddie stared at it. What was going on? Had Bunny moved out?

'Ah Grenville, there you are.'

Eddie turned to find Pops stood behind him.

'Sir,' he said. 'I was going to come to find you. I'm so sorry about Collier. It was my fault, I need to apologise to Captain Milne, and I will do better -'

'We know about Collier,' said Pops, his voice gentle. 'And Captain Milne is fine, in fact he blamed himself for losing you. These things happen.'

'But...isn't that why you wanted to see me?'

'No, no it wasn't. It was about Cavendish.'

'Bunny? I was going to ask you about this.' Eddie waved his hand around the empty room. 'Where is he?'

Pops looked uncomfortable. 'I am afraid that Cavendish had a bad accidental crash taking off from the airfield late yesterday morning.'

'Hah. Bloody typical! He always was ham-fisted. He smashed up three kites in training. I think he just wants to meet nurses,' said Eddie. 'So which hospital is the silly young fool in?'

'He's not in hospital, I'm afraid Grenville,' said Pops. 'He flew straight into the trees at the far side of the field. His neck was broken. It was quick, he didn't suffer. I'm very sorry.'

*

Eddie sat on his bed staring at Bunny's empty one. It could not be true, it simply couldn't be.

He remembered their first meeting, the first day at Sedbergh school. Bunny had always been there, had always been Eddie's little friend, always slightly lost, vulnerable, in need of a big brother to look out for him. Sometimes chaps like that could be irritating, sometimes Bunny was but usually he wasn't, he was just Bunny, well-meaning, someone whose infectious character won through.

And now he was gone. He would never see him again.

'Ah Grenville, good, you're back.'

Eddie looked up, then got to his feet. It was Hastings.

'Right, well now you have finished playing with the PBI it's time to get back to some real work.'

'Real work?'

'Yes, in case you hadn't noticed there's a war on and things are hotting up. Whilst you were gallivanting around yesterday, we had Trenchard drop in. Boom told us straight, it's maximum effort over the next few days. We have to keep the Hun on his side of the lines, deny him sight of what's happening over here.'

'But, how? We're an observation squadron, not scouts.'

'That's by-the-by. There's things we can do, we are on the 11 o'clock show, off up to Vimy with Cooper's on board, shake things up at the station and anything else we can find up there. That should stir up Fritzy.'

'Oh, right,' said Eddie, feeling not a little bit flustered.

'What's up Grenville?' Hastings was frowning. 'You look surprised.'

'It's just, well. With Bunny and everything -' He nodded at the empty bed.

Hastings gave a snort of derision. 'God yeah, him. Cost me a bloody new aircraft he did. Oh not the Quirk, he did everyone a favour by writing one of those off, no the new crate. We're one short now, though Pops says there will be ferry pilots bringing more in today. Hope you're a bit more on the ball than Carter there was.'

'Carter?'

Hastings waved his hand dismissively in the direction of Bunny's bend. 'Him. whatever his name was.'

'Cavendish,' said Eddie coldly. 'His name was Cavendish.'

'Right, well if you say so.' Hastings looked at his watch, one of the new wrist ones, similar to the one that Henry was wearing. 'It's just after 9. Final briefing will be in my office at 10.30. I'll see you there.'

Hastings turned and left. Eddie was stunned. Life just went on then, Bunny was just dismissed. He wasn't someone's loved one, a treasured son, a dear friend, he just had one label; failure. Was life that cheap, that unimportant now?

Would that be his label too, if - when - he went the same way? Eddie was sure that it was going to be.

He had sat down at his desk. He contemplated writing a letter, to do something as a last marker of his presence on Earth. Who to though? To his mother? Hardly, she had never seemed that close, caring, maternal. She always seemed to be irritated rather than pleased by his presence. Certainly not to his father though, with him Eddie associated brusqueness, coldness, everything was business to him. Eddie always felt like his father always regarded him as if he was an asset, something of potential monetary value, a long-shot investment that he had held on to in the hope that it might come right and give him some sort of return. Eddie almost felt that his father was coming round to the opinion that he should cut his losses and cash-in. So not Father.

It would normally have been Alice, gentle, kind, patient Alice, for ever his big sister, where he went to as a child for comfort, solace and closeness. But he could not write to her. She was in Berlin, a widow now, an alien in an alien world, what was now an enemy world. Poor Alice, what would she do without Siggi? How would Siggi's family be treating her? How would the German state? Alice the war widow.

A widow because of Percy.

Percy. Eddie could not, would not write to him. Not ever again.

Annie then. The woman he hardly knew. The one whom he had embarrassed himself with.

He picked up the pen, hoping that inspiration or resolve would come.

It didn't.

He decided to write to Bunny's parents. They were a lovely couple, rather older than the rest of the parents of his friends and completely contrasting with his own in that they were loving, open and caring. They had confided in Eddie once when he had been to stay with them one Summer. It had been an idyllic visit, two weeks in the Norfolk Broads spent sailing and generally having the greatest fun, that long summer of 1914. Bunny's father was in his sixties, his wife was perhaps ten years younger. He had told Eddie that they had resigned themselves to being childless but then, out of the blue, Bunny had come along and made their happiness together complete. Now it seemed to be fate being cruel, given then taking away again.

He had paused over his letter, trying to fight back the tears, when the thought struck him. Cursing, he put the pen down and hurried off to find his flight commander. He found him sat in the mess, a cup of tea on the table in front of him, reading the News of the World.

'Captain,' he said. 'I've just realised something, well two things actually.'

Hastings put down his paper and looked up at Eddie.

'What?' he said.

'Today's mission, I guess we'll be flying the new machines? The RE8s?'

'The Harry Tates, yes of course. You wouldn't get me up in a Quirk again. Not for a watch as big as a shovel.'

'But I've never actually flown one before.'

Hastings looked nonplussed. 'So? What's the problem?'

'Well, don't you think I should at least try one before I fly one in action?'

Hastings crossed his arms. 'It's hardly my fault that you haven't now is it? You had the chance to try one yesterday, you are part of my flight after all. As it was you chose to go swanning off with Davy's mob and left me with the squib. Well hard cheese, old chap. You'll just have to sink or swim.'

'Swanning off?' Eddie could not help his voice rising. 'Do you think I was on a pleasure flight? My observer died.'

Hastings was instantly on his feet. 'I know he died. Bloody good chap he was as well. Milne was a bloody fool to let him go with you.'

Eddie knew he should back down but he found he couldn't. 'I don't care. That was who I was given and he was happy to fly with me. And as for that so-called squib, he was my bloody friend, and he was a bloody good chap too, if anyone had given him a chance.'

Sure enough, this just made Hastings worse. 'Don't you take that tone with me. You'll be on a charge if you go on like that.'

The pair were face-to-face with each other. Eddie was aware that there were other people in the room but he wasn't sure who was there until he felt gentle but firm hands grip his arms and heard Pops voice say, gently. 'Now then, Lieutenant, and you too, Clive. I don't think this is going to help anyone is it?'

Eddie expected Hastings to continue to bristle and to shout further, but instead he seemed to relax. 'Yes, sorry Grenville, that was out of order, careless of me. I know you're a good type. As I'm sure was your friend...er...'

'Cavendish,' said Eddie. 'But it's me that should be apologising.' he added. 'I shouldn't have spoken like that to you.'

'Let's not speak of it again,' said Hastings, holding his hand out. Eddie took it without hesitation. Hastings sat down and picked up his paper again, leaving Eddie standing, puzzled at the sudden turnaround in his flight leader's mood.

'About the lad's lack of experience, Clive,' said Pops, still standing next to Eddie. 'On the new type. Surely it would be better for him to have a quick test to get used to it before he goes out with you? He will be better able to do the job then.'

Hastings lowered the corner of his paper. He looked irritated again and checked his watch. 'Pops, there isn't time for that. It's quarter to ten. Chiefy will be up to his arse getting the kites ready as it is. No, and that's an end to it.'

Eddie was now resigned to his fate so was surprised when Pops continued to push. 'Actually I have a solution,' he said. 'One that might work in your favour.'

Hastings sighed. 'Go on then, tell me.'

'We've got Armstrong and Kerr down to do the shoot at Vimy Ridge. Kerr is the only wireless trained observer free at the moment.'

'They're A flight,' said Hastings, his tone dismissive.

'Yes but Armstrong has flown the Harry Tate. He flew one of the trial machines when it came over in February. When they came back, they were down to ferry their old bird to St Omer and pick up the first of A Flight's. I'm sure Armstrong would be keen on getting his hands on one early. He can go with you and Eddie can fly with Kerr on the art obs. Then he can pick up the one Armstrong was going for this afternoon and get used to the beast then.'

'Hmm, yes,' said Hastings suddenly looking happier. 'Good team that pair. Alright, let's swap then.'

'You'll have to ask them.'

'They'll do as they are bloody well told,' Hastings snapped. Eddie saw him look at Pops and then his eyes dropped. 'Of course, I mean, yes, we'll have to ask them. Actually would you mind doing it, Pops old boy? It would come better from you.'

'Of course, Clive,' said Pops. He gave Eddie a grim smile. 'Do try and see if you can bring this one back this time, they don't grow on trees you know.'

Eddie smiled out of politeness, though he could not help but have the picture of Collier's shattered head come into his mind. He followed Pops out of the mess in search of Armstrong and Kerr.

'You have to handle Captain Hastings carefully,' murmured Pops as they walked.

'What do you mean?' said Eddie.

'He's a good pilot,' said Pops. Eddie could not help but notice that Pops had not really answered his question, and that there was a distinct air of something that had remained unsaid about the end of Pops' last sentence.

Eddie was sure the next word that Pops almost said was 'but'. He wondered what went after it.

They found Armstrong and Kerr together outside the armourers office where the Lewis guns and ammunition were stored.

They were sat together at a trellis table checking through cartridges, discarding bulged ones into a bucket that had a single word roughly daubed on it in white paint; 'Duds', and feeding the good ones carefully into the Lewis's drum magazines. Eddie recalled Percy writing in a letter that he did this too and resolved to do the same from now on.

Pops explained to the pair about the proposed swap. Armstrong and Kerr looked at each other and pulled faces. Eddie instantly assumed the reason for this.

'Look, I'm sorry,' he said. 'I can understand you not wanting to fly with me - ' he began to say to Kerr, but the latter interrupted him.

'Oh hell, Eddie, I don't mind that. You did a decent enough job first time, I'd be quite happy to fly with you, any day.' He gave Eddie a reassuring pat on the shoulder.

'Then what?' Eddie said, puzzled.

'It's me having to fly with the death-or-glory merchant,' said Armstrong, his face set.

'What do you mean?' said Eddie.

'Pops knows, but he won't say, will you Pops?' Pops did indeed just sit quietly at the end of the table. 'It's why we like it on our side of the hangar with Milne.'

Pops sighed. 'Come on, old man,' he murmured. 'That's enough.'

'Milne knows how dangerous this job is, how vulnerable we are with the old buses to Richthofen and his like. He looks out for us, weighs up the risks, does the job without getting us into too much bother where he can. Hastings on the other hand he...'

'Careful, old man,' said Pops. 'Remember *Captain* Hastings is a superior officer, and Grenville has to fly with him eventually. It wouldn't be right to let me hear you undermine an officer in the presence of someone new, would it now?'

Armstrong smiled and nodded. 'Too right, Pops. We need to give some semblance of actually being a military unit or else the whole thing will descend into a shambles.' He looked around him and gave a little chuckle. 'Well *more* of a shambles anyway. Right, I'd better go. Who's my observer?'

'Smith. Well, Hastings is going to have a word with him anyway.'

Armstrong gave a snort. 'Poor bugger,' he said. He got to his feet. 'Right , you two look after yourselves won't you. I'd better report to Albert.'

'You too.'

Eddie shook hands with Armstrong, who then embraced his observer. The two did not exchange any words, but they did not need to. Eddie could see the closeness between the pair, though this was nothing effeminate, it was a clear bond, something more than friendship. They could almost pass for family.

Brothers.

Eddie felt a lump in his throat. It took several swallows to move it, by which time Pops and Armstrong had left. He sat opposite Kerr and started to sort through the bullets in the boxes of ammunition.

'Do you know what you are looking for?' Kerr said, glancing across. 'Bulged cartridges, the case or head out of shape?'

'Yes, I was in the cadets. We had Lee Enfields and a Maxim. We were taught how to do this,' Eddie replied, squinting at a bullet.

'If in any doubt, chuck it,' said Kerr. 'These are one of the few things not in short supply around here, believe me!'

They worked in silence for a few minutes before Eddie stumped up the courage to ask the question that he had been itching to ask. 'Why did Armstrong call the Captain Albert? He's called Clive isn't he?'

Kerr laughed. 'It's his nickname, but don't, for God's sake call him that to his face. It's because he wants to be Ball, well a scout pilot anyway. He reckons he's good enough. He's got three Huns you know?'

'What on Quirks?'

'One of them was, yes, hard enough though it is to believe. Got an Aviatik in February with the front gun on the Strange mount. Don't know who was more surprised, him or the Hun. The others were on a Bristol Scout in his old squadron at the beginning of '16. Every squadron used to have a couple of scouts then. That was how Ball got started.'

'He's been out before then?'

'Yes. He had a year over here, then was posted back to a training squadron for a rest. God only knows what the students made of him, he's not known for his patience as you might have seen. All the time he was over there he was pestering the Brass Hats to get back to France in a fighter squadron.'

'But he got posted here,' said Eddie, the realisation setting in.

'Yes. A new observation squadron, needed some experienced hands to guide the new chaps. We got Milne, a Canadian called McKenzie who went west a couple of weeks ago. And angry Albert.'

'Is that a problem?' said Eddie.

'Just a bit, at least for the poor sods who have to fly with him. Hastings is trying to prove the High Command wrong. He's hankering for combat, that was why he was so keen to get the Harry Tates. It's not just that they have got more chance of defending themselves, it's more because they have a front gun and interrupter gear.'

'But...they're not fighters, are they?'

'Hardly. But that's not going to stop old Albert trying to add to his score. I think he's willing to do anything to make ace. And I mean anything.'

'Oh great,' said Eddie. 'That's really reassuring.'

'Look, I'm sorry,' said Kerr, reaching over to give Eddie a pat. 'Don't listen to my moaning. Pop does his best to keep him in check as well, keeps an ear out, listens to what the other chaps say. I have heard that he has threatened to scupper any chance he has of a transfer by shopping him to Trenchard. That tends to keep him in line.'

Eddie nodded, the scene in the mess and Milne's sudden about face now made sense.

Kerr leant back and stared reflectively out of the door through which Armstrong had departed. 'Still, I have to admit I'm glad I'm in Milne's flight. Looks after you does our Captain.' He sighed. 'Come on, we'd better get this finished. It's almost time for us to be somewhere else.'

Eddie was quiet for the remainder of the time the task took. Partly this was apprehensive about flying over the lines again but mainly it was a thought that went round and around in his head and would not leave him. Milne looked after his pilots, yet that had not saved Collier. So what chance did he have flying with Clive Hastings?

*

'Right, so are you clear on the route?'

Eddie nodded. The trouble was that he was not sure he had taken in what Kerr had told him and shown him on the map. He had tried to concentrate, tried to tell himself to be professional but this was difficult as he was fighting off a growing feeling of nausea that had started as they walked across the grass to the hangar. It must have been last night, he told himself, the brandy was still in his system, though he had a nagging feeling that it was actually the dread of what he was about to do that was the true cause.

Whatever, he was determined not to disgrace himself.

'Good, let's go then,' said Kerr. He paused, and looked more carefully at Eddie. 'I say, are you alright? You look awfully white.'

'I'm fine,' said Eddie, but knew instantly that he wasn't. He only just made it outside before his stomach heaved up what little it contained. It was awfully painful, Eddie was sure that his insides must be damaged by the retching, yet he could not stop the dry heaving. He was also dreadfully conscious of all the riggers and fitters staring at him, he was not sure whether the shame was a greater pain.

'Don't worry about it, Eddie,' said Kerr, who had come to lean solicitously over him. 'Better out than in. You'll feel better for it. And for this too.'

He thrust a flask at Eddie. Assuming it was water, Eddie tipped it back. Too late he realised it was brandy. The spirit burned his throat and made him cough, which amused the ground crew.

'Bloody hell, Kerr,' he spluttered. 'Are you trying to kill me?'

'Nah, you'll be fine. Do you a world of good,' Kerr said, taking the flask back and taking a sip himself. 'You'll find it helps.'

Oddly, Eddie found that it did. The nausea vanished, he felt good. With a spring in his step, he headed towards their machine, pausing only to watch the five aircraft of B flight taxi out, Cooper bombs under the centre section, and start their take-off runs, Armstrong waving at the pair as they passed.

Five aircraft. A flight was usually six. Eddie was puzzled for a moment. Then he remembered; the sixth machine would have been Bunny's, and he felt sick again.

He had recovered a little by the time he was strapped in the machine. He thought that seeing Kerr in the cockpit in front of him would bring back memories of the previous morning, but Collier had been so big and bulky he was unmistakeable whilst Kerr was slight and jockey-like, totally different. Still, Eddie's heart thumped as the engine started, and thumped even more when he faced the machine into the stiff breeze and took off.

As they passed over the edge of the field, Eddie noticed a tree. It had a vivid, fresh scar high up on its trunk, the type of scar that would be caused by a four-bladed propeller hitting it full on.

Trying to put this out of his head, Eddie started to climb.

*

Eddie managed to find his way to the target with minimal problems. He assumed that Kerr was happy with his flying and navigation, whatever he received a cheery thumbs up from his observer. He still felt the butterflies in his tummy as they approached the line, but they had, at least, not had the tension of the long climb that he had experienced the previous day. The downside of this was that they were a lot lower, at around 5000 feet, as Kerr needing to see where the shells burst. This made them very vulnerable, with the cloud base so low, an ambush would be easy. Hopefully though, a single aircraft would be hard to pick out against the ground, though Eddie wished that the unseasonal snow would melt a little so they would stand out a little less. A muddy brown and green aircraft above fields and the trenches was fine, above flecked white meant they would stand out like a butterfly on ice.

Kerr gave him a signal, making a figure of eight with his fingers, then pointing at a ruined church below. That had to be the return point. Eddie nodded and started to fly the pattern. The predictable, repeating pattern that Kerr would need so he could guide the battery

Perhaps Archie wouldn't see them, he thought. Or perhaps they wouldn't work out the pattern he was flying, fail to work out their altitude.

Some hope.

Still, at least he felt like he was doing a proper job now, unlike yesterday when everything seemed to be wrong. He was earning his corn, doing his bit for the war effort.

He half watched the sky, looking for enemy scouts and half watched Kerr setting up the Sterling transmitter, He had seen the equipment on the ground and had learned Morse as part of his training and had been fascinated, amazed that it was possible to at least communicate from the air to the ground even if it was only one way. Kerr was bent down, he would be feeding out the copper wire, all 120 feet of it with the lead weight on the end. Eddie looked behind him, sure enough, he could see the weight bobbing about in their slipstream.

He was brought out of his daydream by Kerr waving at him.

He had forgotten to turn. Obediently he swung the aircraft around. Aiming the nose at the stump of the church tower. Kerr gestured again, this time pointing at the sky all around. The message was clear, Eddie's role was now to watch and fly, Kerr would be occupied.

He did as he was told.

He knew what Kerr would be doing, sending some rapid 'Bs' on the Morse key; the 'Are you receiving?' question to the battery to wake them up, followed by 'KQ' for ready to fire?' and then 'GG' - 'Fire'. He tried not to look but found he couldn't help it, his natural curiosity overcame his desire for self-preservation. He thought at first that the guns had not fired, that the battery was asleep, but then a series of white puffs appeared to one side of them, further into German territory. Kerr plotted these on his board and was about to send his Morse message to the battery when he saw Eddie looking. Angrily he pointed upwards and over the lines. He was telling him again what he was supposed to be doing. Flushing, Eddie tried to concentrate on just doing his pair of jobs.

It was perhaps two minutes later that he saw it. It was a chance that he did, just the slightest bit of movement against the background and from a direction that he did not expect but it was enough to give him a jolt of pure fear. Something black was rising up towards them, very quickly and it was coming from the British side. What on earth was it? An aircraft? But it was surely travelling too fast.

He was about to give Kerr a shove to warn him when the object got level with them and Eddie could see what it was. For what seemed like a minute but which he knew could only be, in reality, a second at most, they were flying in formation with it. It was a huge shell. It hung in the frigid air, copper-coloured, deadly, so close Eddie could even see the fuse on its nose. It then fell steeply away, down, down towards the target.

Eddie felt sick again, almost rigid on the controls. They were in line and on the trajectory of the very shells they were directing. If that had hit them, if any one of the others hit them that were going to be fired, they would be history, either obliterated, swatted out of existence like a fly or else consigned to a long trip down to the ground to be smashed to pieces.

A salvo of Archie burst nearby, Eddie instinctively jerked the aircraft away from them. Kerr looked over his shoulder, gesturing again. Back on course, Eddie was to get back on course.

Every nerve in his body, every sense of reason that he had was screaming at him to get away, away from the Archie that was targeted at him, away from the path of the howitzer shells that would crush him, turn away, get back to the safety of the ground.

Eddie turned the aircraft back onto its figure-of-eight course.

He was shaking, cold yet drenched in sweat at the same time. His breath came in shallow, ragged, rapid pants. Every one he was sure would be his last. What would it feel like? Would it be quick? Or would he be a helpless passenger tangled in the remains of the aircraft, knowing that there was no hope as he fell? He would prefer the Albatros. At least there was a chance then, you could fight back.

Aircraft! Damn, he had not been looking. He searched the skies, above and behind them, looking in the gaps between the clouds. His heart skipped again, there were small dots above them. Again he almost turned the machine west, he felt his hand start to push to that side. It was a mental battle not to do it. Think, he told himself, think. They were just over the British side of the lines. They were probably friendly, high cover. Just watch them, watch for movement, watch for any that dove down towards them.

Time to turn again. Kerr was still watching over the side, then busy on the Morse key.

There was someone speaking, shouting. How could there be voices all the way up here?

Then Eddie realised it was himself, shouting, 'Come on! Come on you dozy bastards, hit the damn thing,' over and over again.

He shut up.

Then Kerr was signalling again. Thumbs up. Mouthing 'Home', leaning down in the cockpit to wind the aerial in.

Eddie gratefully turned and put the nose of the aircraft down, heading West, still battling the stiff breeze that was straight onto their nose, but at least on their way home.

He found he was still trembling, though it felt like the huge weight that had been sitting on his chest had been lifted. They flew into a shaft of light, watery but dazzlingly bright after the gloom of the morning, it seemed like an omen, a good one at last.

He could do this.

When Kerr passed the flask of brandy back to him, Eddie took it with pleasure and took a good, warming mouthful.

He could get through this. He could.

*

When they landed, Kerr briefly thanked Eddie, then went off to the office to report to Pops on the shoot. Eddie had a quick walk around the aircraft. He was surprised to see holes in the rear fuselage and rudder.

'Shrapnel, sir,' said one of fitters, sticking his finger into one of the holes and probing around inside. 'That must have been a near one.'

'I didn't notice anything,' said Eddie, peering at the damage.

'Cor, you're a cool customer, sir, begging' your pardon,' said the fitter. 'Nothing major, we'll get her patched up for you this afternoon.'

'Thanks,' said Eddie. He could not help but feel pleased. His embarrassment of this morning seemed distant now. He felt part of the squadron.

He noticed Captain Milne was also in the hangar, signing off some papers for Chiefy. Eddie swallowed, he had to face up to this. He walked over, saluted and then waited for them to finish their conversation. Milne acknowledged him but went on discussing the various ailments of his flights' aircraft. It was quite a long list of problems.

Once Chiefy had left, Milne turned to Eddie. Eddie expected him to be angry, but Milne looked far more concerned.

'Grenville, I'm so sorry I haven't had chance to see you since you got back. I'm afraid I was out on the early show. Are you alright?'

'Yes sir,' said Eddie, rather taken aback. 'I'm just really sorry about what happened. It was all my fault.'

Milne shook his head. 'No, Grenville, the fault was all mine. I should have kept a better eye out for you, not let you get separated from us.'

'But Collier -'

'No buts, Eddie. None of that was your fault. Get those thoughts out of your head, brooding will do nobody any good. You have a job to do and a responsibility to who you fly with, so that's the end of it, understand?'

'Yes sir.'

'I was really sorry to hear about your friend too. Poor show that, damned unlucky. Must have knocked you a bit for six. How are you bearing up?'

'Alright sir. It was good that I was able to go over with Kerr this morning. Took my mind off it.'

'Good, that's the spirit,' Milne gave a grim smile. 'I understand you're with us again this afternoon when we pick up the new machines?'

'Yes sir.'

'Good. And you can drop the sir when the CO and Clive Hastings aren't around. I'm David or Milne, whatever you prefer.'

'Thank you, and I'm Eddie.'

'Good Eddie, now go and get some lunch. We're off for St. Omer at two.'

*

Eddie was somewhat disquieted when he found that he had been assigned the same machine that he had flown the day before with Collier. It had been checked over, the bullet holes patched with doped cloth but there were still signs of blood on the cockpit floor. He tried not to look and sought out Milne for the signal as to when to take off.

There were only three aircraft from A flight making the shuttle to the depot, all that could be spared. B flight, complete with Armstrong, had to scrub their earlier mission due to three of their number having engine troubles, much to Hastings' chagrin and were down to have another go later in the afternoon, the flight commander's rage spilling over into him shouting at Chiefy, accusing him of being slipshod. Chiefy, holding his tongue but, red with anger, then took it out on his mechanics. As other pilots were required for yet more Art Obs missions, it was a bare rump that were free to go and collect the new machines, Eddie, Milne and a pilot Eddie had barely spoken to before, Vaughn.

The wind had abated slightly though the cloud was still low when they took off. They flew in loose formation, Milne taking them well away from the line for they not only had no observers but they were completely unarmed. There was little chance of any German scouts venturing much beyond the front line but Milne's caution was both understandable and welcome.

The landing at St.Omer was uneventful. The three machines rolled up to the hangars and switched off. The ground crew took charge of the aircraft and immediately wheeling them away towards a large park of other aircraft. They all had a similar look; tired, worn out, war-weary, a collection of BE2cs and 2es, Morane Parasols, a Bristol Scout. Eddie knew that they would not be wasted, over the next few days and weeks they would be ferried back to England by any lucky pilot given leave, although, considering the state of many of the machines, 'lucky' might not be the right term for the pilots given the dubious honour of flying them. In time these worn out aircraft would be allocated to the flying schools. Eddie wondered what the pupils following in his footsteps would make of his battered, stained BE2.

'I've got to go and see to the paperwork in the office,' said Milne. 'You two can go and see if you can get a cup of tea in the mess. I'll see you outside dispersal in, say, 40 minutes?'

'Fine by me,' said Vaughn.

'I'm going to try and find a friend of mine,' said Eddie. 'If that's alright?'

Vaughn shrugged. 'Fine by me,' he repeated.

Eddie walked with his comrades to the main administration buildings where he left them. He had a job to do, something that he did not relish; he had to tell Bean about Bunny.

It was odd walking back towards his old sleeping quarters. He had spent nearly a fortnight here, waiting for a posting and it had almost become a home-from-home. He had only left it three days before but it was already unfamiliar, he felt he was intruding, out of place. His time in St. Omer seemed a long time ago, not the bare 72 hours that it had been.

He hesitated briefly outside the door of the hut, steeling himself, then walked in.

He found himself staring at three strangers.

'Oh,' he said. 'Sorry.'

The three scrambled to their feet. Although he could see from their uniforms that they were second Lieutenants like him, they came to attention.

Eddie was puzzled for a moment, then realised. He was still in his flying gear, grimy, stained in oil from the RAF engine's leaky valve train. He was also stained in something else, the dark mark of Collier's blood. He decided he might as well not enlighten them.

'At ease,' he murmured. 'I was looking for Bean, I mean, Lieutenant Monroe. This is his hut.'

'I'm sorry sir,' said one of the three, 'We've only just got here ourselves, came from England this morning. We got allocated this billet. There was no one in it when we got here.'

'Oh right,' said Eddie. 'No problem, he must have got a posting. Thanks, carry on.'

He turned to leave.

'Sir?'

He looked back. 'Yes?'

'Are you at the front, sir?'

'Yes, are you a combat pilot?'

Eddie hesitated. He had caught his reflection in a mirror that was set upon one of the tables, behind the bowl used for shaving and washing water in a morning. Momentarily he was transfixed. The person staring back was not familiar; he looked older, more worn, certainly more tired.

'Sir, are you sir?'

Eddie broke away from staring at himself and smiled at the three. All were wide-eyed, pink cheeked. They looked a generation younger than him. 'Yes, I am.' he said.

'What's it like sir? What's it like in combat, going over the lines?'

'It's...It is,' he began. 'It isn't like anything else. You probably need to find out for yourself what it's really like. It's different for everyone.'

He turned away and, this time, did not look back.

As he walked back over to the mess he glanced across at the park of the worn-out aircraft. He wondered if there was, somewhere, a similar collection of worn-out aircrew.

*

The three pilots met outside the admin building as arranged then walked over to the hangars where their new machines were waiting for them. After the old, patched, stained BE2s, the RE8s were pristine, the markings sharp, the lettering perfect, the machines still smelling of the last coats of dope and newly-applied paint. They walked around them, taking in the detail.

It was the first time Eddie had had chance to see one close up. It seemed much bigger and more strongly built than the BE2, though one thing seemed familiar; the wings. He asked one of the senior ack-emmas about them.

'Yes sir, that's right, uses the same wings as the 2e, just tacked a bit extra on in the middle. Think it saved the blokes at the factory time designing it.'

'Oh right,' said Eddie, looking at the wing extensions that cantilevered out beyond the lower wings a further 6 feet each side. 'But it's a much heavier machine isn't it?'

'Yes, much bigger engine too, you have 140 hp to carry you, but don't worry, the wings are plenty strong enough. Well, the boffins say they are.'

'Right,' said Vaughn, frowning and staring at the front of the machine which was dominated by a wedge-shaped aluminium tank that sloped back towards the pilot, the top of the cylinder heads and twin stack exhausts that turned at right angles as they reached the leading edge of the upper wing so they stood vertically in front of it. These reminded Eddie of the stacks of a paddle steamer. Vaughn walked up to the cockpit and peered forwards and pulled a face. He rested his hand on the Vickers machine gun that almost seemed to be an afterthought, tacked as it was onto the left side of the fuselage and also protruding into the airstream. 'I presume the designers have heard of streamlining?' he murmured. He looked again at the pilot's cockpit. 'That's a long way back too,' he added.

'That's enough, Vaughn,' Milne said quietly. 'It's what we are flying from now on. We just have to get on with the job.'

'Yes sir,' Vaughn muttered, but Eddie saw how tight-lipped he looked. He could guess why. All those things sticking out into the airstream would slow them down, although their job was often done at relatively low speeds, having a turn of pace to get out of trouble would be helpful. And having the cockpit where it was meant that the view forward would be greatly obscured whilst the wings would substantially mask the sky in front and the ground below, so that trouble would be harder to spot. At least the observer was now in a place where he could better defend the tail and his gun mount was one of the new Scarff ring types. That was more reassuring.

Milne turned and looked outside the hangar. The rain had stopped but the cloud base was low, the windsock showed that the wind was still strong and gusty. Eddie saw him frown as he looked towards the west

'Better get off,' he said. 'I don't like the look of what's coming in. You two ready?' Both Eddie and Vaughn nodded.

'Right then, let's go.'

They each went to their aircraft and climbed aboard. Eddie

spent a few moments familiarising himself with the controls and instruments. Except for the Aldis sight and the trigger for the forward machine gun it was quite similar to the old BE. Looking forward, though, he could see what Vaughn meant. The nose seemed to go on for ever, and, at the angle they sat on the ground, the view forward was pretty poor. Peering around the side of the cockpit, he gave the signal to the ack-emma at the prop to be ready to swing it to start it.

His engine caught first pull, and he settled down to warm it up. He was about to look for the signal to roll when he saw the crew chief walk over to Milne in his cockpit and shout something to him. Milne nodded, then pointed up at the eastern sky. Eddie looked and saw two dots that quickly resolved into aircraft and understood. There were two machines landing and they were going to wait until they were down before taking off themselves.

He left his engine idling and watched as the two machines came in, one about 200 yards in front of the other. He could now see that they were RE8s like his own machine, and these too were factory-fresh, probably being ferried over from England.

The first made a good landing, straight into the wind and bumped to a halt on the grass. The second was to be doing the same but then the pilot changed their mind, perhaps worried that they were too close to the first machine and might collide with it. The nose of the aircraft lifted, Eddie could see the speed bleed off.

It happened very suddenly. The nose of the second machine dropped abruptly, the aircraft completed one half spin and nosed into the ground.

Eddie was not sure whether he imagined or really heard the splintering crunch, probably it had to be the former given the noise that his and the other machines' engines were making. He had heard it too many times before in training though, it had an unwelcome familiarity about it

Men were already running towards the crash, which was no more than 100 yards from where Eddie sat. The wings of the machine had folded forward and sagged, the undercarriage had been shattered and the fuselage was broken, but the wreck looked to have been survivable. Sure enough, Eddie could see the pilot moving, tearing off his goggles and flying helmet. He stayed in the cockpit, however, although he appeared to be trying to lever himself back and out. He's trapped, Eddie thought, as the pilot slumped forward again, his legs are pinned, something in the aircraft has folded back on him.

The rescuers arrived, one was talking to the pilot whilst another pair leaned into the remains of the cockpit, clearly trying to see how the man was stuck.

The fire was like some tropical flower opening, red and yellow, it burst from the wreckage and rolled upward, wide at first, then narrowing into a fierce column. The rescuers threw themselves away from the inferno, the two that had been trying to free the pilot's legs were briefly on fire themselves, rolling on the ground until the flames could be smothered by their companions who pressed coats on their bodies.

And now Eddie could hear it, even over the engine. It was a scream, a high pitched, unearthly wail, the cry of a human being in agony.

It was only stopped when an officer, shielding his face from the heat, stepped forward from the ring of men, once rescuers, now helpless spectators, and raised his service revolver.

Eddie looked away.

He saw that Milne was still looking, goggles raised but then looked at both of his pilots in turn and gestured forward. They were to go.

Eddie's hands were shaking on the stick and throttle as they taxied away from the hangar and onto the field. They passed close by the pyre. He tried not to look but at one point they had to pass through the smoke. The combination of smells was nauseating; petrol, oil, cellulose dope and something else, he was sure it was burnt meat. It lingered even when they were through it, it seemed to have permeated the scarf that he had wrapped around his face. He pulled it down, seeking clean, untainted air but still the scent was there.

Milne's aircraft turned into the wind and pulled away as he opened the throttle. Vaughn followed suit and Eddie did the same. The wet grass swished underneath them and then he was airborne, climbing with the other two machines away from the field.

He was no more than two hundred feet up when there was a sudden change in engine note, followed by a massive bang. The engine stopped, as did the big prop in front.

Eddie had to fight the instinctive move: to turn back. Perhaps if he had not just witnessed the crash he might have done, done what he had seen half-a-dozen pilots do in the last six months, turn and try and get back on the airfield. But turning cost speed, and speed gave you lift, and this aircraft particularly seemed to lose speed very easily.

He pushed the nose down, even though the ground seemed awfully near.

He was detached, like someone else had taken over, was making the decisions, was flying the aircraft on its brief trip down to the ground. Eddie was there though, saying over and over again, 'please don't burn, please don't let me burn.'

He lifted the nose a little. The machine crossed a road. He saw soldiers throwing themselves flat as he passed over them almost close enough to touch. Then there was a wall, dead ahead, so close he was sure he must hit it. He pulled back on the stick slightly knowing that he was using the last of his flying speed. He felt the undercarriage impact the wall and splinter. There was a thump just underneath his seat, the rudder bar kicked hard back against his feet. He noticed a wheel fly up alongside the cockpit as the aircraft slowed and then pancaked hard down into the field beyond the wall. It seemed to slide forever.

Eddie did not remember undoing his belts, nor of actually getting out of the aircraft but realised that he must have done because he found that he was running, and running very hard.

He stopped and turned around.

The RE8 was on its belly about 50 yards away. It was steaming slightly but showed no sign of bursting into flame.

It was only then that he noticed how much his foot hurt and decided that falling over was now quite in order.

*

'Engine threw a rod, sir,' Eddie could hear the chief mechanic talking outside the medical room. 'Came straight out the side of the block.'

Eddie did not hear the reply because the doctor chose that moment to manipulate his foot, accompanied by the traditional medical phrase: 'Tell me if this hurts.'

It seemed such a redundant question that Eddie felt the need to add to his kick and yell of pain with the equally traditional patient's reply: 'Yes, it bloody does hurt!'

The doctor was obviously used to this sort of response for he ignored it. He went to the washbowl in the corner of the room and started washing his hands. He was just drying them when Milne came into the room. He had landed in the field next to where Eddie had crashed and had accompanied him back in the ambulance.

'How is he, doc?' he said.

'I think he's got a small break in one of the bones in his left foot,' said the doctor. 'It might just be bruising but we can get him to the x-ray unit at the main hospital to be sure. They are rather busy though, as you can imagine.'

'Is he fit to fly? Or is he going to need to have time to recover?'

'He can't fly. He will probably need to spend a few weeks not putting any weight on it.'

Eddie had been slightly resenting being talked about as if he wasn't in the room but this had gone too far. Suddenly he realised what the implications of all this were. He might not be going back to the squadron, he might have to kick his heels in a hospital somewhere or, even worse, be sent back to England. Although the last few days had been pretty ghastly, the thought of not doing it, of not doing his bit was appalling.

'I'm fine,' he said, swinging his legs off the bed where he had been examined. 'It's just a bit of discomfort, that's all.' He stood up, gingerly trying to bear weight on his bad foot. The pain shot up his leg, he did his best not to show it in his face.

He saw the doubt show in both Milne's and the Doctor's faces.

'I'm not sure it's wise,' said the Doctor. 'The swelling is going to get worse.'

'Please, sir. David...' Eddie said. 'I want to carry on. Surely you could just strap it up, give me some pills, doc?'

Milne looked at the doctor. 'The lad's keen,' he said. 'Shall we let him try?'

The doctor stared at Eddie's foot for a few seconds, as if he was waiting for the answer to appear on his skin. 'Oh very well,' he said at last. 'But only in the morning. If he's able to stand the pain then and the swelling isn't too bad, I'll send him on his way.'

'Can't I go now?' protested Eddie.

'No, you better do as the doc says,' said Milne, checking his watch and looking out of the window. 'I need to go and get back to Acq whilst there is still enough light. Hopefully we'll see you there tomorrow, Grenville. But only if you really can manage, understand?'

'Yes sir.'

Milne nodded and left the room.

Eddie felt suddenly bereft, alone.

The doctor had gone to his cabinet. He came back with a bottle of pills.

'Take one of these now, and another before bed tonight, more if the pain gets too bad.' he said. 'But don't overdo them, they are Morphine Sulphate - opium.'

Eddie nodded and took one of the pills. He then lay back down whilst the doctor strapped up his foot.

'Right, try that,' he said when he had finished.

Eddie swung his legs off the bed and tried to put some weight on his foot again. If anything it was worse.

'Fine,' he said. 'Much better.'

'I'll get you a stick,' said the doctor, barely hiding his smile.

*

Eddie went to bed early that night. It had been a long day, he was tired, but that was not the main reason. He did not want any conversation, he did not want any questions, he just wanted to be alone. He did not care what his roommates for the night thought of him.

He just wanted to get back to where he belonged.

DAY 4

APRIL 5, 1917

Eddie opened his eyes.

Opposite him in the next bed he could see familiar blond hair poking out from beneath the blankets.

Bunny, it was Bunny.

Eddie sprang from beneath his own bed, eager to rouse his friend, ask him what had happened. Had there been a mistake? Or was it a cruel joke that had been played on him.

In the fraction of a second it took to get to his feet he had gone from elation to anger. Bunny was dead so it had to have been a practical joke. Well it was in damn bad taste.

Although there was only perhaps three feet separating him from his friend, he was somehow getting no closer. Desperately he tried to run but Bunny's bed was getting further away, not nearer. Then the flames appeared, just a little yellow tongue licking around the blankets at first but quickly developing into a roaring inferno that consumed everything it touched. Bunny sat up in the bed, wreathed from head to foot in flame, turning black, screaming. Eddie ran harder but still he was getting no closer.

Then there were no flames, just screaming. It went on and on.

The flame reappeared, right in front of his face, the screaming went on.

It was himself.

'Are you alright? I say, are you alright?'

There were hands on him, they were trying to drag him into the fire. Eddie fought them off, shoving punching.

'Hey, stop it! Bert, grab him will you?'

Eddie was awake. He was in a hut, there were two men, in pyjamas, holding him down. One was holding a lamp.

He stopped struggling.

'Sorry,' he said. 'Sorry.'

The two let go of him and stood back. There was shock on their faces, one had a dribble of blood running from the corner of his mouth. He dabbed it away with his hand, then looked at his fingers. Now he looked more annoyed than concerned.

'Sorry,' said Eddie again. 'Did I do that?'

'Yes you bloody did,' said the man who he now recognised as one of his roommates. 'Bloody lunatic.'

'Steady Freddy, the poor chap was having a nightmare,' said the other.

'It doesn't mean he has to lash out,' said the first, taking the lamp and inspecting the damage to his mouth in his shaving mirror. 'Nor use filthy language like that. Where the hell were you brought up? It's not right you know.'

The other one sat on Eddie's bed.

'You alright, old boy?' he said.

'Yes,' said Eddie. 'Well mainly. My foot hurts.'

That was an understatement; in fact it was throbbing like it was about to burst.

'Oh poor you,' said Freddie from across the room. 'You should see what you've done to my lip, you damn thug.'

'Leave it, Freddie. Remember what the orderly said, he had a crash yesterday.'

'That doesn't excuse him waking people up in the middle of the night screaming his head off and swearing like a Navvy.'

'Swearing?' said Eddie. 'I never swear.'

'Well you do now, old boy,' laughed Bert. 'Let's all get back to sleep, should we? Forget it all happened?'

He gave Eddie a reassuring pat on the shoulder, then went back to his own bed.

There were a few muttered grumbles from Freddie, but he too got back into bed and extinguished the lamp.

Eddie lay on his back in the darkness.

His foot was throbbing worse than ever. He thought about getting his pills but did not want to risk disturbing his companions again.

He was glad that the pain kept him from sleeping at first for he was scared at what he might see in the dreaming world.

*

When he woke again it was light, and he was alone. The other cots in the room were empty and neatly made. He was grateful that the other two were not around, it would have been too embarrassing to face them.

His foot was hurting very badly. He could see that it was swollen. Gingerly he swung out of bed and tried to put some weight on it. Even with his stick it was almost unbearable.

There was a knock on the door of the hut.

'Come in,' Eddie called, hobbling over to the washbowl.

It was one of the hut orderlies.

'Begging your pardon, sir,' he said. 'The MO was asking to see you. Wanted to check how you were, sir.' Eddie saw the man look at his foot and pull a face. 'Looks like I could tell him for you, sir. Looks like you've done yourself a mischief.'

'Thanks,' said Eddie. 'I wouldn't have noticed if you hadn't pointed it out to me.' He peered into the mirror and ran his fingers over his stubble. 'I didn't bring my wash kit with me. Didn't think I'd be staying. You couldn't get me some could you?'

'Certainly sir, we do have a few things that some of the gentlemen who...er...leave us suddenly, so to speak, leave behind.'

Eddie's thoughts immediately went to both Bunny and the unknown pilot whose end he had witnessed the day before. How many more had there been? He didn't like to think.

'Thanks,' he said, turning to sit back on the bed. Without thinking he put his foot down. The pain shot up his leg and he gave an involuntary yelp.

'Looks like you've got a Blighty there, sir,' said the orderly coming over to help support Eddie.

'Why don't you mind your own damned business?' Eddie yelled, shaking the man's hands off him and then sinking onto his bed. 'Go and get me that wash kit and look sharp about it.'

The orderly reddened, mumbled 'Sir,' and left.

Eddie winced. That was uncalled for, why had he done that? The man was only being helpful. And wouldn't going home get him out of this nightmare? No, the thought was appalling, he never ran away from anything, that was cowardly.

But what good was he doing? He had killed his observer, smashed up a brand new machine, not been able to save Bunny and now hurt himself. That was quite a roll call.

Still, none of that was his fault. If he gave up now it would haunt him, eat away at him, nag him and remind him. He had to face his demons. He had to do his bit.

Eddie reached for the pill bottle. He took a couple out and swallowed them with some water.

He would apologise to the orderly when he came back.

He would wash, shave then go and see the MO.

He would get back to the squadron.

*

'I'm sorry, I just can't sign you off as fit to fly.'

'But sir, it's not that bad, really.'

'It is and you know it is, Grenville.' The doctor's face was set firm. 'I'll put it in a cast. That will at least keep it immobile and help with the pain.'

'But I couldn't wear a flying boot over a cast could I?'

'No, you couldn't. You would be on light ground duties only.'

'And how long would it be on?'

The doctor shrugged. 'Six to eight weeks.'

'What? Surely there must be something that you can do?'

The doctor sighed, crossed his arms and stared at Eddie.

'I suppose if you rest it...' he began but then stopped.

'What? Please doc.'

'If you rest it, the swelling may start to go down and the bones will start to knit together. If you catch it wrong though it will hurt like the devil.'

'That's fine, I can put up with that.'

'You will probably end up with a limp, be in pain for life. Come on, lieutenant, you could be at home and out of things for a month or so. No one would judge you for it. You have a genuine injury, you are certainly not swinging the lead, everyone will see that.'

He was right, he knew it, the doctor was right. The prospect of being out of this nightmare was tempting. But at some point he would have to come back. Could he face that? Did he have the courage to walk away and come back. He was not sure. Eddie tried not to think about the possibility. He shook his head. 'No. I want to be with my squadron. What do I need to do?'

The doctor sighed. 'We can see if we can get you a flat shoe to fit you. Something with a really stiff sole. That will at least give you some support. Then I'm afraid that you will have to keep the leg raised for at least 24 hours. Keep walking about to a minimum. What shoe size are you?'

'Eight,' said Eddie.

'Orderly!' called the doctor.

The man appeared almost immediately.

'Go to the stores and draw three pairs of flat soled shoes, sizes 8, 9 and 10 and bring them back here.'

'Sir.'

'With your foot swollen, you'll need a bigger size for the bad one,' the doctor explained. He sighed again. 'It may not be any good you know. If it's no better this time tomorrow I will sign you off as unfit for flying.'

'Yes sir, I understand,' said Eddie. 'Thank you.'

'Don't mention it,' muttered the doctor. 'You know, I took the Hippocratic oath to save people's lives. I'm not sure how this fits with that.'

'Sir?'

'Forget it Grenville. I'll send a telegram to your squadron, explaining everything. I'll see you again tomorrow. I can't do anything more than that.'

*

Eddie was not one for just laying down and doing nothing so the rest of the day was miserable. He lay on his bed, his bad foot, inside the size 9 shoe he had managed to force on over the swelling, raised up, resting on a blanket. It never stopped hurting, it throbbed and pulsed. He was convinced that it was not getting better but worse, that he might not even be able to get the shoe off in the morning.

It was hard to think much beyond his injury. It became his world. He tried writing a letter to Bunny's parents but, even writing in pencil, the flimsy war department paper crumpled and tore and he eventually tossed it angrily away.

His two roommates did make an appearance at midday. Freddie, with his swollen lip, made a point of ignoring Eddie. He only stayed a few minutes before announcing that he was going to the mess to find someone to have a game of chess with and 'where the company is a little more civilised.'

Eddie was not sorry that he had gone.

Bert was a little more solicitous, asking how Eddie was, sympathising with him about the pain and saying all the right things about how dashed unlucky he'd been.

Eddie knew he should have been pleased, knew he should have been glad of the company, glad of someone to talk to but he found himself being surly and resentful, answering only in grunts or monosyllables. In the end even the sunny disposition of Bert seemed to wilt on the stony ground of Eddie's mood and he also made his excuses and headed off to the mess, though still rather more graciously than Freddie had. He did pass over a book and a newspaper and put them on the table by Eddie's bed before he left, and Eddie was grateful for these once he was left in solitude, for, despite his resentment and irritation of the company, once he was alone he found the silence and loneliness almost unbearably oppressive.

Why had he acted that way? Why had he been so unpleasant. Manners are cheap, it does not cost you much to use them, that was something that he had always lived by. Why was he changing now? It was the pain, he told himself, it had to be the pain. The pain and the pills.

The pills. He could have one, it would dull the throb, give him a bit more peace. But it had only been, what, an hour since he had had the last one. Better not have another just yet, the doctor said he had to be careful with them.

He picked up the book, finding it was one he had read before, John Buchan's *The 39 Steps*. It was a good yarn though. He started reading.

'John, my name is John.'

Collier's face swam into his thoughts. Yet was it his face? Eddie was not sure anymore. He only remembered his size, the bulk of the man. How he had resented it for blocking his view, for slowing them down as they had tried to run for safety.

And he remembered Collier's head. His ragged, shattered head, obscenely pink and grey.

The bile rose in Eddie's throat again. Quickly he took a drink of water from the mug on the table, washing the acid back down again.

His foot, disturbed by his movement, throbbed even more.

Eddie reached for the pill bottle and swallowed two of the

pills, then went back to reading.

*

'Shut up, shut up, you annoying little prig.'

Eddie opened his eyes, it was dark. He couldn't breathe, something was stopping him breathing. Something was round his throat. He felt for what it was, hands, arms. Someone was half-throttling him. He fought against them, scrambling to pull the hands away.

'Freddie, stop it, let him go.'

There was now someone else, another pair of hands. Fighting, struggling.

Then suddenly the pressure was gone.

'Bloody lunatic, he should be locked up.'

Freddie's voice.

'He's not well. He's on morphine.'

Bert.

Calm.

Placating.

'If he's not well, why is he here? Why is he allowed to disturb a chap's sleep like that? Screaming, I ask you, screaming.'

'I'm sorry,' said Eddie.

'You bloody well would be if I could get hold of you,' said Freddie. 'I'm not putting up with this any longer. Either he goes or I do.'

'Leave it, Freddie. Try to get back to sleep.'

The pair settled back into bed. This time, Eddie noticed, Bert did not bother to try and comfort him. He just got into bed and rolled over. Well, he couldn't blame him for that, Eddie had hardly been friendly.

He wondered what he had been screaming about. Normally he could remember his nightmares, but not this time. He did not even remember going to sleep.

His foot was hurting again, but it seemed a little easier. The rest must be helping, he decided, and the pills must be helping him rest.

This time he did not hesitate. He reached out and found the bottle in the darkness, ignoring Freddie's grumble when he knocked it over. He took the top off and tipped two pills into his hand, then swallowed them without water.

DAY 5

APRIL 6, 1917

'The swelling looks to have gone down, are you sure that this doesn't hurt too much?'

The doctor pressed his finger against the top of Eddie's foot. Even after the morphine he had been taking every hour since breakfast it felt like razor blades being forced into his skin.

'No, it's fine,' he said, trying his best to control the look on his face.

'Yes, of course it is,' The doctor shook his head. 'You're a stubborn bugger, aren't you Grenville?'

'Sir?'

'Don't try and look innocent. It hurts like the devil, doesn't it?'

Eddie stayed silent.

'Well, I suppose I can't stop you being a bloody idiot. This whole war is full of bloody idiots from top to bottom, what's one more?' The doctor turned to his desk and reached for his pen. 'I'll sign you off as fit. Make sure you take a stick with you, you're going to need it.'

'Thank you, sir,' said Eddie. He pulled his sock on, then gingerly eased the shoe back on. 'I don't suppose -' he began.

'No,' said the doctor.

'I haven't asked yet, sir.'

'You were going to ask for some more Morphine tablets. Well, the answer is no, at least not from me. You'll need a clear head where you're going, not doped up to the eyeballs. Anyway, perhaps a bit of pain will remind you what a bloody idiot you're being. Dismissed.'

'Sir.'

Eddie limped his way out of the room.

*

Two hours later, Eddie found himself back in the cockpit of another new RE8, the engine ticking over as it warmed up. His foot was throbbing in his flying boot. He experimented with the rudder bar; it was bearable as long as he pushed gently.

Just about bearable anyway.

The ground crew were looking at him expectantly. Well, hard lines. He was not going to be rushed. He checked the map, marked with waypoints, railway lines, roads, canals, large churches, anything that would help him work out where he was. He had never done this trip alone before, the only previous time he had Milne to navigate and he had not paid attention. He wanted to be damned sure that he could at least find his way back.

He put the map board back on its clip on the dashboard and checked the instruments again. Everything looked fine.

He should go.

He knew he should.

Yet he did not raise his hands to signal that he was ready. As much as he willed himself to do it he just could not make them move. This was stupid, he did not have to go back, he had a decent enough excuse.

But it was just that, an excuse, wasn't it? A bit of a sore foot, just an accident, not even caused under fire. Coward. He might not be called that by anyone else, but he would know that he really was one, a stinking, snivelling coward, hiding behind his injury, letting others do the job whilst he put his feet up.

So go then. Tell the chief mechanic that you were ready.

Still he couldn't.

He could see them looking at one another, see them doubt him, give each other knowing looks. One of the fitters turned to his mate, said something. They both laughed.

Sod that. He would not be made fun of. He was a war pilot. He was going.

Eddie found that his arms and hands worked. He waved the

crew away. Opening the throttle, began to taxi.

He tried not to look at the burnt patch of grass where the pilot had been immolated and euthanized 36 hours or so before.

He turned into the stiff breeze and opened the throttle to begin his take-off. The RAF engine roared, the lightly laden machine sprang into the air.

Immediately the aircraft abruptly swung sharply to the right under the torque of the big prop. Eddie instinctively pushed hard on the opposite side of rudder bar, the left side, the side with his bad foot. He felt the bones grate, a flash of agonising pain shot up his leg.

It was so intense that he pulled his foot up off the bar, the aircraft, which had just left the ground, swung even more sharply towards the right, towards the last of the hangars and the park of elderly aircraft. It took all his willpower and strength to level the wings, to give it a boot of left rudder, to ignore the pain. Even then he was sure that a crash was inevitable, indeed if the machine had lower wings of equal length with its upper ones the tips must surely have brushed the grass. As it was, he found himself hurtling towards a pair of BE2s at the edge of the park. Heart pounding, well aware that he might stall, Eddie lifted the nose and pushed the throttle forward, even though it was already against the stops. The RE8 barely scraped over the parked aircraft.

Shaken, Eddie started to climb.

*

He arrived at Acq around an hour later, still sweating. The flight should perhaps have only taken 30-40 minutes but Eddie, conscious that he had no observer and that the Vickers gun was unloaded had kept well back from the front. As a result he had twice got lost and had to descend to see if he could spot landmarks that might help him. At one point he was convinced that he would have to land, particularly when the clouds closed in forcing him yet lower. At the last minute he spotted the steam of a train in the distance and turned to follow it. Soon he realised it was the line running in the direction of Arras and he was able to leave the labouring locomotive behind and follow the iron compass beneath towards the city. As soon as the wrecked cathedral was in sight, finding the village and the airfield was relatively simple.

As he taxied up to the hangars and switched off, he saw that another RE8 was being wheeled out for a mission, the pilot and observer muffled up and ready to go. As the mechanics wheel him into the hangar, the pilot looked over at him and waved. It was Milne. Eddie retrieved his stick, gingerly climbed out and went across to the pair.

'Grenville, good to see you,' Milne said. ' I thought you'd be laid up for a month. Are you alright?'

'It's just a bit of pain, I can handle it.'

Milne frowned but then patted Eddie on the shoulder. 'Good man, we do need every pilot we can get. It's been pretty bloody the last couple of days. We lost one crew yesterday and two more haven't come back this morning.'

Eddie could see the strain on Milne's face. He looked to have aged 10 years since Eddie had last seen him just a couple of days before.

'I had better be off,' Milne said. 'Another Art Obs over Vimy. Report to your flight leader, he's in the office.'

'Sir.'

Milne gave a terse nod to Eddie then headed for his machine where his observer was already in the cockpit. Eddie watched Milne start the engine, then headed for the office to report in.

*

'Well look what the cat's dragged in.'

Hastings was leant on his desk talking to another pilot and Kerr when Eddie got to his office. Eddie recognised the pilot as Finch, of C flight. Hastings stared at Eddie in disdain.

'I'm here to report for duty, sir.'

Hastings looked surprised. 'Really? What duty do you think you can do? Other than to destroy more of my machines?'

Eddie stared in shock at Hastings. What had brought this on?

'Are you a Hun, Grenville? Should we start calling you The Baron?'

Eddie had to control his anger, though he was fit to explode. Still he managed to say; 'No sir.'

For a few seconds Hastings stared at him, then Eddie saw

him back down, seemingly accepting that Eddie was not going to rise to the bait.

'It's your bloody types that's caused the mess. The old machine with the small fin was fine but apparently you blokes find it too hard. Fantastic, now we experienced types have to put up with the damned mongrel.'

Eddie was puzzled by this. What was he talking about? Before he could work it out, Hastings continued. 'Right, let's see if we can find something you can actually do. I might have the very thing. Alasdair, this could help you out.'

'How, Clive?' said Finch. 'What did you have in mind?'

'Here's your readymade ferry pilot. Whilst we are up doing the big boys work, young Richthofen here can take your old BEs to the depot and pick up your new grids. What do you say?'

'That could work,' said Finch, nodding.

'But sir, I want -'

'I don't care what you want, Grenville. Just be thankful I'm not sending you back to England for retraining. Right some of us have some war flying to do. Grenville, take your orders from Lieutenant Finch here. He's now acting C flight leader. Alasdair, he's all yours. You're welcome to him. Come on, we'll go and see Pops, sort out the paperwork.'

Hastings picked up his coat, goggles and helmet and pushed past. Finch, with a glance at Eddie, followed leaving him alone in the office with Kerr.

'That was damned out of order,' said Kerr. 'You alright Eddie.'

Eddie nodded.

'Don't know how you kept your cool. I'd have been tempted to thump him and take the consequences afterwards.'

Eddie shrugged. 'What good would that have done? I'd have just been in a worse state. What's wrong with him anyway? And what was that stuff about "our types causing the mess" and the fin?'

Kerr gave a sigh. 'I think he's finding that the Harry Tates are not going to be the ticket out of here that he thought they might be.'

'What do you mean?'

'Well you know that he's after his ace status?' Eddie nodded. 'Well the original RE8 was quite a lot less stable. Lots of chaps over here and at home were spinning them and not being able to get them back before the lights went out. They stuck a bigger fin on it. Phil Armstrong flew the original, says the new one with the big fin is a lot more sluggish. I think old Albert has found that the new machine isn't much better than the old Quirk and that he's going to be with us for the duration.'

'So in the meantime he's taking it out on me,' said Eddie.

'Oh it's not just you, old boy, he's being pretty beastly with the rest of us too. I say have you eaten? You must be famished. Let's get you to the mess before he sends you back out on his errands.'

*

Eddie looked disconsolately across to the other side of the hangar as he pulled on his coat and put on his scarf. Over on that side Hastings was briefing the other members of B flight. His flight. Their machines, the new, still fresh looking RE8s were lined up waiting for the off, fully fuelled and armed and ready to go to war.

He turned to his own mounts. There were three of them, one a BE2e, the other the even older 2cs, tired, decrepit, unloved. This was his job for the day given to him by Finch, taking these old machines back to St. Omer and bringing the new ones for C flight back.

It *was* a useful job. He was doing his bit for the war effort. C flight would be thankful for the new machines. It was safe, well as safe as you could be flying these old museum pieces. He did not have to face the terrors of flying over the front.

It was also demeaning.

He pulled on his flying helmet with little enthusiasm, feeling a dunce's cap might be more appropriate. How long would he have to do this? Would Hastings relent, give him a chance to prove himself? Or would he ask for Eddie to be transferred back to HE, washed out as a failure?

It was all out of his hands, all out of his control. He had been given a job, he resolved to do it in the hope that things would change. Perhaps Milne would take pity on him, take him into A flight? Kerr had told Eddie that Hastings had been pushing to have him and Armstrong transferred permanently across, something that both the pair and Milne were resisting.

No, thought Eddie, that would be running away too. He was in B flight, under Hastings. That was where he would stay and prove himself.

As he climbed into the machine, his flight was already taxiing out onto the field, leaving him behind.

His bad foot throbbing like the devil, Eddie signalled to the mechanics to push the BE out of the hangar.

*

It was on his third flight into St Omer that the problems started.

The third Quirk was by far the worst. It was not one of his original three, it had been changed whilst he was bringing the second RE8 back to Acq. He had heard one of the mechanics say to another that he did not understand why they were bothering to send it home, it would be better off as firewood, and he could see what they mean. All these machines were old, tired and patched but this one was like an ancient, arthritic Labrador, slow, creaky and most definitely on its last legs. The whole frame of the aircraft looked warped, like it hadn't been built of properly seasoned wood and had been left out in the rain.

It did occur to Eddie to refuse to fly it but then he saw Hastings, who had returned from his patrol and was in conversation with Finch again, keep glancing over at him. There was something about him, about the way he was looking, that suggested that he thought this was all a joke. Perhaps it was, perhaps getting Eddie to fly this particular aircraft was something that he had contrived with Finch. Certainly the two were watching Eddie, and both had expectant smiles on their faces.

For a moment Eddie was angry. But then why was he surprised? Wasn't this type of childishness typical of Hastings? Sod them, joke or test, he would show them.

When he had been strapped into it, the rigger who had passed him his goggles had given him a particularly sympathetic look.

'Good luck, sir,' he muttered to Eddie. He wouldn't have been surprised if the words: 'You're going to need it' were added but the look on the man's face was just as eloquent.

As soon as he got it into the air he understood. The engine was down on power, would not give full revs and kept coughing alarmingly. The machine itself would barely climb and showed a marked reluctance to fly straight and level. He had to hold the stick to the right and push down on the right-hand rudder bar to persuade it to fly even approximately in the right direction, though exactly what that was he wasn't certain because the compass was u/s too. He was at first thankful that he did not have to use his injured foot but soon found that even the process of bracing himself against the opposite pressure made it hurt again.

After just two minutes of this he found himself disliking Hastings. After five the feeling had morphed into downright hatred. This had to be a joke, it just had to be. He had been set up. God only knew how this was supposed to be funny. Eddie could only wonder what on earth this Quirk had gone through to get like this.

He considered turning around but was not going to give Hastings the satisfaction of seeing him fail, whatever the reason. Then he thought about putting it down somewhere, anywhere, and just leaving it but then he would have to face getting back to either Acq of St. Omer, as well as trying to negotiate this barely flyable antique into somewhere not prepared for aircraft. In the end he just stuck with it and navigated using half-remembered landmarks to get to the depot.

He had just sighted St Omer when the misfire got worse. The revs and the power started to drop alarmingly, as did the aircraft. He had not been able to get it to more than 1500 feet, so he had very little height to play with. Within 30 seconds he knew he was not going to make the field and started to look for somewhere to put down.

Spotting what looked like a suitable field, Eddie side slipped towards it, almost stalling as he did. The Quirk, as it slowed, became even more left wing heavy and seemed determined to end it all with one last dramatic gesture, and take him with it. Fighting it all the way and trailing a stream of black smoke, Eddie swept over a hedge and somehow made a near perfect landing, bumping to a halt almost in the centre of the field.

He did not wait, he made a careful dismount, cautious not to jar his broken foot.

He stood shaking by the Quirk, vowing never to get into a machine that he had any doubts about ever again. Typical; this machine had survived whilst the brand new RE8 he had crashed two days before had been a total right off. Pity the poor bastard who had to fly this thing back over the channel. And pity the poor recruits who might have to learn on. Boys like Bunny.

Bunny. The poor sod. He would never even have got to France if he had had to fly something like this. Something should be done about it.

There were already men coming into the field and heading

in his direction. He glanced at the aircraft. He did not want it repaired, he certainly did not want to fly it again, even the short hop to St. Omer. There was only him there to do anything about it.

He limped to the far side of the machine and felt for his lighter.

By the time the rescuers reached him the Quirk was well alight.

*

'There must have been a leak in the tank, I tried to save it but it just went up.'

The officer said nothing, he gave Eddie an impassive stare. It was so intense that Eddie was sure that the man was trying to get him to crack, to own up, admit that he was lying. At school he had been renowned at being pretty awful at it, the teachers could always tell when he was fibbing and, if there had been any rumpus involving a group of boys, they always picked out Eddie for interrogation. This tended to both keep him on the straight and narrow and found him excluded from many joint enterprise japes. So why had he done it now, and in such a huge way?

For the greater good, he told himself, for the greater good. If they were going to court-martial him, so be it.

The officer continued to stare him out. Eddie was on the point of giving up and confessing when the officer, sighed, reached for his pen and signed the form that was on the desk between them.

'Very well, Lieutenant,' he said. 'We will consider the matter closed.'

Eddie released his own sigh, though his was from relief not exasperation.

'May I go, sir?' he said.

'One moment, Grenville,' said the officer, reaching into his in-tray. 'We received this telegram from your Squadron adjutant this afternoon. You'd better read it.'

Eddie took the paper.

Urgent attn station cmdr St.Omer.STOP. 2nd Lt.Grenville due you 1600 hours. STOP. Accidentally detailed aircraft declared unflyable. STOP. Imperative repeat imperative that machine is struck off charge on arrival and not transferred HE. STOP. Please report if Grenville arrives. STOP. If no show please advise and initiate search. ENDS

It was signed by Pops.

Eddie look up into the eyes of the officer.

'Looks like you had a lucky, escape, lad,' he said, 'Next time though, if you get given a crock to fly, let us take the decision to put it out of its misery, agreed?'

'Agreed, sir.'

The officer smiled. 'On your way, Grenville. We'll find you a bed for the night.'

Eddie looked at him in surprise. 'I thought I could - '

'It's getting late, Grenville and you've done, what, four flights today. I think that leg of yours needs at least another night's rest. No arguments now, off you go.'

'Yes sir.'

Miserable, Eddie limped away to find somewhere to sleep.

*

Hours later, he was laid in another strange bed, under another strange blanket, in yet another hut. Would he ever spend another night in Acq, with his squadron? He seemed doomed to wander France and stay anywhere other than with his squadron mates. No wonder they were so hard on him, no wonder that he was the butt of practical jokes; he was never there, they did not know him.

Was war always like this? You were surrounded by millions of people in the self-same state as yourself, thrown together yet you ended up alone.

I suppose, Eddie thought, that we all die alone. We might be with people, someone might be holding your hand or mopping your brow but, fundamentally, everyone goes through it as an individual.

He shivered. He wasn't ready to die, not just yet.

He also did not want to be alone.

DAY 6

APRIL 7, 1917

'I can't bloody well conjure a machine out of thin air for you, Lieutenant.'

'But I need to get back to my squadron, sir.'

'Don't get shirty with me, remember I outrank you.'

The admin officer was indeed a full-lieutenant, only one rank above Eddie's, but one rank, nevertheless. He was also paunchy, pernickety and fastidious, his piles of paper, pencils and forms all neatly lined up. Eddie suspected he was some lowly clerk back home in England, probably never had had so much power at his fingertips and thoroughly enjoyed exercising it. He had seen both his mother and his father put down such people at home, they made such types squirm as they reminded them of their status in life.

Then Eddie remembered how much he hated them for doing it, how embarrassed he felt when they did. He also recalled the looks of pure hatred the poor tradesmen had flashed at his parents when they thought they were not looking. Those times were changing, the days when his parents could act like that were coming to an end. Whatever, he felt guilty for the thoughts he had had about the clerk and decided to meet officiousness with civility.

'I know, sir, and I would like to apologise. I know you have a job to do - '

'I do, and a damned hard one it is too,' interrupted the clerk.

'I do realise that, sir, it must be really difficult with everyone wanting things from you yesterday.'

The clerk frowned. Eddie knew that he was searching his face for signs of dishonesty. For the second time in as many days, Eddie found himself practicing duplicity. He suspected he was at last cracking it.

'That's good of you to say it, Lieutenant,' said the clerk at last. 'Most of you pilots have no manners at all. Every squadrons needs new aircraft it has to be done properly. I can't just issue them willy-nilly. They have to get in line and wait their turn.'

He was talking like each one of the machines were his own property, Eddie thought.

'I appreciate that,' said Eddie, easing the weight on his bad foot. He could not help but wince.

The clerk looked down at Eddie's foot. 'You did that fighting the Huns?' he said. 'Have you come up against the Baron?'

'I don't like to talk about it,' Eddie said, quite truthfully.

The clerk's eyes widened in admiration. 'Good heavens, I'd love to hear about it. Must have been bloody scary.'

Eddie just looked down.

'Sorry, thoughtless of me, it must be difficult to talk about. Still I wish I could have a crack too but...' he waved his hand vaguely in the direction of his flabby frame. I wish you could too, thought Eddie but said nothing because there was now a glimmer of hope. 'Look, I shouldn't do this but...' The clerk glanced to either side of him as if expecting people to be interested.

'Yes?' Eddie urged him. 'Don't worry, this will go no further.'

The clerk nodded.

'Right, good.'

'So what is it?' Eddie was struggling to hide his impatience.

'We have one of the machines from 59 squadron in for repairs. It should be finished.'

'So?'

'So it would be fairly easy to misread the paperwork.'

'What do you mean?'

'To put a one in front of the squadron number, a very easy mistake to make in the heat of things. It shouldn't but it does happen all the time.'

He winked at Eddie.

Eddie grinned back. I'd love to show you somewhere really hot, he thought, but said: 'Thanks awfully, sir. I really appreciate it.'

The clerk smiled back. 'Anything for our brave boys, Lieutenant. I will send someone down to the mess to find you when it's ready.'

Feeling slightly grubby, Eddie limped out of the office to wait.

*

In fact, flying that morning was ruled out.

The machine was still not finished, some problem with a magneto had taken longer than expected to trace but it was the weather before lunch that was the problem with low cloud, heavy rain and a squally breeze.

Eddie feared that he would have to stay yet another day, but the fitters got to the bottom of the problem by eleven and one of the old hands in the mess, a delivery pilot, had squinted at the clouds and had pronounced that it would clear up after lunch.

He had given up trying to get find some enthusiasm for day-old copies of the London newspapers and was struggling with a letter to Annie when he noticed that the other members of the officers lounge in the Mess had, to a man, stopped what they were doing and had either gone to a window or actually ventured outside. As the weather was still bitter with snow flurries in the air, this suggested that something out of the ordinary was in the offing.

Eddie left his letter and joined the group stood by the largest window.

'What is it? What's happening,' he asked a dark-haired young man who bore the single wing on the chest of his tunic that marked him out as an observer.

'Bit of a flap, apparently there's a new squadron coming in.'

'A new squadron? What's so special about that?'

'This one is different, or so they say. New aircraft and some really hot pilots,' said the young man. 'I say, we haven't been introduced. I'm Morris, just over from England. Are you the same? Waiting for your posting?' He offered Eddie his hand, who took it.

'Grenville. No, I'm with 159 Squadron. Just waiting to pick up a new machine.'

Morris gave a little whoop of delight. 'Oh the very chap I was looking for. I've been posted to your outfit. They said you were heading back and that I might be able to cadge a lift. What a stroke of luck!'

'It certainly is, and yes, I should be heading back this afternoon. What -'

'Here they come,' interrupted Morris. 'Look.'

Eddie looked to where Morris was pointing. He realised that most of the aircraft had already landed and were taxiing towards the hangars. They were a scout, snub-nosed and rather angular biplanes. All but one had a large celluloid windscreen which gave cover to the pilots, who seemed to sit quite high in the machines. Eddie could see that they had a Lewis gun on a curved mount above the top wing with the barrel of a Vickers machine gun protruding from a streamlined mounting on the cowling above the engine.

'They're the new SE5s,' said Morris, 'And this apparently is 56 squadron, our answer to Richthofen and his mob. I say, they do look rather splendid don't they?'

Eddie had to admit to being impressed. For once, these aircraft looked like they were thoroughbreds, purposeful, solid and dangerous. And yet, although he was happy to see them, he could not help but feel jealous. How come the Royal Aircraft Factory could produce something like this for the scout pilots whilst foisting a creation like the RE8 on him and his ilk?

'They look pretty good,' he said, deciding that he would feel better finishing his letter off rather than getting into a black mood about an aircraft he had yet to go to war in. He turned away from the window, only to hear Morris murmur:

'I wonder which one is Ball?'

'Ball?' said Eddie, turning back to the window. 'What THE Ball?'

'The very same. Oh look there he is, that must be him, isn't it?' Morris pointed excitedly.

Eddie could see that Morris was right, stood a little way away from the rest of the pilots was a man whose face was very familiar to Eddie, given the number of newspaper clippings that he'd collected charting Ball's exploits.

Despite this, Eddie found himself doubting that this was his hero. He expected someone taller, someone with a more imposing manner that all the other pilots would, quite literally, look up to, would defer to and whose lead they would follow. Instead, although distinctly handsome, he was small and slight and there was an air of diffident aloofness about him. His very position in the group that was now listening to the squadron leader was telling: in the group but not fully part of it. The pilots looked eager and determined. Ball looked neither.

The group broke up and headed towards the Mess. Ball trailed along behind them.

'Come on,' said Morris. 'Let's go and say hello.'

Eddie and Morris found themselves behind a scrum of pilots. The newcomers came into the Mess like a victorious first XV, fresh from the rugger field, Eddie was familiar with this sort of entrance from his schooldays. There was another similarity, the way that the majority of the pilots - the players - were greeted with a polite level of enthusiasm whilst it remained obvious that the crowd were reserving their warmest welcome for the real star of the match. With rugby it would be the scrum-half, here they were quite clearly waiting for Ball.

The object of their affections, pockets bulging with pyjamas on one side and towel, presumably holding a wash kit, on the other, ignored them all and went and sat at the end of the table that had been set for lunch. Close to, he looked more than sulky: he looked angry.

The squadron leader, who had been talking to the Mess orderly, turned to find his seat had been taken. For a moment Eddie thought he was going to have a word with the Ace, ask him to move, but, instead, he quietly took a seat next to Ball.

'Now then, gentlemen,' said the orderly, coming over to the spectating pilots. 'Let's leave these good sirs to their lunch. They've had a long flight over here. We don't want to bother them, do we sirs?'

Reluctantly, the pilots and observers slowly returned to what they were doing in the lounge, though a few ventured out into the cold towards where the fitters were working on the newly arrived aircraft.

'Shall we go and have a look?' said Morris.

'Alright,' said Eddie, though really he wanted to stay and hopefully get a chance to talk to his hero. This looked unlikely, Ball did not seem to be in any sort of mood to talk to anyone. 'I wonder what's wrong with him?' Eddie asked on the way over to the hangars.

'It must be quite wearing on a chap, everyone wanting to talk with you, wanting your opinion on everything. He probably never gets a moment's peace.'

'I suppose so,' said Eddie, glancing back at the mess. 'I hadn't thought of it like that. But is it really that bad?'

'Well it must be bad enough to want him to come back here.'

'Oh but Ball would want to do that. He's that sort of chap, isn't he? Wants to keep doing his bit for the war effort.'

'Maybe so, but he didn't look too happy to be back, did he?

Gosh, this is a fine looking machine isn't it?'

They had arrived at the hangars, the 56 squadron machines having been wheeled inside, so Eddie had no opportunity to answer. The fitters were busy refuelling the aircraft and topping up the oil and water, riggers were checking the flying and landing wires for tension. Meanwhile the spectators were milling around like small boys around a racing car or locomotive, stepping up to peer in the cockpit, touching fabric and struts and generally getting in the way of the ground staff.

Close to, Eddie's feelings of jealousy returned. He glanced over to where 'his' RE8 was parked. It looked anachronistic, angular, slow, ugly. It was hard to believe that it, too, was a relatively new design. It was also neglected, the mechanics that had been working on it had abandoned it when the new scouts had arrived. Eddie could understand it, the RE8 was the plain girl who had arrived early at the dance. Once its more glamorous sisters had turned up it could not get a look in.

Eddie turned away from the SE5s.

'What's up old chap?' said Morris, looking puzzled. 'Don't you want to take a closer look?'

'No,' said Eddie. 'I'm going to see if our machine is ready. I want to get off whilst the weather isn't too bad.'

He strode away from Morris without a backward glance.

He had lied to him, there was no-one near his machine to ask anyway. The truth was he did not want to feel like a second-class citizen anymore. Damn it all, didn't his life, the life of all his friends and colleagues matter that much to the War Office? Wasn't the job that he did important, no not important, vital? Why then did they get fobbed off with this mishmash of an aircraft whilst the fighter types got all the fame and glory - and the decent aircraft that they bothered to spend some time designing properly?

His aircraft looked to be finished, the cowling back on it. He looked around; a fitter came out of the stores, wiping his hands on a rag.

'I say,' said Eddie. 'Is this machine ready?'

The fitter hardly glanced at him. 'How would I know, mate? It's not one of mine.' He shrugged.

'Well bloody well go and find out!' Eddie said, his temper boiling over. 'And look sharp about it, I haven't got all day!'

Eddie was not sure which he was more surprised at; the fact that he had shouted or that the man had reacted like a kicked dog, instantly subservient, apologising, dropping his rag and hurrying off to find someone to ask.

He felt sick. He had sounded just like his father, arrogant and overbearing, all of the things he hated about him. He had had no call to be like that with the fitter, why had he done it? Eddie decided he should go and find him and apologise. The fitter had gone through a door at the back of the hangar, Eddie followed.

There was no one in sight, but Eddie could hear voices from around the side, between the two adjacent hangar buildings. Presuming it was the fitter and his chief, Eddie went in that direction. When he turned the corner, he realised he was wrong, and the mention of a name stopped him in his tracks.

'What up, Ball? You're a flight commander. You're meant to set an example to your men.'

'I hate that machine. I can't fight in it.'

'Ball, it's brand new. You have to give it a chance.'

'No. It's an utter dud. I want a Nieuport. If I don't get one, I can't do my job.'

Eddie could see the CO bristle and heard him sigh in exasperation.

'A Nieuport? How's that going to work? The SE is a much faster machine. We can't run mixed patrols like that.'

'The Nieuport is much faster and I won't fly with anyone else.'

'That won't work. Things have changed since you were last over. You won't last five minutes.'

'I don't care. I want a Nieuport. I'll go and see Trenchard. He'll give me one.'

The CO looked like he was going to explode, but then saw Eddie.

'This isn't the place to have this out,' he said. 'We'll discuss it when we get to Vert Galland.' He turned and walked away.

Ball stayed where he was, just staring at the ground. Eddie also had not moved. He wondered if he should say something, go up to him, introduce himself, or just walk quietly away, back from where he had come, avoid giving any embarrassment. He was still trying to decide when Ball seemed to notice Eddie for the first time.

'Oh hello,' he said, giving Eddie a surprisingly shy smile. 'Sorry you had to see that.'

Eddie could not find his voice to reply.

They stared at each other for a few moments then the ace gave Eddie another shy little half smile. 'I have to go,' he said then turned and walked away

Eddie was stunned. In those few moments he had seen so

much; someone who looked trapped and haunted, yet exhilarated and excited at the same time. What shocked him most was that Eddie had seen someone look like that before. One of his brother's friends had badly broken his arm playing rugby a year or so before the war. The pain was so intense, he had been given opium by his doctor and had become hooked on it.

Ball looked exactly like he had.

He looked like an addict.

*

By the time the RE8 was wheeled out of the hangar, 56 Squadron had long since departed. Eddie and Morris walked out to the machine together, Eddie found that his foot, which had settled down overnight, had chosen now to start hurting again. He had taken a couple of the doctor's pills after lunch and was praying that they would start to work soon.

Before starting up, the crew chief leaned into the cockpit.

'Watch out, the Vickers is loaded,' he said, pointing at the front gun. 'The chaps who brought it here had just done a patrol.'

Eddie nodded, then checked with Morris, safely sat in the rear seat who gave him a thumbs up, before giving the signal to the fitter to swing the prop.

Although his foot was still throbbing, Eddie was now ready for the swing on take-off and, as a result, their departure was a lot less dramatic. He settled the machine on course for Acq. The wind seemed quite strong and the cloud cover, although less than it had been in the morning, obscured much of the ground.

He found concentration difficult, his thoughts drifting to Ball. He was not at all what he expected, but then, what had that been? In Eddie's imagination, Ball had been dashing, confident, assured. The person he had just seen was shy, awkward and difficult. He did not strike Eddie as much of a leader, not like Milne, for example. Yes Milne was just what you wanted in someone to guide you. He was patient, careful, considerate. In fact he was a lot like Percy.

Percy? Why had he thought of him? Damn him, no he was not going to think of his brother in the same way as he thought of Ball and Milne, whatever that damn rag of a paper made of him. He was no hero, what had been written was all lies.

But then what did he know about Ball? What he had read,

what he had been told. Was what he had seen, the insight into the real person he had been given, was that really like what the papers had written about Ball? Well yes, it had to be, didn't it, there was what Ball had done, the exploits that had so stirred Eddie and driven him to become a flyer.

*

It was warm. Warm and so relaxing. Eddie could not work out where he was.

Ah yes, he was sat with Percy, the sun on his face. They were on a river bank. Where? Oh yes, it was the Arun, on one of those long summer days when the birds sing so sweetly, insects buzz lazily and the air is heady with the perfume of meadow flowers. Percy is reading, clearly only half listening to him. What was he talking about, he had forgotten? Oh yes, it was about engines, how he felt that he, Eddie, could build a better one than was in Father's car.

A little further on are Siggi and Alice, sat close together. Siggi used to be so much fun but then Alice got in the way. What on earth did chaps bother with girls for anyway? Eddie could not imagine, surely fishing and boating is so much more interesting than being sat there making small talk?

This is good: Siggi is not dead, he is talking to Percy again, and Alice looks happy.

But... none of that was right. This has to be a dream. But it can't be a dream because he's flying. Was flying? Is that he was flying the dream?

There is a sudden bang.

*

Eddie was awake.

He was cold, freezing in fact.

To his shock he found he was indeed flying. He could not have been asleep, could he? Where was he? Was he back flying from Acq?

There was another bang, the RE8 was thrown bodily to the

right. Eddie caught the machine before it tipped over. Urgently he looked around him, everywhere were black puffs of smoke. Hellfire, German Archie. They were over the lines! How the hell had that happened?

He turned around to look at Morris. He was looking over the cockpit sides, down at the trenches beneath them. Why the hell hadn't he said anything?

Eddie swiftly banked the RE8 and headed it west, his heart thumping. How on earth had he got himself into this mess? The pills, it had to be. The pills and four nights with next to no sleep. How stupid was he? How stupid was Morris not to notice?

But then, would he notice? How was a new chap to know what was normal? Perhaps he thought Eddie was showing him the lines? But why would he do that without his observer having a gun? That would just be suicidal.

How far over were they? How long had he been asleep? He looked down and saw, with some, relief the British front-line pass beneath them. Thank God, they were safe.

Ratatatatata

The sound of the machine gun gave him a second start. Where was it? Was it an Albatros? Eddie swung his head around. To his horror he saw a pair of black shapes behind him, framed against the grey of the clouds. God, oh God, they were going to be shot to pieces. All because of his stupidity.

Panicking he kicked the rudder bar and banked the aircraft over, anything to get away.

For a moment he thought he was going to collide with one of their attackers. He had a brief vision of a startled looking pair of Germans, pilot and observer, the latter clinging on to his Parabellum, as they flashed by the banking RE8 not more than twenty feet away.

Two seaters, they were two seaters, reconnaissance machines like his, probably doing the same job, taking photographs over the lines. And they had attacked him, although whether this was from pure aggression or because they saw he was dozing, he could not be sure. Thank God they were not Richthofen, or any scouts in fact, he and Morris would have been dead meat if it had been.

Where were they? He had lost sight of them in the clouds. Good, well perhaps they had lost him too, maybe he could get away still.

Eddie looked at his compass. It was useless, still spinning around after his manoeuvre. With one eye on the sky for the two-seaters, he scanned the ground for something to tell him which way he was flying. Which was the wind blowing when they left? Oh yes, it was from the north-west. Now he needed some smoke. He couldn't see anything. The sun then, he would use the sun to give him a rough bearing. He looked up.

His heart skipped, then thumped painfully. There was another machine just above them. It had to be one of the Hun two-seaters, coming back to shoot them down.

But no, he realised. He was beneath it, they couldn't see him. Not yet anyway but they soon would, it would only take a dip of the wing, and they had to be looking for him.

He should bank away, put the nose down, get away whilst he had the chance.

Something stopped him.

With cold precision and a sudden clarity of purpose he reached across and cocked the Vickers gun. He let the nose come up, squinted through the sights, though he did not really need them he was so close.

He felt like it was someone else, not him, that pulled the trigger, he was so detached from the real Eddie at that moment.

The banging of the cartridges exploding in the breach of the gun seemed so loud, the pace of fire seemed so slow. It was almost magical the way the holes appeared in the underside of the aircraft above him, so small, so many.

The crew would be sitting just above there, he thought, men like you. You are killing them, the lead will be tearing them apart.

But he did not stop.

It was only because his aircraft, slowed by the nose being lifted and by the recoil of the gun, stalling and falling away, could no longer keep his gun to bear on the two-seater that Eddie took his finger off the trigger. He put the nose down to recover flying speed he saw, out of the corner of his eye, the cloud next to him illuminated in red and yellow by flame.

He no longer felt any pain from his foot but had started to shake again. He did his now normal trick of resting his left hand on his right to stop the aircraft from oscillating.

He felt a thump on his back and turned to find Morris waving his arms in triumph and giving him a thumbs up sign. Morris then stood and leaned back over the cockpit, clearly looking for signs of the German machine.

Eddie did not want to look. He quartered the sky, looking for the other two-seater who he was sure would want to exact revenge for the loss of his comrade but there was no sign of him. Satisfied, he searched the ground for a landmark, something that he could recognise that would give him a course back to Acq. It took a few minutes to spot a church he thought he recognised, then a minute more to locate the railway line which he followed back towards Arras, by which time his foot was throbbing again.

There was enough time for the doubts to start. Was that really one of the German aircraft? He had not looked, he had not checked. The wings were squared off, where they shorted on the bottom than the top? If they were then it was another RE8 or maybe a Quirk. Oh hell, had he killed one of his own? Now, in his mind's eye, he could see the roundels underneath the lower wings.

No, he had to be imagining them, surely he would have registered them before he pulled the trigger.

Twenty minutes later, with Eddie still full of doubt, they were on the ground back at base.

*

'I don't understand, Grenville,' Major Reeves eyes were boring into him. 'This was supposed to be a ferry flight. What on earth were you doing over the lines?'

'I don't think I was over the lines, sir,' Eddie said, standing to attention and focusing his eyes on the far wall rather than on the commanding officer.

'The artillery unit report quite clearly say you crossed over from occupied territory. Are you saying they were mistaken?'

Eddie did not fall into the trap of hesitation. If he admitted it, if he told the truth, that he had fallen asleep in the cockpit because of taking the pills and from lack of sleep he was sure to be grounded and sent home in disgrace. He had to be brazen, he had to lie. 'Yes sir, they must be.'

Reeves did not look like he believed him. 'Well, even if they were, what on earth were you doing so close to the lines anyway? Risking a new machine, one we desperately need, when you knew full well that your observer was unarmed?'

'I was wanting to show him the lie of the land. I got a bit closer to the lines than I intended, sir.'

Eddie knew this sounded awfully weak.

The was a knock at the door.

'What is it?' Reeves looked up angrily. 'Pops, can't you see I'm busy?'

'This just came in sir, from Boom's office.' Pops handed over a telegram to Reeves, who took and read it. He pulled a face, then, scowling, handed it to Eddie.

It said,

Congratulations second lt grenville stop trenchard delighted with his success and aggressive approach stop keep it up stop

Signed Baring

'Seems you've cheered the General up,' said Reeves. He shook his head. 'I suppose you should be congratulated, Grenville.'

'Thank you, sir.'

Reeves continued to stare at him, Eddie felt himself almost whiting under his gaze. It was a relief when the Major finally turned back to his paperwork.

'Off you go, Grenville,' he said.

'Sir.'

Eddie sighed and turned to leave.

'You were lucky, boy,' Reeves said. 'Very lucky. You know it and I know it. Risk your own life if you must but don't risk my observers or my aircraft.'

'Sir.'

Eddie left with Pops.

'He's quite right, you know,' murmured Pops, when they were out in the corridor. 'It was a very silly thing to do.'

'I didn't mean to do it,' Eddie said, without thinking.

'You didn't mean to cross the lines?' Pops said, frowning. 'What do you mean by that? Visibility wasn't that bad, was it?'

'No,' said Eddie. 'Look, I've learned my lesson, can I go now?'

'Yes but Captain Hastings wants to see you in hangar one right away.'

'Really? Do I have to?'

'The captain was most insistent about it.'

'Right,' Eddie said, trying to mask his lack of enthusiasm. 'Thanks, Pops.'

What now, he thought as he trudged from the admin block to the hangar. Haven't I been the butt of enough jokes?

At the hangar the canvas doors had been pulled closed across the front, which was unusual. He was just about to look for a way in when, very theatrically, the flaps were pulled back by some of the mechanics. He was greeted by an almighty cheer and a round of applause. From what he could see the entire squadron was assembled inside. Behind them was the RE8 that he had flown in earlier that afternoon. It was bedecked in ribbons, and, by the cockpit, the words 'Hun Hunter' written in white.

'Hail, the mighty Hun killer,' said Hastings, stepping out from the crowd. He had a bottle of champagne which he expertly opened. 'Come on, someone, look lively, get some mugs organised, we need to toast the conquering hero.'

Dazed, Eddie found a mug full of warm champagne thrust into his hand and staggered under the weight of all the backslapping. In the scrum, it took a few moments to realise that someone was calling his name, and a few more before it sank in that the voice was very familiar.

'Bean! Bean old chap, what on earth are you doing here?'

'Posted here yesterday, old man,' said Bean, grasping Eddie to him. 'I couldn't believe when they said you were stuck at St. Omer.'

'Bean, have you heard about Bunny?' he said but then found himself dragged away by Hastings.

'Come on, Grenville,' he said. 'You have things to do before you make small talk.'

'Things, what things?

'Well, first things first, priorities, lad, priorities. First you have to down that mug in one.'

Hastings slopped more champagne into his mug. To more cheers, knowing he had no choice, Eddie did as he was told.

'Secondly you have to make a speech.'

'Oh no, no I can't, really.'

'You've no choice, Grenville, you *are* making one,' Hastings said then yelled: 'Pipe down, everyone, quiet! Now, when young Grenville joined us a few days ago I think we all had a few doubts about him -'

There was a chorus of 'No!' and someone at the back, Eddie suspected it was Kerr, said, 'Only you, Hastings, only you.'

'Yes, yes, all right, perhaps it was only me,' said Hastings, smiling. 'And I'm happy to admit I was all wrong. Grenville is not only a good sport - sorry about that last Quirk, by the way, no hard feelings, I hope.' There were hoots of laughter.

'None,' said Eddie, though inside he was seething.

'Anyway, you have shown you have the makings of a first-class Hun killer. Gentlemen, I give you, one whole fifth of an ace, Edward

Grenville. Eddie the floor is yours.'

Everyone was looking, everyone was waiting to hear what he had to say. Eddie's mind wouldn't work, what could he say, that he was a fraud? That it was all an accident? How could he do that now that everyone had accepted him at last? What did the truth matter anyway?

What did the truth matter? Yes, that was right. Sometimes it did, certainly, but here, wasn't a white lie right?

'It was simple,' he said. 'It was him or me, and I seemed to be the one who could shoot straighter, that was all.'

Judging by the cheers and applause, this seemed to go down very well and, to Eddie's relief, satisfied the audience, who now started to drift away. He noticed Milne stood by the RE8. He was not drinking, in fact had his arms crossed and was looking angry. Eddie wondered what had upset him and whether he should go and talk to him. First, though, he wanted to find Bean, there was so much that they had to talk about, but, before he could, Hastings grabbed his arm and steered him out of the hangar.

'Come on, young man. Flying is scrubbed for the rest of the day and we haven't got much in the way of daylight left.'

'I don't understand, where are we going?'

'We're going to find your kill, lad.'

Eddie stopped, and resisted Hastings' attempts to pull him forward. 'What? No, I'd rather not.'

Hastings looked surprised.

'Oh come on, everyone does it. You'll need a souvenir and we want a trophy for the mess. Don't go letting the side down now.'

Eddie could tell that what he was really saying was 'Don't let me down.' Reluctantly he allowed himself to be led to the Crossley.

They set off at Hastings' normal pace, splashing through puddles and bouncing over the potholes on the road.

'It's not far,' he said. 'Well, about 15 miles I suppose. It came down next to a battery, the ones that confirmed your kill.'

Eddie just mumbled a reply.

'You know, I really had doubts about you,' Hastings said, blowing his horn to clear the road. 'I didn't think you were going to measure up at all. Sorry, old chap, but I have got to be straight. Some men, even the best of types, just can't. I got you wrong. We will get you on the rota starting from tomorrow, no more ferry flights, how does that sound?'

'That sounds good,' said Eddie, because it really did. 'Thanks.'

'Don't mention it old boy,' said Hastings, grinning, swerving around a team of horses pulling an ammunition cart, barely missing the troop of soldiers who walking along on the opposite side of the road towards them. 'It's good to have you on board.'

*

It was over an hour before they reached the village near to where the aircraft had come down, and another twenty minutes before they found the right battery, by which time the light was fading. Eddie was secretly hoping that they would be too late, that they would be forced to give up and head back to the airfield but, after talking to the battery commander, he and his second in command agreed to show them where the wreck was. Hastings took a back of tools from the Crossley and he and Eddie followed the artillerymen into the next field.

All around them the heavy guns were firing, the flashes of the muzzles lighting up the ground all around them followed shortly after by the report that shook the ground. The air was rich with the smell of cordite and chemicals and the sweet aroma of corruption. Eddie decided it was the very way that Hell itself must sound, look and smell.

The aircraft had crashed at the edge of a small wood. By the look of things it had spun straight down in one piece because all the wreckage was clumped together in a tangled mass, a jumbled pile of smashed wood, crumpled fabric, splintered plywood and twisted metal. Parts of the remains were blackened, confirming Eddie's impression that the machine had caught fire as it went down. Only the fin and one wing tip, both of which had broken off, were recognisable as parts of a German aircraft, though Eddie had no idea what kind it was. Despite all the congratulations he had received, he was still haunted by the idea that he had made a mistake, that when he had got here it would be a British aircraft. This was, at least, a relief.

A group of Tommies, stripped down to their shirts, were working with spades and shovels, digging around the wreckage. Despite the chill of this unseasonably cold April they were sweating profusely, and only barely acknowledged the officers who had come to interrupt their work. Eddie wondered what they were doing and stepped closer.

'We still haven't recovered the pilot,' said the artillery captain, anticipating Eddie's question. Eddie quickly turned away. He had caught a glimpse of white and red and the whiff of burned flesh, and felt sick. 'It looks like it's going to be a pretty messy job recovering him. He went in pretty much nose first. The engine...'

If he completed the sentence Eddie did not hear it. He had turned and walked away, pretending to be interested in something that was covered by a tarpaulin that lay on the edge of the wood.

'Ah yes,' said the Captain, coming over to join him. 'That's his observer. It took us a while to find him. He jumped you see, think it was the fire.'

To Eddie's horror Hastings walked up to the tarpaulin and pulled it back. Lying on his back, his blue eyes still open, his gloves and coat blackened, his face streaked with soot, was a young blonde-haired man of about Eddie's age.

He was the image of Bunny.

Eddie turned away, acid bile in his throat.

'I put a guard on him otherwise some of the chaps would have stripped him for souvenirs,' said the Captain, walking over and looking down at the dead man.

'You should really silence the observer first, you know,' said Hastings, ignoring the captain and dragging the tarpaulin completely off the body. 'When you attack a two-seater. Silence the gunner. This chap hasn't got a mark on him. You must have riddled the pilot and the petrol tank though, I'll give you that.'

It was almost like Eddie was receiving the criticism for a bit of prep: Not bad, you covered the main points but your attention to detail was sloppy.

Hastings meanwhile was pulling the boots off the dead German.

'I say, that's a bit off,' said the Captain.

Hastings took no notice. 'Come on,' he said to Eddie. 'Don't just stand there, give me a hand. These are for you, after all.'

The captain pulled a face and walked away from Hastings, a look of disgust on his face.

Eddie found his legs would not carry him over to Hastings, who, having succeeded in removing one of the boots, smirked at him and started on the second.

'All right,' he said. 'I suppose it is your kill, I'll do the dirty job. We need a trophy for the mess though. Something to put on the wall. Go and find something.'

Eddie went back to the wreck. There was a pile of metal by

where the men were still digging. They were the remains of the observer's machine gun, mounting and camera, all of them smashed and twisted by the impact. There was also something white by the pile that Eddie initially could not make out in the gathering gloom; stepping closer he recognised it was a finger, cut off cleanly just below the second joint.

He recoiled but found it difficult to take his eyes off it.

Managing it at last, his gaze fell on the broken off fin. That would do. He went and retrieved it.

He joined Hastings and the artillerymen who were stood staring at the wreckage. Hastings had the observer's flying boots in his arms, saw the fin that Eddie carried and nodded in approval.

'That will look fantastic on the mess wall,' he said. 'Every time you see it, you'll remember this. A reminder of a job well done. Good work, Eddie.'

Eddie could not think of anything he wanted to be reminded of less.

*

He sat on his bed, staring at the boots that Hastings insisted that he was to take. He was hoping that he could find an excuse not to wear them, that they were too big or too small but his flight leader had insisted he tried them on when they got back to the Crossley. Typically, they were a perfect fit.

'Don't get into a funk thinking about it all,' said Bean. 'It's not good for a chap.'

'That's easy for you to say,' Eddie replied. 'You're not a killer.'

Bean gave a rueful smile. 'We are all killers, Eddie, all of us. We just don't normally get to see the results of our work. Come on now, pull yourself together, there's a good chap. We have a job to do. It's a beastly one, certainly but it's a beastly war.'

'Yes, you're right, I know.'

'Of course I'm right. Now let's settle down and get some sleep. We're on the early show tomorrow. What a way to spend Easter Sunday, eh?'

Eddie looked up, 'Easter? Gosh of course it is, I'd quite forgotten.'

'Easy to forget.' Bean sighed. '"I am the resurrection and the life",' he muttered, turning down the light. The party, part celebration of Eddie's kill and part wake for a crew that Eddie had not had time to meet was still in full swing in the mess and their third roommate, Daley, still had to find his way back.

The resurrection and the life, Eddie thought as he lay in the darkness. Instantly he thought of the German observer, and of Bunny. Their life on Earth was over. Would they have been resurrected; would they be at peace in heaven? Or had God forsaken them, washed his hands because of all the madness that the world had descended into.

Madness. Not madness. Call it what it was: bloodlust. Killing.

He had killed.

He had killed them both in fact, the unknown German directly and Bunny effectively. Him, he had, him, young Edward Grenville.

But what worried him most was not the fact that he felt guilty but the that he did not feel guilty enough. If he was truly honest with himself, he wanted to do it again.

He tried to think of something else but the image of the dead German would not go, and with that image came obvious thoughts of someone else.

'I wasn't there, you know,' he said.

'Pardon?' Bean sounded sleepy. 'What do you mean?'

'I wasn't there when Bunny was killed.'

There was silence for a few moments.

'That was probably a blessing, Eddie. It would have been frightfully upsetting to see.'

'I know, Bean, I know. It's just...'

'It's just what, Eddie?'

'I just don't like the idea of him being alone when he died. It must be beastly dying amongst strangers.'

'We all die alone, Eddie. It's a journey one has to take all on your own, whether there are friends and family around you or not.'

'I suppose.'

There was silence again. Eddie wondered if Bean had fallen asleep.

'Don't dwell on it, Eddie,' Bean said. 'I believe in fate, you know. That was Bunny's time and there was nothing you, me or anyone else could have done to change it. There is no point wishing it was different, even though we all wish that it was, it can't be. Don't dwell on death, Eddie, you need to live for the now. We need to look out for each other, keep each other as safe as we can.'

Eddie did not reply, though he knew Bean was right and thinking that way helped.

'I don't want to see you hurt,' Bean suddenly said, from the darkness. His voice had a strange quality to it, there was definitely a degree of emotion to it, Eddie was sure.

It must have been because they were talking about Bunny, he decided. He had been selfish, concentrating on his own problems and, as a result, had upset his friend. Well, enough, he just had to get on with it.

'And I feel the same way about you, Bean,' he said. 'Goodnight, Hector.'

'Night, Eddie.'

Although he was calmer, sleep still took a long time coming.

DAY 7

APRIL 8, 1917

Easter Sunday dawned fresh and cold, with broken cloud. It was, at least, a better day for flying.

Eddie and Bean found that they were not on at first light but were down for the 9.30 show, a photo reconnaissance towards Douai, so they were able to have a leisurely breakfast alongside Morris. Phil Armstrong and Kerr were also there which puzzled Eddie as he knew that Milne and A flight were down for the 6.00 am patrol. He asked Kerr about it. Immediately, Eddie could tell that this was a sore spot.

'It's bloody Albert,' Kerr said. 'He's been agitating again, getting in the CO's ear. He was complaining that all his crews were inexperienced, that he needed a deputy that he could rely on to take the lead if he couldn't, so the next thing we know we get transferred into his flight.'

'There's no wonder he's short of experienced crews, the way he leads,' said Armstrong, his face grim. 'We're not happy about it, as you can imagine but there's no changing Reeves's mind. He can be a stubborn bugger, pardon my French.'

'What do you mean, the way he leads?' asked Morris. Both he and Bean were looking worried. Eddie saw Kerr and Armstrong exchange glances.

'Oh don't worry about it,' said Kerr. 'It's just us old hands having a grumble, we don't like change that's all, do we Phil? Just ignore us.'

'I say, you can't just say something like that and then just leave us hanging,' said Morris. 'We need to know.'

Armstrong shook his head. 'Nah, Alan's right. Hastings does things his own way, we're just not used to it. We should go and sort out the ammunition.'

Kerr nodded in agreement, finished his tea and the pair left.

'What was all that about?' said Morris.

'Hastings has a bit of a reputation for being aggressive in the air,' said Eddie.

'Aggressive?'

'It's just what people say. It's probably an exaggeration'

'Oh right,' said Morris. 'Well, that's not a problem is it? Taking the fight to the Hun? I mean you had no problem yesterday, did you Grenville? How you handled that two-seater. Bloody spiffing it was, sneaking underneath him like that.'

'It was nothing. I was lucky,' mumbled Eddie, not wanting to be reminded about what he had done.

'Lucky nothing,' said Morris. 'I say, look at the time. I had better go off to pick up my plates from the photographic boys. Shall I see you at the hangar, Grenville?'

'Yes, see you there.'

When he had gone, Bean leant over to Eddie.

'Are you alright, Eddie? You look troubled, old chap. Anything you want to talk about?'

'No.'

'Are you sure, I -'

'Just bloody leave it, will you?' Eddie did not mean to snap, but realised that he must have done, because everyone in the Mess had turned to look at him. He had also half got to his feet. He sat down again. 'Sorry, old man,' he said quietly. 'That was uncalled for.'

Bean rested his hand on Eddie's. 'That's alright. You've been through a lot over the last few days. It's bound to affect a chap.'

Eddie found himself looking into Bean's eyes for a moment. Then he pulled his hand away.

'We should get ready too,' he said, rising from the table.

*

Eddie started to feel sick just before Hasting's briefing. He hoped that it would go away but the now familiar feeling of nausea increased as he was walking to his aircraft.

Once again he had to dash behind one of the hangars to vomit. When he limped back to the waiting RE8, Morris looked at him with puzzlement written on his face.

'Bad egg for breakfast,' Eddie said.

'Oh,' said Morris. 'I thought you just had toast.'

'Well it must have been something I ate anyway,' muttered Eddie, climbing into the cockpit. The truth was he suspected he knew exactly what the problem was, and it was not food. He did not want to think too much about it, he was sure it would pass anyway, as he went over the lines.

He hoped it would anyway.

He knew he had other problems. His foot was throbbing, in fact it was almost as bad as it was the day after he had had the crash. Still, there was no way that he was going to take any more of the tablets, not after what had happened yesterday. He could not risk it. He would have to find another way, either to live with the pain or to mask it.

The take-off was uneventful, though the usual butterflies made an appearance in his stomach as Eddie opened the throttle.

They were to go over the lines at 6000 feet. Although the RE8 climbed better than the Quirk, it still took over twenty minutes to get that high. As soon as they had, Hastings turned towards the lines and set course for Douai.

Eddie was sweating, despite the chill. His foot was worse, not better. The more he tried to put it out of his mind the more it dominated his thoughts. It almost became his world, it was hard to concentrate.

Soon though, they were over the lines. Eddie had the presence of mind to check that Morris was paying attention. He found that his observer was looking down at the trenches beneath rather than the sky around them. It was understandable, he had done much the same thing on his own first flight over but he could not let him, they needed Morris's eyes. Eddie got his attention then shouted his instructions. He was pleased to see Morris turn around and start scanning the skies, his hand on the Lewis Gun.

A green flare arched through the sky on his right-hand side. Eddie looked over, his heart beating faster for a moment until he remembered what the signal meant: It was a red flare for danger, green meant 'I am turning back'. He looked back, one of the machines was indeed, straggling. Who was it? Bean? No it had a white letter G on the side in front of the roundel, that was Francis and Lloyd-Davies. They must have engine trouble.

Eddie looked across at Hastings machine. Even though he could see nothing of his Flight-Leader's face, he was sure he could detect anger in the man, particularly when Francis turned for home. It was obvious to Eddie that this had not been taken well, mechanical problem or not, it was a sign of weakness, an almost personal affront to Hasting's leadership.

It made Eddie more determined to continue, pain or not.

The five remaining machines crossed the German front and second lines. It was a scene from Hell below. Shells were exploding all over the line, the barrage was intense. How long had this been going on for? Eddie thought back. Today was the 8th, it had started the day before his first mission which was on the 3rd. Four days! What must it be like down there? How could anyone live through it? And how could there be that many shells in the world? He thought of all the metal and money that was going into this battle, then of the guns and men up and down the line, from the Belgian coast at Zeebrugge to the Swiss border. All that effort, all that cost. For what? How was it that man could put so much effort into destruction and so little into peace? It didn't seem right.

Four days, and that meant five days since that first mission. Only five. Five days since Collier had died, Five days since Bunny -

The thump of Archie brought him back to the present. There were black puffs of smoke all around. He shook himself, he had drifted off again, he could not do that, he had to concentrate. And so did Morris. Eddie looked behind him, Morris was doing his job. Good.

Hastings was waving, then pointing down. They were coming up on their target. Time to do what they came to do. They had been briefed to disperse slightly, flying around fifty yards apart and take a series of photographs of the ground beneath them from Esquerchin northward. Eddie shouted instructions back to Morris, who nodded and reached for the wooden film plate magazine for the camera. Eddie positioned his machine in what he judged to be the right distance from the rest of the flight and started the run.

He found that he was remarkably calm now that he had something to do, keeping his course and speed, ensuring the wings were perfectly level, that their machine did not get too close to Armstrong and Kerr on his right and Bean and Smith on his left, the idea being to cover the ground beneath as completely as possible. Morris started to expose the plates, clicking the shutter of the camera clipped to the side of the aircraft then replacing the plates one by one. Eddie did not watch him, his job was now to keep watch.

They were in hostile skies, after all, with no escort.

They had been running straight and level for only two or three minutes when a red flare arched across the nose of Eddie's machine. He immediately looked at Hastings's aircraft. He was pointing, not upwards as Eddie expected any danger to come from but down and to his right. Eddie looked. There, against the brown and greens of the ground was a dark dot, an aircraft heading east, perhaps a thousand feet below them.

Eddie's heart had thumped at first when he saw the flare, memories of the Albatros attack being very fresh, but he calmed down when he saw the aircraft. A single machine down there was going to do no harm to them, even if it was a German. He was surprised when Hastings gestured at it, waved that they should follow, then banked towards it.

'What's he doing?' Eddie said out loud, though only him could possibly have heard what he had said. Obediently though, he banked round to follow.

He glanced back at Morris who looked both bemused and startled. He had been caught with a new plate in one hand and the old in the other and was now trying to stow both whilst looking around for the danger.

Eddie also looked. This was not right, he knew that, they had not completed the photo run, that was their mission, why then was Hastings attacking something that was no danger to them? And what was it doing on its own just stooging around? This felt all wrong, why was he going along with it?

Hastings was now almost on the other aircraft. It was, indeed, German, an LVG two-seater. The observer was stood up, gun ready in the rear cockpit. Hastings fired.

Morris thumped Eddie on the back. He turned, looking back and up.

There were Albatros coming down on them, at least a dozen. It was a trap.

Morris opened fire as Eddie turned the aircraft towards the lines. There was a rattle of machine guns, tracer rounds were passing them, just over the top of the wing, then the Albatros was past them, the pilot looking back over his shoulder as he overshot. Eddie looked around; if the formation kept together the combined firepower could help to deter the attack but, in Hastings sudden attack, the five aircraft had been left straggling in the wake of their leader. He could see one RE8 to his left and slightly above but nothing else but brightly painted enemy aircraft, wheeling, turning, banking and firing.

Eddie and Morris were on the edge of the melee, their comrade above was in the middle of it and in desperate trouble, three aircraft were harrying it, two from above and to the side but the third was the real danger. It was beneath the big British machine, in its blind spot, gradually getting closer, a shark closing in for the kill.

Eddie found himself yelling at the crew to watch out, he turned but knew he couldn't help, he was too far away, too low, had too little performance to get anywhere near the hunter and the prey. Even as he pointed their nose at them and started to climb, the Albatros beneath the other RE8 fired.

The effect was immediate. The RE8s nose jerked up, a tongue of flame streamed back from beneath it, then the wings on its right side folded back and tore off, fluttering down behind the rest of the wreckage like a sycamore key in autumn.

Eddie had only a moment to see this horror unfold in front of him and to wonder who, of his comrades, had just met their end before he realised that they were the next target. The three Albatros had climbed above him and were turning to attack. Eddie wheeled the RE8 round, heading for home, desperately looking for someone to help them but, apart from the three enemy scouts, they were alone.

Morris opened up with the Lewis from the rear cockpit, Eddie kept straining his head, trying to keep all three Albatros in sight, to make sure that none of them got in a position underneath to deliver the coup de grace. It seemed inevitable; his foes were so nimble, so powerful, they could seemingly go anywhere, surpass any move that he made.

Tracer rounds whizzed past them, just under their port wing, Eddie banked away, only for another stream to come from the starboard quarter, tearing into the wing, pinging off the metal of the cowling and the engine, splintering the plywood panel of the instrument column. He jerked the aircraft over, more bullets hit them, somewhere further back. Morris was still firing, at least he could defend them but Eddie knew it was only a matter of time; they were being chewed to pieces, their aircraft was clumsy, slow - and alone.

He spotted some cloud just below them and to the right. Perhaps if he could get them in there, they might have a chance? He banked, losing height. More tracer came in, from almost directly behind them, tearing through the lower wing, whistling by the cockpit. He kicked the rudder bar and swung to the left.

There was a sharp crack, the RE8 abruptly turned right, the wing on that side dipping towards the ground. What was happening? Eddie had not turned that way. He looked across to the right. To his horror he saw that the wing extension, complete with aileron, had snapped off and folded back and down, being held on only by the sagging flying wires from the kingpost. Shorn of lift on that side and with the remnant of the wing acting as a second rudder, the aircraft was turning and falling, he was sure it would spin. He kicked hard down on the left side of the rudder bar and pulled the stick to the right to put on full opposite aileron, hoping that this would push the left wing down. He was amazed when it worked, the wings levelled though they were losing height.

He was just congratulating himself on the recovery when the machine guns started again, first the distant rat-tat of the Albatros, then Morris's reply from closer behind his ear. Eddie knew now that it was hopeless for them, they could not manoeuvre, they could barely keep flying. They were sitting ducks; it was all over. Any moment the bullets to kill him would come. Would it be quick? Or would they tear at him, rip his insides out?

Or would they burn? Would the bullets set them on fire, incinerate them as they sat here, thousands of feet above the ground. If they did burn, could he do what that German observer have done, end it all, leap out?

He was not sure, but he was going to find out. The Albatros were coming in for the kill, showing no mercy. He could not blame them; he was sure that they had lost friends too. He had killed, somehow it was right that he should be killed in the same way. It was the way of the world, the new lore.

The guns started their chatter again. He braced himself, waiting for the inevitable impact.

There seemed to be a lot of guns suddenly, more than before. Perhaps he was hearing things?

He heard Morris shout, felt a thump on his back. He risked a glance to the left just in time to see a sleek biplane with straight, equal length wings flash by, gun firing. A SPAD! A British one too. More than one, a whole flight!

Then, suddenly it was like they were alone in the sky. He heard Morris cheering, felt him pat Eddie on the shoulder. Eddie wanted to shout back, not in elation but to tell Morris that they might have escaped the bullets but that it was far from over. They could barely fly, he was struggling to keep the wing up, the aircraft was wanting to plunge down to right and he was convinced that the damaged wing would, at any moment, tear itself off completely plunging them into the ground.

And now, once the danger of instant death through bullets had gone, his broken foot which was pressing hard on the rudder bar, started to protest at its treatment. It was pure agony, yet he could not reduce the pressure for a moment.

He looked down, they were low, they had lost a lot of altitude in the fight and they were losing more now. They were still the wrong side of the lines, putting them down here would see them become prisoners, yet surely they must land. How the aircraft was still flying he wasn't sure, the rest of the wing could collapse at any moment, plunging them to certain death.

Yet he did not put them down. Something kept him flying, though he was so tempted to try and get to the safety of the ground. Instead he increased the throttle slightly, trying to slow their rate of sink. The RE8 was hardly flying smoothly before this, it was crabbing through the air, now it creaked alarmingly as the extra power was applied. Eddie knew it was virtually fighting itself, one half of the machine was trying to turn to the right and plunge down, the other half, the side he was controlling was pulling the other way. Eddie felt like he and Morris were like the rag tied in the middle of a tug-of-war rope and that, any moment, the other side would win.

He had very little directional control but luckily they were heading virtually due west. The lines, the dark stain across the landscape, were now approaching. They started being Archied, they were close enough to the ground for Eddie to see individual soldiers raise their rifles and take pot shots at them. Several rounds hit them, one pinged off the Vickers, taking a chunk out of the cooling jacket. He wanted to shout at them, tell them to stop it, that they were dead anyway but could not find the energy to do so. He was convinced that they were bound to be hit and was sure that the bullet would hit him in the behind and travel all the way up his body, tumbling and tearing as he went. For some reason, being shot in the bottom seemed worse than anything else he could imagine, it was so squalid, so ignoble, not a war wound one could boast about, not one he could show his mother.

He found himself laughing at this thought. He stopped himself, this was serious, he had to concentrate. Being shot was never funny. There would be no wound to show anyone anyway, he would be dead if he was hit.

And even if it did not hit him then surely one of the bullets was bound to hit something vital on the aircraft, cut a flying wire, puncture the radiator, or hit the petrol tank, there were so many of them now. They buzzed past them like wasps from a broken nest.

Yes, the petrol tank, that would be it. It was right in front of Eddie. It would be hell, like sitting in a furnace. He would jump if that happened, he decided. But was he too low to be certain that the jump would kill him? He might end up burnt and paralyzed.

He found that he was rigid, almost frozen with fear. He had to snap out of it or they would be dead for sure.

A shell burst on the ground almost beneath them, reminding him that they were in the firing line. The concussion wave hit the aircraft and lifted it; his foot slipped off the rudder bar. The machine slewed to the right, it almost spun, just in time he was able to bring his right foot over and kick down hard to stop it. A spin would be fatal, they were too low and he doubted that he had enough control to even begin righting it. The RE8 returned to its semblance of level flight, though they were now even lower.

He realised they had crossed the German front line. They were out over no-man's-land. It had been raining, the landscape beneath looked cold, alien, deadly. It was riddled with craters, most flooded. A crash there would probably kill them anyway.

There was a sharp crack, something hit him in the face, a sharp pain slapped his cheek, the shock almost caused him to lose control again. What was it, what had happened? Eddie put his hand to his face, pulled down the scarf that covered his face, then looked at his gauntlet. There was blood on it. He was hit! How? A bullet? Surely that would hurt more? Then he noticed the strut in front of him was splintered, the front half shattered. Ah, that was it, a bullet had hit the strut, he had got showered in splinters, got one in the face.

Then he realised that the strut had been hit from the front. The bullet had come from the British lines.

'You stupid bastards!' he yelled, though he knew only Morris was likely to hear. 'Can't you see I'm one of yours?'

By this time they were over the British trenches. Eddie could see the faces looking up at him. They looked cold and miserable but, at that moment, he could not feel sorry for them.

As soon as they got beyond the support lines he would find somewhere to put down, he told himself.

But there was a problem with this. Wherever he looked there seemed to be obstructions, troops, guns, horses, stacks of ammunition, cans of food and fuel. And by the time he had flown five minutes beyond the lines the prospects of a crash landing did not seem so appealing. Now he was using his good foot on the rudder it was not so bad and he was getting used to straining to hold the stick over against the strain of the broken wing. Sod it, he thought, it had flown this far, he might as well get them home.

He found landmarks he recognised and that, with a little careful adjustment, he could get them pointing on roughly the right course.

Fifteen minutes later, they were approaching Acq. He knew that he would only have one chance at landing so aimed the aircraft at the centre of the field to give himself most room. He caught the windsock, he knew he was coming in slightly cross wind but there was nothing he could do about it, he would have to accept what he got. He risked a glance back at Morris, he was gripping the cockpit sides and kept looking at the broken wing. Well at least he knows the trouble we are in, Eddie thought, turning back to concentrate on his approach.

It had been about five minutes out when he had thought of something: how would the loss of lift affect the stalling speed? He had seen what had happened with an intact RE8 at St. Omer when a pilot had slowed too much, what would happen here, particularly as the damaged upper plane was already acting as a brake on the aircraft. He decided they would have to come in fast and use the elevators to control their sink rate rather than throttle back. How fast he should come in he had no idea, no one in all probability could know but, in any case, his air speed indicator had been shattered by the Albatros's bullets.

As they flashed over the perimeter fence of the airfield, Eddie realised that they were probably going too fast but there was little he could do about it other than push the stick forward.

The wheels touched the grass, bounced. Eddie quickly closed the throttle and was about to switch off the magnetos when the machine returned to earth rather more rapidly and much harder than he intended. There was a splintering as the undercarriage collapsed, the prop shattered, one wing dug into the grass, and Eddie's world became a jumble of grass, flying mud, sky, fabric, wire and breaking spruce.

Abruptly, the aircraft was gone and Eddie was rolling, bouncing, sliding along the grass. He could smell it, fresh like it was newly mown, like the beautifully manicured lawns of home, tended so carefully by father's gardeners.

It took him a few moments to realise that he had stopped and all was quiet. Was he dead? Did heaven have lawns and gardens?

Would there be flowers too?

Then his foot started hurting and he knew he was alive.

He was face down in the wet grass. He rolled over onto his back. He could not see the aircraft at first, so sat up. He realised he was in a little dip, one that he did not know existed but which he now made a mental note to avoid for future, more conventional landings.

He almost laughed at the thought.

The remains of the RE8 were about 30 yards away. All that was recognisable was the fuselage, wingless, broken, draped in wires, lying on its side. Further back he could see pieces of wing, the tail fin, the Vickers gun and various bits of wood and fabric.

Men were sprinting towards the remains, as was the Crossley tender.

It was like having the front seats for a play, he was watching it all happen in front of him. He saw Bean's long frame, sprinting ahead of the rest. Of course, Eddie thought, he was a runner, quite the athlete, remembering that school's competition they had both been in.

I should get up, tell them I'm alright, he thought but he was filled with a sudden immense tiredness so he just lay where he was and watched it all unfold.

Bean got to the wreck first, even beating the Crossley. He dashed to the far side, to the cockpit. He looked frantic, kneeling down, trying to right the fuselage.

He thinks I'm underneath, Eddie realised but still couldn't find the energy to get up.

More people arrived and pulled Bean away. He looked distraught. There were dozens there now, all concentrating on something just out of sight, towards the middle of the broken machine.

It was then he remembered Morris.

He was still in there.

It was like a slap in the face, or the shock of diving into cold water.

Eddie did not remember getting up, though he did note with some surprise that he could still walk and that he was not in any more pain than he had been before he had crashed. He walked around behind the riggers, fitters and pilots who were gathered around the wreck.

'Steady, you man, get some cutters in there, easy!'

Milne's voice. Of course, he had taken charge.

There was a groan, some swearing, followed by a gasped,

'Sorry sir.'

'Don't worry about it lad, we'll soon get you out.'

Eddie pushed his way to the front of the crowd. He found he was standing next to Bean.

'How is he?' he said.

The next thing Eddie knew was that Bean had grabbed him and had tugged him to his chest.

*

'He got off lightly,' Milne was saying as Eddie reached the squadron office. 'The MO says he's got a broken leg and arm. He'll be out of action for a while but he'll mend.'

Eddie had just come from the doctor himself so knew this. Milne was with Hastings and Pops so, although the door was open, felt the need to knock to announce his presence.

He could not help but notice that it was only the latter two that seemed pleased to see him.

'Ah, Grenville,' said Pops. 'What did the MO say?'

'He said I was fine, apart from the foot and I didn't do that today,' said Eddie.

'Yes, you must get out of the habit of smashing up our aircraft,' said Hastings, smiling.

'He was damned lucky,' said Milne. 'What the hell did you think you were doing, Eddie?'

Eddie was rather taken aback by this. 'But...we got hit, we got into a fight with some Huns.'

'I know that,' snapped Milne. 'That was bloody obvious. What on earth possessed you to try and fly your machine back here in that condition?'

'But - ' began Eddie, but Milne was in full flow.

'It was bloody irresponsible; you should have put it down as soon as you could. It's not just your life, you know.'

'I know but -'

'It's not the first time you have been so bloody stupid.'

'What do you -'

'There was that jaunt over the lines yesterday. That could have killed both you and Morris for no bloody reason.'

'I say David, ease up on the boy.' To Eddie's surprise it was

Hastings who had come to his defence. 'He's just keen. He's got the right spirit. He just wanted to get the machine back to us to give the lads a chance to repair it and get it back into action. He knows how precious the new machines are. We need every one.'

Milne stared at Hastings. 'Not as precious as the men who fly them,' he said. 'And if they are so precious, why are you risking them breaking off from doing the job that you were sent out to do just to attack a two-seater?'

'I beg your pardon? I...what are you saying?' Hastings said, looking affronted.

'I'm saying that we lost two good men, Daniels and MacKenna because of it and the job you were sent out to do is only half done, probably less if they are not able to recover the plates from Grenville's machine.'

'I don't like what you are insinuating,' Hastings blustered. 'You don't know what happened, I'd mind you to keep your opinions to yourself. You don't know what happened.'

'I've heard,' said Milne, coldly. 'I've talked to some of the chaps.'

'Which ones?' demanded Hastings.

Milne did not answer.

'David, you have clearly been misinformed. That LVG attacked us, are we not allowed to defend ourselves?'

'An LVG *attacked* you?' There was incredulity in Milne's voice.

'Absolutely,' said Hastings. 'Young Grenville will back me up on that, won't you Eddie?'

Eddie found himself under the gaze of the three superior officers. He felt himself flush. It was obvious what Hastings wanted, he wanted Eddie to lie. He had backed, Eddie up though, swung to his defence. Yet it was still a lie, the truth was important wasn't it?

'Yes,' he said at last. 'The LVG moved to attack us.'

He could see in Milne's eyes that he did not believe Eddie. He also could see disappointment and some disgust in his face. Hastings on the other hand, looked triumphant.

'I got it too, didn't I, Grenville. You'd have seen it go down smoking then?'

'Well, I...' began Eddie, then decided it was easier to continue with the lie. 'Yes, I think so.'

'Good,' said Hastings, his eyes gleaming. 'I'll amend my combat report. I should get a probable for that. You'll sign it, won't you Grenville?'

'Yes sir,' said Eddie, dully. He felt a little sick and did not think it was the after effects of the crash.

'Right,' said Milne. 'Well, whatever, we still have to go back and do the job that B flight didn't finish, don't we Pops?'

'I'm afraid so David,' sighed Pops. 'HQ said it was vital that we get new pictures of that area, given what is going to happen tomorrow.'

Milne also sighed heavily. 'Which, as we are down for the next show makes it down to us. I'd better go and brief my boys.'

He pushed past Eddie, giving him neither a glance nor an apology.

There was an awkward silence, finally broken by Pops who looked at Eddie and said: 'So you're fit to fly, Grenville?'

'Yes sir.'

'Good, stand at readiness. We might be called on to do some Art Obs this afternoon. I'll also find you a new observer.'

'Sir.'

'Good. Right, we might as well fill in the Combat in the Air form now. No time like the present is there?' Hastings smiled. 'This is victory number four, you know. Dashed important.'

Eddie just nodded.

*

Eddie left the office half-an-hour later and made his way to the the mess. His throat was dry and he was in desperate need of some tea. As he was walking over he saw A flight taking off, heading back to complete the job they had left less than half done that morning. Eddie could not bear to watch them.

Most of the members of B flight were in the lounge, including Bean, Armstrong and Kerr. Bean looked pleased to see Eddie, jumping up when he came through the door. Armstrong and Kerr were slumped in armchairs, looking glum.

'You alright, Eddie?' asked Kerr. 'That looked nasty.'

'Yes, I'm fine, just a few bruises,' he said. 'Morris is a bit banged around though,' he added. 'I did the wrong thing, trying to get back. I should have put it down straight away.'

'Don't be so hard on yourself,' said Armstrong. 'It was a damned good bit of flying. With the aircraft in that condition you needed a big field and I don't suppose you know yet where the other airfields are yet?'

'No I don't,' admitted Eddie.

'Anyway, it wasn't your fault you were in that condition,' Armstrong continued. 'It was bloody Albert. He's going to get us all killed with his antics.'

'Er, yes,' said Eddie, finding a seat.

'What the hell did he think he was doing? That LVG was no danger, it was just stooging home, or, even worse, it was a trap. It was obvious that there would be Huns about above just waiting for some damned idiot to have a go at it,' said Armstrong. 'And we were those damned fools,' he added, bitterly.

'Can't we do anything about him?' said Bean.

'Phil and I have had a word with Milne, told him what happened. It's just our word against his though. Did any of you see what happened?' said Kerr.

'No, I was too busy trying to make sure I didn't mess up,' said Bean.

'Eddie, you were over on Hastings side, you must have seen what he did.'

Eddie felt himself redden. What could he say? That he had seen Hastings break off the reconnaissance just to attack the two-seater? Or that he had not seen anything at all, deny everything? Both contradicted what he had just told Milne in Pops presence and would certainly contradict the account that Hastings had just virtually dictated to him and was now winging its way to headquarters for verification. He had painted himself into a corner. He had left himself nowhere to go.

'To be honest, I thought it was threatening us too,' he said.

Armstrong and Kerr just stared at him with their mouths open.

'Really?' said Kerr at last. 'You really thought that?'

'Yes,' said Eddie firmly.

'Right,' said Kerr, slowly. 'So that's the way the land lies, is it? Well, fine, Grenville. We should be going, Phil. I'm sure there is somewhere else we need to be.'

'Absolutely, Alan,' said Armstrong, giving Eddie a glare as he left.

Bean frowned, looking from the pair's retreating backs then at Eddie. 'Have I missed something?' he said.

Francis and Lloyd-Davies both stirred uncomfortably and looked at the floor. Eddie just mumbled: 'I'll tell you later,' partly because he wanted to move the conversation on but mainly because

Hastings had just walked into the lounge. He had a huge smile on his face. To Eddie's discomfort he walked straight over to where they were sitting.

'Good news, chaps,' he said. 'Well, actually of course, the second bit of good news of the day after my fourth Hun.'

'Fourth Hun?' repeated Bean. 'Did you get one of the Albatros then?'

'No, I got the two-seater.'

'But I saw that LVG nose down heading safely back to Hunland.'

'You must have been mistaken, Monroe,' said Hastings. 'I got it. No doubt about it. Positive flamer. Your friend Grenville here backed me up.'

'Oh, right,' said Bean. Eddie saw him glance over in his direction. 'But you said two bits of good news?'

'Ah yes. We're stood down for the day. Tomorrow is the day of the big push, the day we rout the Huns and send them back to Berlin with their tails between their legs. It's maximum effort for us from 4.30 am. We need all the machines serviceable for contact and flash patrols from first light.'

'Alright, good,' said Bean.

'Doesn't mean we can't have a quick celebration early doors this evening though.'

'Celebration?' Bean looked puzzled.

'For my Hun of course! What else?' Hastings shook his head in amused exasperation. 'Gosh, you can be a bit slow, can't you Monroe?'

'Er, yes sir, but...'

'But what, Monroe?'

'I was just thinking about Daniels and MacKenna, sir.'

'What about them?'

'They did die today.'

Eddie groaned inwardly. He knew Bean was right but also that this was exactly the wrong thing to say to Hastings.

'It's what they would have wanted. Life goes on, Monroe, we can't get all maudlin or we'd all be in a proper funk. You'd better learn that.'

'Yes sir,' mumbled Bean.

'Now, you two,' said Hastings, turning to Francis and Lloyd-Davies. 'I want an explanation.'

'Sir?' said Francis, looking shocked. 'What for?'

'For leaving the formation early like that. What happened?'

'We had a dud engine; it wouldn't pull full revs.'

Hastings gave a snort of derision. 'Really?' he said. 'You realise that being one aircraft short probably caused Daniels and MacKenna to get shot down?'

Frances looked shocked. 'You can't believe that, sir?'

'Don't tell me what I can and can't believe, Francis. I'm just pointing it out that's all. Remember young Grenville flew his machine back here with half a top wing yet you turned back for a little misfire. Not good enough, both of you. I'll be keeping an eye on you from now on. Understood?'

'Yes sir,' said Francis.

Eddie could see he was trembling, though whether this was with barely suppressed rage or indignation, he was not sure.

'Right, let that be the end of it then. I will expect to see you all in the mess after dinner,' Hastings looked around the mess. There were some nods and a few muttered 'Sirs' which seemed to satisfy him, for he left, heading in the direction of the squadron office.

In the room silence reigned. No one seemed to be much in the mood to say anything.

*

Hastings' 'celebration' was, as Eddie suspected, a damp squib. Even with alcohol no one was much in the mood to party, in fact the event turned into more of a wake for Daniels and MacKenna, much to their flight leaders' chagrin.

Eddie noticed that the atmosphere in the mess had changed. It was not just that they were mourning lost friends, there was something else, a tension, a sense of foreboding. No one spoke about it but this did not make it any less real. Eddie decided that it must be because of the start of the offensive in the morning. Whatever, the event broke up early and most of the crews returned to their billets to sleep, talk, listen to music or write letters home, Eddie and Bean among them.

They both lay on their beds, the light on but neither seemed in the mood to talk. Eddie certainly did not want to; he had had quite enough of the day. Even though it was very early he considered sleeping but, just as he was about to ask Bean whether he minded the lamp being turned down, the blanket covering the door was pulled back and Milne, Pops and Sergeant Evans came into the room. Milne still had his flying gear on.

'That's 'is bed, sir,' said Evans. 'And 'is bag's is under it.'

'Thanks,' said Pops. 'We'll see to his things then you can do the bedding.'

'Sir.'

Milne said nothing. He reached under the bed, pulled out Daley's suitcase and started putting his books and clothes in it. Milne's face was set, grim.

'David,' said Pops gently. 'You don't need to do this. Evans and I can deal with it. You go over to the mess, get something to eat, some tea.' He placed his hand on Milne's shoulder who angrily shook it off. Undeterred, Pops took hold of the flight leader's arm and pulled him away from Daley's possessions. 'Off you go now, David, go and get something inside you. We'll finish up here.'

Milne turned and walked to the doorway. As he pulled aside the blanket he looked across at Eddie, locking eyes with him momentarily. Then he was gone.

Eddie was shaken, the look was more of an eloquent accusation than any words could have framed.

'They were jumped by Richthofen's crowd,' Pops said. Eddie realised that Bean must have asked what had happened. 'Sinter and his observer went down with a stopped engine but landed alright behind the Hun lines. Jenkins and Daley went straight in though, didn't stand a chance according to David. The rest of them only got out by the skin of their teeth.' There was a chink of glass; Evans was gathering up Daley's stock of brandy and Irish Whiskey he kept under his table. 'Leave those, sergeant,' Pops said.

'Sir,' said Evans, putting the bottles back.

Eddie let his head drop. This was their job, the one they hadn't done.

'All done, Pops,' murmured Evans.

'Right, try to get some sleep, chaps,' said Pops. 'Very early start.'

Bean acknowledged this with a 'Sir.' Eddie just nodded.

When Pops and Evans had gone, Eddie and Bean just stared at Daley's bed in silence for some minutes.

'Knocks a chap for six, something like this, doesn't it?' said Bean at last. 'Such a nice chap.'

'Yes,' said Eddie quietly. 'That was our job,' he added.

'Don't think about it, Eddie, it could have happened at anytime. And it was Hastings who broke off. We have to follow his lead.'

'I know,' said Eddie but knew he did not believe that deep down. 'There's something else too.'

'What?'

'Daley and Jenkins had been out here for nearly a year. They were probably one of the most experienced crews in the squadron. If it can happen to them...'

Bean pursed his lips. 'We'll get through this, Eddie. I know it looks black now, we're having a rough time but it will settle down, it has to. It's got to get easier. Come on, we need to get to sleep.'

Bean started to get ready for bed. Eddie did not feel like it. He did not want to risk trying to sleep now with all the dark thoughts going round and around in his head.

'I'm going to write a few letters,' he said. 'I'll keep the lamp low.'

'That's fine, old boy,' said Bean gently. 'Don't stay up too long now.'

'Don't bloody well tell me what I can and can't do!' The flash of anger surprised himself as much as it seemed to shock Bean.

'Sorry, Eddie, you know I didn't mean anything by it. Good-night, old chap.' Bean got under the blankets and turned his back on Eddie.

Eddie sat at his desk, the blank paper in front of him. Where had that come from? It was uncalled for, he should apologise. Yet he couldn't, he was gripped in inertia, he just could not be bothered to do or say anything. But he had hurt Bean's feelings by snapping, he really should say something, but in the morning.

The morning might be too late. He might forget and then...

Bunny had gone without them saying goodbye to each other.

'Sorry Bean,' he said. 'I think I'm tired.'

There was no reply. It didn't matter, at least he had said it.

He picked up the pen.

Dear Annie,

I am sorry that it has been such a long time since I wrote to you.

He paused. Had it been so long? He had written to her just before he had left St.Omer to catch the train to Arras. How long ago was that?

He was shocked to realise that it was just seven days ago. Seven! So much had happened, it was like living several lives. He understood now why the instructors who had been in France had seemed so old, every day was like a month of the 'old' time, the time at home. Those long, lazy days which seemed to go on forever, it was so easy to be casual about that sort of time, to just use it up like it was inexhaustible.

The experience here showed that your days were most definitely finite.

But, Eddie realised, had he ever felt more alive than he did now? When the blood pounded in his head as his heart beat in fear as the Archie buffeted them, when the machine-guns rattled? Didn't it feel good to press the trigger and send his bullets into the body of that German pilot?

Then the vision of the observer, lying broken on his back on the chalk-soil swam into view, followed by his last memory of Bunny, laying in the bed where Bean slept now, his tousled blonde hair just sticking above the blankets.

And of Daley, dead not two hours, who he hardly knew yet would remember all his life, a man who died doing the job he failed to complete.

What kind of monster was he to be enjoying this life?

He sighed. He did not want to think of the answer to that question because he knew it would take him to Percy.

He picked up the pen again and began to write.

DAY 8

APRIL 9, 1917

'Sir, sir, wake up, sir.'

For all the time that Eddie had sat up writing his letter, he was already awake before their batman had come in to wake them up.

He had lain listening to the murmur of voices in the background, heard the pumping of pressure into the Tilley lamps and the soft roar as they were lit. He knew it was early, probably around 4 am but somehow the noise was not foreboding but comforting. It reminded him of something, and it took a while to remember what it was. When he did, he smiled; it was like when he was a small boy, perhaps six or seven, waking up early on Christmas morning, hearing the household come to life, feeling the expectation and excitement build but knowing he could not get up until he was allowed. This day was like that, this was the day, the day of the big push that they had been building up to and, now that his tea had arrived, it was time.

He swung his feet out of the bed. Once out from under the covers he realised how cold it was. He felt for his tea. He had hated the taste of the rough Army tea when he had joined up but now it was the sweetest elixir, strong, warming and reviving.

Would he live through the day? Oddly, with all the death around him, it was the first time that he really thought that he might die, probably would, in fact. It was always going to be the other chap, he, Eddie might have scrapes but he would always survive, that is what his half-formed, subconscious thoughts had been, all the way from training until now. Now, once he had thought about it, he was sure that he would die, and probably today.

Strangely, it did not bother him.

He wondered whether his pre-flight nerves would now be gone. Would he still want to be sick after the briefing? Perhaps not. His gaze fell on Daley's collection of spirits. He resolved to take one of the small bottles of brandy with him. Might as well, it had worked on that flight with Kerr, better to be safe than sorry.

Bean was stirring. For all that he had several hours longer in bed he looked haggard. Perhaps he did not have it in him to get through this, thought Eddie, perhaps he wasn't strong enough. Only the strong would survive, that was what Darwin said, the survival of the fittest. Men like Hastings. Men like Eddie.

Men like Percy.

Eddie shook himself. He was disgusted with himself for what he had just thought, not only about Hastings and himself but what he had thought about Bean. Bean was his friend, a good friend, sensitive and thoughtful, a poet, a musician, a brother, a son. A good man. A good friend.

'Morning, Bean old chap,' he said, smiling.

'Morning, Eddie,' said Bean.

'Sorry about last night.'

'There's nothing to forgive.'

Why doesn't he stand up for himself? Because he's weak, thought Eddie.

*

The weather was foul. Raindrops, driven by a gusty wind, stung Eddie's face as he headed for the mess. It was bitterly cold too, there were flecks of snow on the grass and the ground was sodden. This did not bode well.

Breakfast was a hurried affair, toast, tea or coffee, and most people did not even sit but grabbed what they could and headed for the squadron office to get their assignments. It was clear to Eddie from the number of crews up that both A and B flights had been mustered, only C had been given the luxury of staying in their beds.

Reeves, Pops, Hastings and Milne were gathered round the desk. All looked grim faced.

'We can't send the chaps up in this,' said Milne. 'I'm not sure they would even get off the ground.'

'Oh come on, David, it's not that bad,' said Hastings. 'Once we are up it will be fine. We have a job to do.'

'I'm not sure it will be fine,' said Pops. 'But you're right about the job. Trenchard wants maximum effort. Like David, though, I don't like sending the boys up with the weather like this.'

'We haven't got a choice, let's get everyone assigned,' said Hastings, getting to his feet.

'No! Half the chaps are new, straight out of training. It would be suicide sending them up in this weather,' said Milne. 'Murder in fact.'

'This isn't a game, David,' said Hastings.

'It isn't me who plays with men's lives,' said Milne.

'What do you mean by that?' Hastings bristled at Milne.

'Enough,' barked Reeves. 'Both of you. This is not going to help anyone. Pipe down.'

'Yes sir,' said both Milne and Hastings though neither looked at all placated or admonished.

'Clive and Pops are right,' Reeves continued. 'We don't have a choice. We have to report the gun flashes back to field HQ.'

'But that's crazy. Even if we get the chaps up, they won't be able to see anything.'

'We have no choice. That's my decision.'

'But -'

'We'll ask for volunteers. The chaps won't have to go up if they don't want to.'

'That's not going to help,' said Milne, shaking his head. 'You know what the new chaps are like. They all want to do their bit, they don't know any better.'

'Then we'll make it experienced crews only, at least first thing,' said Reeves. 'It will probably clear up later.'

'Great, the squadron will lose the best chaps. That's wonderful.'

'It's war, David, in case you hadn't noticed,' said Hastings.

'Enough,' said Reeves. 'Most of the chaps are outside anyway. We will ask them.'

'I want to fly,' said Eddie.

Milne threw his hands up in exasperation.

'That's exactly what I meant. He's not been here a week. It's madness.'

'The boy's keen, and he is a good pilot, he got that wreck of a machine back yesterday, remember?' said Hastings.

'I bloody well do remember,' said Milne. 'Well damn you all, I'll be in the hangar with my machine. Just let me know what my sector patrol is.'

Milne angrily pushed by Eddie. He could be heard slamming the outside door.

Eddie saw that Pops and Reeves looked embarrassed but Hastings was smirking.

*

In the end, of the eleven crews mustered, all but one volunteered to try to get up. Reeves, with Hastings assistance, selected six of them to fly the first patrol.

Eddie was one of them.

He was amazed at how much pride he felt. Then he remembered that he didn't have an observer.

He was about to say something when Hastings beckoned him over. He was stood next to an older man, also a second Lieutenant like himself but with the single wings of an observer on his chest. The man was gaunt, he looked pale. Eddie wondered if he had been ill. He saluted Eddie as he came over, which Eddie found odd. Clearly Hastings did too.

'Steady on, old chap, you're an officer now,' he said. 'Well it says so on your shoulders anyway.'

'Oh aye, sir, I forgot,' said the newcomer.

'Well don't forget again,' said Hastings. 'Grenville, this is Brown. He's new in from blighty but he's been out here since the start, did a tour as an observer last year. You're in need of a good chap in the rear seat so I thought of you straight away.'

'Thank you sir.'

'Thought it would be good to put our pair of limpies together.'

'Sir?' said Eddie.

'I got shot down last November,' said Brown. 'Busted me legs up a bit. The docs did a good job but I've ended up with one peg a bit shorter than t'other.'

'Oh right,' said Eddie.

'There's something he's not telling you, Grenville.'

'What's that sir?'

Brown sighed. 'I was with your brother when he had his bad prang. How is the Captain?'

Eddie opened his mouth but could not get anything out. This was not at all what he was expecting this morning. He was glad when Hastings looked at his watch.

'No time for chit-chat,' he said. 'We have to get up. You can catch up with all the family news later.'

Rather stunned, Eddie fell into step with Brown and Hastings as they made their way to the hangar with the rest of the crews. He could see what Hastings meant about the limp, both he and Brown had problems with their left feet. In other circumstances he might well have seen the joke.

Once in the hangar, they received their assignments. It seemed that 159 had been assigned to the central zone just beyond the city of Arras, flying RP patrols.

Eddie knew this job; to spot flashes from any enemy batteries that survived the artillery barrage. The aircraft were bombed up with 8 Cooper bombs under the centre section showing that they were not just spotting.

Hastings confirmed this.

'These are for any targets of opportunity you might see,' he said, slapping his hand onto one of the bombs. 'Machine gun nests, surviving trenches and the like.'

'Just make damn certain they are German,' muttered Milne.

'Of course,' said Hastings. 'Goes without saying.'

'And keep an eye out for other machines,' Milne went on. 'It will be damned easy to get lost and it's going to be dangerous enough without dodging other chaps. Keep your eyes peeled.'

Eddie saw Hastings give a lift of the eye, clearly feeling Milne's warning was unnecessary. He was sure that most of the other crews had seen his dismissive gesture too.

Eddie and Brown had been assigned a section just South of the Railway Triangle, adjacent to Hastings' own area. As soon as the crews had marked up their maps they went to their aircraft. There was no need to take off en-masse, indeed, Eddie realised, it would have been downright dangerous to try. They were going to be on their own on this trip.

The realisation of this and what they were about to do brought on his usual feelings; the nausea, pain that gripped his stomach. This time he was determined to act first.

'Are you fine with our route, Brown?' he said.

'Yes sir...er...Grenville,' said Brown. 'Sorry, still not used to havin' the pips on me shoulder.'

'Eddie is fine,' said Eddie. 'You'd better give your wireless a check over, check your ammunition drums are properly stowed and so on.'

'I already have, sir... Eddie.'

'Give it another look over,' said Eddie. 'I just need to have a last walk around.'

'Fine,' said Brown, though he looked slightly puzzled.

Eddie walked around the port wing, past the fuselage then around the back of the tail fin. There, in the gloom of the hangar he retrieved one of Daley's brandy bottles from his coat pocket, pulled out the cork and took a good swig. The spirit seemed even stronger than Kerr's, Eddie almost choked as it seared his mouth. He forced himself to swallow, forcing it down his throat. He felt it burn all the way down to his stomach. Although it made his eyes water, he was in no doubt that it had done his job. Silently thanking Daley, he put the bottle away and walked to the cockpit.

He saw Brown frown.

'You all right, Eddie?' he said.

'Fine,' replied Eddie, trying to keep his mouth turned away from his observer in case that he caught the brandy fumes.

'You're not checkin' t'other wing then?'

Eddie glanced at the starboard side. Of course, he had had forgotten to complete the pantomime. Nodding, he walked around the wing, checking the tension of the wires and pulling on the strut. All seemed fine. Hoping that he was not blushing he went back to the cockpit and carefully climbed on board. Even as he was fastening his straps they were pushed out into the darkness. He didn't feel at all ready for this. Suddenly he realised he was wishing that Reeves and Hastings had chosen someone else.

The mechanics were waiting to start the prop, they were clearly going to do it inside the hangar, get it warm so they would be ready for the off. In a daze Eddie went through the start-up routine. The engine started at the second pull.

Out of the shelter of the hangar, the RE8 was buffeted by the wind. Two mechanics where on each wing tip, straining to keep the machine from tipping over. The crew chief looked anxious to see them off, and gave the order to swing the prop almost before Eddie was ready. In front of him another machine, he was not certain whose, started its take-off run, the mechanics running alongside holding the wing tips as long as possible before it reached take-off speed and disappeared into the darkness.

Eddie's machine's engine coughed once, picked up, then coughed again and stopped. An Ack Emma dashed to the front, signalling a restart to Eddie. He swung the prop but the RAF V8 was reluctant to start, was it dirty petrol? Bad magnetos? Whatever, Eddie wondered if it was a degree of self-preservation, that it wanted to stay on terra firma. Whatever it meant that, other than the flapping of canvas in the wind and the whine of the wind in the wires, it was relatively quiet so, therefore, it was easy to hear the crash.

The crump and splintering of wood was now a familiar soundtrack, what was more unusual was the fire and the explosion as at least some of the Coopers detonated. Eddie felt the pressure wave and the heat on his cheeks. Briefly the ground crew and the RE8 were bathed in a ruddy glow, Eddie could not avoid the notion that the men looked just like demons holding onto one of Satan's evil devices, ready to unleash it onto God's servants.

Then the glow faded, the prop swung and the engine caught and kept running.

The mechanics stood back, expectantly. It was time to go.

Eddie looked back at Brown, who gave the thumbs up, then signalled the ground crew that he was ready. He opened the throttle and their aircraft began to roll.

He felt the strength of the wind immediately . It was gusting unpredictably, threatening to lift one wing tip and plough the other through the grass. Perhaps that was what had happened to the other aircraft? No, he thought, they must have been well into the air when things went wrong.

He was still speculating when he felt the wheels leave the grass, but this was driven from his mind because he had his hands full trying to keep control. He was still fighting the aircraft when they passed over the scattered fires that marked where their companions had died.

Who was it? Milne was long gone, he was the first off, it could not have been him. Hastings? He was around them in the line. Or Armstrong and Kerr? When had he last seen them?

Well their problems were long since over, he had his own worries.

It was still dark, the wind was strong, even more so at a thousand feet and now it had started to snow. It was light at first, a few swirls, but then it came on stronger, huge white clumps that whirled, and spun around them, hurtling past like the thickest of tracer bullets. It was hypnotic, distracting. It was also settling on his windscreen and on his goggles, he kept having to wipe them but, when he did, the lenses were no clearer. The snow landing on his coat was melting in places, the water finding its way through to soak his legs, making him yet colder.

Panic hit him. He was flying blind, he could not see a thing. How high were they? Were they really at a thousand feet or were they lower? It was impossible to tell. There were hills and the remains of the steeple of the cathedral. What if they were over the town, oh God, they could blunder into something and get swatted out of existence in a second, oh hell, were they even flying level, perhaps they were diving into the ground already. Yes, he was sure that they must be...

He almost pulled back on the stick. It took all his will to make the rational side of himself win over the instinct. He had to rely on his instruments, had to believe that they were flying straight. If he pulled back they could well have stalled, particularly with a strong wind behind them. This low, with what he had already seen with the RE8, that would almost certainly have meant a crash. Their petrol tanks were virtually full, they were bombed up. It would have meant immolation.

He breathed more deeply, trying to calm himself. He desperately wanted another drink, to warm himself, not to give himself courage, he told himself.

Almost magically, as if someone had thrown a switch, the snow stopped. He could at last see where he was going.

It was still dark, and, although he had been trying to follow the right compass bearing, he had no idea where he was. He turned to Brown in the rear cockpit and saw that he was looking over the side at the ground, map folded up in his hand, obviously seeking some sign as to where they were.

Eddie also looked down, then forward, over the nose. That was odd, there was a firefly, just over to the right, looking like it would pass in front of them.

Odd, he thought, how could there be -

He pulled back on the stick and pushed the throttle open so hard that his hand slipped off the lever and he thumped the dash.

In his peripheral vision he saw the black shape and two goggled faces staring up in horror passing just beneath them.

Shaking, he levelled out and throttled back.

Fear hit him like a bitter cud in the back of his throat. He was trembling so violently that not even the two-handed trick worked. How close was that? He wasn't even sure what sort of aircraft it was, a two-seater certainly but whether it was a Quirk, another RE8, one of the new Bristols or even a Hun he wasn't sure. Now he definitely needed a drink. Risking taking one hand off the stick, he pulled off his outer glove with his teeth and felt for the bottle in his pocket. Using his teeth again, he pulled out the stopper, then took a huge swig. The bottle's cork, which he tried to hold in the same hand as the bottle itself, slipped from his grip and was torn away by the slip-stream. Involuntarily, Eddie turned to watch it go - and found him-self staring into Brown's eyes.

Eddie knew that his observer was looking at the bottle. Well, thought Eddie, my secret is out. He took another swig, then offered it back to Brown. 'No point in wasting it,' he shouted, though whether he could be heard, Eddie very much doubted. Whatever, Brown only hesitated a moment before taking the Brandy from him.

Eddie turned back to flying. The spirit had held him, the sour taste of fear had gone and he felt so much warmer. Now to find out where the hell they were, he wasn't even sure whether they were over the front.

As is in answer, beneath them, stretching as far as the eye could see, the ground in a line seemed to flash red and yellow, a roll-ing, spitting fire that banished the night that was followed by the concussion that was like a thousand bass drums all beaten at once. Moments later, as if in an echo, there were flashes over to their front and right, hundreds, no thousands of them, one after the other. This did not stop, it went on and on, the bright flashes and gouts of flame from one side, the duller red/orange detonation from the other.

Eddie knew what this was. This was the final barrage, the lighter guns targeted at the German first and second lines, the prel-ude to the attack proper. Down below them, in the British trenches, men would be lined up ready to go over the top, cold, wet, probably terrified.

Eddie thought about all the shells passing them in the dark-ness. How could they not be hit? He turned back towards the British lines, anxious to get out of the trajectory. If they were directly over the gun line then they would surely be safe.

As he banked around to run parallel with the lines there was a massive flash to the north followed moments later by a second one. He wondered what they could be, clearly they were explosions but what could have made them? He did not have time to think about this before he noticed that the intensity of the artillery fire beneath them had diminished.

Cautiously he edged lower. It was getting slightly lighter. They were approaching the British lines from the rear. There was movement, men were clambering out of the trenches, scaling the ladders and moving out into no-man's-land, in fact it had been clearly going on for some time for, in the gloom, Eddie could make out figures walking forward. Then, from behind them the guns started up again, with answering flashes further into the German lines.

This was the rolling barrage, the line of shells moving forward to hit the enemy, giving the British troops cover. He looked at the line of shell bursts, how could anything survive that? And how much guts did it take to walk right up behind it, trusting that the chaps doing their calculations back at the guns would get their sums right and not drop a deadly load of red-hot iron and copper onto their own?

Possibly the same amount needed to fly an aircraft up through the shells to scout out resistance, Eddie realised.

And now that he had had that thought he found that he was quite unable to make the turn to bring themselves into the line of fire. He knew that he should, must indeed, it was the job that they were there to do but the thought of what that meant filled him with dread. There's no point anyway, he told himself, he had no idea where he was, it was still virtually dark. Even if they did find something, there was no way of calling down a barrage on it because they would need to know the map reference.

But they had the Coopers, a voice inside him told himself. The bombs could do the job that the artillery couldn't do. All he would need to do was see the target.

Still he let the RE8 fly along the British lines.

What would Brown be thinking? Eddie could almost feel the man's eyes boring into his back. He would be comparing Eddie to Percy, thinking what a coward his younger brother was.

Percy would have done the right thing.

Visions of Siggi swam into Eddie's mind.

He banked the aircraft over, following the British troops. It was beginning to get much lighter; he could see where men were looking up at them as they passed over. A few holes appeared through his lower plane and he knew that some of them, high on fear, were taking pot-shots at them, roundels or not. He found himself oddly indifferent to this, compared to the shells, the bullets seemed a trifling matter, mere flea bites, though his rational self told him that their effects would be just as deadly.

They were over the German front lines now, though to call it a line was rather an oxymoron. He had noticed before that the Germans seemed to have a different philosophy about defence, their front line was less strong than the British, more a skirmishing line than fortress. Their main defences, the hard points and the prepared defensive lines were further back, away from the point of the first shock. Eddie could see the logic, if you were fighting defensively it made sense. Whatever, the bombardment had largely obliterated what there had been and, all down the line, he could see that the Tommies had, at least made this first line and were occupying the positions.

There were some points where there was resistance, there seemed to be one point where there was a concentration of British troops in shell-holes about thirty or forty yards from the German lines. Eddie flew towards and over them. Anxious faces looked back up at them. One, carrying a revolver waved up at Eddie and then pointed towards the lines, then jerked back and fell, sliding down into the water at the bottom of the hole. At the same time Eddie felt their machine get hit and banked away. Brown thumped him on the shoulder, Eddie glanced back, his observer leant forward and shouted 'Machine-gun,' though he had already worked this out for himself.

He found that he was surprisingly cool and detached. He kept the point from which he had seen the firing come from in the corner of his vision as he turned back towards the German lines, crossing them he turned back in a wide arc until they were pointing back the way they were come. He couldn't see the machine gunners now because the nose of his aircraft was in the way but he looked down and forwards alongside it trying to catch sight of the denuded tree that he had seen next to the position. He felt bullets striking them but ignored them. Somehow they seemed so insignificant, a part of him wondered why? He felt that he - they - were invulnerable. Suddenly the fear of just a few minutes ago was gone. It was just him versus the machine gunner, no one else mattered. No one else could get in the way.

He saw the tree, a little to the right. He corrected his course. He reached forward and cocked the Vickers gun, then kept his hand on the release for the Coopers.

A star shell went off. The light seemed dazzling after the gloom of the sleet-laden, pre-dawn. He realised that they would be lit up, a clear, slow moving target for everyone, friend and foe, to shoot at, but he did not care. The flare also illuminated his target. He could see the machine gun crew, the gunner himself crouched behind it, the loader feeding the belt and a third man, possibly an ammunition runner, knelt behind the pair. This man was looking back at him. Eddie saw him shake the shoulder of the loader, pointing back at the British aircraft, then reach for his rifle, struggling to swing it around behind him in the confined space, trying to bring it to bear on the approaching RE8.

Eddie fired the Vickers. Dispassionately he saw that bullets were going beyond his target. He pushed the stick forward. The was a spray of mud, water, then flesh and blood mingling in a mist that hung glistening in the fading light of the star-shell. The flare fizzled out, to Eddie it seemed apt, it was like the end of a play, no, not the end of the whole thing, just the end of a scene, a dramatic interlude. Still he fired, then lifted the nose to make sure that he did not fly them into the ground. Even though he was sure that the Germans were dead, he pulled the toggle of the Cooper release twice, then pushed the throttle open and started to climb away.

They were so low that the detonation of the two bombs was almost immediate. The flashes lit up his aircraft again and the concussion lifted them. He felt something strike the tail of the aircraft then they were away. Their path took them over the shell hole where he had seen the officer. There was no sign of him that Eddie could see but the Tommies were advancing again.

'Yes!' he shouted. 'Yes, yes!'

Another flurry of sleet and snow hit them. The flakes flashed and swirled around them like bullets. He could not see again and now he knew for definite that they were very low. He had to climb and had to trust his altimeter that they were doing so. He had to concentrate on keeping the wings level, it would be easy to become disorientated, to spin in.

And suddenly, as if the floodgates had been opened, fear swept over him again. He couldn't see, they were going to crash, he was sure. He was rigid at the controls, he was sure that even if a church spire or another aircraft loomed up out of the gloom now there would have been nothing he would or could have done to stop it, he would have flown them straight into it. He had to fight to get himself to relax, to will his arms and legs to give up their rigor. Even when he felt it ease, he let them keep climbing, the engine at full throttle.

Abruptly they shot out of the cloud into a clear sky.

The sun had not yet come up, Eddie glanced at the clock on

his instrument panel; it was 6.20 am, the first glimmer of light was already turning the sky from black to a myriad lighter shades of blue graduated towards the east. Moonlight bathed the top of the clouds, giving them a gentle soft, silver sheen. The combination of colours was beautiful, almost mystical, restful. It was almost impossible to believe the nightmare that lay beneath. It seemed to Eddie that God had drawn a veil over what was happening below, that he no longer wanted to look, to see the horrors.

Horrors like Eddie himself had just caused.

Now he was up here in the calm beauty of the retreating night, his thoughts turned to what he had just done. It was not the act that disturbed him as much, that was his job, he knew that, his country was at war, killing could not be avoided. No, what bothered him was how it had felt when he was doing it. He knew that what he had done had gone beyond duty; he had enjoyed it, the act and the exultation he felt afterwards.

He was disgusted with himself. How could he feel that? He had killed those men, granted they had killed themselves, they were holding up the attack of the Tommies. He had done his duty, done his job, cleared the way.

But that was not enough to salve his conscious. He had gone beyond that. He had done enough to kill them three or four times over, what he had done was driven by a pure bloodlust.

What had he become?

He felt a thump on his shoulder. Brown! He had almost forgotten about him, he must be wondering what on earth he was doing, flying up above the clouds. Eddie had not even checked the direction he was flying, looking at his compass he found that he was indeed flying virtually due East, deep into enemy territory. He should turn them back, he knew that.

But, for a moment, he was tempted not to. He could keep on flying, land somewhere. They would be taken prisoner certainly, but they would be safe.

Below the clouds were illuminated from beneath, flashing orange and red like a Chinese lantern, hinting at what was happening beneath. Down there men were dying, up here it was so peaceful, beautiful even. It reminded him of what he loved about flying, why he had fallen for its charms in the first place.

Oh to be somewhere so peaceful. To stay here for eternity.

He turned back to Brown and gave him the thumbs up, then swung the machine around to the West, for a moment staying in level flight but then putting the nose down, heading for the clouds and what lay beneath.

It seemed to Eddie that the wisps of grey reached up to them, seemingly determined to drag them back into the darkness.

Back in the clouds, the snow had given way to rain. The visibility was still awful.

Eddie nosed the aircraft down, hoping to see the ground. After the relative lightness of the pre-dawn sky above the clouds he found that, if anything, it was more difficult to make out features than before. He forced himself to fly lower. At last he could see the battlefield, pockmarked with shell holes. He guessed that they were still behind the German lines so pulled the nose up again to climb higher.

As soon as he did, they ran into snow again, even thicker than before. It collected on Eddie's goggles which were now also smeared in oil from the engine. Soon, despite wiping them repeatedly with his gloves, he could see virtually nothing. In desperation he took the goggles off. Ball never flew with goggles, Eddie knew that from the newspapers, so why couldn't he? Well because the snow and sleet stung his eyes, that was why.

He soon knew that it was impossible. They were doing no good here, they had no idea where they were and they could not see what was happening on the ground. It was pointless.

Even then he hesitated. What would Hastings say if he got back to find that Eddie was already there? Would he think him a coward?

Brown thumped him on the shoulder again. What now? Eddie turned around. Brown was shaking his head, pointing back towards the west, mouthing 'Home'.

Eddie nodded and swung them around. There was no choice.

It took half-an hour, battling against the wind to get back to the airfield but, even then, it was with a feeling of dread that he landed with. Eddie was convinced that he would be hauled over the coals for coming back early. He even wondered if they might court-martial him.

It was with some surprise that he found that there were three other machines from the patrol in the hangar already being tended to by the mechanics, two of which had the flight leaders streamers attached to the struts. That meant that both Hastings and Milne were back.

When he switched off and got out, it was Milne who came out of the hangar to greet him. He was frowning, he looked anxious.

'Eddie, are you alright?' he said.

'Yes, fine. I'm really sorry.'

'Sorry? What on earth are you sorry about?'

'For coming back early. We had no idea where we were, did we Brown?'

'No sir, it was bloody awful.'

'Grenville, we've all been back more than half an hour,' said Milne. 'We thought we'd lost you too.'

'Too?'

Milne nodded. 'We lost Johnson and Arnold on take-off and Francis and Lloyd-Davies haven't come back yet.' Eddie saw him look towards the east, scanning the sky. 'It was bloody stupid sending us up in this,' he muttered. 'And for what?' He shook his head, then looked at Brown and Eddie. 'Ah forget it. Good to see you back. Go and get something hot in the mess, there's fresh coffee waiting.'

'Sir,' they both said, and headed off.

Even before they had reached the mess, Bean came loping over. Eddie thought for a moment that his friend was going to embrace him but, perhaps seeing Brown limping alongside him, contented himself with just squeezing Eddie's shoulder.

'Good to see you back, old thing,' he said. Eddie could see that Bean's eyes were red and wondered, albeit briefly, whether his friend had been crying.

*

They had been in the mess for around twenty minutes before Eddie thawed out enough to join in the conversation.

The A and B flight crews who had not flown were there as where some of C flight who were not due to fly until later in the day. All wanted to know what was happening with the attack. Luckily, Eddie found that Brown was able to field most of the questions.

'Yeah, no question, it looks to be going alright,' he said. 'Nothing like the Somme. I was over there on the first day. That was bloody murder. No it looks like the Huns are really on the run this time, good'n proper.'

'Perhaps it will all soon be over,' said a young pilot who Eddie did not recognise. He was sat next to another fresh-faced stranger, an observer, Eddie noted.

'Strachan and Simkins,' murmured Bean in Eddie's ear. 'Replacements for Daley and his pilot.'

'Oh,' said Eddie, sipping his coffee.

'No empty chairs,' whispered Bean.

Eddie knew what he meant. It was one of Trenchard's maxims; there were to be no empty chairs at breakfast. It was meant to stop people moping, missing their pals. The trouble was it was both too well known and totally ineffective. You still did miss people, you were bound to.

'That was a good bit of flying,' Brown said suddenly.

'Pardon?' said Eddie.

'The Hun machine gunners. The way you pinpointed them, well, it just reminded me of flying with your brother.'

Eddie just stared at the table.

'Brother?' said Bean. 'You flew with Eddie's brother?'

'Yes. I was his observer for a couple of months late last year. Mind you I was just a sergeant then.'

'Gosh and you've ended up as Eddie's observer. Well it is a small world isn't it Eddie?'

Eddie allowed himself a monosyllabic 'Yes'.

'So what was he like?'

'The captain? Oh he was the best, very caring for the chaps under him. Always took on the hard jobs, always seemed to be in the air, I think he would have flown night and day if he could 'ave.' Brown was holding a mug of tea. He looked thoughtful as he took a drink from it. 'Mind you, takes its toll that does you know. Hard on a chaps nerves. Some people are just too damn brave for their own good, if you know what I mean.'

Eddie abruptly stood up. Bean and Brown looked up at him in surprise.

'I need to go,' he said. 'Call of nature,' he added in explanation.

'Oh all right, old chap,' said Bean.

Eddie strode out of the messroom. He was at a loss as to where to go. The truth was he had heard enough. He did not want to hear about his brother, good or not. He certainly did not want to hear how much he, Eddie, was like him. That was too much.

He was still dithering in the hallway, wondering whether he should go back to his billet, when Hastings strode in.

'Ah Grenville, good I was looking for you.'

'Sir?'

'We need to be back up. HQ wants us to run RP patrols. Your machine serviceable?'

'I'm not sure. We took a few rounds.'

'Oh yes, I saw you had dropped a couple of Coopers. What on.'

'A machine gun nest that was holding up the advance.'

Hastings looked impressed. 'Good man, that's the spirit. You and your navvy up for another trip?'

In the glow of pleasure at the praise he was feeling in the moment Eddie nodded. 'Yes, absolutely.'

'Fine. Get your man and get over to the hangar. We will be off in ten minutes.'

It was as he was walking back to the mess that Eddie realised what Hastings had called Brown: navvy. For a moment he had wondered, did he mean navigator? Now though he understood. It did seem rather unfair to pick on a chap just because of his lowly birth. Still each to his own.

These thoughts were crowded out by the realisation of what he had volunteered them to do. They were going back over the lines, once again.

Eddie stopped. He turned and ran back to his billet to retrieve another of Daley's bottles.

*

Initially, there were only five crews at the briefing in the hangar. He had an odd feeling when he saw that Bean and his observer Smith were one of them. He could not at first identify the emotion. He wondered at first whether it was fear for his friend but then realised it was something less noble; it was jealousy. Somehow, Bean's presence undermined his own, though why this should be the case he did not know. Trying to put these thoughts out of his mind, Eddie thought about the significance of their only being five crews. He wondered if they were just going with the reduced numbers given their losses that morning, but then Armstrong and Kerr arrived.

Hastings gave a deep sigh and frowned at them.

'So glad you could join us, gentlemen,' he said.

'Sorry,' said Kerr.

Armstrong said nothing. Eddie noticed that there seemed to have been a change in the pilot. He looked gaunt, his eyes were set, rarely blinking. He appeared in a daze. He saw Kerr glance at him a few times whilst Hastings continued with his instructions. Although Eddie was trying to concentrate on what his flight leader was saying, he could tell that Kerr was concerned about Armstrong, deeply concerned.

When the briefing ended and they turned to their machines, Eddie found himself alongside Armstrong. 'Are you alright, Phil?' he asked but Armstrong did not reply, simply walking off towards his RE8 .

'Sorry, Eddie,' said Kerr. 'Leave him be, I'm sure he'll snap out of it.'

'What's the matter?'

Kerr puffed out his cheeks and gave a little shake of the head. 'We had a bit of scare this morning, it's shaken him up a bit, me too, to be honest but it's hit Phil pretty hard.'

'What happened?' asked Brown. 'A Hun? Archie?'

'No, nearly got wiped out by another aircraft. British one too. God knows how it missed us.'

'Oh that was-' began Brown but Eddie quickly interrupted.

'That was terrible. Did you see who it was?'

'No,' said Kerr. 'Think it was a Quirk. Might have been a Harry Tate. Still, dozy idiot, God knows what he was doing.'

'Quite,' said Eddie, giving Brown a warning stare. Fortunately his observer seemed to have cottoned on.

'Anyway Phil has really got the wind up. He was all for throwing it all in, going to the CO and asking to be taken off flying. He's convinced he's on borrowed time. I had a hell of a time persuading him not to, to get back up and get it out of his system. Look, he's watching us, I don't want him thinking we're talking about him.' Kerr gave a little wave of his hand to Armstrong, who was already in the cockpit. 'Look after yourself, Eddie. See you back here for lunch.'

'Good luck, Alan,' said Eddie.

He watched as Kerr walked to his RE8, then turned back to his own machine. He saw that it was a different one to the one he had flown earlier, A4571. One of the Ack Emmas saw him look.

'This morning's kite had a bullet in the front spar, sir,' he said. 'This is a good bus though, sir.'

'Good oh,' said Eddie and climbed into the cockpit.

The butterflies started almost straightaway. He cursed himself for not remembering to have a walk around so that he could have a drink. Well it was too late now, but still he knew that he needed something. He pulled the bottle out of his pocket, uncorked it and took a swig. This, if anything, was more fiery, it reminded him of what he'd drunk with the Australian gunners. He looked at the label: Calvados. He had not heard of it before, he wondered if it was a brand name. Whatever, it had had the desired effect.

He was ready to go again.

*

The flight over was largely incidental. The weather, whilst still cold and cloudy had improved slightly over the previous two hours. Eddie noted that the wind was still strong, though it was coming more from the north, running almost parallel to the lines. At least they would not have a headwind against them when they were coming back.

Eddie did not hesitate as they approached what had been the British lines, he put the nose of the aircraft down, crossing over at around 200 feet. He could now see the scaling ladders in place where the men had gone over the top a few hours before. Further to the east were the first of the bodies, lying where they had fallen, some with limbs thrown wide apart, others curled up in a foetal position. The wounded were being ministered to by medics, the white field dressings standing out like beacons amidst the brown-churned ground, others were being carried back by stretcher-bearers, the latter slithering on the mud as they maneuvered their loads across the broken landscape. Most looked up as Eddie past overhead, none waved.

They were soon at the old German lines. Everywhere Eddie could see khaki, here at least the attack seemed to have been a complete success. Tommies could be seen either making their way forward or else escorting lines of dejected looking, grey-clad men back towards the British support lines. He felt a lift of elation, perhaps it was all over? Was this the great breakthrough? Might they all soon be home?

Eddie suddenly felt another emotion, a sinking, empty feeling in the pit of his stomach. It was a feeling of impending loss, not of any person but this life. What would he do without it?

Those feelings were soon snatched away for they were approaching the line of shell bursts that marked the line of the rolling barrage. Now Eddie felt the familiar prickle of fear, they were flying into the path of the shells again. He could not help to recall the poem about the Charge of the Light Brigade, the Tennyson that he had detested learning at school. He said what he could remember over in his head:

"Forward, the Light Brigade!"
Was there a man dismay'd?
Not tho' the soldier knew
Someone had blunder'd:
Theirs not to make reply,
Theirs not to reason why,
Theirs but to do and die:
Into the valley of Death
Rode the six hundred.

Cannon to right of them,
Cannon to left of them,
Cannon in front of them
Volley'd and thunder'd;
Storm'd at with shot and shell,
Boldly they rode and well,
Into the jaws of Death,
Into the mouth of Hell
Rode the six hundred

Someone had blunder'd? He was not sure about that but there was so much that he understood about the poem now, that you just had to do what you were told and gallop in front of the muzzles of the guns into the valley of Death.

But there were not six hundred, there were just the two of them and, unlike the Light Brigade, they did not do it once but they had to do it time and time again. If you keep knocking on the doors to Death's domain, Eddie thought, one day it is bound to open.

He was shaking again, and this time he let his instincts take over, he pulled the machine away to the right and flew away from the line of bursting shells. Out of the corner of his eye he saw Brown swing the Lewis gun and knew he was quartering the sky, searching for what he thought Eddie must have seen. How was Brown to know that it was sheer funk, sheer cowardice that had caused him to turn away.

'Damn you, Grenville, get a grip,' he said out loud and swung the RE8 back towards the lines. He felt his stomach churn but still he held firm on course.

There were tracks on the ground beneath them, heading in the direction that they were flying, towards the German lines. He had little time to think about it before they crossed over what was creating them, a giant iron monster crawling towards the trenches with a group of Tommies following on behind it. He could hear it clanking and creaking even above his own engine. Almost forgetting where he was, he could not help but circle around it. A tank, the first he had seen in action. He shuddered, what on earth must it be like to see that heading towards you? What could hope to stop it?

But then he got his answer. A fountain of mud and stones erupted just in front of the tank. The shell burst was close enough for the compression to lift Eddie's machine and for him to feel the pressure change in his ears. It reminded him that they were most definitely in the firing line and that they were not there to sightsee. He was about to complete the turn and continue over the front line when a second shell detonated with a savage yellow and red flash on the tank's hull.

For a few seconds the machine was obscured by a cloud of black and brown smoke that bubbled and boiled into the sky, quickly reaching Eddie's level but then it cleared so could see what it had done. The shell had opened the tank up like a tin can, peeling back the metal like the petals of a flower though, instead of stamen and pistil, the centre of this specimen was a fiery heart, more blast furnace than botanical. The Tommies were scattered around the tank like fallen leaves and Eddie did not want to think about what it was like inside. He was convinced that no one could have survived so was surprised when he saw a hatch in the side open.

He continued to circle the wrecked machine - and soon wished that he hadn't. What came out was not a man but something from a nightmare.

It was all on fire, from head to toe, and illuminated all around it, like a beacon in the gloom of the morning. It was not just that tanker's clothes were on fire, his very essence seemed to be burning, the flames rising to at least the same height again above the man's head. What really struck Eddie, shook him to the core in fact, was that the glowing figure moved with no haste. The man did not run, did not roll around in the mud to try and put the fire out, he just clambered slowly out of the tank and walked a few feet away from it before sinking to his knees.

Eddie did not want to see any more. He turned the machine back towards the barrage. They were here to do a job, to spot the very guns that had just done that. That was the brutal answer to the question as to why they were there. He could not help but think that he had failed, that his cowardice had caused the death of the tank crew and the Tommies around it, if he had been on patrol where he should have been he might have seen the flashes of the guns, given Brown the chance to call in the counter barrage. Even though he knew this was silly, that there would not have been time to do anything about it, still the all-consuming guilt drove him on, over the line of bursting shells out into the German held land beyond.

He wondered how the Germans had spotted the tank. It can't have been luck, the fire was directed, he told himself. He searched the horizon and was not surprised to see three Drachens, noses pointing into the stiff breeze. The balloons were perhaps 3 miles inside the German lines and the observers would have a perfect view of no-man's-land.

He felt a sudden flush of anger, a need for revenge. Without thinking he swung the machine around and cocked the Vickers, firing a few rounds to check that it was working. Almost immediately he felt a thump on his shoulder. He turned to find Brown gesticulating, pointing away from the Drachens and shaking his head. Eddie turned back, determined to ignore his observer but Brown was persistent. He thumped Eddie again and leaned forward shouting something. He heard the word 'No!' but knew that Brown was saying something else. He looked back over his shoulder again and saw that Brown was pointing at something on the ground a way to the right of the balloons. Eddie did not at first see what Brown was pointing at but then a series of flashes lit up the spot. Of course, the guns, probably the very ones that had destroyed the tanks. Eddie gave a thumbs up to Brown and turned the RE8 towards their target.

Whilst Brown wound out the aerial for the Morse transmitter, Eddie took over checking the skies around them for hostile aircraft. He also had time to think about what he had been about to do. Had he really been going to attack the balloons? Captain Hollingsworth had told him stories about his attempts at balloon busting, it sounded a deadly business, the Drachens were well defended both by Archie, machine guns and flaming onions as well as often having enemy aircraft nearby waiting to pounce on anyone having a go. Attacking balloons was best left to a nimble scout yet here he was in a lumbering RE8 about to try. It would have been suicidal, what was he thinking? Well, that was the problem, he wasn't thinking, he'd just been out to avenge the tankers.

The vision of the burning man, the human candle, came back to him. He tried to push it away but it wouldn't go.

Brown tapped him on the shoulder again and traced a figure

of eight with his gloved finger in the air. Eddie nodded and started to fly the pattern. This was it, this was the job, this was what they were here to do, this was how they could best help chaps like the tankers. It was not death or glory, teeth into battle, it was not the glamour of the Light Brigade, or the dash of Ball, it was simply the job. He had to do it to the best of his ability, Milne was right about that.

Whilst flying the figure of eight he thought about that. Milne's way, not Hastings', his own flight leader? Yes, although it seemed the safe, cautious way, it was probably the right one.

Something caught his eye, what was it? An aircraft? For a moment Eddie was not sure what it was, only that something had moved in his line of sight. He looked across to the left of the aircraft, wondering what he had seen. Then he saw it, a hole appeared in the fabric of the lower wing, then another. Instinctively he kicked the rudder, dipped the wing to see whether there was an aircraft underneath them that he had not seen but there was nothing. Someone was firing at them, but from where? He looked down, they had passed over a small wood a few moments before. Although he had not reached the end of his pattern he swung them around. He looked back at Brown, he was looking bemused and slightly annoyed and Eddie could understand why; the first shots from the battery were landing around the German guns, Eddie was making the job of correcting the fire more difficult. Feeling slightly guilty at this he persisted, Milne or not he was going with his instincts on this one. He pointed down at the wood which they were rapidly approaching again. Brown followed his gaze, then animatedly pointed himself. Eddie could see what he meant, the wood was twinkling as if it were alive with a thousand fireflies.

Bullets started pinging off their machine. Eddie hurriedly banked away and climbed for height. He looked at Brown who nodded and pulled down the cloth covering his face and mouthed 'Zone Call' at Eddie, who nodded. They had clearly found a concentration of troops, perhaps the reserve about to be thrown into the line to stop the advance. They would not have seen them if they had not given into the temptation to take a pot-shot at the British aircraft. Brown busied himself with the Morse key as Eddie completed the climb and started to fly the pattern again, keeping an eye on the sky around them. He could not help but feel a frisson of excitement rising, he knew that Brown would be signalling to the artillery corps they were assigned to the map reference and then sending 'LL', the signal for 'all'. Every gun in their sector were required to act on it until they were signalled to stop. Eddie and Brown suddenly had the power of a General, albeit fleetingly, and that was all down to him, it was him, Eddie Grenville who had seen it.

The thrill rose as the first shell landed, followed quickly by several more. Soon the whole wood and its surrounds seemed to be erupting, trees, mud, rocks being thrown high into the air.

Eddie's elation disappeared as the true horror of what he had done hit home. Men were dying down there, not just one or two, dozens. They were being lacerated, eviscerated, pulverised.

'You spot them, we shell them,' that was what the Australian Captain had said. 'We all kill.' They had just been words before but now they were real. Now he didn't want to see what he had done, he wanted to go, to get far away from what he had done, but Brown was still at his Morse key, was calling out corrections to the shell falls. They had to stay.

They are the enemy, he told himself. They would have killed our troops if they had the chance.

It didn't make him feel any better.

He could not face looking any more, he searched the sky around them, looking for enemy aircraft. Oddly, even though he knew what the consequences would probably be, he found that he wanted there to be some. At least that would give him the excuse to turn them away from the carnage being wrought beneath them.

And there was something.

At first he thought it might be a drop of oil on his goggles but it was still there after he wiped them and it had moved relative to the clouds. It was slightly higher and heading in their direction. Eddie looked back at Brown, he was still staring over the cockpit side, his hand on the Morse key but he saw Eddie looking at him. Eddie pointed at the incoming aircraft. Brown nodded and swung the Lewis around.

Eddie was not sure what to do, whether to run for the lines or to face the attacker. He was still trying to decide when he saw the machine bank turning slightly away from them, before resuming straight and level flight. Eddie was pretty sure that, even from a distance, he could make out roundels painted on the lower wings. Within another ten seconds he was sure; now he could see the aircraft in profile he could tell that it was a Quirk, and an old one at that, a 2c. He turned back to Brown and gave a thumbs up, although he was sure that his observer had also recognised it and was already relaxing.

Eddie swung them back towards the other machine. He

caught it up within a few minutes and flew alongside it. The pilot waved a gloved hand at Eddie, who waved back. The observer, in the front cockpit, was busy with his camera and plates. Eddie was now used to the RE8s, he found it a shock how slight and frail the Quirk looked. It was like something from another age. He could not believe now that he had gone to war in anything like that. It seemed so long ago.

He glanced away for a moment, checking where they were. A shadow seemed to flash over them, though it came and went so quickly he wondered whether he had imaged it. When he looked back, the Quirk had gone. Puzzled, Eddie dipped his wing, wondering if the other machine had dropped down below them.

There were things fluttering down towards the ground. Was it paper or cloth? He wondered where it had come from, it looked like confetti, twisting and swirling in the morning light. He was entranced, it looked quite pretty. He wondered where it had come from. Then Brown gripped Eddie's upper arm so tightly that he winced. He looked back, his observer's eyes were bulging. Suddenly Eddie knew; the confetti that was all that was left of the Quirk. It had been hit by a shell, almost certainly one that they themselves had called in.

*

They landed back at Acq around forty minutes later. Neither he nor Brown exchanged a word, they just went through the motions of handing the aircraft over to the ground crew as if in a daze. Eddie did glance at Brown as he dismounted the Lewis gun and passed the gun magazines down to the Ack Emmas. He looked ashen faced, numb, in fact mirroring just what Eddie himself was feeling like at that moment.

Eddie waited for him to finish then walked alongside him back to the admin block.

'We need to report to Pops,' he said. 'Pinpoint where we called in the Zone Call.'

Brown just nodded.

They walked on.

'Did you get the serial number of...' he paused. 'That other...' His voice trailed off. Somehow he could not bring himself to utter the words "machine" or "aircraft" though he had no idea why.

'No,' said Brown.

Eddie nodded and the pair carried on into the office.

*

Although it was lunchtime, Eddie did not feel like eating.

His eyes were sore, they felt like they were rotating in sand in their sockets. He had never felt so tired. It was an odd sort of tiredness too; he was not sleepy as such but had a grey weariness that sapped all energy.

He made his way back to his billet. He just wanted peace and quiet, a lie down.

He found himself hoping that Bean was not there.

He wasn't but there was someone in the room. A red-haired young man was laid on Daley's bed. He swung his legs down and stood up as soon as Eddie came into the room.

'I say,' he said. 'You must be one of my dorm chums. Pleased to meet you.' The redhead was smiling as he thrust his hand out towards Eddie.

'Who the bloody hell are you?' said Eddie, keeping his hands by his side.

'I'm Slade,' said the newcomer. 'I've just arrived.'

'Good, well now you have just be quiet, will you?'

Eddie lay down on the bed and closed his eyes.

'That's not very friendly,' said Slade.

'Well I'm not in a friendly mood,' said Eddie.

There was silence for a few moments, broken only by the sound of Slade moving as he sat on the bad. Eddie sighed, it really wasn't friendly, it wasn't the lad's fault. It also wasn't like himself. What was happening to him?

'Sorry,' he said, sitting up. He leant over and offered his hand. 'Grenville. Eddie.'

Slade took the hand and gave a little nod of greeting. Eddie could see that he was wary.

'It's been a tough morning,' he said. 'Good to have you here.'

He did not wait for Slade's reply. He just laid back on the bed and shut his eyes.

He needed to shut out the world.

*

Eddie woke. He was lying on his bed. What time was it? It was dark out, how had that happened? Was he due back on patrol, had he slept in? Hastings would be furious. Panicking, he swung his legs off the bed.

Percy walked into the room. Eddie stared at his brother in shock.

'What are you doing here?' he said. 'When did you come back to France?'

Percy did not answer. Instead he was enveloped by a pillar of flame that twisted and turned, yellow and white, lapping at the roof tiles above his brother's head. Percy did not try to beat the flames out, instead he looked almost serene. He looked at Eddie and smiled as his flesh turned black and his skin blistered.

Eddie screamed.

*

He woke.

It was still daylight.

He looked around. Slade was lying on his bed reading. Bean's was still empty. Slade showed no sign of having noticed anything unusual.

Eddie was relieved, at least he had not cried out in his sleep, though he found that he was bathed in sweat. He felt for his watch. He found, to his surprise, that he had only been in the room perhaps twenty minutes. It felt like he had been asleep for hours although he felt no rested than he had before.

The blanket covering the door to the billet was pulled back and Hastings stepped through. Slade scrambled to his feet. Eddie sat up. Was this real? Was Hastings going to turn into flame too? Momentarily, Eddie was sure that he was still dreaming.

Hastings gave a brief glance at Slade then looked back at Eddie. He frowned. 'What's the matter Grenville, you look a little queer. You're not sickening for something are you?'

Eddie got to his feet.

'Er, no, sorry, I've just been asleep.'

'Well get yourself awake, we've got a job. The Brass want some plates of beyond the Railway Triangle. You up for it?'

'Yes, of course.'

'Good, get your man Brown and get down to the hangars. We leave in twenty minutes.'

With that he was gone.

Eddie sighed and started to get his flying gear back on.

'I say, this is really something, isn't it?' said Slade.

'Is it? How?' said Eddie, pulling his over-trousers on.

'Well this is the real thing, helping out our troops, the generals, helping to win the war.'

'Yes,' said Eddie.

'I can't wait to go over myself. Captain Milne said I would be on this afternoon if the weather clears.'

'I'll keep my fingers crossed for you,' Eddie said.

'Thanks, old chap.'

Eddie did not reply. He checked how much was left in the bottle of Calvados. As there was not much left he uncorked it, swallowed the contents in one go, threw the bottle in his wastepaper bin and took another from Daley's dwindling stock. He walked out of the room without another word.

'Good luck!' Slade called from behind him.

He walked down the billets. He realised that he had no idea where Brown's was. He looked in a couple before he found him.

He was billeted with Finch, the C flight leader, who was sat at his desk writing a letter. Brown was sat on his bed, staring at the ground but he looked up when Eddie came in. He was holding something.

'Oh, we on again, sir?' he said.

'Brown, you're an officer now, well in name at least,' said Finch. 'I know it's difficult for types like you to remember things like that but do at least try to keep up.'

'Oh yes,' said Brown.

'But it's 'sir' when you address me, of course,' said Finch, without looking up. 'I do outrank you - and in more ways than just what the army says.'

You insufferable prig, thought Eddie.

'Yes, Brown, we're on again,' he said.

His observer nodded and stood up. Eddie could now see that he was holding a small photo frame. In it was a picture of three quite small children, two boys and a girl, stiffly dressed in their Sunday best. The boys were staring into the camera, looking serious but the girl, who must have been about 5 or 6 had a mischievous grin on her face. Brown carefully put the photograph frame on the table at the end of his bed.

'Yours?' asked Eddie as Brown started to get into his flying gear.

'Yes,' Brown smiled. 'They are.'

'You and your wife must be very proud,' said Eddie.

'The wife's dead,' said Brown. 'Zeppelin raid. They're with her mum and dad now.'

'Oh right,' said Eddie. 'Is that why you-'

'Yes,' Brown said quickly.

Finch gave a loud sigh. 'If you don't mind, I am trying to concentrate here you know. I'm sure Brown's domestic arrangements are fascinating but I, for one, really don't want to hear about them,' he said. He looked at the picture. 'It's bad enough having the blighters staring at me all day,' he added.

Brown said nothing, though Eddie could see the anger in his face. He picked up his gloves and flying helmet. 'I'm ready,' he said.

As the pair turned to leave, Finch called out, 'I'll leave my boots out for you, Brown. See they are cleaned and polished and by my bed for the morning, there's a good chap.'

Eddie turned around, his own temper rising, but Brown grabbed him by the arm.

'Leave it,' he said. 'Pay no mind to it. It's just the Lieutenant's bit of fun.'

Eddie was reluctant to leave but Brown firmly guided him out of the room, leaving Finch smirking at his desk.

'What's wrong with him?' Eddie said as they headed for the outside. 'And why do you put up with being spoken to like that?'

Brown shrugged. 'It's just his way. He doesn't think I'm the right sort to be an officer. He's right too, I don't know why I agreed to it, but that's by the by now, I did and I'm here.'

'But still -'

'Still nothing, sir...I mean Eddie. He's still my senior officer. I've been in long enough to know that I must defer to him, right or wrong. It don't matter, it's just words. Words can't hurt me.'

Eddie nodded. 'I suppose not. How long have you been in Brown - I say, I can't keep calling you that, what's your name?'

Brown smiled. 'It's Alfred sir, I mean Eddie. Everyone calls me Fred though. And I was a territorial. Joined up in '12 into The East Riding Yeomanry. I volunteered for overseas service in August 1914. Other than being in t'hospital I've been out here ever since.'

'Good heavens, Fred, how have you stood it?'

'Oh it's not that bad, you know. And this life is a damn sight better than being up to your armpits in mud, believe me!'

'I can understand that.'

Brown had been smiling but then it was almost as if a cloud had gone over his face. 'It's different now though than when I was out before. The machines are better but…'

'But what?'

'It's harder, more dangerous. There's more Huns about. And what happened this morning. That other machine. I don't know about you but it shook me. I've seen lads killed before but that.' He gave a little shudder.

'Yes,' said Eddie. 'Me too.'

'Before I just wanted to get my own back, for Mary, that was the wife you know. Now I'd really like to get back for the nippers. I really would.' They were almost at the hangars now and Brown abruptly stopped. 'Eddie?' he said.

'Yes, Fred.'

'I know you carry a bottle with you.'

Eddie felt himself flush. 'Yes, it's just for a bit of warmth. It calms my stomach too.'

Brown gave a rueful smile. 'I know. I just wondered if I could have a shot of it now.'

Eddie smiled too and pulled out the bottle and passed it over. When Brown had finished with it he took a mouthful too. For the first time he realised that this one was whisky. It did not burn quite as much as the Calvados but still had the desired effect.

Inside the hangar the machines were being prepared. Eddie could see that there were three of them and that Armstrong and Kerr were already waiting. Armstrong face still looked strained but he looked rather better than he had this morning, though Eddie noticed Kerr still glancing at him. The lower cowling was still off one of the machines with ack emmas working on it. Kerr stepped closer to have a look at what they were doing and Eddie joined him.

'This one yours?' he said.

Kerr nodded. 'Yup. It's got an oil-leak. We're a bit short of serviceable grids today but they reckon they can get it fixed.'

'Good,' said Eddie. He glanced over at Armstrong who was stood by the tail. 'How's Phil?'

'He's all right,' said Kerr. 'Well, better anyway. Still a bit quiet but he seems to have grown out of the idea that he is going to buy it at any moment. Good bloke is Phil.'

'I know.'

Kerr glanced at Armstrong again. 'Although…' he said then

stopped speaking, his lips set straight.

'Although what?' Eddie asked quietly, making sure the mechanics could not hear.

Kerr said nothing at first, indeed the pause was so long he wondered whether he had not heard or was unwilling to answer.

'We did turn around on the last one,' he said at last. 'Engine trouble. At least that's what Phil said, that it wasn't giving full revs.'

'Well, it did have this leak.'

'It wasn't this machine, we had 4048. It's being checked over now, that's why we've had to take this one.'

'I'm sure Phil wouldn't -'

'Hold up, here comes Albert,' interrupted Kerr, nodding over to the entrance to the hangar. Sure enough Hastings and his observer had just walked in, the latter carrying maps. Hastings noticed them standing by the engine and came over.

'Problem?' he said.

'Just a bit of trouble with an oil leak,' said Kerr. 'It'll soon be fixed.'

'Well make certain it is. You know what I feel about chaps dropping out of formation and turning back for trivial reasons. There's too much of it.'

Kerr's face was set. 'Phil and I have never turned back for no reason,' he said.

'I wasn't saying you, I was just talking generally,' said Hastings. 'There's too much of it. You have to admit that.'

'If you say so. Sir.' said Kerr. The coldness in his voice was obvious. Hastings either was unaware of it or chose to ignore it.

'People in my flight need to pull their weight or they can ship out. Let's do the briefing,' he said.

'Perhaps we'd like to ship out,' said Kerr.

Hastings turned, his face angry.

'I beg your pardon? What did you say?'

Kerr glanced at Armstrong. 'I think you heard me, sir. We were quite happy flying with Captain Milne. It wasn't our choice to come over to your flight. Sir.'

Eddie wanted to tell Kerr to stop, he could tell that this was doing no good. Hastings came closer and got right in Kerr's face.

'That's enough of your lip, lieutenant. I don't give a damn how David runs his outfit but, like it or lump it, you are flying with me now and you'll do things my way. Yes, you can ship out but you'd so under a charge, I'd see to that believe me. Do you want it to be that way?' Hastings' eyes were bulging as he leant over Kerr. 'Well do you?'

Eddie saw Kerr swallow 'No sir,' he said.

Hastings continued to stare threateningly at the observer for a few more seconds, then relaxed a little. 'Right, then that's the last I want to hear about it. Come on, let's get the briefing done. We should be away by now.' He turned and walked away.

Eddie and Kerr followed him over to where the others were waiting. Eddie could tell that Kerr was seething and was struggling to hold his tongue. He saw him look over at Armstrong but the pilot's face was pale but impassive.

He doesn't care, thought Eddie. Why doesn't he care?

*

Although it had improved, the weather was still poor, at best marginal for flying but the three aircraft had successfully taken off and had spent the first twenty minutes climbing for altitude before Hastings signalled for them to head for the lines.

As they did, Eddie noticed that Armstrong's machine was trailing a light smoke trail, not so much from the exhausts but from the engine itself. He drew his own machine closer alongside and waved to attract the attention of the other crew. He saw Kerr look down and behind him, then lean over and talk to Armstrong who did the same. It was obvious to Eddie that there was some discussion going on in the RE8.

A rattle of a machine gun made Eddie jump and look around him. They were still on the British side of the lines, surely there wasn't a Hun scout over this far? Quickly he realised that it was Hastings firing his Vickers to get their attention. He was on the far side of the pair, looking over at them. Eddie could see him shake his head and point forward, over the lines towards enemy territory. The message was clear; keep going, don't turn back.

Eddie saw Armstrong nod and turn his head forward again. Kerr looked across at Eddie and gave a shrug, then look behind him at their smoke trail.

Eddie let his machine drift away from the other aircraft. Hastings was right, he was sure, the smoke trail was probably just the remnant of the oil leak. The mechanics had been working in a rush to get the machines ready and had probably not had time to clean up the mess properly. The smoke trail was almost certainly just the residue burning off against the hot engine. Still the smoke trail was alarming, it was like a finger pointing straight at Armstrong and Kerr. In their stead he would have been very tempted to turnaround.

At least the cloud cover, though intermittent, gave them a degree of cover. It would make taking photos harder but against a clear blue backdrop they would have stood out far more.

They crossed the lines with little trouble. It seemed that the British advance and the artillery barrage which was continuing before them was disrupting the Archie batteries. Eddie was glad of that at least.

As they approached their target, however, their problems increased. The cloud cover below them was more continuous with only a few gaps below which the ground could be made out. Hastings signalled for them to circle. Eddie realised that he was waiting, hoping that a gap would appear in the clouds driven by the stiff breeze. Looking down he tried to gauge whether this was likely. It did seem possible but how long it would take was anyone's guess. He could not help but look back at the trail of smoke that was coming from Armstrong's aircraft. He suddenly felt very exposed.

Hastings was signalling. He was pointing at Armstrong and Kerr then pointing down at the clouds beneath. Eddie looked, there was a gap in the cloud approaching. Ah, he thought, he wants us lower, that would give a better chance of getting some plates over the target. Armstrong was nodding, conferring with Kerr, and put the nose of his machine down, aiming at the gap.

Eddie was just about to do the same when he saw that Hastings was now waving at him. He pointed to himself, then at Eddie, then put the palm of his hand flat, then circled his fingers around. He had to repeat this twice before Eddie got it. The pair of them were to stay up high, to circle.

He nodded his agreement but was puzzled. Why were they doing this? The briefing was that they should all photograph, the more aircraft they had, the more of the ground that could be covered. Granted this depended on them being able to see the battlefield below but still, why was Hastings only using Armstrong and Kerr? It seemed very strange but Eddie did as he was bid, indeed followed Hastings in climbing slightly.

When Hastings levelled out and started circling above the third machine, the truth dawned. Looking down, although the smoke had diminished somewhat, the trail was clearly visible against the grey clouds beneath. His instructor, Hollingsworth had told Eddie about these tactics when it looked like Eddie was going to be a scout pilot, about how to use another, slower, machine as bait. Hastings had put them in a perfect position, using the broken upper layer of cloud as cover.

Eddie felt sick, it was fine to talk about this on paper, sat safely on the ground, it was exciting to hear about how Hollingsworth had used this in France over the Somme in his little DH2. But they were not in a speedy scout, they were in a lumbering Harry Tate and down there was not some anonymous reconnaissance aircraft, down there were his friends, Armstrong and Kerr. Phillip and Alan.

Hastings was using them as bait.

It didn't seem right.

The next twenty minutes were wearing on the nerves, scanning the skies above and around and casting anxious eyes down a thousand feet of so to where the other RE8 was flying backwards and forwards, chasing the gaps in the clouds. He was sure that at any moment that they would be attacked, but no other aircraft appeared. Eddie could see Kerr working the camera, gradually working through his stock of plates.

He urged him to hurry up, to expose all the plates as quickly as possible but he knew that Kerr was not like that. He would want to do the job properly.

Eddie thought of Armstrong. He could see the pilot scanning the sky as well as flying a straight as path as possible for his observer. What demons was he fighting off? Armstrong' nerve was shot, how he was still able to fly was beyond him.

At last, it seemed they were done, either because Kerr had run out of plates or because the clouds cover was just too bad for them to continue. Whatever, he fired a green Very Light and Armstrong swung the machine around to the west.

Eddie breathed a sigh of relief. At last it was over. They could go home.

He looked across at Hastings and was relieved to see him nod and point towards the lines. For a moment he had wondered if Hastings would insist on them continuing the patrol.

As he banked the aircraft around he put his nose down slightly so that they would gain a little speed; Armstrong and Kerr were a little way in front, he saw something that puzzled him. There was briefly a dark shadow behind and beneath Armstrong's aircraft. It was such a fleeting image that Eddie was not sure whether it was there at all or whether he had imagined it.

Had he seen it? If he had was it just a trick of the light, a shadow cast from the other machine perhaps? He kept staring at the relative point in the sky where he had seen it, perhaps a hundred yards or so behind the other RE8. After a minute when nothing appeared he was sure that he must have imagined it.

Then, rising like a shark from the depths, an Albatros ascended through the clouds.

Eddie yelled a warning though he knew it was pointless. He put the nose of his machine down and opened the throttle. He did not look to see whether Hastings had followed suit, his concentration was on the German machine.

It was not gaudily painted like the others he had seen, this one was a soft honey colour. It was gradually overhauling Armstrong and Kerr, sitting in the blind spot under their tail. Eddie saw the pilot leaning forward, concentrating, but then look back over his shoulder right at Eddie's machine, stare at him for a moment, then turn back to look forward again.

He knew they were there! He knew they were there and it didn't bother him, the glance was one of dismissal, it said quite clearly: I'm going to do this and there's nothing you can do to stop me. The worst of it was that Eddie knew that he was right, they were too far back. He would never get there.

In desperation, Eddie cocked the Vickers and fired, hoping to get Kerr's attention. He saw the observer look up at him, then scan the sky above and behind them.

'No, you idiot, look below you,' yelled Eddie.

He had a grandstand seat for what happened next. It seemed to happen in inexorable slow motion.

The nose of the Albatros lifted slightly. The twin machine guns over the nose fired. Eddie could see the tracer bullets pass up into the RE8, through the centre section, the wings and the cockpit. There was a burst of vapour - steam probably from the radiators - then the machine turned sharp left and corkscrewed down into the clouds.

Someone was shouting, swearing, mouthing obscenities at the top of his voice. Eddie realised that it was himself. He fired the Vickers again, even though he was still over a hundred and fifty yards from the German machine. The pilot looked back at him again then, with a casual, almost dismissive wave of his hand, banked down and disappeared into the clouds.

The sky above the clouds was now clear. There was nothing left to indicate what had just happened, no smoke, no debris.

There should be blood, he thought, blood in the water.

Eddie was almost at the top of the clouds himself now. He hesitated, lifting the nose slightly to skim the tops. It was like the surface of some milky sea. What lay beneath? There was at least one predator, he knew that. Would he be waiting in ambush for them? No, he would be more likely finishing off Armstrong and Kerr. That made the decision for him, he had to help if he could. He pushed the nose down, then, out of the corner of his eye, saw Hastings' machine speed by him and plunge into the vapour, turning in the general direction of where the Albatros had been.

Then he was in the cloud. Usually he enjoyed this plunge, when the light dimmed, when you felt the chill of the moisture all around you. Now it was threatening, terrifying, he had the notion that there were ghosts all around them, chill wraiths that plucked at his machine and the bodies that sat within, insubstantial, yes, but ones intent on sucking the life and warmth out of them.

Then they were through.

Above the clouds, other than when the Albatros had intruded, it had been peaceful, beneath them lay the battlefield pockmarked with shell holes, full of smoke and noise. He could hear the crump of the shell bursts even above the engine and the roar of the wind through the airframe, he could even smell the bitter tang of chemicals and cordite.

Eddie searched for the Hastings and the German aircraft. He could not see either, though he presumed the former was still around, waiting to ensure that Armstrong and Kerr were dead and also for the chance to add to his score with one of the other machines. Eddie looked back at Brown, he was facing back, his hand on the Lewis, scanning the sky. Good man, thought Eddie, at least our tail is covered.

Knowing this, he started to scan the ground, convinced that he would see the crashed remains of Armstrong and Kerr's machine. To his shock he could see not one crashed aircraft but several. Which was theirs? Were they all British? Surely not.

He was about to go lower when a movement to the left caught his attention. It was an aircraft, low down but in the air, perhaps at 500 feet or so, heading north. That was parallel to the lines. What was it doing? Was it a Hun? Or one of theirs on a reconnaissance flight? Eddie turned towards it.

He soon saw it was an RE8 trailing vapour. He opened his throttle and flew a course to intercept it, checking that Brown was still covering the skies behind them first. The other machine was flying slowly so he soon caught up with it. Even before he did he could see from the markings that it was one from his own squadron. As he drew alongside he could see that it was Armstrong and Kerr.

His surprise - joy even - of finding them still flying quickly vanished. Their aircraft was a wreck, the central part of the fuselage was shredded, the windscreen shattered, part of the cowl was gone and strips of fabric was torn from both wings and trailed backed in the slipstream.

Both Armstrong and Kerr had been hit, the pilot was hunched forward, his left hand gripping his own upper arm, whilst Kerr's head was lolling against the cockpit side. For a moment Eddie thought he might be dead but, as he edged closer, Eddie saw him look across and raise a weary hand in acknowledgement.

A sharp crack made Eddie jump and look around him. Black puffs of Archie were all around reminding him they were; well over the wrong side of the lines and over the German rear area. At least the Albatros was not back, he reflected, but then realised that they would not stay away for long if they continued to fly this course and attract this amount of attention. Armstrong and Kerr were in no state to defend themselves, they should change course, fly west, back over the lines.

Eddie had another thought: Armstrong and Kerr were both wounded, they needed medical attention. Wouldn't it be better for them to land as soon as they could, even over the German side of the lines? Eddie looked down, the attack was still going on, would they have the common decency to look after the crew if then did manage to land?

More Archie burst around them. The gunners were getting their range and they were flying straight and level. That was suicide, he would have to do something. He made a decision.

He waved at Kerr, attracting his attention, then pointed firmly to the west with his outstretched arm, jabbing his hand in the direction of the British lines. Even so, it took some time for this to sink in with Kerr, he seemed bemused about what Eddie was telling him. At last though, he seemed to understand. He nodded and leaned forward, bringing his head alongside Armstrong. Eddie saw Armstrong nod his head and start a slow turn in the right direction. The RE8 wobbled and dipped halfway around, Eddie was afraid that they might stall and spin they were going so slowly but, eventually, it righted itself on roughly the right course, so he closed up alongside again.

He was having to throttle back to keep in station with the other aircraft. He looked down, the ground beneath them was barely moving. He knew the wind was strong and they were virtually nose into it now. He estimated their ground speed to be no more than 30 knots.

They suddenly seemed even more vulnerable, the pair of them. This was taking too long, surely some German patrol would see them, or Archie get their height and range, they were a sitting target. A chill of fear rose within him, he started to imagine the pain that the red-hot shrapnel would cause as it ripped through his soft innards, or the tearing of bullets through flesh and bone.

Bone.

He remembered John, his skull shattered by the bullets.

He began to shake, his broken foot started to throb, to hurt almost as badly as it had the first morning after he had done it.

'Come on, come on you miserable bastards, go faster, go faster can't you? You're killing us all here.'

As soon as he had yelled it this the guilt hit him. It was almost as bad as the pain. This was Armstrong and Kerr he was shouting at, his friends. They couldn't help it, they were wounded, their aircraft was a wreck. He had to stay with them.

But did he? What good was he doing flying alongside them? What could he do?

Just be there for them, he told himself. Just being there was enough, it gave them a companion, hope.

What would Hastings do in these circumstances? Eddie was sure that he knew. Milne though, he would do what Eddie was doing, it was the right thing, even though it was also foolhardy. But where was Hastings anyway? Eddie looked around, there was no other aircraft in sight. Had he seen them? Had he abandoned them, done the rational thing?

Well he was right, wasn't he? Eddie needed to get him and Brown out of here. He moved his hand to the throttle, he so wanted to push it forward, to accelerate away. It took all his willpower not to do it.

He looked back across at the other aircraft. The crew had returned to the positions that they had been in when he had first seen them. It was clear that they were badly wounded, barely able to keep going.

Yes, they were finished, leave them, they knew the risks.

Eddie shook his head. How could he think things like that? The poor sods.

Then he saw something that chilled him. There was a tongue of flame just under the engine of the other machine. It was only small, just a small yellow flame coming from the very end of the engine bay where the metal gave way to canvas and ply.

Eddie waved frantically at the other machine, pointing down underneath them. Armstrong and Kerr paid no attention.

'Look, you damn bastards, look,' Eddie yelled.

There was no reaction. The flames were growing bigger but were still underneath the aircraft.

Eddie continued fired his gun. There was still no reaction.

A rattle of a machine gun behind him made jump, tracer arched close over Kerr's head. Eddie looked back, it was Brown, of course, good old Brown, he was alive to what was going on, it was he who had fired over the other crew.

This time Kerr did stir. He looked across. Both Eddie and Brown were pointing down at the fire which was now streaming underneath the fuselage of the RE8 and leaving a ragged black smoke trail behind them. Kerr looked over the side. Even now he did not react as Eddie had expected. He just stared at the flames and smoke as if he had never seen such a phenomenon before.

'Get down, land you fools!' Eddie yelled, even though he knew it was a pointless thing to do.

Once again Brown fired over the head of Kerr. This time when he looked both Eddie and Brown pointed down. He nodded and leant over to Armstrong, Eddie could see the effort that this was taking.

He saw Armstrong look over the cockpit side, saw him nod. The nose of the RE8 went down.

There was a flash. The entire front part of the machine erupted in a ball of flame. It enveloped all of the cockpit, Armstrong was totally surrounded. The slipstream bent the flames backwards over the rear cockpit, though Kerr was protected from the worst of it by Armstrong's body, and then arched it down to the tail which quickly blackened and blistered, the fabric burning away, as it was on both wings.

Amidst the flaming comet, Eddie saw Kerr look straight across at him. The observer lifted his hand and gave a little wave.

Then the aircraft turned on its back and plunged straight down. It was only a few hundred feet, taking perhaps only five seconds but in that time the wings folded back and the flame turned from yellow to blast-furnace white before the machine hit the ground with a thud that Eddie could hear even above the noise of his engine. Mud and stones were flung in the air and there was a gout of flame. A mushroom shaped cloud of black smoke boiled up,

Eddie had, without thinking, banked round to circle the falling aircraft and could not avoid flying through it. The smoke was hot, it smelt of petrol, oil, dope from the fabric and - he could not help but think - of the smashed and burnt remains of Kerr and Armstrong.

There was no point staying, he did not want to look anyway. He levelled out and flew away.

This was a nightmare, he thought. Please let it be a nightmare, let this be something I can wake up from, let Alan and Phil be still alive.

He knew he was not asleep. This was not a nightmare.

At least one he could not wake from.

Then Brown was thumping him on the shoulder. What did he want? Eddie looked back, puzzled. Brown leant forward and yelled, 'Where are you going?'

Eddie looked at his compass, it was no help, it was still spinning from the sharp bank he had done over the crash. He tried to work out where the sun was, the clouds had closed over. Looking down he quickly found some smoke and understood; he was flying East, away from home.

He could carry on this way, he thought, tell everyone he had got lost. It was cowardice though, it was against the Military Code, he could be court-martialled for it, shot even. But when would anyone find out, when the war was over? When would the war be over? From what he had seen it looked like it would never finish, you could easily imagine this stalemate going on forever. He would be a prisoner, certainly, but he would not have to see any more of the things he did not want to see.

He was tempted. Would the truth ever come out?

He thought of Percy. Who cared about the truth anyway?

He still did. He thought he did. Truth and honour, if you don't believe in that, why bother with anything at all?

Eddie turned to Brown and gave him a thumbs up, then turned them back to the west. Back home.

*

They landed in the middle of a rain shower.

The grey skies and dampness gave Acq an appropriately dull and dour atmosphere. It felt like there would never be any more joy in the world, that it would be sad, cold and wet forever. As Eddie taxied up to the hangars it was like he was wading into a sea of memories. It was from about this spot that he and Kerr had taken off from just a few days before. Over by the hangar was where Kerr had stood over him and passed him the flask of brandy to ease his nausea. Kerr, smiling and helpful. Alive.

No more.

Eddie stayed in the cockpit of the aircraft for a few moments. The ack emmas seemed to sense that he needed time and hung back. He suddenly felt very weary, that he did not have the energy to get out. He wondered why; he was 19 for God's sake but suddenly he felt 90.

What was wrong, surely he could cope with...?

He tried to think, how many flights had he made today? Three? Four? He just could not be sure. He closed his eyes. He felt like he could sleep, right there in the cockpit. Perhaps he could, perhaps they would refuel and rearm the machine around him, wake him up when it was time to go again.

But then visions of Armstrong wreathed in flames and Kerr looking over at him came, like dreams - nightmares - crowding into the waking world as if they could not wait until night so he opened his eyes and climbed out of the aircraft. Brown was already out. Neither said a word to each other. There was nothing to say.

Eddie saw that Hastings' machine was already back and was being wheeled into the hangar. Of Hastings himself there was no sign but Milne was stood under the cover of the entrance, staring out into the afternoon's drabness. He saw him glance across at Eddie then look back away to the east.

He's waiting for Armstrong and Kerr, Eddie realised, then also became aware of his responsibilities. He had to be the bearer of the news, only he and Brown had witnessed it.

Steeling himself, he walked towards Milne. His limbs felt leaden, his foot throbbed and he knew he was limping. Milne looked straight at him as he approached.

'They're not coming back,' Eddie said.

Milne's face was impassive, set almost as if it were made of stone.

'Is there any hope?' he said.

'No,' said Eddie.

Milne said nothing, then gave a little nod. He looked across at Hastings' machine.

'Did he cause it?' he said.

Eddie hesitated, and knew in his hesitation that he had given himself away. Milne interrupted.

'I bloody knew it,' he said, turning away. 'The bastard.'

Eddie was shocked. He had never heard Milne swear before.

'It wasn't Hastings' doing. They didn't keep a proper lookout. A Hun managed to get behind them. It was their own stupid fault.'

Eddie was shocked to realise that it was himself who'd said this. Was that really what he believed? Milne clearly felt the same because he turned around sharply and stared at Eddie.

'I beg your pardon?' he said. 'What did you mean by that?'

'I meant just what I said, they were careless. It was no surprise that they got it in the neck.'

Milne just stared at him, then shook his head.

'I don't know what's happened to you, Grenville, I really don't,' he said then turned and walked away.

Eddie stayed where he was. Why had he said that? Did he believe it? Really believe that? If he didn't why had he said it? It was like he was cursing his friends, insulting their memory. Yet, despite this he knew, deep down, that he *did* believe it. They died because they were weak and careless, that was all. It would not happen to him.

It was that thought that made him feel better.

He realised that he was not alone. Turning he found Brown stood a little way away from him. Eddie knew that he had heard everything. Their eyes met briefly, long enough for Eddie to see the disappointment written in them. He could tell what his observer was thinking.

'I'm not my brother,' he said.

'No, you're not,' said Brown, then walked off towards the squadron office.

Eddie stayed in the hangar. He looked across at the point where he had been sick and Kerr had stood over him.

'Sorry, Alan,' he murmured then he, too, headed into the warmth.

*

After making his report to Pops, Eddie headed downstairs, There were half a dozen other crews in the mess, mainly from A flight. There was a buzz of conversation when he stepped through the door but this died away to nothing as he walked into the room. Puzzled, he said nothing but sat in one of the old armchairs, leather-covered but rather tatty, apparently recruited from the neighbouring chateau, next to two of the A flight pilots who he recognised but had barely talked to. He saw them glance at each other, then get up and move to the other side of the room.

Eddie was nonplussed. They were cold-shouldering him, but why? What had he ever done? Then he realised. These were Armstrong and Kerr's former flight-mates. They would have known them well, they would be mourning them. But why blame him?

Then he remembered what he had said. Milne probably would not have passed it on but there were witnesses. Armstrong and Kerr's flight sergeant and crew were around, they had come across to B flight with them. That was not uncommon, his brother had written to him about it the previous year, about how the ground crew had formed a bond, almost like family and how his crew had been really upset when Percy had been transferred into another squadron and that they could not come with him.

He recalled the look on the crew's faces when he had told Milne. The Flight-Sergeant had looked pained but was stoic but one of the mechanics had turned away, clearly distraught. And then he had gone and said what he had. They had overheard and then word would have been passed around, this was like a little village and, in such places, it was impossible to keep confidences.

Eddie's mood rapidly shifted from guilt to anger. For God's sake, he had risked his life to go and help them, he had flown alongside them, tried to get them home. Didn't any of that matter?

Well damn them all, they could go to hell.

He needed something to warm him. One of the mess orderlies was cleaning some cutlery and putting them in the drawers of the dresser that was up against one of the walls.

'You man, stop doing that and come over here,' Eddie said loudly.

'Yes sir,' said the man, 'I was just -'

'Don't give me any lip, get your arse into gear and get me some tea.'

'Sir,' said the orderly.

'And put something in it,' Eddie shouted after him.

The man hurried off. He saw some of A flight looking at him in some disdain.

'And you can sod off too,' he muttered under his breath and picked up an old paper to read.

Over the next minute he first seethed but then realisation of what he had said and done sunk in. Hell, he had acted and sounded just like his father. He loved the old chap, he had to, he was his father after all but he had always hated his bombast and the way he had treated people who he considered his inferiors. Percy hated it too, it had been a source of friction between father and elder son.

He had sat with Percy, Siggi and Alice once whilst the other three had discussed the world and where it was going. They had not included Eddie, perhaps not even really noticed that he was there but he had listened as Siggi had talked about the socialists in his country, how they were millions of them in Germany, how they were one of the biggest parties in the German parliament, how he could see that one day it would be them in power and not the Kaiser and the army as it was then. Percy had agreed, he had said that he could see it happening in Britain too but that it would be slower, that it would take time unless something like a revolution happened and the British did not go in for things like that.

'Or a war,' Alice had said, quietly.

Percy and Siggi had disagreed, they said a war could not happen, that politicians were too careful but Alice stuck to her guns. She said war was inevitable, that people were too proud, too stupid, too intent on building armies and dreadnaughts not to want to use them, to prove that they were stronger, to impose their wills and philosophy on others.

And she was right, wasn't she? She was right and Siggi was dead, she was a widow and Percy was his killer.

And Eddie was not becoming like his liberal siblings or Siggi but was turning into... Into what exactly? Into his father he was going to say, but he was not sure exactly what he was turning into. Whatever, he wasn't himself anymore.

He would try to do better. Starting by apologising to the orderly when he returned.

*

He opened his eyes. For a moment he did not know where he was. There was an engine, oh God had he fallen asleep flying again. He felt for the joystick, there was nothing. He yelled out in horror, kicked out with his legs to find the rudder bar. His bad foot hit something solid and the pain jolted him back into full consciousness.

He was still in the mess. People were looking at him, other pilots, observers, two of the mess orderlies, Finch, the acting leader of C Flight. He had kicked the table in front of him, upsetting the cup of tea that was sat on it.

'Sleeping beauty awakes,' said Finch loudly. 'And without a kiss from his Prince too.'

'His Prince is missing,' said another voice.

'Sorry,' said Eddie, moving to right his teacup.

'Let me do that for you, sir,' said one of the orderlies, pushing him to one side, taking the cup from him and mopping up the spilt tea.

'Sorry,' said Eddie again.

'That's all right, sir,' accidents will happen. Shall I bring you another one sir?'

Eddie just looked at him. He was trying to work out whether this was the same orderly that he had been rude to before. It bothered him that he could not remember whether it was or not. Hellfire that was a man, with feelings, yet he had treated him like he was a piece of the furniture.

'No,' he said at last. 'No, thank you. Sorry about before.'

'Sir?' said the orderly, looking puzzled.

'Nothing, forget it,' said Eddie. 'What's your name, corporal?'

'Hickson, sir.'

'Thank you, Hickson, for clearing up after me.'

Hickson smiled. 'That's alright, sir, just part of me job.'

Hickson took the cup away. At least Eddie felt a little better, he was acting normally. He looked across at Finch and the other man, whom he did not know but suspected was Finch's observer.

'What time is it?' he said.

'Time you got a watch,' said Finch, not looking up from his paper.

'It's just before five,' said his observer, who at least looked a little friendlier.

'Oh right,' said Eddie. The engine which he had heard before coughed into life again. 'What's that? Which flight is going out?' He got to his feet.

'Don't panic, Princess,' said Finch, now lowering the corner of his paper. 'The war isn't going on without you. Well it is, it just doesn't need us at the moment.' He lifted his paper again.

'Flying's been scrubbed for the rest of the day,' explained the observer. 'The wind's too strong and too gusty. Corp HQ have seen sense. That's just the AMs trying to get the grids in some sort of shape for tomorrow.'

'Right,' said Eddie and sat down. He wondered if he should ask the man's name. Did he know it? Was he at the party on that first night? He just wasn't sure. There were so many new faces, those in A flight just before, how many had he actually known? He wracked his brain, he could not put a name to any of them. Surely there could not be that many lost or missing? Was he just losing his senses, losing touch with reality?

Something else struck him. Something that the observer had said.

'Missing? Who's missing?' he said.

'What? Oh, sorry old chap, thought you knew. That tall chap you room with, now what was his name, MacKenzie?'

'Monroe...Hector.'

'Oh yes, thought it was something scotch. Yes, afraid he didn't come back from this lunchtime's contact patrol.'

*

Eddie sat on his bed in a daze. It was 8pm and the sun was setting. He had gone to see Pops who had confirmed the news. He was ringing around the other fields searching for news of Bean and his observer Smith as well as two other crews that were also missing.

'Don't worry too much yet,' said Pops. 'There's no point in getting into a funk about it. Chances are he's safe, just landed somewhere, just like you did. He'll turn up, don't worry. Go and get something to eat, you'll need your strength for tomorrow.'

The trouble was that, although he had indeed gone through a forced landing and a night away from the squadron, he just did not believe that the same had happened to Bean. He was dead, he was sure of it.

He had tried to eat but he just could not force more than a few mouthfuls down. His mouth was dry and his body did not seem to want to go through the effort of swallowing let alone digesting food. He sat at the table in silence whilst the conversation buzzed all around him. He could not understand how people could do that, seemingly forget those they had sat with last night and over breakfast that morning who were no longer with them. Perhaps it was the best way, to move on, not dwell.

He just couldn't do it. There were too many ghosts sitting with him.

He made a mumbled excuse he doubted anyone had heard and returned to his room, alone.

Bean was dead. Just like Bunny. Worse though, he had tried to help Bunny but with Bean he had just ignored him. Worse, he had considered him weak, bound to fail. And he had, hadn't he?

No, no, he told himself, don't think like that. He'd let his friend down by doing nothing.

But he'd killed Bunny by interfering.

He couldn't win.

He had sat there for twenty minutes or so in the gloom with his thoughts going round and round in his head when there was a knock on the door frame.

'Grenville, are you awake?' The curtain covering the entrance was pulled back.

It was Pops. Eddie sprang to his feet.

'Is there any news? Have you heard from Bean, Monroe I mean?'

'Ah, no, sorry, nothing yet,' said Pops. 'As I said before, that doesn't mean anything bad. With the push on things are very fluid at the front and there are other things more pressing for corps headquarters than missing crews I'm afraid.'

'So why…?'

Pops held out an envelope. 'There's a letter for you. Came this afternoon but with all the flap and commotion I quite forgot about it.' He held it out. 'Thought it might give you a little boost. You look like you could do with a little fillip.'

Eddie stared at it for a few seconds then took it.

'Try and get some sleep, lad,' Pops said, then left.

Eddie looked at the envelope, he did not recognise the handwriting. It had been addressed to him care of St.Omer and had been opened and presumably read by the censor. He almost put it to one side, he was not in the mood to receive news, good or bad but found himself opening it almost as if he was in a dream.

Dear Eddie,

I have found it difficult to write this letter. I have begun it several times but have given up in despair. This time I am determined to see it through. Please accept my apologies if you find it confusing or if you do not understand what I am trying to say. The truth is, perhaps, that I do not understand what that is myself!

Firstly, thank you for your letters. I did not expect to hear from you, not after the way we left things at the hospital, though I think that I hoped you would write which was why I gave you leave to do so.

Oh gosh, 'leave to do so', that sounds so formal. This is just one of the problems I have had, I want to be right and proper, I am a widow after all and the memory of David is still raw and I want to do right by him, yet inside I feel quite differently. I am churned up and confused and do not quite know exactly how I really feel.

I have left a gap here because the previous line was where I got to before I contemplated giving up again. However, I put the page aside, did my shift and then came back to it. All the time I was doing my work I was distracted - Matron even called me a 'silly girl' and that never happens to me, other girls are silly and frivolous but never me - but now I am back and I am determined to finish.

I am going to be honest. Although we have met only once I feel I know you already, and not just through your letters. You seem genuine and sweet and kind and caring and, if you can excuse me being so bold, I am attracted to you. I am blushing as I write this, I have never been so direct to anyone, not even to David but perhaps there is something about these times and this beastly war that have changed things. I am still conflicted, my moods are very much up and down as they have been since David was killed but I am beginning to feel that there is life beyond him and that I should not deny myself feelings any more.

So please accept my apologies for my behaviour on the night we met. I hope you understand why I was the way I was. I hope too that you wish to continue writing to me even though this is the first time that I have been able to write back. It was not because I did not want to it was because I found it so difficult to frame what I wanted to say, possibly because I did not have it straight in my own mind before now. The truth is I have come to look forward to your letters arriving and have been accused of being in a beastly bad mood when one has not come - oh dear, I have read that line back and it sounds like I am being critical, I promise you I am not.

Perhaps I had better get onto news. To be honest there is not much. There is much talk about when the Zeppelins might return and whether our aircraft and guns will be able to turn them back now. Here we are as busy as ever with casualties. I had thought about volunteering for service in France and talked to Matron about it but she said that there were jobs to be done here that were equally important and that not everyone had to be in France to do their bit. I suppose she is right but still I wonder whether I should be doing more. What do you think?

I also need to tell you about your brother, although I know you were angry with him after your visit. I hope that you can put that behind you and that you have come to some kind of understanding about his condition and how war changes people, though not, hopefully, permanently. I have no wish to preach or make you angry, suffice to say that I do believe he is a good man deep down and that the act he did, unspeakable as it was, was out of character. Anyway, I have good news about him. He made very good progress both physically and with his nerves and was discharged last week. I believe he has gone home. There is also talk about him receiving a gallantry award for saving his observer. He was very upset about your visit but it seems to have been a Godsend in a way. It seemed to rally him, make him more determined to recover himself. He certainly made more of an effort and I certainly saw the man that you described to me return. I hesitate to interfere in your family affairs but I hope that you can consider this and perhaps write to him? I know he would appreciate it.

Well Eddie, it is late and I must sleep or Matron will be shouting at me again on my shift tomorrow. I hope that you are well and are keeping safe. Please do, I really do want to see you again when you return to England.

Now I do not know how best to sign off this letter. Rather than make a fool of myself I will just sign my name at the bottom like a coward.

Annie

PS Please write again soon. If you want to of course.

Eddie lay back on his bed, his mind reeling. She liked him, she actually liked him. He found himself smiling, but then remembered Bean. How could he feel happy when Bean was missing, no not missing, dead, yes he was sure of it, Bean was dead, like Bunny, like Kerr and Armstrong, like...oh God he could not even remember the name of his first observer, What was it? John, yes. But what was his surname?

He found his eyes were filled with tears. He was crying. He was crying because he could not remember the name. This wouldn't do, men did not cry.

To his horror, the heard voices outside and the curtain was drawn back again. Quickly he turned his head away, then rolled over on the bed, wiping his the tears from his eyes. It must be Slade. He'd been a bit abrupt with him earlier. He should try to be his old self, be more friendly and welcoming. The chap seemed nice. He would make an effort once he had composed himself.

'You're in here, sir, with Lieutenant Grenville.'

'I say, thanks awfully.'

Eddie was surprised. He expected it to be Slade or even Pops come back.

'This one is your bed.'

This made him sit up, the anger coursing through him. Bean was only missing, for God's sake, yet they were giving someone his bed already.

'What the hell do you think you are doing?' he said sharply, then stopped. The newcomer and Evans looking at him in surprise, the pilot having placed his bag on Slade's bed.

'I was just showing the young gentlemen his billet, Lieutenant Grenville, sir,' said Evans. 'This is Lieutenant Moorhouse.'

'Lance,' said the young man, holding out his hand. 'Just over from good old England. I say, is there something wrong with your eyes?'

Eddie stared at him for a few moments, then shook his hand. 'Good to meet you. I'm Grenville. Sorry, I just got something in them and was rubbing them.'

'Oh, righty oh. Looked like you'd been crying, that's all.'

'Well I bloody well haven't,' said Eddie, raising his voice more than he intended and making Moorhouse jump backwards a little. 'Sorry,' he added. 'I'm a little on edge. It's been a long day.'

'That's all right, old chap,' said Moorhouse. 'Didn't mean anything by it, dash careless of me, always putting my boot in things.'

'I'll leave you two gentlemen to settle in,' said Evans. 'The Major will want to see you in the morning, Lieutenant.'

'Righty oh.'

'Evans?' said Eddie.

'Sir?'

'What happened to Slade? He'd only got here this morning.'

Evans face darkened, and Eddie saw him glance at Moorhouse before replying. 'Lieutenant Slade has gone, sir. He went over with C flight at about 1pm.' Evans did not add anything further, there was no need.

'Oh, right, thank you, Evans.'

Evans saluted and left. Slade gone already? If his billet was being given up already then they must be certain that he was not coming back. He shook his head; this was a living nightmare. Kerr, Armstrong, Slade, Bean, all gone today, and the others earlier. What chance did he have of surviving? What chance did he have of seeing Annie again?

'Have you been out long?'

Moorhouse's voice made him jump. His new roommate was unpacking his things.

'Long?' Eddie repeated.

'Yes, how long have you been at the front?'

How long? It felt like a lifetime. Two lifetimes. How long was it really? He had arrived on the 2nd, today was the 9th. A week, only a week!

'Ages,' he said, and lay back down on the bed again and rolled over.

*

He lay for hours in the darkness with his eyes open. He had pretended to sleep whilst Moorhouse was unpacking, then whilst he lowered the lamplight and wrote a letter home. He did not care that he might be considered unfriendly or unwelcoming, he was just too tired to talk, yet also he did not want to sleep.

He went over the reasons for both, time and time again in his head. Why wasn't he showing the common decency that he had been shown when he arrived? He and Bunny had felt like outsiders, some people had treated them that way but others, John, Kerr and Milne had gone out of their way to make an effort and that had made it all feel less strange.

But what was the point? Slade had only lasted a few hours, what was the point in getting to know someone? All that meant was that it hurt more when they were no longer there, and there was no doubt that they would soon be gone. It was selfish, he knew that but, to survive, you had to be selfish. Like Hastings, like Finch. They didn't care. And they were alive.

But Milne was alive too, and he cares. No, he was lucky, he could dismiss that notion. He had to be selfish to survive.

So no conversation. No friendship.

So why couldn't he sleep?

Was it because he had slept earlier in the mess? Possibly, but Eddie became convinced there was another reason: he was scared to sleep. His sleep was not dreamless. In his dreams the dead came back.

Some were friends once. He did not want to face them.

He sat up, then felt for the lamp. He fumbled for matches and lit it.

Moorhouse grumbled in his sleep and rolled over. Eddie ignored him. He got up and sat at his table. He reached for one of Daley's bottles and uncorked it. He took a drink straight from the bottle, scotch this time.

It burned straight down to his near empty stomach but, still, he felt better.

He looked at the letter that was on the floor by his bed.

Annie's letter. He picked it up. He caught a faint whiff of scent. It transported him back to that night in her bedroom, how her body, warm, firm yet soft, felt when she pressed herself close to him, how excited he had felt. The excitement grew in him again. He wanted her there, now.

He wanted her.

He wanted to lose himself in her.

He picked up his pen and drew a fresh sheet of paper towards him.

DAY 9

APRIL 10, 1917

Eddie woke.

Where was he? He opened his eyes. He was laying on his bed, fully clothed. How did he get here? The last thing he remembered was writing to Annie, he had no recollection of going to bed.

What time was it? It was light, where was everyone? Where was Slade - no not Slade, Slade was gone already, the other chap, what was his name? Whatever, he was not there. And neither was Bean.

Bean.

No, of course, he wouldn't be there.

There would soon be another young man sleeping there. Someone else who would come and go and whose name would quickly be forgotten.

Eddie felt the dampness on his cheek again. Annoyed he wiped his eyes, crying again? This would have to stop.

So what time was it? Why hadn't anyone come for him? There was no sound of engines, had they all gone on patrol without him? Perhaps they had, perhaps his batman had come for him and this was as far as he had got. He would be in trouble.

He quickly put his shoes on and grabbed his flying gear, throwing most of it on the bed and pulling on the underlayers as he left his billet.

Outside his face was stung by rain. It was freezing cold and the wind was strong. During the short walk across to the admin buildings it got worse, a flurry of snow blowing across the field almost blotting out the hangars from view. Even through the white haze, Eddie could see that the hangar's canvas doors were pulled to, the machines inside.

What was going on? Why weren't they flying?

He had a sudden jolt, a feeling of pure pleasure. Perhaps the push had succeeded, the breakthrough so complete that the Germans had been routed, had offered terms for surrender? If the war was over then he had survived, he wouldn't have to go up again.

He stopped, almost at the door to the building.

The elation had been followed straight away by a strange feeling inside of him. What was it? Eddie struggled to identify it.

Then he knew, it was loss.

How could he live without doing this? This was his life now; this was what he did. Everything after this would be dull and mundane.

Then he heard, over the howl of the wind, the guns, the heavy crump of artillery in the distance. It wasn't over.

The door to the admin block opened. Finch leaned out, squinting up at the sky, wrinkling his nose in clear disgust at the sleet and snow. He dropped his gaze to Eddie.

'What the bloody hell are you doing stood out there?' he said.

'I was just...listening to the guns,' Eddie said.

Finch stared at him for a few seconds. 'You really are some kind of imbecile,' he said at last.

He turned away before Eddie had time to answer.

He realised how cold and wet it was. Finch was right, he must have looked a complete idiot stood out there. And what stupid thoughts, that the war was over. How could he think that? The war was never going to be over, well not until everyone was killed or maimed or captured, he would have to keep on flying until then. He shivered at the thought of having to get back in the cockpit, of having to face the Archie and the fighters and the shells that could pluck you out of the sky, swat you out of existence like a fly. How could he do it again?

'Good morning, sir. There's coffee and tea in the mess, sir.'

The voice jolted him back into the present. It was Evans, his coat on, clearly ready to go outside and over to the billets.

'Thank you, Evans,' Eddie said, stepping to one side to let the man pass.

'Foul day, eh, sir?' said Evans, opening the door allowing a flurry of snow inside. 'Hope it clears up a bit for later.'

'Yes, hope so,' said Eddie, though the door had already been shut.

He was tempted by the thought of hot coffee but wanted to know what was going on. He made his way up the stairs to the squadron office.

'I say, what...' he began as he stepped through the door but then stopped instantly when presented with the tableaux laid out before him.

The three flight leaders were all there, Milne, Hastings and Finch. This was the first time that he had seen them all in one place at once with Pops and Major Reeves.

'Sorry sirs,' he said quickly.

'Not now, lieutenant,' said Reeves. Eddie could see that he was angry in fact there was a palpable level of tension in the room.

'Go and get something warm in the mess, there's a good chap,' said Pops gently.

'Yes sir,' said Eddie and went back down the stairs again.

He did not go all the way down, however, for he heard Hastings say: 'I just don't know what the problem is. The weather is no worse than yesterday.'

He knew he shouldn't, he always hated eavesdroppers, but he could not help himself.

'There is a huge difference,' Milne said.

'What? I don't see it.' Hastings sounded like he was up for a fight.

Milne was being equally stubborn.

'Do I have to spell it out for you?'

'Yes why don't you? We're all ears.'

'Clive, please,' growled Reeves.

Milne sighed. 'We are not in any fit state to do the job.'

'Rubbish.'

'It's not rubbish, it's a fact. Firstly we've lost five crews since yesterday morning, and eight since the beginning of the month, plus we are two other observers down.'

Eddie realised that these were his observers.

'So? David, that's our job. It's a damned dangerous one in case you hadn't noticed.'

'And some people make it a damned sight more dangerous too.'

Eddie knew exactly what Milne was saying, and quite clearly Hastings did too.

'What the hell do you mean by that?' he snapped.

Milne started to reply but Eddie heard Reeves' weary voice interrupt.

'That tack is not going to do anyone any good,' he said. 'Move on, both of you, that's an order.'

'Sir,' said both men.

'David, go on,' said Reeves.

'We've lost a quarter of our active pilots, over a third of our observers. What makes it worse is most of those crews we've lost were our most experienced. Add to that the fact that the machines that have come back have mostly needed repair and it's obvious that we are grossly under strength.'

'Tell us something we don't know,' said Hastings. Eddie could imagine the sneer on his face.

'That's not all. These machines are new to us. None of us have had time to work up and get used to them, to work out how we can get the best out of them.' Milne was clearly not going to give up.

'So what are you saying? That we should give up, go home, leave the field for the Krauts just because we think it's all a bit dangerous? That reeks of cowardice.'

Eddie heard a chair being thrust back abruptly, as if someone had leapt out of it.

'Enough!' yelled Reeves. 'Stop it, the pair of you. Hastings, you will apologise for that remark.'

Eddie heard Hastings mutter something, though he could not hear exactly what it was.

'Right,' said Reeves. 'Good, though I have to say that, although I object to the language, I can see what Captain Hastings is getting at. Are you suggesting we should ask Corp Headquarters to be withdrawn from the line?'

There was a pause. It was a long ten seconds before Milne replied.

'We are having to send inexperienced chaps up to do the job,' he said. 'The weather is awful. We are asking boys barely out of training with little experience to take aircraft they don't know up in terrible conditions that even the best of us would find next to impossible. Even if they do get up, the chances of them finding their targets are slim. The German aircraft our better than ours, Our scout squadrons are spread thinly and are too busy trying to survive themselves to spend much time protecting our boys. Essentially we are sending our crews on near suicide missions with very little prospect of them doing anything useful whilst they are risking their lives. Certainly it's dangerous, I know that, we all know that. But I think we have reached a point where enough is enough. It's not fair on them, it's not right that we should be asking these boys to do it.' Eddie heard Milne sigh and the chair grate on the floor as he sat down. 'The squadron is no longer effective, so, yes, I am saying that we should ask to be stood down.'

There was an immediate reaction from Hastings.

'That's crazy!' his voice was raised, angry. 'It's tantamount to giving in to the Hun, surrendering,'

'No it's not. It's a sensible, tactical move.'

'You've lost your bottle, David. You should damn well go home and take up knitting. Oh no, it involves sharp needles doesn't it? That might be too dangerous for you as well.'

'Clive,' said Reeves sharply. 'I've told you -'

'It's murder,' interrupted Milne. 'What we are ordering our men to do is tantamount to murder. And the worst of it all is that it's all so bloody pointless. We are sending chaps to die doing a job they can't do.'

'David! I won't have that sort of talk either.'

There was movement in the corridor down at the bottom of the stairs where Eddie stood. Someone was coming. Not wanting to get caught he quickly made his way down the stairs and was just in time to meet the chief mechanic at the bottom. He held a bit of paper in his hand, Eddie guessed it was the up-to-date position on the serviceability of the aircraft. The chief nodded and said 'sir' in greeting as they passed.

Eddie's mind was in a whirl as he headed for the mess. Milne was arguing that they should be taken out of the line, given a rest. That would mean safety, at least for a while. He'd not have to face the Archie, the shells, the ground fire, the deadly Albatros. He'd train, get better, he'd survive.

A hollow feeling developed inside him. It was the same feeling he had had before, the feeling of loss. Then the prospect was remote, a hope not anything that was likely to happen like the war ending. Now, though, it was real. It could happen, it could all end today.

And he did not feel elated. He felt sick. He felt like a big part of him had died inside.

And now, as well as feeling physically sick he was also revolted with himself. This existence had killed Armstrong and Kerr, and Daley, John...whatever his surname was, the RE8 delivery pilot at St. Omer, the BE2 crew that had been swatted out by the shell and...and.

Bunny. And probably Bean too.

Yet he loved it. How sick does a man have to be inside to actually love this?

Hastings loved it too. Did that make him sick? It had to. Didn't it?

'I say old chap, you were a bit restless last night.'

The voice made him look up. It was Moorhouse. He was holding a mug in one hand and a plate of toast in the other. In the daylight Eddie was struck at how young he looked.

'Yes, sorry about that,' he said.

'Oh no problems, Grenville, I can sleep with any disturbance.'

'That will be useful.'

'Always has been, old boy, always has been.' Moorhouse took a bite of toast. 'Aren't you getting some brekkie, my man? The toast is top-notch.'

'I'm not hungry,' said Eddie, which was true, though this surprised him as he could not remember the last time that he had sat down to a decent meal.

It also seemed to surprise Moorhouse. 'If you say so, old chap, but you look like you could do with -'

'Just leave it will you? I said I wasn't hungry, didn't I?'

Moorhouse looked abashed. 'Sorry, Grenville. Didn't mean anything by it.'

Eddie's temper cooled almost as quickly as it had flared. 'Sorry,' he said. 'It's been a difficult few days. Didn't mean to snap.'

Moorhouse just smiled. 'It's okay, old boy. Shall we get a seat?'

'Yes,' said Eddie, finding a space on one of the battered leather settees. 'I'll get some tea,' he added in the direction of a passing orderly.

Moorhouse joined him. He looked around. 'Is it always this busy in here?' he said.

Eddie could see what he meant. Virtually every seat was taken, at the tables, the armchairs, two people, a pilot and an observer, were even sat together on the piano stool. He realised that he had never seen it like this before.

He also realised how few of the people in the mess he recognised. He was surrounded by strangers.

'What a lot of chaps. Bit like being the new boy at school, isn't it? You'll have to introduce me to them.'

'I don't think that's the done thing,' said Eddie to cover himself. 'Everyone else will come over and say hello if they want to, otherwise it's best to just let people be.'

'Oh, alright,' said Moorhouse 'Oh look, we can squeeze in together on that settee there.' He pointed across the room. Eddie could see that it was amongst a group of A flight crews, the ones that had cold-shouldered him the day before, so it was with some reluctance that he followed Moorhouse over. He saw a couple of them talking quietly to each other when they saw he was heading over and felt the familiar anger and resentment build within him. Sod em, sod the lot of them, he thought and sat down, ready and waiting to give back as good as he got.

One of them, Palmer Eddie thought his name was, yes Palmer, one of the older observers in the squadron and someone Eddie had seen Kerr spend time with, leant across.

'Grenville,' he said.

'What?' Eddie's voice was sharp and cold.

To his surprise Palmer held out his hand. 'I think we did you an injustice. I heard how you went to help Alan and Phil. Did your best to get them back. Sorry we were so hard on you.'

Eddie stared at Palmer for a moment, then took the hand.

'Thanks,' he said.

To his horror he felt tears start to form. Why was he crying? And why here in front of everyone else? He let go of Palmer's hand and turned his head away. Luckily, at that moment, everyone's attention was caught by the arrival of Major Reeves, Pops and the three flight leaders in the mess.

'Pipe down, everyone, pipe down,' Pops said loudly. 'The Major has an announcement.'

Wiping the moisture away from his eyes, Eddie, along with everyone else in the room turned to face the group of senior officers. Eddie could see that Hastings and Milne were on either side of the squadron leader and that neither looked happy.

'Men, as you know things have been pretty rough for the last few days. The weather's been foul and Fritz has been worse. We have lost a lot of good men.'

There was a murmur of agreement around the room.

'What has made it worse, of course, is having to bed in the new aircraft. At this time we need our most experienced crews, yet the demands of the front and the big push have meant that we have not had the time to learn our new mounts properly. The ground crew as well are having a hard time, working through the night to keep our aircraft serviceable. They aren't complaining but they are at the end of their tether.'

'What's he saying?' Moorhouse whispered to Eddie.

'That we are being taken out of the line,' he replied, scarcely able to believe it himself. It was true, he was being given a stay of execution.

'They need a break, a little time. We all do in fact. We need to catch breath. That's not what I told Corp HQ of course but that, in essence, is what we need.'

Eddie could feel the realisation sink in. There was a collective sigh in the room, a lifting of mood. He felt it himself, the mixed feelings he had had were gone, now he wanted this time more than anything. Safe time, he could be trained properly, heal properly, learn to love flying again.

'So what we have decided,' Reeves went on. 'Is that we will not fly this morning, or the first part of this afternoon.'

It took a few seconds for this to sink in but when it did it was like a knife in the gut. A few hours? Was that it? What good was that?

Eddie was clearly not alone in thinking this. Palmer looked stunned.

'Really sir?' he said. 'Just until this afternoon?' There was a clear note of incredulity in his voice.

'Yes Palmer,' Reeves said sharply. 'There is a war on, we have to do our bit. This is going to be hard enough to swing with Trenchard as it is.'

'But sir,' said another voice. 'You said yourself, with our losses -'

'That's enough, Paul,' interrupted Milne, his voice calm but authoritative. 'Major Reeves is quite right; we can't just be taken out of the line on our wishes and whims. We still have a job to do which we will do to the best of our abilities.'

'But David -'

'That's sir to you, and that's the end of it, understand. This is a decision that all of the flight commanders support.'

The mess fell silent. Eddie looked at Milne in surprise, then at Hastings. It was quite clear from his face that he most certainly did not agree with the decision, but said nothing. Finch was just staring at the floor. He looked very pale.

'Good,' said Reeves. 'You can step down until 4pm this afternoon. Your time is free until then. Good day gentlemen.'

As soon as the senior officers had turned to leave the mess started to buzz with conversation.

Eddie took a deep breath. Now he understood why both Hastings and Milne had looked unhappy: neither had got their way. Yet Milne had supported Reeves's poor compromise. Why had he done that?

Of course, he thought, collective responsibility. Argue against something, certainly, but once a decision had been made back up your leader.

Eddie's admiration for Milne rose. And then he thought of Hastings. He had said nothing, he had looked surly and petulant throughout. He had made it patently clear that he did not agree with decision.

Was Eddie following the right course by following Hastings' lead?

'Well,' sighed Moorhouse. ' That's a bit of a relief. Thought I was going to miss out on all the action before I started. At least I can get my crack at the Hun now.'

Eddie just stared at him. He looked so young, so innocent. Was this how he had looked just over a week ago. He looked over Moorhouse's shoulder at the window. With the overcast and rain it was relatively dark outside and the lamps were lit, so he could clearly see his own reflection in the glass.

He barely recognised himself, he looked so old.

*

Eddie pulled his flying coat around himself. The weather was improving but the wind was still gusting and occasionally flinging ice-cold raindrops into his face that stung and then numbed.

He had had to get out, he just could not settle inside. He had tried to relax, there were a number of chaps playing cards in the mess, poker, cribbage, even a Bridge four but that had never been his thing. Moorhouse had suggested chess, a game that he had excelled at in school but that had been a failure. He found that he had no capacity to concentrate, and soon got irritated by Moorhouse's poor play and puppy-like personality.

So he went for a walk, though he had no idea where he was going to go.

He realised that this was something that he had had no time to do, explore the airfield, the village and the surrounding countryside, though he had flown over it so many times already.

It was quite beautiful even in the awful weather. It was odd, it was like England in so many ways but was, still, even without seeing any signs, or hearing the natives talking, somehow distinctly French. It looked different, smelt different.

He walked around the perimeter of the airfield, revelling in the solitude. He longed for it to be a warm day, then he could lie on the grass in the sun and listen to the birds sing. Would he survive long enough for the weather to warm up for him to see it? However, even this cold stroll was entrancing.

But then he stumbled over a rabbit hole and the pain shot up his leg from his injured foot. He was instantly reminded of how he had done it and what had happened to the delivery pilot on the same day. He suddenly smelt the aroma of burnt flesh, though his more sensible self told him that it must just be the smell of cooking from the village. Then, on the wind, the distant rumble of the guns reminded him where he was and why they were all there.

The war.

They were at war.

He was at war.

He did not think he could ever escape that.

With timing that matched his sudden change of mood, a heavy shower of rain swept across the airfield. Eddie at first hunched himself deeper into his coat, then made a limping dash for the shelter of a nearby line of trees. It was poor cover but, by pressing himself up against one of the trunks, he was at least able to ride out the worst of the rain.

He noticed that the trees were not in a single row, as he had seen alongside some of the roads in France, but were in a distinct line about five deep stretching away from the field. He guessed they were to provide shelter from the wind for something that grew in the fields beyond, though what this was he was not sure. The barrier was not complete, there were areas where perhaps trees had been blown down and new ones had not grown to replace them. He was sheltering at the edge of one of these gaps.

Whilst he was stood there he noticed something, a flash of colour, in the grass in front of one of the trees where the line resumed. It was just peeking out into his line of sight beyond another of the trunks. They had to be flowers, which was odd as there did not seem to be any others nearby, not that any showed their heads above the long grass anyway. Puzzled, as soon as the shower passed, he set off to investigate.

When he got within ten feet of the flowers, he knew just

what they were and just which tree it was.

He hesitated, almost turned away but forced himself to go on.

The bouquet was nothing much, just some early spring flowers tied together with a blue ribbon. There was a piece of paper tucked inside them. Eddie looked up. There was the vivid white scar on the tree trunk, about twenty feet up, the smell of oil and petrol mingled with tree sap. The latter was dribbling down from the scar making it look like the tree was bleeding - or crying. Eddie quickly looked down again.

He squatted on his haunches, ignoring the pain in his foot, and reached for the note. The envelope it was in was damp, as was the note inside but the paper was of good quality and the writing perfectly legible. He did not need to read it, he knew who it had to be from.

Sleep well, old friend. I'm so sorry I wasn't here with you. I will never forget you, my brother.

Bean

Eddie gulped, then found himself crying again. This time he did not try to stop it. He allowed himself to fall forward onto his knees and let the tears flow freely down his cheeks, dripping off his chin and onto the ground, onto the petals of the spring flowers, onto the note and the soil of France that was littered with pieces of fabric and broken propeller.

*

He was not sure how long he had knelt there. He did not care that his trousers were wet, the cold and damp against his skin was, in some way, soothing. At last though, he got to his feet. He knew where he had to go, where he should have gone before. He had no idea where it would be, or how long it would take him to get there, only that he needed to go.

He limped off in the direction of the village.

He soon spotted the church. It was a squat, solid building with a square steeple, in the very heart of the settlement. He headed towards it.

He had perhaps 500 yards to walk. His path along the road

took him past a farm and a barn. There were three women outside the barn. They were dressed in thick skirts, men's shirts and jumpers, and had their hair in headscarves. They were clearly agricultural workers; their clothes and faces were muddy and pink with exertion. They were washing down a plough or a harrow - Eddie was not sure what, his knowledge of country life was hazy at best - heaving wooden buckets from a nearby spring up to the implement. Two of the women were older than him, one perhaps in her thirties, the other perhaps a decade older than that. One though was young, it was hard to tell but she might have been his age, and although it was difficult to tell under her bulky garments, seemed to Eddie to have a good figure.

He realised that he was staring just as one of the older women noticed him and nudged her companion, saying something to her that made her laugh. The other called something out to the younger girl, Eddie had always been poor at languages and his French was rudimentary at best so had no idea what had been said, but the girl smiled, looked up at Eddie then quickly back down at her work. The older women both laughed and called something out at Eddie this time, he just shrugged at them and hurried on. This seemed to cause even more amusement.

He arrived at the church. It was set on the edge of the village square, opposite a cafe and a small shop. There had been fighting around here at some time; part of the church roof was damaged and covered in a tarpaulin, and there were bullet holes pockmarking the stonework. Eddie stepped over a filled in shell hole and through the gate into the graveyard beyond.

It didn't take him long to find what he was looking for.

On the far edge of the burial ground there were three graves where grass was yet to grow. One was freshly dug. It had a cross on it and , in black paint, was the name 2nd Lieutenant E B Cavendish. On the grave beneath was another bunch of flowers, the same types as were by the tree.

Oddly, Eddie did not feel the need to cry this time. He had been steeling himself, he told himself, he knew what he would see unlike on the field when he had stumbled on the accident scene unexpectedly. Still though, his lack of tears, of real emotion disturbed him. Here was his friend, someone who he had known half his life, lying just six feet or so beneath his feet, less than a week dead, probably still intact, still recognisable, yet he was feeling - nothing.

Now he did feel the prick of tears in his eyes, and a deep sadness inside and quickly turned away because he knew that these were not for Bunny, they were for himself.

He was along the road away from the churchyard before he knew it and heading back to the airfield. When he passed the farm, he saw that the yard was empty and the woman were gone. This was at least a relief; he would rather not be the source of amusement for French women.

'Hello, monsieur.'

The voice was soft, the solitary word of English heavily accented.

It was the younger woman. She had come out of the barn that was set on the left side of the farmyard.

'Oh, hello,' he said.

'You...?' she began. 'vous êtes un pilote?'

Close to, Eddie could she that she was pretty, a little plump and stocky perhaps but with a sweet, regular face and soft brown eyes.

'Pardon? Oh, am I a pilot...yes...I am. Oui'

'Comment vous appelez-vous?'

He stared at her for a moment, trying to work out what she was asking. Then he got it.

'Edward. Eddie.'

'Eddie,' she said, and smiled.

'What is yours? Er..Quel...nom?'

'Je m'appelle Sophie'

'Sophie. That's a nice name,' Eddie replied.

There was an awkward silence. It was if she was expecting something. What was he supposed to say? His experience of girls his own age was limited, there was his sister of course but she did not count. And Annie of course, but she was older, more confident too. And there was not the language problem.

'Well,' he said abruptly. 'Please excuse me. I must be going.'

'Non!' she said and stepped towards him. She slipped her arm through his. 'Vous ne voulez pas venir ici avec moi ?' She started to pull him towards the barn.

'What, no, why do you want me to go in there?' said Eddie, resisting.

'Viens s'il te plait,' she said. She was now tugging his arm.

'I don't understand you,' he said. 'Why do you want me to go inside there?'

'Inside, oui, good,' she replied.

'What, good things? Inside there?'

'Oui,' she nodded.

Another shower of rain swept across the village. Suddenly being under shelter seemed appealing. Eddie reluctantly allowed himself to be led into the barn. He half expected the other women to be there, for it to be some kind of joke, but there was no one else there, just the hay and the smell of animals and must.

Sophie led him towards the hay then turned around.

'Dix francs,' she said.

'Pardon?'

'Dix francs,' she said again. 'Avez-vous un préservatif?'

'Preservative? I...what?'

Sophie stepped forward and, to his alarm started to try to unfasten his trousers.

'No, stop it, what are you doing?' he said, trying to push her off.

She stepped back, a look of surprise and puzzlement on her face.

'Qu'est-ce qui ne va pas chez toi? Tu ne veux pas me baiser?' she said, then pulled her blouse and cardigan out of her skirt and lifted them up to her chin, exposing her breasts.

Eddie stared at them. They were full, slightly pendulous, creamy white, with large nipples. Suddenly, he understood, and felt a range of emotions; embarrassment, panic, in fact he felt like a total fool.

'No, no, I don't...I...I've got to go.'

He turned and ran out of the barn. Behind him Sophie started shouting. He did not know what she was saying but the soft voice of before was gone; now it was harsh, the unknown words cutting.

He ran as far as he could bear before the pain got too much and he had to stop. Hell, she was a street girl, a prostitute, why hadn't he seen that? Because he had no experience, in fact, her's were the first breasts he had ever seen. And they were beautiful, desperately exciting. Eddie was aroused

He had never been with a woman, and, other than his sister and mother he had spent very little time around them, the type of interests he had did not bring him much into contact with them, though he had started to notice how pretty one of the housemaids were at home in his last Christmas holiday home from school. He had caught her eye a few times, caught her smiling at him. He later realised that her mother must have seen this too for, when he came back home at Easter, she was gone.

He thought of Annie.

He recalled how it felt to have her close, her warmth, the feeling of closeness and excitement. That moment made him understand how Siggi had looked and acted around Alice, how, when they had got together, he had changed, become softer, more gentle, caring, nicer. He might never feel that, given how precarious his life was now, what were the chances of him getting those feelings with Annie.

His thoughts drifted back to the French girl, her body, the creamy softness of her breasts, the fullness of her lips. He could...no, that would not be right, he was writing to Annie, he had developed feelings for her.

But then he thought of the girl, and the war, the bullets, the shells, the ways that he could be killed or maimed so badly that no woman would ever look at him again. What would happen if he ended up like the man in the hospital? The one with no arms or legs? No hands to hold, no fingers to caress soft skin, what then? And Annie, was she really interested in him? She was older, she had been married, he was just a boy. His family too, his mother certainly, she would put a stop to things. Annie was not what she would call 'their sort of person', he could imagine her being dismissed as someone far too common to associate with her son.

That made him burn with anger, he had always hated that attitude but now it looked even more stupid, this war had shown that. It was a great leveller. Why shouldn't he be with who he wanted to be with? Life was too short to have regrets, Siggi and Alice showed that.

But then his resolve melted. He was being stupid, infantile even. He was a boy, that was all, and he had fallen into the trap of a youth: infatuation. He had no future with Annie, he was clinging on to a vague hope. This girl was here and now, warm, willing - well, for money at least - available.

He was back at the airfield now, the guard at the entrance was still sheltering inside his hut but was watching him, fag end clutched in cupped hand, clearly ready to challenge and show that he was really doing his duty. Eddie stopped. Why not, he thought. Why not take what might be his one chance to enjoy the 'sins of the flesh'? Sins of the flesh, yes that was what his school padre called it, warned against, that any boy that indulged in it out of wedlock would burn in the fires of hell. That always made it sound interesting, something like drinking and smoking, things that grown-ups told you not to do whilst enjoying it themselves.

But then burning, his soul burning throughout eternity. He

had seen quite enough people burning for a lifetime, let alone eternity. It was starting to haunt his dreams and his waking life. Did he want to risk it?

He took a step towards the gate. The guard took a last quick drag on his cigarette and then stubbed it out.

Did he believe that would happen? Did he believe anything at all now? He could not honestly say that he had any faith at all.

He stopped, then turned around and began walking back to the village. He was sure he heard the guard curse quietly behind him.

He had got twenty yards when he remembered he had no money on him. His soul and body slumped together. How stupid was he? He had not taken any money, why should he, he had got up expecting to fly. Would Sophie let him anyway? No, of course not, she wanted the money, why else would she be doing it otherwise?

He stopped. Why would someone do what she was doing? Not out of choice, why would you? She was doing it not because she wanted to, but because she had to. Eddie was taking advantage of her. He was disgusting, a user.

But she offered. She needed the money. And he needed...

He turned back to the airfield. He was going to get his money.

As he walked through the gate, the guard came out, saluted but gave him an exasperated look.

'Made your bloody mind up have you now, sir?' he said.

Eddie knew that he should put the man in his place, remind him that he was an officer and that cheek should be kept to himself but somehow it didn't matter, in fact he found it really funny, the funniest thing that he had heard in months. He started giggling, and once he had, he could not stop. The guard, a man perhaps a few years older than himself, just stood bemusedly shaking his head as Eddie laughed.

'You, alright sir?' he asked at last.

'I'm fine, yes I'm fine,' Eddie got out between giggles. 'And yes, I've made my mind up.'

'That's really good, sir. Of course you have.'

'Carry on, soldier.'

'Oh I will, sir, don't you worry.' The guard retreated into his hut. Eddie was certain that he muttered 'what a bloody lunatic,' under his breath as he did. He didn't care. He had made a decision. He just needed his money.

As he stepped into the courtyard, the sun came out. It was weak, veiled behind thin cloud but it seemed to lift his mood still further. He was not sure what had just happened, but he was aware that something significant had. He had changed, grown up perhaps? Whatever, he was going to take another significant step into adulthood with the help of a girl called Sophie.

Across at the field, he saw that there was a lot of activity around the hangars. Aircraft were being wheeled out whilst others were being tended to. Eddie wondered if they were taking advantage of the weather improving to do some air tests. He wondered who was going to do the flying, not him, he had other better things to do.

'Ah, Grenville, there you are, we've been looking for you.'

Eddie turned around.

'Oh hello, Pops,' he said, 'I've just been for a...er...a walk. To the village.'

'Well, good that you're back. We need you.'

Eddie glanced at the RE8s now lined up on the field, some with their engines being run up. 'Well, actually sir, I don't really want to fly any air tests, not just yet anyway. I've got...er...' He pointed vaguely back in the direction of the village.

'Oh it's not an air test. Trenchard has put his foot down. The push has stalled, they need all the eyes they can get. We need to run contact patrols.'

Eddie felt his elation leave him like a deflating balloon. He stared at Pops in disbelief.

'Sorry Eddie, we've got no choice. Half of the lads took the tender to the depot for baths. We are having to put up a makeshift flight with who we have.'

Eddie still stared at him, then nodded and trudged off towards his billet.

'It's not all bad news,' Pops called after him.

Eddie looked back over his shoulder. 'Right,' he said, flatly. 'Really? How so?'

Pops smiled. 'You'll see.' He turned and walked back into the admin block.

Puzzled, Eddie continued his trudge to get the rest of his flying gear. What could make things better? It was like escaping a fight only to have someone jump you with a knife. He was going to die, now he was convinced of it, he had had his chance and he'd blown it. He was going to fly, he was going to die and die a virgin.

His gloom had deepened by the time he reached his billet. He hoped Moorhouse was not there, the last thing he needed was a surfeit of cheerful optimism. Angrily he tugged back the curtain.

Bean was sat at his desk writing.

'Oh hello, Eddie,' he said. 'I'd wondered where you'd got to.'

Eddie just stared at him. He did not move when Bean got up and came over and gave Eddie a hug. 'I've really missed you, old chum,' he whispered. 'I thought you might have bought it whilst I was away.'

'Well I haven't,' said Eddie, shrugging Bean off and pushing him away. 'Not yet anyhow.'

He saw Bean looked surprised. He was surprised himself; he wasn't pleased his friend was alive, somehow he felt - the opposite? Really, did he want Bean dead? He turned and started to gather his flying gear together. 'Where have you been?'

'We got hit by Archie, came down in no-man's-land. At least we thought it was, turned out that it was in our hands, taken it that morning.'

'Why didn't you let the squadron know?'

'Couldn't old chap. The boys were rather busy fighting. Had no time for us,' Bean sat down. 'Had to stay the night. It's pretty bloody up there.'

Eddie pursed his lips. 'I know.'

'Oh yes, of course, you've done pretty much the same, haven't you?'

'Yes.'

'Except of course your observer didn't make it.'

Eddie did not want the vision of John's shattered head at that moment but it came nonetheless.

'No,' he said.

'I say, old chap,' said Bean. 'Are you alright?'

'I'm fine,' said Eddie, tugging his flying coat on.

'Oh, right. You just seem...'

'I just seem what?'

'You don't seem very pleased to see me, that's all.'

Eddie turned angrily to him. 'Oh dear, oh dear, I'm so sorry. I'm sorry I haven't put out the flags but I really don't really feel like celebrating.'

'But, but...' Bean stammered, astonishment written on his face. Eddie knew he had already gone too far, nor why, in fact he was doing this, the words just seemed to want to spill out.

'I flew four missions yesterday, or was it five? To be honest I can't remember. All I know is that on one of them I watched Armstrong and Kerr die. They didn't go prettily, Do you want to know what happened? Well do you?'

'No. No I don't. Eddie...'

'Well tough, I'm going to tell you anyway. They were riddled by a Hun, then they flew on wounded, probably in agony, barely alive until their sodding aircraft caught fire. Even then it wasn't quick, they had to ride it all the way down.'

'Oh God, that's awful. But...'

'Oh it was pretty bloody awful, believe me, but then I was right with them about 20 yards away when they burned to a crisp. Then today I thought I was going to...' Eddie paused for breath. 'Today I thought I'd be getting a rest but it seems not. And I can't help but notice that you're not getting ready to fly.'

'Well no, Pops said that I could sit this one out because -'

'Do you know why that is?'

'Because I'd only just got back and Smith is a bit...'

'Because you're useless that's why,' interrupted Eddie. 'Well not useless, you're a damn sight better than Bunny was, now he really was useless.'

'Eddie! How can you say that?'

'Because it's true. But you, you could be all right but your problem is you're too bloody cautious, too careful, everything has to be so precise.'

Bean just stared at Eddie, blinking.

'You were just the same in training. We could all see it, but no one wanted to hurt your feelings about it. War's not like that. Well don't let it worry your pretty little head. You sit here and rest. You stay away from all the nasty rough boys whilst we go and do the dangerous stuff.'

'Eddie, that's enough. Stop, please, you're being beastly.' Eddie saw a tear roll down Bean's cheek. 'Why are you being like this?'

'Oh stop crying, you baby,' he said, and, picking up his gloves and helmet, walked out of the billet without a backward glance.

In the corridor he stopped. His head dropped, his shoulders slumped. The anger within him vanished almost as quickly as it had come. Why had he done that, to Bean? He had only known him a few months but Eddie had come to consider him the closest friend that he knew, perhaps even had ever known. Bean was quiet and sensitive, and there was another thing.

He had gone with him to the Lily Pond at Lyons Corner House in Piccadilly Circus on one of their leaves. Well to sit near to it, Bean typically lost courage when he got there and he and Eddie had sat with all the other customers whilst the decorous young, and not so young men, took tea and cakes and chatted extravagantly.

He knew what Bean was suppressing, constantly fighting, he'd felt for his friend. And yet Eddie had done that, kicked him where it really hurt, found all his friend's sensitive points and made sure he ground his fists into them.

All because Eddie was angry that he had lost his day off. Or lost the chance to spend half an hour with a common prostitute. What was important?

He turned back, intent on apologising, but then stopped.

He turned and carried on walking towards the hangars.

It was better like this. He was being cruel to be kind; it was in both their best interests. It was better not having friends here, who needed them? They could help for a while but everyone was better alone. You wouldn't get hurt then. You'd learn self-reliance.

It was what Bean needed.

It was what Eddie needed.

Just take what you wanted. Maybe that's what he should have done with Sophie.

On the way, he called into Brown's room. His observer was sat on the bed, dressed and ready to go. They did not exchange a word, Brown just nodded at Eddie and followed him outside.

In the hangar were five crews, amongst them the three flight leaders, Hastings, Milne and Finch, It was clear that Milne was giving the briefing.

'Nice of you to turn up, gentlemen,' said Hastings, tartly.

'At least we didn't bugger off to the nearest bar,' said Eddie, meeting Hastings' stare with a cold one of his own. 'We're here now, let's get on with it.'

To his surprise - and gratification - he saw Hasting's discomfort. He looked down, ostensibly at his map but, in fact, Eddie could see that he was backing down.

'Well that's told you, Clive,' said Milne. Eddie could see that, for all his weariness, he was smiling. 'Good to have you with us, Grenville. Right as I was saying...'

Eddie was only half listening to what he was saying from then on. His heart was beating hard, thumping in fact. Was it because of his confrontation with Hastings? Or for the words with Bean. No, he was just keen to go, keen to get back up in the air, over the lines.

This was what he was living for. It was what his whole life was aimed at getting to.

'Right,' said Milne. 'So we need to establish where our troops have got to, and, above all where they are having the most trouble.

Observers, take photographs where you can but notes are more important. Always know where you are, mark everything on your maps.'

'We're not carrying Coopers,' said one of the observers, nodding towards the six aircraft.

Eddie noticed Hastings give an exasperated sigh.

'No. That's deliberate. The information we are collecting is vital. If you don't come back, it's useless.'

'But...' protested the observer. Eddie realised it was Kirk, Hastings' rear seater. Kerr had told him at the first night's party that he had lost two brothers in the war and had served in the trenches himself as a machine gunner. He was almost as belligerent as his pilot, having a real hatred of the Germans.

'Dead men can't report,' said Milne. Hasting's quietly shook his head. 'I know it's tempting to help out the ground troops, but sergeant, the best way we can do that is by bringing back the information - and yourselves - intact. Yes?'

'Yes sir,' said Kirk.

'Perhaps we should drop a note to the Huns and ask them not to be nasty to us,' muttered Hastings.

'Pilots, the key thing is getting back,' said Milne. He checked his watch. 'Any questions? No, take-off in five minutes.'

'There's nothing to stop you using your guns, if you get the chance,' Hastings said quietly to Kirk as they passed Eddie.

The crews walked towards the aircraft, or at least, Eddie thought they had all set off. He saw Finch's observer pause and look back. Eddie did the same. His pilot was still inside the hangar, staring at the floor.

'Finchy!' The yell was Hastings. 'Wake up, man! Get your arse into gear and get to your aircraft.'

Finch seemed to shake himself, almost as if he was waking from a deep sleep. He seemed startled to see the rest of the crews halfway across the grass to the waiting RE8s. Even then, he didn't look right to Eddie. He was white, distant. When he reached his observer he muttered, 'Sorry Thomas,' and continued to his aircraft. Eddie saw the observer's eyes follow him, and the man bite his lip pensively. Eddie could guess why; the normal, abrasive, superior Finch was gone. Above all, although he did not know either very well, Eddie was sure the way that Finch had talked to his observer was not in character. He had seen how Finch was with Brown, an officer yes, but someone from a class he considered inferior. Finch's observer was a sergeant, yet he had called him by his first name.

What had happened?

'I think he's snapped, Eddie,' said Brown quietly. 'I know he's difficult, he's been a sod to room with, but he's not a bad 'un really.'

'Right,' said Eddie. 'I'll take your word for it.'

'He's got a young wife, a baby on the way. She's a nervous sort, I think she's been writing the wrong things to him, though he's not letting on. This morning, when we were told to take a rest, he was like a spring lamb, like he'd been given a new lease on life. When Pops came and broke the news...well I think it's just broken him.' He looked across at the other aircraft. 'A few have got started. We should get going, lad,' he said.

Eddie nodded, and put his feet into the footholds in order to climb into the RE8. Around 30 yards away, Finch was doing the same. Unlike Eddie though, he did not swing his leg up and into the cockpit. Instead, he stood there. He looked frozen in fear, like a nervous diver on the high platform, unwilling to step forward, to take the plunge. Eddie found himself whispering "Go on Finch, go on, get in". It had suddenly become somehow personally important to Eddie that Finch conquer his demons and go and do his job, his duty.

The demons won. Finch stepped down and walked away from the aircraft, throwing down his gloves and stripping off his flying helmet, tossing it onto the ground along with his goggles. The ground crew were stood around in shock, his observer shook his head slowly and sadly then began to climb out.

'Fuel on, switches off,' called Eddie's mechanic.

Eddie just stared at Finch.

'Eddie,' Brown said sharply from behind him.

Eddie did as he was told in something of a daze, barely watching as the cylinders were primed and the prop walked through four turns.

'Switches on!' called the mechanic, and Eddie switched on and cranked the starting magneto as the prop was swung. The engine started first pull and he waited whilst it warmed up, hoping that his nerves would calm down. His confidence seemed to have evaporated, Finch, a flight leader, one of his leaders, cracking, walking away from the job. How could he be expected to carry on when someone like that couldn't?

A Very light arched from Milne's aircraft and it started to roll. Eddie pulled his goggles down and, when it was their turn, opened the throttle and followed, not giving himself chance to change his mind. The RE8 wobbled a little as he left the ground, he put it down to the strong breeze though knew that it was his own shaking hands that were causing it.

*

The first burst of Archie as they crossed into German held territory came as a shock. He'd been daydreaming, thinking about everything except the job in hand, Finch, Sophie, Annie, anything but the fact that he was going back to war. But wasn't that good? That he could think about such 'normal' things rather than the prospect of his likely death?

Death? Did it bother him that much, dying? Would there be an afterlife? Or would it just be blackness. It would be simple; it would end the torture of this life. He would be at peace.

There was a thump on his shoulders. Brown. What did he want? Eddie turned around. Brown was pointing at the ground, what did he want? He looked annoyed.

Eddie understood. Brown had his own map, they were off course, away from their designated area.

Eddie kicked himself. What was wrong with him? He was drifting, hazy, not concentrating. He needed to get his mind on the job, this was not just his life, this was Brown's too. Where the hell were they? He looked at his own map, then down at the ground, then at the map again, desperate to find a landmark. He wished that the formation had stayed together, but that wasn't what they were doing this afternoon, they were all flying alone, trying to get over and back without attracting attention, get the photos, do the observation and get back, as quickly and efficiently as they could.

Yet here he was, already lost.

It took him a good few minutes to at last find a landmark, a stream near the remains of a wood, that he could locate on his map. Good, he told himself, they were a bit off course, but he knew where they were, it wouldn't take them too long to reach where they were meant to be. He banked them round in the right direction and turned back to Brown, giving him a thumbs up.

Brown was not looking. He was gripping the Lewis, scanning the skies, but looking mostly over to their left. Eddie did the same and saw dark spots, weaving like gnats on a Summer's evening. Aircraft, Huns? Probably, and they were swirling around something, it had to be another aircraft. One of their flight? They were in trouble then, Eddie thought, then looked away.

It was a minute later that he thought about what he had just done. He had just been watching one of his squadron mates fighting for their lives and he felt - well he felt, nothing. Empty. Completely emotionless. Was that normal?

It had to be.

It was sensible anyway. All it meant to him was that he could get on with the job without being bothered.

Still, deep down, in a detached way he found his reaction disturbing, though he could not work out why. He looked back, there was a descending trail of smoke in the sky, the dots still weaved around it as it fell.

He still felt nothing. Brown was still facing backwards, hand resting on his gun, but he turned his head to look at Eddie and shook his head.

Eddie turned around to check their course.

There was a flash of red.

*

It was quiet, yet somehow there was a pounding in his head. Had he been drinking? It must be morning; he had his eyes shut but he could tell that it was light.

It was cold, so cold too. It must be bitter out. Was it raining, snowing? If it was he might get another morning off. He could go and find Sophie, take his money with him this time. But what about Annie? Should he really be doing that to her?

How would she know?

He would know.

It really was cold. And windy. The wind was whistling past his head, was the window open? There was the sound of an engine in the distance. It was muffled, like he was hearing it from under water. It was a sick engine, and he could just about make out some other noises. Flapping, yes something flapping in the breeze. There was a smell of hot oil and dope. It felt like he was flying.

He *had* been flying. When had he landed?

There was someone shouting.

Eddie opened his eyes. He could see a dial. It was a compass. Down there was the throttle, beyond that the joystick. He jerked back in his seat. They *were* flying.

It was Brown, Brown that was shouting. Eddie turned his

head to look at his observer, raised a hand in apology. How had that happened? How had he fallen asleep in the air again? He was useless, a danger, after he had got the aircraft back under control he would fly back, take himself off flying, like Finch, yes like Finch. If he could do it...

But first things first: they were falling, quite rapidly too. He pulled back on the stick. He felt a jolt of fear. There was nothing, no resistance. It was like the stick wasn't attached to anything.

And now the engine was coughing, was stopping. Eddie checked the switches, all on, the fuel cocks - open. He reached forward and switched on the gravity tank, at least he had remembered that this time. The engine still popped and banged. Why was it stopping? He looked over the cockpit side, they were trailing steam or smoke, it was hard to tell, where had that come from? He looked out of the other side and saw something which caused him to give an involuntary shout. The wings on the right side were shredded, riddled with holes, fabric trailing back from all surfaces, one of the flying wires was snapped and was whipping back against the fuselage like a frantic jockey beating extra speed out of his tiring steed. There were rips in the fuselage side and, looking down, he could see that the elevator controls were gone.

The engine stopped completely with a final bang and a spray of hot oil. Eddie was frozen with fear, there was nothing he could do anyway, he had no engine, no elevator, no ailerons. They were on a one-way trip; they were going to crash.

The ground was coming up rapidly. He saw them cross some trenches, he saw men in field grey raise their rifles at them, saw the puff of smoke from the barrels, heard the bullets pluck at their machine.

A shell burst beneath them. The blast lifted them bodily upwards then seemed to throw them forward.

Stony ground leapt up and started smashing them to pieces.

*

Eddie was shaking. God, he thought, that was a dreadful nightmare. Thank God he had woken up.

He wasn't very comfortable. He shifted his body, something hard dug into his leg. He opened his eyes. There was mud and stones, water, barbed wire, the stench of corruption, the sweet, acetone smell of cordite and the smell of unwashed, sweaty bodies.

He sat up, tried to get to his feet but something heavy fell on him, dragged him back down hard onto the ground, the sharp stones digging into his flesh even through his bulky flying gear. He fought back, tried to shrug off his assailant. He got one hand free and blindly started thumping whoever it was. There was a dull roaring in his ears, like everything was far off, he was sure he could hear someone shouting in the distance.

Then something hit him in the nose, giving him a flash of red and pain and made him stop fighting. He clutched his hands to his face.

His gloves and goggles had gone.

The heavy weight was holding him down, pressing him into the ground. Someone was right by his ear; he could feel the breath on it. They were whispering, why didn't they speak up?

Then, through his other ear, he made out what they were saying.

'Eddie, Eddie! Keep still, keep down!'

It was Brown. Of course it was Brown.

He stopped struggling.

'Sorry,' he said. 'Sorry Brown.'

He was shocked. He could hear his own voice but it was muffled.

'I'm alright, leave me be,' he said.

The weight lifted off him Eddie was able to look around him. They were in a shell hole. Half in the pool of water at the bottom was a khaki-clad corpse, contorted in death, bloated, the face greenish-black. Two rats were squealing at each other, rearing up, paws clawing momentarily before one gave in and scurried over the body to the other side. The victor raised its nose briefly then sank its rodent teeth into the rotting hand by its side.

Eddie quickly turned away.

'You alright, Eddie?'

Brown's voice was still muffled, even though he was crouched next to Eddie. He put an exploratory hand up to his right ear, he felt roughness on the skin and was not surprised to see dried blood on his fingertips when he looked at them.

'Yes, what happened?' he said.

He more saw than heard the word 'Archie' come from Brown's lips. He rolled over on his back so his left ear, which seemed to be less affected was closer to his observer. 'Archie burst,' Brown continued. 'Lucky shot, got our range and height straight off. Stunned me for a few seconds it was so close. Thought you were a goner.'

'Might as well have been for all the use I was afterwards.'

'You got us down.'

'That wasn't me, believe me, I had no hand in it,' said Eddie.

There was a shower of mud.

'Look out,' said Brown, covering his head with his arms. Eddie was a bit slow doing the same and so received a few sharp cracks on the head and body as a rain of stones, fortunately mostly quite small, rained down on them.

'Bastards,' grunted Brown. 'Mortar, they know we're around here somewhere.'

Mortar? Eddie had not heard a thing. Was he going to be deaf for the rest of his life? Then again, given where they were, the rest of his life might not be that long.

Eddie felt his ear again, then, as his nose was sore, tentatively touched it and inspected his fingers again. There was more blood, fresh this time.

'Sorry,' said Brown. 'That was more me than the shell. I had to drag you away from the wreck. You were spark out. When you woke up you wanted to stand up. I didn't think that was a good idea.'

Eddie tested his nose gingerly. It didn't seem to be broken. 'Thanks,' he said. 'For both of those things.'

Brown just shrugged. 'It's nothing Eddie. Anyway, I'm just paying a bit back for what your brother did for me.'

Percy, always Percy. He'd gone through this, just like Eddie was now.

Another shower of mud landed on them, but this time Eddie both heard the dull thud of the explosion and covered his head before the heavier stuff landed. A larger lump of stone thudded into his thigh, making him yelp in pain.

'This is getting a bit hot, I thought they might have given up by now.' Brown edged up the slope of the shell hole towards the lip but then hastily slid back down again. Eddie's hearing was coming back so he was able to make out the heavy thumps as bullets impacted the rubble at the rim. Brown blew his cheeks out and shook his head. 'There's at least one machine gun nest and a lot of rifle fire. Not just from t'other side either. We're in the middle of a battle.'

'Great,' said Eddie. 'What do we do?'

'Sit it out I guess.'

Another shower of mud and stones rained down on them. The two covered their heads again. Something zinged off the lip of the shell hole and cut a furrow through the soil, coming to rest hissing in the water. Some part of it must have nicked the corpse because it started to hiss obscenely and deflate, filling the air around them with noxious gasses. Eddie could not help but retch and was now glad that he had not eaten because it limited the amount he brought up. The body gave a twitch and a final groan. To Eddie it seemed it was saying, 'What, more? I'm already dead, leave me be, I've had enough.'

They lay, faces pressed against the stone-covered ground, hands over their heads. The mortar fire did not decrease, quite the contrary in-fact. Was this how he was going to meet his end, cowering in the mud, blown apart, eaten by rats? He looked at his companion. They locked eyes. Eddie knew that he and Brown shared the same thought: it could only be a matter of time before one of the mortar shells dropped right on them.

'We can't stay here,' Eddie said.

'But we can't go,' said Brown.

'Which side are we nearest to?'

'Does it matter, they're both shooting at us.'

Eddie looked at Brown in surprise, it was the first time he had heard him lose his cool. Brown must have realised that his irritation had shown. 'Sorry sir, I mean Eddie. It's hard to tell. The trenches look pretty smashed up by the attack. I reckon the Germans are closer, maybe a hundred yards. Perhaps one-fifty. Why?'

'Can we wave a white flag?'

Brown looked astonished.

'Surrender?'

'Yes.'

Another shower of mud and stones landed on them, interrupting their stand-off and making them cower again.

'Yes, surrender, why not?' Eddie persisted.

'To the Huns? No way,' said Brown.

'But we'd be alive.'

Brown just shook his head. 'No chance. I'm not doing it. Anyway, we've not got anything white.'

Eddie had thought of that. 'I've got a vest on. That's white.' He waited. 'Come on, yes or no.'

'No, damn you, no,' Brown yelled. 'I'd rather be dead. I've got to get back for my kids. ' He stared at Eddie. 'Captain Grenville wouldn't have suggested that. I can't believe you did.'

'Well I'm not my brother, am I?'

'No,' said Brown. 'You're not.'

They lay in silence, their arms over their heads. With each passing moment Eddie knew that the final, fatal shell was closer to arriving. It had to come, it just had to. Would it be quick or would the red hot metal slice into his body, split him so his insides spilled out? He could not help but look at the corpse again, it was now covered in a wriggling mass of grey and was twitching and jerking as the rodents forced their way inside. The thought made him retch again. He had the urge to get up, to run, to escape the horror even though he knew it would be certain death to do so. It began to rain, adding to their misery, now they were soaking wet. Eddie began to shake uncontrollably.

'It wouldn't work anyway,' said Brown.

'What wouldn't?'

'The white flag, surrendering. They're not in the mood, neither side. They'd just shoot us.'

Eddie knew that Brown was right. He also realised that his observer had been thinking about it, that he had planted the seed in his mind. Eddie knew that was why he would never make a good leader. Leaders, be they like Milne or Hastings were definite, even if they themselves were full of doubt. they never revealed what was inside.

Percy was like that too. He decided what was right and then did it. At whatever cost.

'Sorry,' said Brown, interrupting his train of thought.

'Sorry? What for?'

'For what I said. About what I said about you and your brother. You're a good man Eddie. Just like him.'

A good man.

Just like Percy.

A good man.

The man who had murdered his best friend and brother-in-law.

A good man.

A man that can watch one of his friends be attacked by enemy scouts and feel nothing but relief that it was them and not him. A man who would seek pleasure and solace from a French whore rather than wait for the girl that was waiting for him at home. The man that would stand over the grave of a school friend and shed no tears. A man who would not welcome home another friend who he thought to be lost but had returned but instead had abused, insulted and belittled him, all because he was frightened of the feelings that friendship offered when that friendship could be suddenly terminated.

A good man.

The tears dripped off his cheek, mingling with the cold French rain and dropping into the mud. How many tears had fallen over the last three years? How much blood? What crops would grow from these fields after this was all over? This was a harvest, a time of reaping. A strange harvest.

'Eddie?'

'Yes?'

'I think we should -'

Eddie did not hear the rest.

I'm flying, he thought, I'm definitely flying, though how he was not sure, there was no noise, he was floating, amidst the dirt and the stones.

I was born to fly, he thought. Was he flying up to heaven?

DAY 10

APRIL 11, 1917

'Eddie, Eddie!'

Eddie was in the mess. Milne, Brown, Hastings and the rest were looking expectantly at him , empty glasses in hand.

'What?'

'It's your round of course,' said Hastings, thrusting his glass at Eddie.

'Oh right.'

Milne and Brown finished their beers and did the same.

'Thanks. Same again?'

'Of course.'

Eddie juggled the glasses and made his way to the bar. God, he was woozy, how much had he had? It must have been a skinful. He considered not getting another one himself but found himself giving the order anyway. He did not recognise the steward but then reflected that he had spent very little time at Acq in the evenings. He waited whilst the glasses were filled then carried them back on a tray. There was no sign of Milne and Hastings, though Brown was still there, standing on his own staring out of the window.

'Cheers, Eddie,' he said, taking one of the glasses.

'Where are the others?'

'Oh they're around somewhere.' He nodded into the darkness. 'There's some thirsty chaps over there that might appreciate them though.'

Eddie looked where he indicated. He saw Bean sat on one side of a table with two others. They were in the gloom on the edge of the room so he could not see who they were.

'I'm not sure whether I'd be welcome over there,' he murmured to Brown.

'Don't be daft, lad. He's your friend. Always has been. Go on, you'll be fine.'

Eddie still hesitated, but Brown gave him a firm push towards the table.

He saw Bean see him coming and look away. He knew his first instinct was right, this was a mistake. He should have done this earlier, when they got back from no-man's-land with Brown. It was all too late now. He stopped; he was almost at the table but something had struck him. He could not remember how and when they had got back. He thought hard, so hard that his head started to hurt.

'Eddie,' Bean said. His voice was cold. 'What's the matter. Can't handle your drink? Or is there something else you can't cope with?'

The room started to spin.

*

Eddie opened his eyes.

He was lying on his back. It was dark. He could not see a thing. It must be the middle of the night. Where was he? His billet? Home? No, he was cold, so cold, and wet. His head was spinning, he had a thumping headache and a sharp pain in his ankle. Was he drunk, had he got lost on the way back from the mess on the way to his billet, fallen over somewhere and slept it off?

A bright light suddenly came on. It seared into his brain. He screwed his eyes tight shut.

'Stop it, turn the bloody thing off, will you?' he shouted but the light did not fade.

Odd, he thought, I can hear it hissing. What sort of light hisses?

He opened his eyes again and sat up.

Around him was no-man's-land. The light was high in the air, a parachute flare, falling slowly the ground.

The pain in his ankle was suddenly so sharp that he shook his leg violently. Something detached itself, rolled on the ground over and over until it found its feet again. It was a rat, fat and sleek, its eyes glowing a malevolent red in the fading light of the flare. It bared its teeth at Eddie, affronted that he had had the nerve to interrupt its meal, then advanced towards him again.

Eddie shrank from it.

'Go away! Ah! Go! Leave me alone you bastard!'

The rat kept coming. darting towards his leg. He kicked out, missing the first time, then connecting, The rat squealed in anger but showed no sign of giving up. Eddie continued to back away. In doing so his hand fell on something, it was smooth and wooden, it felt heavy, He picked it up and swung it without looking at it. He hit the rat towards its back end. It screamed in agony, over and over again, wriggling back on itself and away. Now he felt guilty, it was just instinct with the rat, it was just doing what came naturally, who could blame it. The flare was dying, he could hardly see the rodent now, but he could not leave it. He scrambled after it in the darkness, hitting out again and again until he finally must have connected with a fatal blow and the screaming stopped.

Eddie knelt, panting in the darkness.

He was still here. God, he was still here in no-man's-land. They hadn't got back. Him and Brown, they hadn't made it. Hellfire.

Brown? Where was he?

'Brown,' he called. 'Brown, where are you?'

He listened. There was the sound of guns in the distance. A machine gun opened up a few hundred yards away.

Then he heard a voice.

'Tommy, Tommy can you hear us?'

Eddie said nothing.

'We know you can hear us, Tommy. Lost your friend, have you?'

There was the sound of faint laughter.

'Shall we come for you, Tommy? We can you know. Our knives are sharp, Tommy.'

Eddie started to edge away, desperate for cover.

'Where are you going, Tommy? We can see you.'

The was a flash from the darkness, a crack of a rifle, then another. Bullets thudded into the ground all around Eddie. He got to his feet, head down, started running, but almost immediately tripped over something. He fell bodily forward, sharp points cut into his flesh and knew that he had tumbled into barbed wire.

Eddie fought to free himself but every time he thought that

he had escaped he would find another part of him ensnared and he would be tugged back into the wire's grip. It was as if it were alive, a monstrous creature of the battlefield intent on keeping him to devour at its pleasure, as a spider cocoons it's still living prey. It took all his will to stop struggling, for he knew his panic was making things worse, somehow to submit to the wire felt all wrong but eventually he did, lying panting amidst the jumble.

Immediately he heard the mocking laughter.

'Tommy, Tommy, we can still see you.'

There was another rifle crack, a bullet pinged off something close to his feet, there was more laughter. He was lying on wire, some of which held one of his hands, his arms and his torso but it was around his right leg and ankle where he was held the tightest. Eddie found that he was able to raise his head and twist his neck to look backward and see how bad things were. He was lying down the slope, one of his feet resting on an iron bracket and tangled up with the barbed wire that was attached to it. It had to be this that he had tripped over and, probably, what the German sentries could see of him. It was pretty dark, though the flashes as shells exploded periodically lit up the battlefield. Actually, Eddie realised, it was probably only his leg that could be seen from the front line. Still, he had seen the effect that a heavy bullet had on the human body with what had happened to John. He did not relish the thought of a round hitting his leg. From his training he knew that the lethal distance of an infantry rifle was over a mile. From a hundred yards or so the bullet would probably tear it right off.

His good leg too. Bloody typical.

The was another crack and he heard the bullet whiz past him, then another and another, interspersed by swearing, laughter and what he assumed to be cat-calling. At least his leg and foot were proving to be a difficult target but how long could his luck last? Each time the Germans fired he flinched, anticipating the impact but each time it missed. He tried to keep calm, to keep still so that the movement he was able to manage did not give the shooters something to focus on. The light was poor so he could not see how badly he was caught, but the gloom was also a blessing; in better light the sentries would be able to hit him easily.

When would it get light? Eddie had no idea what time it was. His pocket watch was in his coat pocket and there was no way he could reach it.

Or was there? His arms and body were mainly trapped by his flying coat which was still fastened around him. Certainly some of the barbs had penetrated his flesh but they mainly held the leather. If he could wriggle his hands free he could withdraw his arms into his coat - and achieve what exactly? He'd be able to get to his watch and find out what time it was, from which he could work out when dawn was and therefore how long it would be before the Germans could see well enough to shoot his leg off.

He slumped down again. Why struggle? Why not just give in and wait for the inevitable? What was the point?

Anyway it probably made no difference. There was bound to be another flare, another star-shell. For ten seconds or more it would be like daylight, more than enough time for a marksman to take aim.

'Just do it, just sodding do it, get it over with,' Eddie yelled.

There was more laughter in the distance, and a volley of shots. These came so rapidly that Eddie was sure that there now must be more than one taking pot-shots at him. Was this how it was going to end, like a target in a shooting gallery at the fair? He needed to get free, before someone launched that next flare at him. He needed help, he needed Brown. Where was he? Why had he abandoned Eddie?

Maybe he hadn't. Maybe he was still around, been knocked out by the same thing that had flung Eddie here. Which was what exactly? A mortar, yes, it had to have been a mortar round. But why hadn't he heard the explosion? He had heard nothing, absolutely nothing. They say that you don't hear the shot that kills you, perhaps that was the same with shells?

It hadn't killed him though.

Not yet.

Not straight away. As good as though.

He had to try.

'Brown,' he called. 'Are you there, Brown?' He listened.

He just heard the Germans talking amongst themselves, laughing. One called out in a mocking, wailing voice: 'Braun, Braun, hilfe...hilfe!'

There was more laughter. Another shot, then another.

Then there was silence.

Eddie lifted his head and twisted back to look at his leg again. Could he get free?

Amid a shower of sparks, Eddie's leg was violently and painfully thrown forward. Although it seemed to be physically impossible, he felt his foot impact with his own head, the impetus of his leg jerking back flicked his body over, so that he performed an involuntary somersault. His palms ripped as his hands were jerked from the wire.

When he came to rest the pain from his leg was excruciating. He lay gasping on his back, tears trickling down his face. So this was it, it had happened, he had been shot, his leg would be gone. The blood that would be pumping out of his body and his life would soon be over and, with injuries like that, would he really want to live? He thought of the legless man in the hospital, the hollow look on his face, the disbelief that the world could be so cruel. Would that man have preferred to drift softly into death rather than be saved to face a lifetime of suffering? It should be relatively painless to go this way. Eddie closed his eyes and waited for death.

It did not come.

Not only that but, although it felt odd, he could still feel his foot, indeed he found he could move it.

He opened his eyes and tried to move. He was still pinned by the wire, some of the strands had wound themselves around him by his contortions, but his right hand, though torn and bleeding, was now free. He was able to lift his head and peer into the gloom at his leg. In the light of the shell flashes he could see that he still had both of them. The right one still had the wire wrapped around it and attached to that was the jagged end of the stanchion. That explained it - and the shower of sparks - a bullet must have hit the metal and broken it, and the kinetic energy carried him forward He shuddered to think of what the effect would have been if it had hit flesh or bone.

Whatever, he was still trapped. He explored the wire wrapped round his chest. It was just a single strand but it was enough to stop him from moving his torso more than an inch and it was too fresh and strong to break. There was a lot more wire round his leg, he could feel it cutting into his flesh, the blood trickling down his calf and ankle.

So he was no better off. He was still alone, in the most dangerous place on Earth, unable to move.

Above him the clouds were clearing. The stars were twinkling against the inky blackness. It was a long time since he had looked at them, he had forgotten how beautiful they could be. Then, abruptly, they were blotted out as the clouds cleared further and the moon, which was just waning from the full, bathed the battlefield in its cold light. It gave his surroundings a ghostly, ethereal, unreal cast. Given the isolation, the destruction, the corruption, the waste, the look seemed quite appropriate to Eddie. He realised that he could not see anything of his aircraft, where was it? Pulverised by the mortar fire he realised. Still he thought there should be something left. It became important to him to find it.

Something caught his eye, something moving in the middle distance, in the direction of the German lines. Then, to his horror, he realised that it *was* the German front line. What he could see moving was helmet-clad heads, and if he could see them then they could see him. He had been flung out of the cover of the low mound that had shielded all but his leg so that now his head and upper body was visible.

He froze. With the moonlight they had to see him, surely they had, how could they not, they had been shooting at him before after all. Why didn't they fire again, he was a sitting target now, even worse a trussed up laying down one. He wanted to shout, tell them to get it over with but he could not find the energy to speak. This was a nightmare, there was a sword of Damocles hanging over him, ready to fall at any time.

The light started to dim. Eddie risked a glance upwards. A veil of clouds had blown over the moon, there looked to be more clouds coming, thicker ones. If the Germans did not shoot quickly, they would lose their chance until morning, he might then have a chance to escape? He knew though that this was clutching at straws; the wire held him in such a tight embrace he was very unlikely to be able to get out himself. The Germans seemed to have the same thought; he was sure that he saw a face look over the parapet then look up at the darkening face of the moon. What were they doing? Why were they putting him through this torture?

The thicker cloud reached the moon and the battlefield was plunged into darkness again. Eddie found let out a long sigh of relief. He had received a stay of execution, some more minutes of life. Suddenly that life seemed precious again, worth fighting for, worth saving. He wanted to live, he realised it, he wanted to live.

And to go home.

He heard voices, low, murmuring, then a scrabbling, the scrape of boot on rock. Someone was coming for him. Oh God, the Germans were coming. This was why they had not shot him, they wanted to dispatch him in a more personal way. What was it going to be? A garrotte? No, it would be a knife. they would slit his throat, or his belly, let his entrails spill out and leave him to a long, lingering death.

He tried again to struggle free of the wire but it was hopeless, all he was doing was weakening himself, the barbs ripping more of his flesh. He sank back. He was exhausted, desperately thirsty, the hope draining from him. He could see the German coming now, keeping low, moving swiftly but carefully over the churned-up ground. He was going from scant cover to scant cover, pausing each time before moving on, ever closer.

Eddie struggled again, then remembered that his hand was now free and that he still had his service pistol in his holster under his coat. He reached for it, fumbling with the strap that held it down. He was still struggling to free it when the man reached him and crouched down. Eddie waited for him to deliver the first blow.

'Good morning,' whispered the German. 'Are you badly hurt?'

Eddie was too stunned to reply. Instead he found that that, once he had stopped thinking about it, he had managed to unstrap the revolver and withdraw it from beneath his coat.

The German noticed but did not seem phased by this. He was running his hands over Eddie, pausing where his gloved hands found wire. 'You really are caught in dis vire aren't you? I can help you. But not if you shoot me, of course.' He nodded at Eddie's gun.

Eddie stared at him for a few seconds then laid the revolver down.

'Good,' said the German. 'I, for one, do not wish to die just as yet.' He reached inside his coat and pulled out, not a knife, but some wire-cutters. He felt again for the wire and cut it, pulling the strands carefully away from Eddie, though he could not stop the barbs tearing as they were withdrawn. He moved on to the next piece, and the next. It took a full five minutes for Eddie to find his voice.

'Why are you doing this?' he managed to say.

'Vy am I cutting you free?' Eddie's eyes were now more adjusted to the light and he could see his benefactor better. He was young, perhaps Eddie's age, perhaps a little older. Under his coal-scuttle helmet Eddie could make out that he was clean shaven, his hair and eyebrows looked dark. Round his neck he had a lanyard from which a gas mask hung. Eddie could see the uniform beneath the coat but could not work out what the man's rank was.

'Yes why? You were shooting at me before.'

The man paused, he gave an anxious glance upwards. The thicker cloud had passed and the faint outline of the moon's disk could be seen. Then the disk faded and the man felt for the next strand of wire.

'It was not I that was shooting,' he said. 'I do not agree with those that were, you were helpless after all, but I can understand them. You are a pilot, yes?'

'Yes,' said Eddie.

'They have been bombed and machine gunned by airmen like you. You can understand them too, yes?'

'Yes.' Eddie tried not to think about the previous day, about the men he had killed in the machine-gun nest.

'Good. Anyway, they did not manage to hit you?'

'No they didn't.'

He saw the young German smile. 'Our battalion needs to improve their shooting,' he said. 'Anyway, when our officers came, they ordered those that were shooting at you to stop. I volunteered to come and get you.'

Eddie saw him glance at the clouds again, then over towards the British lines. It sank in just how much guts that the man was showing.

'You asked me vy I do this? It is simple: It is the right thing to do.'

Eddie just stared at him.

'Thank you.' he said at last.

The German just shrugged and snipped another piece of wire.

'You vill have to come back with me, yes?' he said. 'No trouble? You will forget about your gun? You would not get very far anyway.'

'Yes, I understand,' said Eddie. 'No, trouble.' To reinforce this he pushed the revolver away. So that was it, with a sinking feeling he began to accept that his war was over. He would be a prisoner. He wouldn't see his family, or Annie, or anyone he knew until the war was over.

But he would be alive.

'Right, you should be free now,' said the German. 'Roll over to your right, but do not try to get away, or you will be shot.'

Eddie did as he was told and found that he was, indeed, free of the wire. He was cut and bruised but the feeling of release was like he had been given a new life. He lay on the ground next to his rescuer.

'Thanks,' he said again.

'We still have to get back to our trench,' said the German. He raised his head cautiously to peer towards the German lines. At that moment the clouds drifted from in front of the moon again, flooding no-man's-land with light. There was a crack, a metallic ping, the German swore and quickly ducked down again.

'Are you alright?' said Eddie.

'It seems your men are slightly better shots than ours,' said the German.

There was a volley of shots, bullets started to thud all around them. Eddie pressed himself into the ground, alongside him his rescuer did the same.

'Your friends seem to not wish you to be saved,' he heard him mutter.

There was a volley of shots from the German side, then the rhythmic thud-thud of a machine gun, the tracer whipping just over the heads of Eddie and the German.

'We need to get out of sight whilst we are getting the covering fire,' said the latter. Come on.'

He started shuffling forward on his elbows, keeping his body flat to the ground. Eddie tried to do the same, ignoring the pain he was feeling from his bruises and cuts. The German abruptly turned across in front of Eddie then disappeared out of sight. Eddie felt suddenly exposed and alone, and hurried forward, tipping over a slight rise then sliding uncontrollably down until he splashed into stinking water, some of which he immediately sucked into his lungs. Coughing, he tried to get up, only to feel himself grabbed and pushed down into the ground.

'You cannot get up, my friend, this hole is not that deep.'

Eddie pushed the German off him, then rolled over, panting. He glanced across at him. He was lying calmly on his back, his hands behind his head, one leg crossed over the other.

'We will have to wait for things to calm down,' he said. 'We have not been introduced. I am Max. Max Steiger.' He held out his hand.

Eddie looked at the German's hand. There were regulations against this - weren't there? One of the King's regulations, about fraternising with the enemy, even about communicating with them? But then, he had saved Eddie. And there was Siggi, he was a German, and a good sort.

He reached over and took Max's hand. 'Edward. Eddie Grenville.'

Max nodded. 'It is good to meet you Eddie. It is a shame that it is under such circumstances.'

He waved his hand around the shell hole.

Eddie pulled a grim smile and nodded. 'It is a bit unfortunate, yes.'

Max looked up at the sky. 'I used to pray for clear nights so I could observe the stars. Now I would rather that the clouds and rain came back.' He looked at Eddie. 'I was a student of astronomy before

I was called up. I miss my nights with the telescope.'

Eddie nodded. 'I've never even looked through one,' he said. 'My family had no interests in anything but business and the army I'm afraid.'

'You were in business before the war? That was your career?'

'No. I had no career. I didn't have time. I joined up straight from school.'

Oddly, Eddie found that his eyes were moist. He was feeling sad, sorry for himself. He had never lived, not experienced a 'normal' life. Would he ever now? Then he thought of Bunny. He never had a chance either, and never would now, like countless other young men.

He had thought about death before, before he joined up, in training, whilst he was at 159. He had told himself that his death might happen and he had rationalised that, as long as he was doing it for his country, for his cause, then it was alright, he could accept it. Suddenly, he found that rationalisation false and facile. He really wanted to live, to have that normal life. And he wanted everyone else to do the same, Hastings, Milne, Bean - and Max too. Max wasn't a monster, in fact he seemed so much like Siggi - formal yes, but funny, gentle and self-depreciating, all the things that Alice had fallen for.

And that Percy had loved too.

Yet Percy had...

'Are you alright, Eddie?' said Max. 'You seemed far away somehow.'

'I...was...just thinking of something,' said Eddie, wiping his face with his hand. 'Perhaps wishing I was far away!'

'Wish that for us both, my friend,' said Max. He looked up at the sky and wrinkled his nose in disgust. Eddie knew why. Not only was the sky clear, over to the east there was a distinct pink tinge, a harbinger of the approaching dawn.

'It doesn't look good does it?' he said.

Max just grunted a reply.

'I'm sorry,' Eddie said. 'I got you into this.'

Max gave a wry smile. 'Actually I think it was our Kaiser and his generals that got me into this. And my own sense of ...what is the word I am looking for?'

'Honour?' said Eddie.

'Decency,' Max said. 'I do not think there is much honour in this conflict.'

Eddie nodded.

They lay together in silence whilst the sky lightened. The gun battle continued, tracer bullets whipping just over their heads from both sides, though the firing became more intermittent and desultory, waxing and waning.

'How long have you been at the front?' Eddie asked at last.

'I have been six months in France,' said Max. 'But I also served a year on the Eastern Front.'

'What was that like?'

'Very cold in Vinter, hot in Summer and miserable all year round. What about you?'

Eddie smiled. 'I have been at the front a whole 10 days.'

'Good heavens, not very long.'

'Long enough to be shot down twice and crash twice more. I've had my observer killed in front of my eyes, seen too many friends die.'

'Yes, our flyers are doing well at present. You have seen the Baron, yes?'

'The Baron?'

'Von Richthofen and his little red machine?'

'Ah, no.' Eddie thought for a few seconds. 'I say, did you see my machine crash yesterday?'

'Yes, we saw it.'

'Did you see what happened to Brown? My observer?'

'We saw him drag you from the machine. We have not seen him since. I am sorry.'

Eddie thought of the mortars, and the feeling of him flying. That had to be when. There was still a chance but he knew it was very remote. Brown was dead. He had to be.

They lay in silence staring at the stars for a few minutes. Then Eddie noticed it had gone quiet, the firing had stopped. He saw Max had realised the same thing and had raised himself up slightly to look over the rim of the shell hole towards the British lines.

'What is it, what's happening?' Eddie said.

'I don't know,' said Max, turning over onto his front and crawling up the slope. Eddie joined him.

'Do you think they have given up, forgotten about us? Maybe we can make it over to your trench?'

'Perhaps,' said Max. 'But...'

Suddenly the whole western horizon lit up, sheets of orange flashes. It was like a sudden, repeating dawn, but a dawn in the wrong place and at the wrong time.

'Mein Gott,' muttered Max.

If he said anything else, Eddie did not hear it for everything was drowned out by the whistling of heavy shells dropping out of the sky.

*

The noise was unimaginable, but it was more than noise, the artillery barrage assaulted all the senses. The shell bursts flashed like a million lamps all lit at once. The pressure wave of the explosions assaulted the eardrum and tore the air from the lungs and was followed immediately by the shock transmitted through the ground that travelled through the body shaking the heart and soul and vibrating all the organs within so violently that Eddie was sure that they must be torn from the veins and arteries connected to them. The vibration was numbing, Eddie was not certain whether he was still laying on the ground but was instead floating above it. Then there was the stench of chemicals, chemicals mixed with churned earth, corruption, death, vomit and excreta and all of this rained down on the pair as they huddled together in the scant shelter of the shell hole.

And this did not happen once, it went on and on. It seemed that it would never end.

Eddie found it hard to think, in fact at first the only thoughts that he had was firstly how could anything survive through this and secondly is that this was what he was involved in, this is what he called down when he had been part of signalling in the Zone Call. He had inflicted this on other human beings, men like the one who he now found himself huddled next to. Yes, this was war but...

But what? This was war. This was the reality. There was no heroics, there was nothing noble about it, this was what war was, the industry of each side making the guns and the shells that then were sent to rain down on fragile bodies that huddled in the mud and squalor, shitting and pissing themselves with fear whilst waiting for the white-hot shard of metal to end their suffering.

Or begin it, he thought, as the image of the shattered legless man with the vacant stare came back to him.

Something hit him hard in the back, then something else, heavy, landed on his upper arm. He convulsed in pain, only to receive a stunning crack on the head by something coming down from the darkness above him. He felt something lay on top of him, something heavy covering the top part of his body and head. It was only when he heard the ping of stone on metal between shell bursts did he understand: It was Max, Max who, unlike Eddie was wearing a steel helmet was using himself to protect Eddie's head.

Humanity can be amazing, he thought.

Sometimes at least.

Then it felt like his lungs were sucked out of his body through his mouth and nose.

He gasped, trying to breath. All went black.

*

Eddie put the drinks down on the table. Bean just looked at them.

'What are they for?' he said.

'For you of course,' Eddie said. 'Well for you and your friends.'

'I don't want them,' said Bean. 'And they don't either.'

The light somehow brightened revealing the other people around the table. Bunny, his face smashed and distorted. Collier, with the ragged red and grey shattered skull. Siggi, white faced, rotting features green-tinged staring sightlessly at Eddie.

He vomited onto the table.

*

Eddie opened his eyes.

All he could see was dirt, dirt and stones.

It was light, he realised, light and, although still going on, the shellfire seemed somehow quieter, more distant.

He was being pinned down. What was on him? He was not sure he had the strength but he tried to free himself and was surprised that, by raising himself up on his arms, he was able to shrug off the weight that was on him.

He rolled onto his back. It was daylight, there was no doubt of that but the day seemed misty - or was it smoke? Or gas, oh hell was it gas? Strangely he found that he wasn't worried by this, even though he had nothing to protect himself against it. The world was unreal, dreamlike, he was just a spectator. Perhaps that was it, he was dreaming still. That explained his feeling of invulnerability, you could be petrified in a dream but you couldn't die.

There was a groan to his left. It was Max. Ah, that explained the weight that had pinned him down, it was Max, he had been still laying over Eddie, protecting his head. Good old Max, when he woke up, when they got to safety he would have to stand him a beer.

Where prisoners-of-war allowed beer? He wasn't sure, surely that was one of the things that they should have been told? They never told you anything important, anything useful, the army didn't.

There were other figures in his dream, big, strange figures, looming out of the mist, or cloud, smoke, gas whatever it was. Crouching low, running, running past his shell hole. Where were they going?

Eddie sat up.

'Hey,' he called, but his voice was little more than a croak. His mouth was dry, his throat was sore, very sore. Could you feel pain in a dream? Well apparently in this dream he could. When had he last had something to drink? Had he drunk any of the beer with Bean? No, he was being silly, that *was* a dream, Bunny and Collier were there and they were dead.

Collier! That was John's name, he had remembered. The mind was such a fickle thing.

'John, my name is John,' Eddie said, though it was barely a croak.

Two figures appeared on the edge of the shell hole. They were strange, frightening, khaki-coloured with round heads, big round insect eyes, a proboscis dangling in front. He backed away from them.

The insect-men looked at each other, then to Eddie's left. They were coming into the hole, coming towards him.

Rifles. They held rifles, with bayonets fixed.

This was real, this was not a dream.

Eddie looked at Max. His eyes were open. He was covered in mud but he was in grey, the field grey of the German Army, the only one of the four of them not on khaki.

He looked at Eddie and smiled.

The soldier rammed his bayonet into his belly. Max's eye's bulged. He sighed.

'No!' Eddie tried to yell but did little more than croak. 'Please, no!'

The soldier withdrew the bayonet, red with blood then thrust forward again and again.

The other one was knelt next to Eddie saying something. It was hard to make out through his box respirator but at last he made it out.

'It's alright sir, we've got 'im. You're safe now, sir, you're safe.

*

He was on a stretcher.

He had tried to walk back to the British lines but had stumbled and fallen several times and the stretcher party had insisted. He heard shells fall, the rattle of a machine gun, the crack of rifles but it was all hazy. He only vaguely noticed when the stretcher bearers dropped him and swore when one shell fell close by and pelted them with mud and stones.

'Sorry sir,' they said, but he was beyond caring.

Then he was in a trench. It was virtually deserted but smelt of woodbines, sweat and shit. The stretcher-bearers had apologised, said 'do you mind, sir, can't take you further like, need to get back. Do you mind making your own way from here?'

Eddie stood alone in the trench for some minutes. He was not inclined to go anywhere even if he had any idea where to go. He just stood and stared.

'Hello, my son, are you alright?'

Eddie blinked and tried to focus on who had spoken. Words were still muffled, adding to the dreamlike quality of where he was.

'Are you alright, do you need help?'

The man talking to him was dressed like a soldier, khaki uniform, greatcoat, pudding-bowl helmet but his face was lined, his hair wispy and snowy-white. His blue eyes were soft and gentle.

'Are you God?' Eddie rasped.

The man laughed. 'Hardly, my son, hardly. Just trying to do His work the best way I can. It sounds like you need a drink.'

'Water, just water, please,' whispered Eddie.

As the man passed him a canteen, Eddie saw that he was wearing a dog-collar.

'Thank you, padre, er, sir,' said Eddie, realising that the chaplain was a Captain.

'Don't need to call me sir, we are all the same in the eyes of the Lord,' said the Chaplain, who then looked around him. 'Just don't tell the army I said that, will you?'

'No,' said Eddie, looking back over towards the German lines. 'We *are* all the same.'

He gulped the water down but it came straight back up again.

'Steady, my son,' said the Chaplain. 'How long is it since you last ate or drank anything?'

'I'm not sure,' Eddie shrugged. 'Yesterday sometime?'

'Yesterday? Oh my boy, poor you. You're a flyer aren't you? Were you shot down?'

Eddie nodded and cautiously sipped some water. This, at least, looked like it was going to stay down.

'Come on then, old chap, let's get you back to the medics, let them take a look at you.' The Chaplain took Eddie's arm and tried to lead him away. Eddie's anger bubbled over. He tore free of the grip.

'Get your bloody hands off me, I'm all right.

He realised that he should not do that, that the Chaplain outranked him and, in other circumstances could have led to a court-martial but he did not care.

'My son, what's the matter?' The Chaplain looked more concerned than angry. 'Don't you want help?'

'Not from the likes of you.'

'From me? Why not me?'

Eddie pointed at the man's dog-collar. 'Because of that. How can you preach that what we do is right, that it is right to kill, that our side is Christian and right? How can you? Hypocrite, you, me, all of us are bloody hypocrites!'

The Chaplain sighed. 'I understand, my son, believe me, I do. And I do believe God will judge us for our actions, but, in the meantime, we have to do what we think to be right. It would be easy if everything was black or white, right or wrong, whether we are following the path of the devil or the saints. It is not though, the path is hard to see, all we can do is go where we think the light is leading us.'

Eddie bit his lip and nodded. 'Lead kindly light,' he murmured.

The Chaplain smiled. 'Indeed, "Lead, kindly Light, amid th'encircling gloom; Lead thou me on! The night is dark, and I am far from home; Lead thou me on! Keep thou my feet; I do not ask to see the distant scene--one step enough for me." Old John Newman may have turned to Rome but he could write about faith and doubt couldn't he? Now, shall we get you back and let the doctor look at you? Oh wait a minute, just step back.'

The Chaplain gently pushed Eddie back against the trench wall as a stretcher party came past, a blood-stained casualty on it, gently moaning.

'I'm fine,' said Eddie, once they had gone. 'I don't need a doctor. I'm not badly hurt, just a bit bruised.'

The Chaplain frowned. 'Well, if you say so. Let's get you back for a hot drink and some food anyway. It looks like you need it. Shall we go?'

This time the Chaplain did not lay a hand on Eddie but just raised his arm and opened his hand in invitation to follow, which Eddie did.

'Sorry, sir,' he said.

'Sorry, my son? What for?'

'For what I said, before. I was insubordinate.'

'You were questioning, that's all, I don't mind that, it's to be encouraged.' The Chaplain, stopped, turned and smiled as he whispered, 'Don't tell the army that either.'

He resumed walking and Eddie followed. They soon reached a trench leading away to the right, Eddie realised that this must be a communication trench, leading back to the secondary lines. They had to stop a couple of times to let parties of first soldiers, presumably reserves going forward to the front line, and then the stretcher party they had seen before going out again, past, before resuming their meandering path back.

They reached an area where a larger opening had been dug out. Medics in white, blood-stained aprons were working on casualties whilst others waited, lying on cots on the ground.

'Field dressing station,' said the Chaplain. 'The docs try and stabilise the chaps that can be saved here then they are taken back to the main hospitals. The ones that are beyond their help...well that's my domain.' He nodded towards a row of bodies, covered completely in blankets.

'Brown,' said Eddie suddenly. The Chaplain looked quizzically at him. 'My observer. He was with me in no-man's-land, pulled me out of the wreck when we were shot down. I lost touch with him in the night.' He looked towards where the medics were working.

'You think he might have been brought in?'

'Yes,' said Eddie, though deep down he was sure now that

Brown was dead, blown to pieces by the mortar that had dropped him into no-man's-land.

'I'll ask them,' said the Chaplain. 'Just wait here, my son.'

Eddie did as he was told. He tried not to look at the station station but it was hard not to. Everywhere there were soldiers, some quiet, many moaning, all bandaged. A group of stretchers was laid by the entrance to the dugout, casualties laid on them, covered up to their necks in brown army issue blankets. Most had their eyes shut but a couple stared at Eddie through rheumy eyes.

'Got a fag, guv?' said one. 'I could really do with a drag.' The man was white-faced with pain, the top of his head and one side of his face bandaged.

'Sorry, I don't,' said Eddie.

The man looked away. Eddie felt a pang of guilt, even though he knew it was irrational. He had not deliberately denied the soldier that small comfort but, somehow, it felt that he had. The feeling grew when more of the casualties came to stare at him, he felt their gaze almost as a physical assault, that they were accusing him. He was pleased when the Chaplain came back over, though his heart sank when he saw the grave look on his face. The Chaplain had a piece of paper in his hand.

'What is it?' he said.

'There was a flyer brought in this morning but I'm afraid it's not good news. They found his body in the wreckage of his machine.'

'In the machine?' Eddie's spirit lifted a little. 'It can't have been Brown. We got well away from our aircraft; in fact I never even saw the wreckage. I think it was pretty much smashed up even before the mortars started.'

'Oh that's good then, I'm glad it wasn't your friend.' said the Chaplain. He nodded towards the line of bodies. 'He's one of those. They gave me the number that's pinned to the blanket. He wasn't carrying any identification, or if he was, it had been taken from the body. There's a lot of looting, I'm afraid, from our side as well as theirs. They were rather hoping you could identify him, but it sounds like you've been spared that.' Despite his words, the Chaplain still stared at the paper in his hand. Eddie stared at it too, knowing the last thing that he wanted to look at was another dead body. After a pregnant few seconds Chaplain at last stuffed the paper in the pocket of his coat. 'Well, better get you back to the rear. This way.'

He led Eddie out of the clearing station, though their progress was immediately stopped by a line of troops coming up the communication trench heading for the front. There was also an almighty roar as a shell went off nearby, showering them in mud. It was followed by several more, luckily further away.

'Sounds like Jerry is regrouping,' said the Chaplain. 'Looks like we are getting you out just in time.' He looked down the sap. 'I think we can go now.'

'Yes,' said Eddie, but did not move. The delay had caused his guilt to grow, not about the cigarettes but about the dead pilot. What if he did know them? If he knew them he could give them a name, save them being buried as an unknown. At least their family back home would have some certainty then. If it happened to him he would want someone to do the same. It was not much to ask, he was being selfish otherwise. 'That pilot. I'll take a look,' he said.

The Chaplain's face brightened. 'Oh will you, my son? That is really good of you. You really don't have to.' He turned and walked back into the clearing station, not giving Eddie a chance to change his mind.

And, as they walked towards the bodies, Eddie really did want to reconsider. Being noble and selfless was fine but now it did not seem such a good idea. The trenches stank but, this close to the bodies, the stench of death was almost overwhelming. It was obvious that some of the bodies had lain out in the open for some time, Eddie was surprised that they were placed here, so close to those fighting for their lives.

The Chaplain was bent over the bodies, comparing the number on his paper with that pinned to the blankets.

'Ah, here he is,' he said. He reached to pull back the blanket. 'Ready?'

Eddie wanted to scream that he wasn't ready, he wanted to run away. What if the body was rotting, green. Or blown to bits, missing arms, hands, legs, or with its head shattered like John's had been. Or what if it was Bean? He had lost one friend, could he bear to lose another and see them dead?

Although was Bean still his friend, given the way that Eddie had treated him.

He thought of all this in the time it took him to say the word: 'Yes.'

The Chaplain pulled back the blanket.

*

He only vaguely was aware of walking back to the rear area with the Chaplain, of taking his leave of him, or of what he said or what was said to him in farewell.

He knew he had reported to the field headquarters, that they had assured him that they would ring the squadron and arrange someone to come and pick him up and that he had been told that it could be some time. Someone told him - though whether this was an officer he was not sure - to go still further back, to a village whose name was St. something-or-other which sounded beautiful and perhaps once was but was now little more than a few jumbled heaps of timber, brick and stone. After half an hour or more of stumbling onward, he only knew that he had arrived at the village by seeing the tented field kitchen that he had been told was there.

He sat on a pile of stones that may once have been a wall or even part of a house and waited. It was cold, the clouds had started to close in again, but he was largely insensible to it. He just stared into nothing, trying to get the image of what he had seen out of his head.

He couldn't though, he doubted whether he ever would.

He could not work out why he had been so shocked as to who was lying there. He was not a close friend. It was just so - well, unexpected.

Yet inevitable.

And it had shaken him to the very core of his being.

Of all the things he had experienced, John Collier, being shot to pieces by the Albatros, Bunny, the euthanised burning pilot, the burning tanker, and Max, the noble, kind Max to whom he owed his life, it was this that had affected him the most.

It started to rain harder. Still he did not move.

Someone gave him a mug filled with hot, sweet, tea. They asked him why he didn't move under cover.

He ignored them.

He found some time later that he had only taken one sip of his tea and that it was stone-cold when he tried it again.

Sometime in the afternoon, the Crossley tender drew up next to him. Stiffly he climbed in the back, barely acknowledged the two ack-emmas who had been sent out to fetch him and closed his eyes and tried to sleep on the journey back.

He was not successful but at least it avoided him having to

make conversation.

It was getting dark by the time they drove through the gates and into the courtyard at Acq. He was out of the car and heading into the admin block almost before it had stopped. Behind him he heard the ack-emma's mutter something about him being 'an ungrateful bugger' but ignored them.

The first person he saw was Moorhouse coming out of the mess.

'Grenville, I say old chap, you're alive, what -'

Eddie pushed past him and went up the stairs.

He walked straight into Pops' office. The man himself was sat at his desk and he smiled broadly when he saw Eddie.

'Grenville!' he said. 'We'd almost given up on you. We couldn't believe it when we got the call-'

'Captain Milne is dead,' Eddie said flatly.

'How do you -'

'I saw his body. Bullet through the heart.'

Eddie found that his legs would no longer support him.

Pops and the room faded away in a revolving swirl.

*

He was not sure how much time had passed, an hour, half an hour, but he was now in the doctor's office, laying on the couch that was used for treatment. He had been vaguely aware of being poked and prodded, of being asked questions, though exactly what he had said in response he was not sure. Now he was wide awake but did not seem to have any energy to do more than lay. His arms and legs were aching and he felt more tired and lethargic than he had ever done before.

Outside they were talking about him; the doctor, Pops and Reeves. He could follow what they were saying but could not be bothered to interject.

'Physically he's alright, a bit bruised and cut about and his foot is very tender but that's not the problem,' said the doctor.

'What is?' Reeves sounded impatient.

'Basically he is at the end of his tether, his nerves are shot.'

Eddie was sure that he heard Reeves give a snort of derision. This was confirmed by what Pops said next: 'Don't be like that, Major, he's very young and he's had a hard time.'

'All my pilots are young, they've all had a hard time,' said Reeves. 'That's no excuse for them not to fly.'

'He really isn't going to be much use to you,' said the doctor. 'My recommendation is that he's shipped out. He needs a rest. He should be in a hospital.'

'I don't agree,' said Reeves. 'He just needs a good night's rest. And think of the example he's going to be setting to the other boys if they find out.'

'He needs more than that, sir.'

Pops again.

'I agree,' said the doctor.

There were a few moments of silence.

'Look,' said Reeves. 'We need pilots, we're desperately short of crews. We've lost two flight leaders in the last two days, one already to outright cowardice -'

'I hope you're not suggesting that Grenville is in that category,' interrupted Pops. 'That's not on.'

'I didn't say that, did I?'

'I suppose not.'

'Whatever, with David gone too we're in serious trouble. We need pilots. We can't mollycoddle them.'

David.

David Milne.

The careful, indestructible Captain Milne, who protected his men, who always came back. Eddie decided that this was what had shocked him so much when the Chaplain pulled back the blanket to reveal Milne lying beneath. There was nothing shocking in the way that he had died, in fact he looked very peaceful, it seemed he had had a quick, clean death, even the crash had not seemed to put a mark on him. No, it was the fact of his death itself that was so disturbing. It showed Eddie the certainty that no one was safe. If it could happen to Milne...

Whatever he did not want to fly. He certainly did not want to kill. How could he pull the trigger or drop a Cooper bomb now? He just knew that every time he did, he would see the face of Max.

Outside the room his fate was still being argued.

'We will give him a few days here, he'll come round, mark my words,' said Reeves.

'I don't agree,' said the doctor.

'Neither do I.'

'I'm sorry, that's the decision. I have a squadron to run. He can be excused flying duties until he's ready. Good evening, gentlemen.'

There was the sound of a door closing.

Eddie closed his eyes.

The nightmares continued.

*

The night air brought him fully awake. He was outside. Oh God, was he still in no-man's-land, had he dreamed all that? Someone was holding on to his arm, he shook them free, he was ready to run.

'Steady Grenville, easy there.'

Pops. It was Pops. He breathed easier. He was back at Acq, he wasn't dreaming.

But that meant that Max had really been butchered and that Milne was dead.

'Where am I going?' he said.

'Back to your billet,' said Pops. 'You'll be more comfortable there.'

Eddie allowed Pops to hold his arm again and lead him on, but then a thought hit him and he stopped.

'Is Bean still there, is he alright? He's not dead, is he?'

'Bean? Oh Monroe? Yes, yes, he's there, he's fine. He's been worried about you though.'

Eddie carried on walking.

They were inside, the light was better. Pops pulled back the curtain.

'Here we are. I am sure your friend will deal with you now.'

Bean was stood, facing Eddie, a mixture of concern and delight on his face.

'Eddie, it's so -' he began.

Eddie did not let him finish. He found the energy to step to Bean and take him in his arms and hug him.

'Bean, my old friend,' he said, his eyes stinging. 'I'm sorry, I'm so sorry.'

*

Eddie thought that sleep would come quickly but he found himself lying awake in the darkness listening to Bean and Moorhouse snore. His mind was racing, going over and over in his head what Pop had said to him before he had taken his leave.

'I know the Major needs pilots, but don't be swayed by it, or anyone else. You're not well, it's not just the foot, we've known about that for days, I'm meaning the other thing, your...behaviour. I've seen how you've changed. You can go home, there's no shame. You're at the end of your tether Eddie. Go home, get a rest. Then, when you are able, come back. You'll be stronger.'

He could go home. He could live. There would be no shame. He could rest and recover and come back stronger.

But, now he was thinking about it, he was no longer sure whether Pops had actually said it. Had he? Or had Eddie fallen asleep and just dreamed it? The sleeping and waking world felt just the same now.

What was real?

DAY 11

APRIL 12, 1917

He wakes in his bed wondering whether he is really back at Acq or is dreaming and is really still in a shell hole somewhere.

It's light, the room seems familiar but is frightened to move lest he disturb the image, that the room will dissolve and resolve into churned up earth, wire and death.

There is a low buzzing - no, not a buzzing, a hiss in his head. He cannot not hear the normal sounds of the airfield. There are no voices, no one whistling, no music playing. Above all there are no engines running, no familiar rough beat of the RAF V8s, the soundtrack to his time in the RFC. Now there is nothing but the soft hiss in his head.

It isn't right.

Is it real?

At last he can stand it no longer and finds enough courage to move his head and look around.

The room stays where it is. He is not on the battlefield but he is alone. There is no sign of the others. What are they called? Bean and Slade. No not Slade, Slade is gone, Moorhouse, yes that's his name. What time is it? How long has he slept?

He has a moment of panic. What if Bean has gone up and is now dead? Tears fill his eyes. Bean is his friend, he remembers that. He cannot face losing more friends, he has lost too many, though it is hard to remember now who exactly has gone.

Bunny. Did he know a Bunny? Silly name, childish. A boy, yes he knew a Bunny as a small boy, but was he here? He can't have been.

But Bean is here. WAS here at least. Has he gone?

He is out of bed before he realises it and moves over to Bean's side of the room. Relief, all his things are still there, they have not been cleared out. Good, that means Bean is still around. Last night he had been vaguely aware of being given a box by Pops, and that the batman came to the billet and was hanging his clothes up. At the time, the pleasure of seeing Bean caused him not to think about it. Now he realises that, in fact, his clothes and belongings were being returned to him. that they had presumed him to be dead and cleared his stuff away.

He goes sits on his bed again, and stares at his box of belongings, taking stock.

He decides he does not feel angry with them for packing up his things. It was a logical thing to do and, anyway, he feels nothing now - no anger, no emotion. It is what he imagines being dead would feel like, nothingness, quiet.

He suddenly feels useless. Tears come back, not for Bean this time but for himself.

What use is he? He is a pilot who does not fly. He is a warrior who will not kill.

He tries to pull himself together, he must feel something - but what? Is he totally numb? Detached from the world? He takes stock. Does he have any emotions? Yes, he thinks he does but they are stunted. So what does he now have, what does he feel? Fear, yes. Fear of dying? No, dying doesn't worry him, that means peace, no more worries, dying would be welcome. So what does he fear most? Yes, he knows what it is. It is fear of loss. Of losing Bean, his one remaining friend.

Is that fear drawn from love? Does he love Bean? Not in that way, he isn't like Bean. He loves him like a brother.

A brother. He has a brother. Percy. He loves his brother, what he is, was, not what he became.

But what of Annie though? He has hardly thought of her, not since his encounter with Sophie, not when he was shot down and was facing death. Surely, he should have done?

Perhaps he just needs to be reminded of her. He reaches into his box and draws out her letter. He tries to re-read it but the paper will not keep still in his hand. He is trembling, his hand is shaking uncontrollably.

He looks at his hand in wonder. He remembers this happens when he is flying, when he is afraid. Now it is doing it on the ground and he cannot not make it stop. He stares at his trembling hand for a good minute before he passes the letter into his left and stuffs his right into the pocket of his trousers.

He tries again to read Annie's letter. He is sure that words had been such a tonic a few days - hours? - ago but now they mean nothing, they could be an instruction manual for all the interest they hold for him. The ink but is cold and dead on the paper, the image of warmth, and love, excitement, sensuality that he is sure that he felt when he first read it is no longer there.

Were they ever?

He decides that the words are not written to him. They are written for a different person. Someone he once knew. Someone he once was?

What about the French girl, Sophie?

He tries to visualise her, picture how she looked when she had bared her breasts for him but he finds he cannot remember her face, and the electric thrill of sexuality and excitement he had enjoyed are not there either.

It's him. He is numb. He is as good as dead.

What is the point of existing like this? He is a pilot who does not fly, a warrior who does not fight, a man that cannot kill.

A man that cannot feel.

A drone. Pointless.

He feels the fear of loss though. That is something. He will hold onto that.

He tosses the letter back into the box and stands up.

He needs people around him, even ones he does not know. He does not want to spend any time with himself.

He does not bother to put a coat. He does not notice the cold. Outside it is snowing, thicker than ever before. Surely no one can be flying in this? He knows that he can though.

But he is a pilot who does not fly.

In the mess he finds the crews lazing about drinking coffee and tea, playing cards, writing letters and generally chatting to each other. He cannot not see Bean though, and he finds himself frantically searching the faces - the largely strange faces - for his brother.

Not his brother. Not Percy. His other brother. Bean.

'What oh, Grenville, there you are.'

He turns to see who has spoken, briefly hopeful but finds it is someone else. What is his name? Slade? No, Slade has gone. It's Moorhouse.

'How are you, old chap? You look a bit better than you did last night, I must say. I say, this weather is beastly isn't it? I was hoping I could get over the lines today but if it stays like this it looks like I'll be staying on the ground.'

'Yes,' he says, irritated that he has been interrupted. He is still looking for Bean.

'Not that it concerns you of course, not with you not flying.'

'No,' he says. He is getting angry now.

'What's that?' says a nearby pilot. He cannot place him but thinks he is in C flight. 'Who's not flying? Why not?'

'Grenville here. Major Reeves orders. It was because he had such a beastly time when he was shot down.'

The pilot looks disgusted. 'Bloody hell, we've all had a beastly time! What makes you so damned special, Grenville?'

'I believe his Uncle's a General,' a laconic voice replies, the owner of which is concealed by a cloud of cigarette smoke.

The pilot nods. 'Ah, that would explain it then. Family pulled a few strings to protect their precious little boy, have they?'

His anger rises 'It's not my choice to be taken off flying. I'd rather...I'd rather...'

His voice trails off. He knows what the truth is.

'Yes, of course you would, Grenville, of course you would. What the hell are you still doing here if you're not willing to do the job? Taking up a billet of someone with more backbone, that's what you're doing.'

'I say,' says the other one. Slade. No not Slade. Moorhouse, that's him. 'That's a bit -'

'That's enough of that talk. Johnson, you'll apologise to Grenville.' To his surprise it is Hastings who has intervened. He hasn't seen him in the mess when he had arrived so he assumes he must just have walked in.

'But sir,' Johnson protests.

'I said enough. Grenville is just taking a bit of a rest on the orders of Major Reeves and the Doc. Now damn well apologise Johnson.'

'Sir,' says Johnson. 'Sorry Grenville. Didn't mean anything by it.'

He shrugs. What does it matter? He is a pilot who does not fly. A drone.

'Good, right Grenville, I'd like to see you in the squadron office.' Hastings turns and leaves the mess.

He follows.

Hastings. Does he like Hastings? He is not sure.

The flight leader's' office is deserted. 'Shut the door.' says Hastings. He does as he is told.

Something inside him tells him that he should say something. Hastings has done something for him, though he is not sure what it is.

'Thank you, sir.' he says.

Hastings, who has sat down, looks up sharply.

'What for?'

Yes what for? Oh yes, that other man - boy? - was trying to be nasty to him, though he was right. Hastings though, he stood up for him.

'For defending me in there.'

Hastings gives a snort of derision. 'Yes, well, truth is I agree with Johnson. In my book you're either here to fly or you're not. I'm not one to question Major Reeves's judgement but I'm not sure about this call.' He shakes his head. 'I had high hopes for you, Grenville, I really did. You're a good pilot but you really need to pull yourself together.'

Pull himself together. He can do that. But in what way? He is fine. He should say something again. It is expected.

'Yes sir. Sorry sir.' He realises his right hand is trembling again, so he stuffs it back in his pocket.

'It's alright being sorry but it doesn't help us any, does it? We're in a right fix here, we've lost two of our flight leaders and the crews that might have taken their place are either dead or...' Hastings waves his hand in his direction. 'Like you.'

He wonders what he is like but says nothing.

'HQ have scoured the available squadrons and are sending us some replacement senior crews to act as flight captains but, in the meantime, it's B flight that has to take the load.' He stares at Eddie. 'You're in B flight, Eddie.'

'Yes sir.'

'And you're one of our most experienced pilots. I know you've not been with us long but you've flown a lot of tough missions. You've got nerve.' Hastings pauses, then stares hard straight at him. 'At least I thought you had.'

He swallows. His throat is dry. He should have a drink. What is this man saying? Something about B flight. He is in B flight. So is Bean. Perhaps this man knows where Bean is.

'Sir, Bean, sir. I mean Monroe. Where is he?'

Hastings frowns. 'Monroe? Oh yes, him, one of my - bolder - pilots!' He gives a mirthless chuckle and raises his eyebrows in a little gesture of exasperation. 'I don't know. He's certainly not flying, no one is this morning. You've seen the weather? He's probably in the mess, or in the munitions hut. I saw him there the other day sorting through the ammunition for his Vickers. God knows why, he never uses it. Why do you ask?'

Because he is my brother and I love him. 'He'll be flying later when the weather improves though?'

'Yes. Of course.'

There is a knock at the door.

'Yes?' calls Hastings.

The door opens and someone old walks in. He struggles to think who it is. There are so many people, it's like school. Ah yes, it's Pops. 'Clive, I've got the...oh, Grenville, you're up. How are you feeling?'

'Fine sir,' He is fine. He is at peace with himself. And Bean is alive.

He fears losing him though. He should protect him.

'Well, if you say so,' said Pops,

He sees Pops look at Hastings and frown.

'We were just having a talk, weren't we Eddie?' Hastings says.

'Yes,' he says.

'What about?'

'Well -' begins Hastings.

'I was telling the Captain that I want to fly,' he interrupts.

He is aware of some discussion, raised voices but he ignores them.

He is a pilot, he will fly.

Later Captain Hastings puts his arm around his shoulders and says: 'Good man.'

Good man, yes. he is a good man.

Later he finds Bean. Good old Bean. Friend. He is checking bullets. He is pleased to see him. Bean says that he is going to try to be like him, bolder.

Good old Bean. He can keep Bean safe.

Then they have lunch, though he does not really want anything. He is not hungry. He is thirsty though, like yesterday with Max.

Max. he likes Max.

Max is gone.

Max is finished with this war.

Max is at peace.

It is still snowing. Not all the time but enough to keep them on the ground.

Then it stops. Captain Hastings comes looking for volunteers, The infantry need help, they need a bombing mission. He does not listen where. Bean's hand goes up. He puts his hand up too. Wherever Bean goes he will go too.

There is more talking. He does not listen but realises they are talking about him. He has no observer. He wants to take Brown but there is no Brown. No one seems to want to fly with him. That is fine, he will go alone. But then Slade says he will go as an observer. No not Slade. Slade is at peace. Moorhouse, yes, Moorhouse that's his name. He will go.

He sees Pops looking unhappy. Talking to Reeves. Reeves just shrugs.

Then he is in the aircraft. The engine starts.

He is a pilot. This is what he does. This is his world.

His hand is shaking. He puts his left hand on it to steady it.

Bean is over to his left. Good old Bean. His friend. He will keep him safe.

That's his mission.

His only goal.

There is a flare. Hastings' aircraft is moving.

Bean does the same.

Now it is his turn.

They climb into the sunlight. It is weak, it is cold but he tilts his face to enjoy the rays. He is in his element. This is what he was born to do. This is his life.

Below the land is changing, from green to brown and black. The dark furrow is beneath them, ploughed with Lyddite and brass and fertilized with blood and bone. He wonders what crop will spring from this land.

Has he had that thought before? It seems familiar.

It must have been someone else.

The person before.

The black flowers are around them now. He likes them, they are like the black tulips he once saw, even down to the stamen of red and yellow inside.

Another flare. Hastings is pointing his arm forward and down, then lowers the nose of his aircraft. Bean follows.

He follows Bean. He will go where Bean goes.

There are yellow spots flying up towards him. He ignores them. They cannot hurt him.

Bombs fall from Hastings aircraft. And from Bean's.

He looks down and ahead. There are grey figures beneath. Cowering, running. A yellow flower blooms amongst some of them, and another, a yellow flower with brown petals. They do not get up though some squirm like a worm caught under the blade of a spade.

A spade. Digging over the fertilizer.

Grey uniforms. The grey that Max wore.

Max was his friend.

His hand is on the bomb toggle. He does not pull it.

They are like Max.

There is shouting from behind him. Shut up Slade.

Not Slade.

Moorhouse.

He is a pilot but he is not a warrior. He does not kill.

He protects.

Protects Bean.

Moorhouse is still shouting. He ignores him. Hastings leads Bean and him up and away. Beneath them now are tents. There is a Red Cross on the top. Hospital. He does not like hospitals.

But they do make people better.

Sometimes.

Another flare. Hastings is pointing ahead. He looks. Another aircraft, slightly higher, heading across their path. Hastings heads to cut it off, climbing. Bean follows, black smoke from their exhausts. Full throttle. He does the same.

They are pulling away from him. Why are they slower?

Ah yes, the bombs. He has not dropped them.

He is a pilot not a warrior. He is only there to protect Bean.

His friend.

He sees Hastings fire on the other aircraft. He knows that this is stupid. It is a trap, he knows it but he cannot be hurt.

Then they come. The Albatros. Red aircraft, Red and white, red and yellow, red and blue. So pretty amidst the drabness. So many.

Hastings is gone, spinning down. Bean turns away. He follows.

In a shallow dive he is catching Bean. It is the bombs again. Now the weight helps.

Slade - not Slade - is shouting again. His Lewis gun is firing.

An Albatros appears in front of him. It is like a conjuring trick, a sleight of hand. Hey presto! Here I am! Instinctively his hand has gone to the gun trigger. He does not fire though. The pilot has not seen him, he is looking ahead.

He is like Max, like Siggi.

He is a pilot, not a killer.

The Albatros moves out of his sights. Sparks fly from the nose. Twin lines of tracer. They intersect with Bean's aircraft. It shudders. It burns. It collapses into itself and plunges down.

He's sweating. He cannot breathe.

There is nothing.

A void.

No purpose.

Purpose.

He can breathe.

He can be what he is.

What he has trained to be.

What all this has made him.

No compromises.

Brown...no not Brown, Max...not him either, ah yes, Moorhouse behind him swearing, still firing. He looks behind. Just one Albatros. One will do.

Someone kicks the rudder bar, lifts the nose, chops back on the throttle, then pushes it forward again before they stall. The Albatros skids by them, banking. Momentarily it is in the sights. Someone fires.

Is he doing this? It's so smooth, automatic, natural.

The Albatros's nose jerks up and it falls away, burning. He does not look where it has gone.

He puts the nose down, heads for the ground. Behind him he feels someone give him a pat on the shoulder.

What next?

It's so much easier now.

Now he knows what he is.

He is a pilot.

He is a warrior.

He does kill.

He does his duty.

Complete the mission.

Kill the enemy.

Get home.

Below and to his right, he sees something. Without hesitating he heads towards it.

Bullets are hitting them, plucking at the fabric, splintering the airframe. Behind him he hears shouting, 'Eddie, what are you doing?'

He ignores the bullets; he ignores Brown and Max and Moorhouse.

Something hits his left wrist like a sledgehammer. The hand and arm are useless, the pain intense. His right hand is fine though, and it is not shaking any more.

As they approach the hospital tents, he fires a long burst from the Vickers then puts the stick between his knees and grasps the bomb toggle with his hand, pulling it as they cross the threshold.

He feels rather than sees the bombs burst amongst the tents but can imagine them opening like flowers within them.

Flowers of death.

He does his duty.

Completes the mission.

Kills the enemy.

Goes home.

PART THREE

CHAPTER TWELVE

England, Friday April 20th, 1917

'Lord and Lady Howe.'

Maxwell Fitzroy was being talked at but kept an ear on the barker announcing the guests' arrival, waiting for the right opportunity. It wasn't Lord Howe, despite his estate in Devon, old money and good bloodline, he was little more than a country squire. Not worth crossing the room for.

He took a glass of champagne from a passing waiter and drained it. He grimaced; it had been allowed to get warm. The British, all breeding and class but no style, no taste. He would never fully understand them. Should he have chosen somewhere else to settle? Germany, possibly, the United States, definitely. But he was here, for now. And with the US joining the war alongside Britain and France now, surely then it would only be a matter of time now before Germany was beaten.

And there lay a problem; he only had a little time left to exploit the opportunity the war had brought to increase his wealth and influence. He had the first part: money, but not the latter. He was shunned; he needed to become part of the establishment, one of the ruling classes.

He was running out of time.

Meanwhile, his garrulous American table companion was still talking.

'So you see, Maxwell, I can call you Maxwell, can't I? You see, Max, our aircraft manufacturing company can quite easily produce flying machines that are superior to anything that the armed forces of the Kaiser, your King George or even Uncle Sam himself have produced up to now.'

'Really, Mr...er...'

'Pederson, Hank Pederson, Max, I said so before. Now, you want to know how we can do this, don't you?'

'I am all ears, Mr Pederson.'

'Hank, please. Well I betcha do but I can't tell you that otherwise Tommy Sopwith and Anton Fokker and the like would give their right arms to know why, and Uncle Sam would like as not have me shot as a traitor for giving the secrets away. All I will say is this, our aircraft are 50% faster and climb 50% quicker that the best scouts in the world today. '

'Is that so, Mr Pederson?'

'It sure is. Now, obviously a whole lot of other companies are damned jealous of us and have moved heaven and earth to make certain we don't succeed.'

'Or get contracts from the United States Government, I presume. Or, if I might be so bold to advance, they have denied you access to engine manufacturers and even the basic raw materials necessary to construct your wonder aircraft, is that correct?'

The American's mouth dropped open.

'How did you know?' he said.

Fitzroy gave him a sardonic smile. Because as con men go, you're not even close to being in my league, Hank. You can't con a conner. Still, it was amusing to pretend to play along.

'Because I've seen it happen so many times in this country. I find it sad that the situation seems to be the same on the other side of the Atlantic.'

Pederson took this as an invitation to continue, saying how good it was to find someone who understood and how he was just looking for the right backers and the ear of someone in the War Department, but Fitzroy was not really listening, for the Barker had announced: 'Sir Arthur and Lady Grenville.'

This was it.

What he'd be waiting for.

The Grenvilles.

A good family. Wealthy, in banking and finance, well connected in both political circles and in the military. Above all a son who was a war hero, one who would have stayed unknown if it hadn't been for him; Maxwell Fitzroy and his patriotic magazine, King and Country.

A family that should be grateful.

Pederson was about to start pitching again but Fitzroy rose and said, 'Excuse me, but there is someone I must meet.' He did not wait to hear Pederson's response. He walked straight over to the couple.

'Sir Arthur! Lady Grace. It is such a great honour to meet you at last,' he said.

Arthur Grenville, tall, grey haired, with a belly that was only barely constrained by his cummerbund, regarded Fitzroy with disdain. 'I do not believe we have been introduced, sir,' he said coldly and signalled for a waiter to bring a tray over.

'If you excuse me, that is not to the standard which I am sure you expect,' said Fitzroy. 'Waiter, take that muck away and bring a bottle of the Dom Perignon '97.'

'But sir, I'm not sure…' the waiter protested.

'You have some left, I know that. And it can be charged to my account, Maxwell Fitzroy. Now off you go and be quick about it, these are honoured guests.'

'Sir,' said the man who put his tray down and hurried off.

'And make sure it is properly chilled,' Fitzroy called after him. He turned back to the Grenvilles. 'My apologies, I am -'

'We know who you are,' said Lady Grenville, even more coldly than her husband. He looked at her puzzled. 'He's the proprietor of that dreadful rag, the one that published the story about Percival.'

'Ah,' said Sir Arthur. 'Him.'

Before the Grenvilles could say anything else the champagne arrived. The waiter showed the label to Fitzroy who nodded his approval. Once it had been opened and poured, and the filled glasses distributed, Fitzroy raised his and said: 'It is an honour to toast the parents of a War hero of this great country of ours. To you.'

'Thank you,' said Sir Arthur grudgingly and took a drink. 'Hmm, yes, excellent choice, Fitzroy. Much better than the usual bilge they serve at these War Bond dinners. Dreadful stuff. Almost as bad as the food.'

Fitzroy beckoned the waiter over and, slipping a ten-shilling note into the man's hand, whispered for him to stay and wait on them.

'I'll get into trouble, sir,' he whispered back, glancing over in the direction of the Head Waiter.

'I will see that you don't,' murmured Fitzroy. 'And there will be another of those for you at the end if your service has been acceptable.'

'Thank you, sir,' said the waiter, who stepped back and stood, unobtrusively, against the wall.

Lady Grenville, who had not even sipped her glass, put it down on a nearby table. 'It has been a pleasure, I'm sure, to make your acquaintance, Mr Fitzroy but if you will excuse me, I see an old friend over there. Arthur,' she added. 'I am sure you will not be long, will you?'

She strode away across the reception hall.

'You will have to excuse Lady Grenville,' said Sir Arthur. 'Grace does not like to see the family name bandied around in publications like your own. Not that I decry your motives on this matter.'

'Thank you,' said Fitzroy. 'We certainty did not mean any disrespect. We just felt that your son's bravery should not go unnoticed.'

'And the fact that you could sell more copies on the back of it was quite incidental?'

Fitzroy inclined his head briefly in acknowledgment. 'The public were most gratified to get news of our war heroes. They get such little information as to what is really going on. But that was not our primary concern. All we really wanted was to see your son get his rightful honour. It would be very gratifying to have a Victoria Cross holder in the family.'

Grenville nodded. 'I will concede that, it would be - though that does seem a remote possibility. Perhaps if he was awarded it, that would be enough for Percival to see sense, accept he's done his bit and will return to the family business. If so then I will be in your debt. It is exceedingly busy at present. We need him.'

'Yes, this war is expensive, companies need good sources of finance more than ever. And war creates opportunities as well as distress, does it not?'

'It does,' Grenville conceded. He drained his glass and Fitzroy indicated for the waiter to refill the glass. 'Thank you. If you need the services of a bank, feel free to call my office. Mention my name, that will at least get you through the door.'

'Thank you, that is most kind but my business is quite adequately financed. As I said, I seek no reward but the gratification that your son's heroism is acknowledged by the authorities. Our boys must receive the respect they deserve for the sacrifice that they are making for our country.'

'Our country?'

'Yes, indeed.'

'But I had heard that you were not a native of the British Isles, Mr Fitzroy.'

Fitzroy kept his voice under control. 'Your sources are mistaken.'

'Ah, my apologies. You have son's serving at the front yourself?'

'I do, yes.' Fitzroy knew that was probably true, it was just that the sons he had had with two different women twenty years ago would not be serving with the Allied forces, if they were still alive at all. It did not matter to him; he never had any strong feelings for them. They were useful in these circumstances.

'Ah, my apologies again, you will understand the worry one feels for one's boys,' said Grenville. 'Unless you have at least one of your own at the front it is hard to understand.'

'Indeed, indeed.'

Boys, thought Fitzroy. He said 'Boys' not 'Boy'. Holloman had mentioned another son when he researched the VC story. What was his name? Edmund? No, it was Edward.

'I believe your second son, Edward, is also in the Flying Corp. That must be a further worry to you.' Fitzroy congratulated himself on his memory. It was still sharp, and the recall was still useful for him.

'Yes,' Grenville shook his head and sighed in exasperation. 'I wish he wasn't. I blame Percival for that too. I cannot help but think he has led young Edward astray. Edward is not much more than a boy and they are easily swayed at that stage. Young men these days seem to be always attracted to the latest things. I presume you find the same with your son?'

'Sons, Sir Arthur, I have two. Yes, the same.' Fitzroy's lies were smoothly delivered.

'They will not listen to the reason of their elders. As a result they put themselves in unnecessary peril. They are too brave for their own good, foolishly so. Edward himself has now been wounded, not too badly, thank the Lord, though I understand he could easily have been killed several times over the last few weeks, like so many other young boys have. We will pay the price for this in the future, mark my words. We are losing the cream of our future leaders in the trenches and in the skies above them -'

'-whilst the Socialists and the Bolsheviks plot to take over,' Fitzroy said, nodding sagely. 'That is my big concern.'

To Fitzroy's pleasure he saw Grenville nod. A gratifying sign of respect from the banker.

'Mine too. We must be vigilant.'

'Absolutely, Sir Arthur. They must be stopped.'

Fitzroy saw Grenville glance across the room. Following his gaze he saw that Lady Grenville was looking in their direction. She was clearly not pleased to see her husband was still with the publisher.

'I think you will have to excuse me, Fitzroy. It has genuinely been a pleasure talking to you.' He put his glass down and set off across towards his wife but then stopped and turned around. 'I think I had misjudged you,' he said. 'Perhaps it would be useful to meet again, talk to some like-minded people.'

'That would be most gratifying.'

Grenville smiled, nodded. 'I will be in touch, Mr Fitzroy.' he said, and turned to continue walking over to his wife.

'Thank you, Sir Arthur,' said Fitzroy. 'I hope your sons recover quickly.'

Fitzroy tried to keep calm but under the surface he was exultant. He was beginning to make progress. He was becoming acceptable to the establishment. Influence and power would follow.

His feeling of euphoria carried him through the rest of the evening of poor food, served tepid and the near constant talking of Pederson who tried to pitch his wonder aircraft company to Fitzroy all night.

At one point, he caught a waiter looking daggers at him. Briefly he wondered what he had done to offend the man then realised that he was the one that had got the champagne for him and was still waiting for the second part of his tip.

Let him wait, Fitzroy thought. It will teach him not to expect to be given things but to take what you want. With any luck he would be sacked by the headwaiter at the end of the evening for neglecting his real duties.

Life was hard and you had to be tough to survive.

*

Still euphoric, Fitzroy called Charles Holloman into his office the next day and instructed him to find out all he could about Edward Grenville's service at the front.

'I want a story,' he said. 'Another one. And if the younger Grenville has not also been put up for a medal already, make damn certain that he will be after your article is published. On your way!'

After Holloman had gone, Fitzroy leant back in his chair and put his feet up on the desk. If creating one hero in the Grenville family had gained him great leverage, what reward would creating two give him?

CHAPTER THIRTEEN

England, Monday April 30th, 1917

Annie Ross strode up the driveway to the hospital, her shoes crunching on the gravel. She glanced up at the clock on the tower above the hospital's entrance; she still had five minutes before visiting time.

She stopped before going in. Should she do this?

Why did she feel so uneasy? That was easy to answer. She'd travelled for two hours in trains packed with troops still stinking of France, some leering at her with hungry eyes, changing twice, all to see a man - no not a man, a boy - that she had met only once before. What was she thinking?

But then the world seemed to have gone crazy, why shouldn't she do the same?

'Excuse me, miss?'

The voice from behind her took her by surprise, jolting her out of her train of thoughts. The man who had spoken to her was dressed in a brown suit, worn a little shiny with age, middle-aged, with grey hair, his complexion white and pasty as if he had not seen much sun in his life. His eyes, although sharp, bright and clever, were world-weary.

'Yes?' she said.

'I'm really sorry to bother you, but, well you see, I'm in a bit of a pickle.'

Annie frowned. The man's clothes were old but were smart enough. He did not look like someone who would be looking for a handout.

'I'm sorry,' she said. 'I don't have anything-'

'Oh, no, I'm not after money,' said the man. 'It's just, well...' He looked about them, there was no one within earshot, then stepped closer to her and whispered conspiratorially. 'Well, you see, the thing is, I have a good friend, wounded in the trenches. I've come all the way down here to see him but because I'm not a relative they won't let me in.'

'Oh gosh, that's terrible for you.'

'It is.'

'But how can I help?'

'I think you might be a nurse, am I correct?'

'Well, yes, I am but not here. I'm just visiting someone too.'

'Oh, right.'

The man's face fell.

'I'm sorry...' she said.

'I still think you could help, ' he said, looking eager. 'If you don't mind that is? If I accompanied, you they would think we were together and I could get in to see old Bert.'

'Well, I don't know if I should...'

The man stared into the middle distance. 'Good chap, Bert is, best pal a chap could hope to have. He's pretty poorly too, so his Missus says anyhow. I'm sure it would give him a real tonic to have a visit from his old mate.' He turned his eyes back on Annie. 'Can you help me, miss? Please?'

Annie felt her resolve melt. 'Oh alright then.' But then she thought of something. 'Oh, wait, are they that strict here? It's just that I'm not a relative either. I'm just his...' She hesitated. What exactly was she? She was married, her husband had not been officially declared dead, he was just missing.

And she had met this man - boy - just once. True, he had made an impression, he was young, naïve but there was also something else, an intelligence, a sensitivity that was quite beguiling. But she didn't really know him.

Fortunately the man came to her rescue.

'Ah but you see, for a young lady that does not matter. Nurses like yourself understand the needs of the heart. They will let you see your beau.'

Annie felt herself blush. Her beau.

'Even the fiercest Matron would allow a visit, wouldn't she?'

'Yes, I suppose so,' said Annie. 'But who-'

'I could be your father, accompanying his daughter on her mission of mercy.'

'Oh, right. Yes, I see how that would work. Fine then, should we go in?' The man smiled, and taking her arm, lead Annie inside the hospital.

Despite his pleasant manner and his apparent genuineness, she could not help but feel that something was not right. He was just too smooth, his patter too perfect, like he'd had lots of practice. And how did he know she was a nurse, she wasn't in uniform, there was nothing as far as she could see that gave things away. Yet why would he want to deceive her, what was the point? It was just a hospital.

She still had her doubts when they arrived at the ward. They were not assuaged by the man whispering, 'what's your name?' to her as they walked up to the sister at the desk.

'Annie Ross,' she said.

'And who are you visiting?'

'His name is Eddie. Edward Grenville.'

His grip on her arm momentarily tightened, then released almost as quickly. What was that about, she thought. But he was already addressing the Sister.

'Hello, Charles Ross. My daughter here has come to see Edward Grenville, the young pilot who is recovering here. She is his lady friend. She's so worried about him. May we go through?'

'Oh,' said the nurse. 'You're not family?'

'No but the next best -'

'We have had strict instructions not to-'

'Now come on my dear, my daughter has been beside herself with worry since she heard he was wounded. We've travelled for hours to get here. Surely you can understand her anxiety?'

'Yes, but -'

'And surely it is common decency to let her see him. You're not going to turn her away after she has come so far, are you?'

'I...er...no, I suppose just this once but I should-'

'Is it this way?' said the man, stepping beyond the desk, his arm still through Annie's guiding and leading her onwards.

'Yes, the waiting room is on the end of the corridor on the right.' The sister still looked flustered, 'The staff on the ward will take you through when they are ready. But I really should check with Matron first...'

The man ignored her and lead Annie down the corridor.

Annie feelings that something was wrong had grown. She was being bullied, hurried into a situation that was out of her control.

And something he had said had bothered her, she knew that

but, for the moment, she could not settle on what it was. As they reached the waiting area it came to her. She stopped, resisting his efforts to move her on.

'How did you know he was a pilot?' she said.

'Pardon, my dear?'

'How did you know that Edward was a pilot.'

The man smiled. 'Why because you told me, of course.'

'No I didn't.'

'With respect. my dear, you did.'

Annie shook her head. 'I didn't. I'm not a silly girl who does not know what she is saying. Who are you? And why do you want to get at Eddie.'

'Because he's a reporter with that terrible rag, King and Country.'

The voice was female, and reminded Annie of cut crystal and ice. Annie expected her to be a nurse or the matron but the woman who had spoken was dressed in a simple and elegant black dress, with a black jacket over it. Dark-haired and pale, she looked somehow familiar. Had Annie met her before?

There was something else: the woman was pregnant.

Her train of thought was interrupted by the newcomer.

'How dare you keep bothering us, Mr Holloman. Get out, get out this instant or I will call the police.'

The man gave a little mirthless laugh, released Annie's arm. 'I just have a job to do. I *will* get my story, but it would be better if got it straight from the source, so to speak. Surely you can see that? Why don't *you* tell me all about your brother's heroics?' He pulled out his notebook and pencil from an inside pocket.

'Get out, get out this instant, we have had quite enough of your trash,' snapped the woman. The sister from the desk came into the corridor, clearly having heard the raised voices. The young woman turned to her. 'I thought you knew the instructions about visitors? Weren't they clear enough for you?'

'I'm sorry madam, I..'

'The hospital authorities will hear about this, mark my words. Now do your job and get rid of this man.'

'Yes madam.' said the sister, who was now red and flustered. 'Please, sir, will you go? I'll call for the porters if you don't.'

'I will take my leave.' said Holloman. He doffed his hat to Annie and the newcomer. 'Ladies,' he said and turned and walked out of the corridor back into the hallway. The sister went with him, presumably to check that he had, in fact, left but also, Annie thought, to get away from the sharp tongue which had scolded her.

The woman went back inside the waiting area, leaving Annie in the corridor, uncertain as to what to do. Should she leave too? By the sound of things only family were being allowed in. But she had come a long way, the reporter was right about that at least, and she was worried about Eddie. She was also curious, who was this woman? Was she with Eddie? An old flame perhaps? He hadn't mentioned anyone but that did not mean anything. She was certainly posh enough to be part of his set, she had that aloof superiority that Annie found both irritating and intimidating in equal measures.

And the baby. Eddies? Surely not.

She hesitated. In the end she decided. She wanted to see Eddie and also wanted to know who this person was.

Annie entered the waiting area. The dark-haired woman was sat in one of the chairs. She was ramrod straight, her hands on her lap, her face set.

It was a familiar face, who was she?

She looked up at Annie as she came into the room.

'You're still here then?' she said.

'Yes,' said Annie. 'Sorry about that man. He...he wasn't with me. He tricked me.'

'To be tricked one needs to be gullible in the first place.' The crystal-ice delivery was back. Annie felt herself flush, both with embarrassment and anger. She was about to say something back, to deliver her own tart return but the woman suddenly relaxed. 'My apologies,' she said. 'I didn't mean to insult you. That man is very devious, it would be very easy to be taken in by him. Please, if you are staying, take a seat.' The voice was suddenly gentler, much more tired, and the cold facade seemed to melt away. It was like looking at an entirely different person

And Annie suddenly realised who she was.

'Oh my goodness, you're Alice,' she blurted out, unable to stop herself. 'Alice Grenville.'

The woman gave a little smile. 'Alice Von Leitner, actually,' she said. 'Grenville was my maiden name.'

A chill settled on Annie. 'Oh yes, of course. I'm sorry - about your husband,' she said.

'Why should you be sorry? I married a German and that makes me German, of course. And he was just a bloody Hun, wasn't he? An enemy soldier.'

Annie found that she was trembling. That phrase: 'Just a

bloody Hun'. That was just what Percy had said when he'd shot Siggi. Did Alice know the truth? 'He was your husband,' she said. 'German or not, it's still terrible to lose someone you love.'

'Yes,' said Alice. Alice's gaze dropped to look at Annie's left hand, the one with the wedding ring on it. 'I'm sorry. Sometimes I forget that I'm not the only person to lose someone.'

'Sometimes it just feels you're the only one though, doesn't it?' said Annie.

'Indeed it does,' said Alice. She seemed lost in her thoughts for a moment, but then looked up, straight at Annie. 'Please sit. I believe they are changing the dressing on Eddie's arm. It could be some time before we are allowed in.'

'How is Eddie?' asked Annie, sitting next to Alice.

'Don't you know?'

'No, I've not heard anything other than what his squadron commander wrote to me.'

'He wrote to you?'

'Yes. They found my letters in his things apparently.'

'Ah I see.' Alice nodded thoughtfully. 'Well, physically he is on the mend. He had a bullet in the wrist you know.'

'Yes, I knew that. But you said physically? What else is wrong with him?'

Alice sighed.

'You'll have to see for yourself. But you have me at a disadvantage. You know who I am.'

'I'm sorry, of course. My name is Annie Ross.' Annie hesitated before going on. 'Actually, I know both of your brothers. I nursed Percy when he was first brought back to England. That's how I met Eddie. And,' she added, 'how I heard about your husband.'

'Ah I see,' said Alice. 'Yes. Percy would have been told about him. They were close, you know, before the war. He seems to have taken Siggi's death really badly, perhaps even worse than myself.' Her face darkened. 'Well so I understand, anyway. I've not seen him since I got home. I don't think he can face meeting me and being reminded of Siggi.'

I am certain you are quite right about that, thought Annie.

'Oh, right,' she said. 'Of course, you were in Germany. How did you get back to England?'

Alice sat back.

'It was difficult. My parents-in-law wanted me to stay but I needed to leave. I had to get a steamer to Stockholm, train to Narvik, Then another ship back across the North Sea, always on the lookout for U-boats. I arrived back a week ago.'

'It sounds awful,' said Annie. 'May I ask, why were you so determined to come back? Wouldn't it have been easier to wait until the war was over?'

Before Alice could answer, they were interrupted by a nursing sister.

'You can go in now,' she said to Alice, then looked at Annie questioningly.

'She's with me,' said Alice. 'She is a friend of my brother's.'

The nurse nodded and lead them into Eddie's room.

Eddie was in a private room on the first floor. The window looked out over the hospital grounds. Spring sunshine poured in through the panes, outside England was green, fresh, peaceful, with new growth and Spring flowers in abundance.

Eddie was propped up in bed. His left hand and arm were swathed in bandages, new, white and pristine. Although he did not look particularly unwell, though he was pale and gaunt, Annie was shocked by his appearance. It was how old he looked. She had last seen him towards the end of March, then he was youthful, coltish. Now, at the beginning of May, he could have passed for someone in his mid-thirties. His eyes were open and seemed to be staring at something on the far wall. His gaze was so intense that Annie followed the direction of his gaze. The wall was, as far as she could see, was completely blank.

'My poor baby brother,' murmured Alice. 'What on earth has happened to you?' She leant over and kissed him on the forehead. Eddie did not react, though he did blink his eyes. 'I've got a surprise for you, Eddie. Look, it's…' Alice looked across at Annie. 'I'm sorry, I'm terrible for names.'

'Annie.'

'Oh yes, Annie. Eddie, look, it's Annie, your friend. From Percy's hospital, remember?'

Eddies lipped trembled. He seemed to be on the point of saying something but then it seemed to fade away, like he had given up trying to force it out.

That was at the mention of Percy's name, not mine, Annie thought.

'You may as well sit. I'm afraid that this is about as much as you'll get out of him.' Alice sounded very weary. She pulled a chair across from the side of the room and sat next to her brother. Annie found there was one on her side and did the same. The two women sat on opposite sides of the bed.

'How long has he been like this?' said Annie.

'About three weeks, I believe,' said Alice. 'It is hard to get anything out of the army. My parents did get a letter from his observer, a chap called Moorhouse. He said that Eddie was wounded during a bombing mission but he carried on with it until they were done, then turned and flew them all the way back to their airfield. Moorhouse had no idea he'd even been hit, the landing was perfect. It was only when Eddie slumped forward in the cockpit when they came to a stop did he realise. We think he has been like this ever since.'

She stared at her brother.

'He was a hero,' said Annie. 'Perhaps we should have spoken to that reporter.'

'Don't be so stupid,' snapped Alice, the superiority and ice abruptly returning. 'His sort do not care for the likes of us or for Eddie or the men fighting and dying in our names. All they are interested in is selling newspapers and making money.'

'I'm sorry,' said Annie. 'I didn't think.'

She saw Alice bite her lip, saw the coldness drain out of her again. The caring, vulnerable side was surfacing again. Once again she was reminded of Eddie.

'It's alright, I don't suppose you will have had much dealings with the press. I'm sorry too, I didn't mean to call you stupid. I'm just worried.'

She looked again at her brother and reached across to stroke his forehead.

'The doctor says catatonia is not uncommon with cases of shell-shock. We must keep talking to him, he may well snap out of it. Mind you, I'm not sure that they truly know what they are talking about.'

'They are getting a lot more experience,' said Annie. 'I've nursed many men like this over the last year, more than I care to remember.'

'And do they recover?'

Alice's gaze was steady. Annie briefly considered trying to sugar-coat her answer but swiftly rejected the idea. Alice, even in the brief time she had known her, struck her as a strong character who would not appreciate being told anything but the honest truth.

'Some do improve quite markedly, though whether you could ever call them fully recovered is a different matter. There is always some lasting effect.'

'But some never recover at all?' said Alice.

'Yes,' said Annie. 'Some don't get any better, whatever treatment is offered. The trauma to the mind is too much to bear.'

'Poor Eddie,' murmured Alice again.

'I'm sure Eddie will get better. From what little I know of him he is a determined, strong character. I'm sure he will pull through.'

Did she believe that? Did she really?

Alice just nodded.

In the silence that followed, thoughts were racing through Annie's head. The thoughts that came back the most were about Percy and Siggi and the realisation she had just had - that Alice was someone who wanted to know the truth. But all the truth, however unpalatable?

'Why are you staring at me?'

Annie shook her head, glancing away.

'Sorry,' she said, 'I was miles away.' She turned her gaze on Eddie. 'I was wondering how long it would be before he came back.'

If ever, she thought but did not add this.

There were many things she did not add. Amongst them were questions of why she was there in the first place? What was she doing? This was a boy, one she hardly knew and he was damaged. Would he ever be the same again? Could she handle the loss all over again? And if he did come back what was there in the first place? They had been thrown together by war - and by the actions of his brother. A brother who had wronged the woman who now sat on the opposite side of the bed from her, who seemed to have no idea of the secret that Annie knew. It would help if the dislike of Alice and her class she had felt on their first meeting had been maintained but it hadn't. She had warmed to Alice, she was genuine and caring. Annie could see that she could easily be friends with her - yet Annie knew a terrible secret that could destroy Alice and her family.

This was crazy, she had her own loss to mourn and her own job to do. She should go and never look back.

'Don't worry,' said Alice abruptly, reaching over Eddie and grasping Annie's hands with her own. 'You are right. Eddie is strong. He will come back to us. It will just take a little time. And faith.' She hesitated, then added, 'Will you stay and help?'

Annie found herself nodding before she could say no.

CHAPTER FOURTEEN

England, Monday May 7th, 1917

The man was on crutches, that was not unusual these days. He was noticeable, however. His short dark hair and neat moustache that gave him a dashing edge and, with his RFC uniform, and pale, pain-etched face would. Holloman thought, with not a little jealousy, give him a near irresistible image for ladies young and old in the capital.

It occurred to Holloman that he might, if he had more time, have used that to his advantage. He had, amongst his contacts, several Madams who could supply just the right girl to get someone relaxed enough to indulge in some pillow talk.

But he was here now and time, and Fitzroy was pressing him for a story. He had got himself into the RAC club in Pall Mall by the gift of the gab so he would have to do the same with this young lieutenant.

He waited whilst the young man had been signed in, his coat taken, had a banal conversation with the steward over the luncheon menu and when it was to be served and then had followed the young man into the lounge. Many of the members there were having a quiet drink catching up on the morning paper or were snoozing in a quiet corner.

Once the young man had found an empty chair, Holloman made his move. He grabbed a copy of The Times from a table where it had just been discarded and headed over to the chair next to the airman.

'Good morning,' he said in a soft whisper, putting on his most cultured voice. 'I say, would you mind awfully if I took this seat?'

'Not in the slightest,' the young man gave a little smile. 'As long as I might take a quick look at your paper.'

'Of course,' said Holloman, passing it over. 'Anxious to get some news of the front?'

'Yes, well what little we actually get to know.'

'It is a little difficult to know exactly what is happening,' agreed Holloman.

The lieutenant gave a sigh. 'It looks like the French push hasn't got anywhere,' he said. 'Our boys did alright around Arras though,' he added. 'Good to see that. Feel a bit of a part of it, you see.'

'Oh right,' said Holloman. 'Is that where you were serving? My apologies, I am assuming that you were wounded in action?'

'Yes I was, and you are right on both counts.'

Holloman was not surprised. His contacts in the Army administration had already checked the records.

'In the Flying Corp, too I see,' said Holloman, pointing at the half wings sown in the lieutenant's uniform. 'I bet that was a bit hot, wasn't it?'

'It was a little, er, tricky, shall we say, at times.' He gave a grim smile, then held out his hand. 'I'm Morris, Cecil Morris.'

'Grenville,' said Holloman. 'Charles Grenville.'

Morris looked surprised. 'Grenville. Oh right. That's a bit of a coincidence.'

'Is it?' said Holloman, feigning disinterest and trying to catch the eye of one of the Stewards. 'How so?'

'Well my pilot, the one who I was flying with when I did my leg, he was called Grenville too.'

A steward had now come over and was waiting expectantly by the two men.

'My nephew is a pilot. Young Edward. That's not the same chap is it?'

'Good heavens.' exclaimed Morris, rather too loudly for some of the other members who turned down the corner of their papers and glared at him. 'The very same! Pleasure to meet you, sir.'

'And the same to you. Will you have a brandy with me?' said Holloman. 'I would really love to hear all about the exploits of my nephew.'

The steward took the order and Holloman settled down whilst his story was delivered to him on a plate.

He left an hour or so later, with a slightly fuzzy head from the brandies but with just the information he needed.

France, Monday May 7th, 1917

The girl looked up at the evening sky. The clouds were low, angry, threatening yet more rain, or even snow. It was a dreadful Spring, but then it had been a dreadful year, dreadful years since the Germans had come.

The chatter of machine guns and the sound of aircraft engines was not unusual, the front was so close, closer now the British had advanced at the start of the previous month. Yet she still looked up as she hurried along past the ruined farmhouse. It was dangerous being out, death could come from anywhere, but life had to go on.

At first she could not see the machines but then a small aircraft, shark-like in shape, appeared out of the clouds a few kilometres away. It was descending, its engine stopped. A Boche, she thought. She hoped the pilot was dead, but then shook her head. That was an un-Christian thought, that was still some mother's son, a brother a father in that machine, she should not wish them harm, despite what their country had done to hers. She was relieved to see that the machine appeared to be under control as it disappeared from sight.

Briefly she could hear the sound of another engine somewhere above her but it abruptly stopped. She carried on walking, hurrying along the road.

Something passed over her, so low that it made her duck.

She watched it happen as if in a dream. The something was an aircraft. It was upside down, its propeller stopped, trailing a smoke plume behind it. It seemed to hang there for ever, time was moving so slowly. She could take in every detail, the drab muddy brown of the wings and fuselage, the red, white and blue roundels on the wings, the gun, the tail with its red, white and blue striped rudder, the number, upside down but still recognisable as A4850. The pilot, bare-headed, young, pale.

It was something from a dream, something that was insubstantial, that would vanish as quickly as it had appeared.

But then it plunged into the ground with a sickening thump

and crash, proved it was all too real. The violence of the impact was made even more shocking given the gentleness with which the aircraft had glided over her. It crumpled in on itself, the wings smashed, the nose dipping into the ground, the fuselage, still inverted, breaking and compressing the pilot within.

Then there was silence. A cloud of smoke or steam rose from the wreckage.

She stood for a second, stunned, then hurried to reach the machine which lay only fifty metres or so from her. She hesitated as she reached it, she could not see the cockpit from the side she had approached the aircraft from. She really did not want to see what horror might lay within, but the pilot might be hurt, trapped. It might catch fire at any moment, she needed to put her own feelings out of her mind and help him.

She walked around the rear of the aircraft until she could see the pilot. He was still in the remains of the cockpit, slumped forward, his dark hair resting against the instruments. She was sure that he must be dead given the impact and the degree to which his machine had been smashed but she leaned inside to be sure, ignoring the smell of petrol and oil. To her surprise she could hear him breathing, however the breath was shallow and laboured, as if each intake was an enormous effort.

She must get him out, she could not let him burn. She put her arms under the pilot's and tried to pull him clear. She was not expecting to be able to but he came out quite easily. He was small and slightly built and he did not seem to be trapped. She could see, however, that one of his legs was badly broken and that there was something not right with his chest which had taken the brunt of the impact and was misshapen and collapsed. There was no time to check though, she had to get him clear.

She slipped backwards on the wet grass, the pilot's head and shoulders fell into her lap. His eyes, which had been closed, opened briefly and he looked at her.

He's so young, she thought, so young and so handsome. He's just a boy, he should be at school, not fighting, risking his life, wasting it.

She knew the moment he died. His eyes stayed open but the light behind them faded. The tortured attempts to breathe stopped.

He was at peace.

She was still holding him when the first German soldiers arrived a few minutes later.

CHAPTER FIFTEEN

England, Friday May 11th, 1917

Percy paused outside the house, the porticoed frontage and the street so familiar. The family had this house in Curzon Street for generations, he'd known it all his life. He knew he should go in, this was what he had resolved to do, yet, now he was faced with it, he felt his determination draining away.

The tremor in his hands was back. It just would not stop. The sweats had started too. Damn it, would this never go away? He pushed his hands into his pockets, fighting his body's involuntary actions. He would beat it; he was not a coward.

Or was he? Wasn't what he had done unspeakably cowardly?

Or just unspeakable.

'That is why you are here.'

A couple passing by looked at him oddly, though the man raised his hat in greeting before the pair hurried off down the street.

He had said it out loud. He was talking to himself as well as shaking and sweating. Well he would just have face up to what he had done and stop hiding.

It was about time.

He straightened his tie, smoothed his uniform down and checked his cap. He was pleased to note his hands had stopped shaking. He limped determinedly up the steps and, without ringing the bell, strode into the hall.

He was putting his hat on the stand when one of the maids hurried into the hall.

'Hello, can I...' she began, then her face lit up with a smile. 'Why it's, Mr Percy. Oh sir, it's so good to see you!'

'Hello Lucy, you're looking well,' Percy said.

'Thank you, sir, I'm doing nicely,' said Lucy. 'But how are you, sir? We were all so worried below stairs when we heard you were wounded.'

'I'm very much recovered, thank you Lucy. Is my father here?'

'Oh sorry sir, what am I thinking? Since Mr Parkes went off to the war, I've had to take his duties and they're still strange to me. Yes, he is, sir, he's in the study. I'll go and announce you. He'll be so pleased to see you.'

She turned to head up the stairs but Percy stopped her.

'No Lucy, go back to your duties. I'll surprise him.'

'As you wish, sir.' Lucy curtsied. 'Shall I tell cook that there is one more for dinner?'

Percy hesitated. Would he be staying?

'I'm not sure,' he said.

'Very well, sir, I'll make sure she makes allowances anyway, sir.'

'Thank you,' said Percy. 'Lucy, one more thing.'

'Sir?

'Is Mrs Von Leitner here?'

'Oh yes sir, she's staying in her old room. And young Mr Edward's here too.'

'What? I thought he would be with a squadron by now. Is he on leave?'

He saw Lucy's face darken. 'Oh, you don't know, sir? He was in France but he was wounded, like you sir.'

'Wounded? How badly? Where is he?'

'He got shot in the arm, sir, but that seems to be mending. But...'

'But what, Lucy? What's wrong with him?'

'He's not well, sir. He doesn't speak, he doesn't seem to know there's anyone around him. Poor Mr Edward, such a lovely young boy he was too.'

Percy swallowed, staring at Lucy. He felt the tremor come back into his hands, the sweats starting up again. Eddie, wounded already. This was his fault, this as well.

'Where is he?'

'The mistress has had the old nursery fitted out a bed. His nurse looks after him there.'

'His nurse?'

'Hello Percy.'

The cool voice was familiar. He looked up the stairs.

'Nurse Ross. What are you doing here?'

Annie gave a faint smile, though this faded almost straight away.

'Looking after your brother,' she said. 'I've taken leave from my job.'

'But how? Why?'

She shrugged. 'Your father has very good connections. He made it possible. As to why, well Alice is very persuasive. And I like your brother.'

Percy knew what she could have added but had chosen not to: I like him but not you. The coolness in her voice made it obvious. He stood staring at her for a few seconds, then realized the maid was still there.

'Thank you, Lucy, that will be all for now. I will let you know whether I will be staying for dinner.'

'Thank you, sir.'

Lucy left, leaving Percy and Annie alone.

'You're looking well,' she said at last.

'Thank you,' he said. 'I am a lot better. And, Nurse Ross, I must apologise for how I was in the hospital. I must have been a difficult person to look after.'

Annie gave a little inclination of her head.

'Yes, you were, but you weren't well.'

'Thank you.' Percy could not help but notice that the coolness was still there. 'How is he? Eddie, I mean.'

He saw Annie glance upstairs. 'You can come and see for yourself,' she said.

Percy shook his head. 'I doubt whether he would be at all pleased to see me. Not after the way things were left the last time we met.'

Annie pursed her lips. 'I see you are still selfish,' she said.

Percy felt the insult like a slap. 'Selfish? Is that what you think I am? I thought you said I was ill.'

Annie sighed deeply. 'I'm sorry. I'm tired. That makes me speak more bluntly than I would normally. And…'

'And what?'

'I…regret taking up this post. It may not have been a good idea.'

Percy could guess exactly what she meant. He knew his parents too well.

'I'm sure you have call to say that. Still, I really do feel that Eddie would not want to see or talk to me. He made that quite clear last time.'

'If that's what you feel, fine, but I would think far better of you if you did the decent thing and put your own feeling to one side for once. Believe me, Eddie does need you. I think you might be the one person who can get through to him.' She stepped forward and took his arm. 'Please.'

There were a few moments of silence whilst they stared at each other.

'Fine,' said Percy at last. 'I need to see my mother and father - and Alice too. It would be best if I saw Eddie now. It might be the last chance that I will get for a while.'

He moved towards the stairs but she gripped his arm again.

'Why?' she said.

'Why what?' he said.

'Why might this be the last chance? Are you returning to France?'

'No.'

'Why then?'

He glared at her. 'I really don't think that is any of your business,' he said and tried to shrug her off. She continued to hold his arm.

'Don't,' she said.

'Don't what?'

'Don't tell them. It won't do any good, not to them, not to you.'

'But Alice deserves...'

'Alice deserves to have a brother - both brothers - and to preserve the memory of her husband. She's suffered enough.'

Angrily he pulled her hand away. 'How dare you...'

'She's pregnant.'

'What?'

'What is this noise. You, girl, what are you doing with my son?'

The sharp voice from above made them look up.

'Hello, Mother,' said Percy.

'Percival,' said Lady Granville. 'Whilst it's nice you have bothered to come and see us at last I'd be grateful if you did not pick arguments with the staff.'

'I'm not a servant,' Percy could tell that Annie was seething.

Lady Granville came down the stairs. 'You are paid staff, with duties to carry out. Duties which you appear to be neglecting.'

'I'm not...' Annie began.

'Nurse Ross was the person who nursed me when I was ill. She did a wonderful job, mother,' Percy interrupted, flashing a warning glance at Annie. 'One I know that she will be doing for Eddie, too. It was only natural that she would wish to talk with me and update me on his condition.'

Lady Granville frowned. 'Don't treat me like a fool. It sounded much more like an argument to me.'

'You are mistaken,' said Percy, moving forward to peck his mother on the cheek. 'Nurse Ross, would you be so kind as to go back to my brother. I will be up shortly.'

'But…' Annie began, but once again Percy interrupted.

'I will think over what you said and will give the matter more thought.'

Annie nodded, and then said, very coolly. 'Lady Granville,' before making her way back up the stairs.

'I regret taking on that person,' said Lady Granville before Annie was out of earshot. 'However your sister insisted on having her. Modern women, they have strange ideas.' She sighed. 'Well Percival, shall we go into the parlour? I will send for your father. I do not wish the servants to eavesdrop on any more of our family's business.'

'I will see my brother first, mother,' said Percy.

Lady Granville gave him a sour look. 'We have not seen a hair of your head for nearly a year, surely you can spare us a few moments of your time now?'

'You could have seen me in hospital. You knew where I was.'

'It was a public hospital. I do not care to go to such places. We did try to have you moved to somewhere more suitable.'

'I know. I refused to go.'

'Then you can hardly blame us for not visiting you, can you?'

Percy gave a little smile. 'Indeed not, mother,' he said. 'I promise I will be down and will talk with you and father. However, I *will* see Eddie first.'

'As you wish,' said Lady Granville, and turned and walked swiftly into the parlour. As Percy walked up the stairs he heard the bell ring for one of the servants to attend to his mother. He was sure that they were not going to have an easy time.

He got to the door of the nursery. He hesitated then knocked.

Annie opened the door but, rather than let him in, stepped out into the corridor.

'I am sorry about my mother,' he said. 'She has a very unfortunate attitude.'

'She does. Clearly you and your siblings were brought up by some very nice nannies.'

Percy could not help but smile. 'We were.' he said.

'Did you tell her?' she said.

He shook his head. 'Not yet.'

Annie nodded slowly. 'Well, you know my opinion on it. I cannot see what good it would do, other than to salve your conscience, of course.'

Percy took a deep breath. 'You think that is why I need to do it?'

'Of course, why else?'

'Because what I did was wrong? Because it was deeply repugnant to all human decency?'

Annie shrugged. 'Haven't you just described war, that's all?' She closed her eyes briefly. 'Anyway, I'm more worried about Eddie. What do you know about his condition?'

'Nothing, until today,' he said, so she told him.

When she had finished, he asked, 'So he's not spoken since he came back?'

'He talks in his sleep. Sometimes he seems to be having conversations.'

'Who with?'

'Someone called Bean. And Milne and Brown.'

'What about when he's awake? Doesn't he react at all to people talking to him?'

Annie shook her head. 'Except when your name is mentioned,' she said. 'I've noticed it a few times. He definitely reacts to it.'

Percy gave a rueful sigh. 'He's probably still angry with me, and who can blame him? But, if it will help...'

He put his hand on the doorknob, hesitated for a moment, then turned it and stepped into the room.

Inside he found that Eddie was in an armchair pulled up to the big window that looked out onto the street, wearing pyjamas and Paisley patterned dressing gown. He was not the boy he remembered: he was an older man; gaunt, pale, his gaze vacant.

'Good God,' he murmured.

He walked softly over to his brother and crouched down next to him, laying his stick down on the floor, ignoring the pain from his own injured ankle.

'Eddie. Eddie, old chap, what on earth has happened to you,' he said.

He didn't expect a reaction, even after what Annie had told him.

But Eddie turned his head to look at him and smiled.

'Percy. How are you?' he said.

CHAPTER SIXTEEN

England, Saturday May 19th, 1917

Annie strolled back to the shade of the terrace of the summer house, leaving Eddie and Percy on deck chairs on the lawn enjoying the warm Spring sunshine.

The sun had brought out the insects, bees were busy moving from flower to flower. and the birds were singing. It was a perfect day, the coldness of April now a distant memory, yet still she could not put aside the feelings of disquiet that she had felt since they had come down from London to the Grenville family home in Hampshire.

It had seemed a good idea, giving Eddie, a change, fresh air and some peace and quiet. Annie, stifled and irritated by Eddie's parents had welcomed the idea of getting away, Lady Grenville being 'Far too busy with her charity work' to be able to come down with them.

And it had been good in a way, Eddie had come around, he was talking, interacting with people, particularly Percy.

Yet there were problems, and no one seemed willing to address them.

She sat down at the table and stared at the two men. They were both reading, absorbed in their books, looking relaxed in their civilian clothes. The war seemed a distant memory, something that had happened only in the imagination. Yet Annie knew she was fooling herself, the war was real, it was still going on, it had taken her husband and both the Grenville boys had sticks close at hand to help them walk, evidence of their physical scars.

If only the mental scars were as obvious.

Alice came out of the house. Annie saw her look at her brothers, could see her indecision.

Eddie was better, yes, but he wasn't right. he certainly wasn't the man - boy, Annie Ross, remember that, he's just a boy - he was before. Conversation with him was difficult, he seemed to drift in and out of the real world, sometimes spending hours not speaking. Other times he would switch off in the middle of talking about something; some music, a book he had read, talk about a friend, before returning abruptly sometime later and taking up the thread as if he had never been away and no time had passed.

That was not the problem, Annie was sure that Alice could understand that and could cope with it, indeed, from what Annie had seen, Alice was far more patient than she, herself, was. No, the problem was that it left Alice trying to make conversation with Percy.

Whilst Percy did not cold-shoulder her as such, he was hardly friendly, in fact he was downright awkward, sometimes even making weak excuses to be able to leave the room and go somewhere else. Often that excuse was Annie. 'Well, I'm sure you ladies have things to talk about and don't want me about,' was a line that had been repeated at least half a dozen times over the last week.

Annie had got to know Alice quite well over the time she had been nursing Eddie, know her and like her. She had found herself musing how two such unpleasant parents - actually, she corrected hers, that wasn't strictly true, Arthur Greenville was merely apparently indifferent to his children, Lady Grenville was the unpleasant one - had produced at least two likeable children, and possibly three as well if you accepted that Percy was, prior to his service, also sweet and kind. Whatever, although Alice had not even mentioned it, Percy's behaviour towards had certainly been noticed and it most definitely hurt her.

Annie almost got up when she saw her friend's indecision but she found herself wearied by it all. There was also anger; what exactly was she doing here anyway? Eddie knew her, that was obvious, but he showed no affection towards her. Did he care? Why should she bother helping this family?

She sighed, annoyed with herself for her own selfishness. Eddie was ill, badly wounded, mentally if not physically. Alice was her friend, a new friend but a friend nonetheless, widowed and pregnant. Percy...well Percy had his own issues.

But by the time she had resolved to do something it was already too late. Alice had turned away from the garden and had headed over towards Annie on the terrace. She smiled at Annie, the smile masking the pain that showed in her eyes.

'Hello, it's a fabulous morning, isn't it?' she said.

'It is, it's lovely,' said Annie. 'I was just thinking, it's hard to think we're at war on a day like this.'

Her annoyance with herself deepened. There were serious things to talk about, yet they were discussing the weather.

Alice eased herself into one of the chairs, Annie jumped up to help her down.

'Thanks,' said Alice, patting her stomach. 'He or she is getting heavy to move around.'

'Yes, I can see. Poor you, I hope it won't get too hot before it's your time.'

'It should be just another month. Hopefully I won't get too much bigger!'

'Well, pregnancy suits you. You're blooming.'

A ghost of smile played briefly about Alice's lips, then Annie saw a tear roll down her cheek, which was quickly wiped away.

'I'm sorry,' said Annie. 'I didn't mean to upset you. Thoughts about your husband?'

Alice's eyes widened, then she laughed. 'My, you are direct, aren't you? I'm not used to that. Yes, Siggi said he could not wait to see me pregnant and blooming. He used those very words.' She wiped away more tears. 'Now see what you have done. It's a good job my mother isn't here, I would get told off for not remembering my status.'

'Yes, it's a good job your mother isn't here,' said Annie, with perhaps more feeling than she intended.

Alice laughed. 'Oh you are terrible, but wonderful. Who else could have me laughing and crying at the same time?' Alice pulled a handkerchief from her sleeve and wiped her eyes and cheeks.

'It's one of my few talents,' said Annie. 'Did Siggi know?'

'That I was pregnant? No, and now look you've made me cry all over again! I don't do things like this, really.' She dabbed her eyes again. 'I thought I was. He came home for leave at the beginning of October. When he left again, somehow, I just knew. I waited though, just to be sure. I was going to write to tell him. But then I heard he was missing and never got the chance.' Alice took a deep breath. Annie knew that she was trying to compose herself. 'You and David had no children?' she asked.

Annie bit her lip. 'No,' she said. 'We didn't get the chance.'

She sat back, Alice had said she was direct, honest, yet she wasn't being, was she? Well who was she protecting? Not David, he was long gone, herself then? 'The truth is,' she went on, then stopped, unable to make herself say the words. 'The truth is, I'm not sure that it was right for us to have children. David and I, well, we were friends yes, his parents and mine lived near to each other in Nottingham. It was just…'

She fell silent. It suddenly felt like she was being disloyal.

'It was just what, Annie, my dear?'

Alice's voice was soft and gentle. Somehow Annie knew that she had to answer.

'I had known David for years. We grew up together. I had no more feelings for him than if he was a brother. Yet, I knew he had feelings for me, deeper feelings. It was when he joined up, in that first August of the war, and I saw him in his uniform... He was such a sweet boy, so kind, gentle. I felt, I felt, like I owed him. Isn't that terrible?' To her annoyance she felt wetness in her own eyes.

Annie felt Alice put her own hand on hers and give it a squeeze. 'Not at all,' she said. 'There are a lot of worse reasons to marry someone.'

'What about love? You loved Siggi, didn't you?'

Alice nodded. 'I did, yes. But we have both ended up in the same situation, haven't we?'

'We have indeed,' said Annie.

There was a pause, then Alice said: 'Do you fear that you have done the same thing again? Become attached to someone because they are sweet, kind and gentle?'

Annie turned and stared at her. 'I thought I was the direct one,' she said. She saw Alice look flustered.

'My apologies, Annie, my dear. What was I thinking? That was…'

'Direct.' said Annie.

'Yes, brutally so.'

'And honest.'

'Oh dear yes, please say you forgive me?'

Annie had tried her best to keep a straight face but then gave a snort of laughter.

'Oh you beast,' said Alice. 'That was mean. And we have disturbed the boys' reading.'

Percy at least was looking in their direction. Eddie had not moved.

Annie raised her hand in greeting. Percy went back to his book.

'You are quite right though,' she said quietly. 'I do fear just that.' And, she thought, but did not say, where is sweet, kind boy now? Is he still inside?

'Eddie is still very young,' said Alice.

'Too young for me? Or, rather, am I too old for him?'

'What should age matter? And why shouldn't a woman take a younger man? The other way around is not remarked on at all,' said Alice.

'I am not sure that your mother would approve of that view.'

'I am sure that she wouldn't.' said Alice. 'But that is not what I meant. I cannot think of Eddie as anything other than my little brother. It is hard to think of him grown up and in a relationship with anyone.'

'So you are saying I'm too old for him.'

'Not at all. I was just speaking like an older sister. If it is to be anyone, I would that it was you.'

'Thank you.'

'Whilst we are talking bluntly,' Alice said. Annie waited expectantly, but the rest of the sentence remained undelivered.

'What?'

'Nothing,' said Alice. 'I'm thirsty. We should get some lemonade.'

Annie got to her feet. 'I will go and make some.' Alice looked at her in some surprise.

'Sit down. We have servants to do this. That's what we pay them for.' She picked up the bell from the table and rang it. Annie sat down again.

'Sorry, I'm still not used to that.'

Lucy, who had travelled down from London with them, came from out of the house.

'Ma'am?' she said.

'We'd like some lemonade,' said Alice. 'Percy. Eddie. Would you like some?' she called.

Percy looked up but Eddie stayed as he was. Annie was now sure that he was not reading his book. 'Yes please,' Percy called back, then looked at his brother. 'Eddie, do you want some lemonade? Eddie? Eddie - come on. old chap look lively.'

Annie saw Eddie start, then look at his brother puzzled.

'Yes?' he said.

'Alice wants to know if you want lemonade.'

'Lemonade?'

'Yes.'

'Oh right, yes, that would be nice.' He looked around. 'Does Siggi…?' he began, then stopped.

'Pardon?' said Percy. 'Eddie, Siggi is gone. You know that.'

Annie saw him glance towards Alice.

'Oh yes,' said Eddie. 'I was just looking at Nelson there. I got distracted.'

Nelson was the Grenville's old gun dog, a spaniel. It lived in virtual retirement here, its shooting days long behind it. It had, according to Alice, been particularly close to Eddie as a boy, the two going on long adventures in the countryside. Now it plodded across the garden, stiff-legged, plump from lack of exercise. Nelson's coat was matted and thinning and his muzzle grey, the white of cataracts showing in his eyes.

'Ah yes, poor old chap,' said Percy. 'Come here, boy.' The spaniel turned and walked slowly over to him, its back end giving a reasonable impression of a wag as Percy scratched the dog's neck. 'You're a poor old thing now, aren't you? Not much of a life. No chasing rabbits anymore for you, is there boy?'

'Poor old thing,' murmured Eddie.

Lucy returned with a jug of lemonade and four glasses on a tray.

'Should I take the drinks down to the young masters?' said Lucy as she poured.

'No, thank you, Lucy.' said Alice. 'They can come and be sociable and sit with us around the table. Come on boys. Eddie, come on, come over here.'

Eddie got to his feet but Percy stayed where he was.

'You ladies were having a nice chat,' he said. 'I will have mine over here, please Lucy.'

'No Lucy, leave it on the table. If you want it you have to come over to us.' Annie glanced at Alice. Her mouth was set, she was a picture of determination. This was a battle of wills and Alice look to be set on winning it.

Percy, with great reluctance, rose and came over, though Annie noted he had put his book on his deckchair as if emphasising that he would soon wish to get back. He sat down. Annie could see that he was tense, his body nearly rigid. Eddie looked like he was going to follow suit, but at the last moment he turned and walked towards the main house.

'Eddie, where are you going?' said Alice. 'What about your lemonade?'

Eddie stopped and turned around to look at them. 'Lemonade?' he said, looking puzzled. Then his face brightened when he saw the jug and glasses. 'Oh yes, that would be nice. But I need to get something first.' Annie saw him look across at Nelson, then continue off into the house.

'I wonder what he is going to get,' murmured Alice, watching him go. 'He's not right yet, is he?'

'No. Not yet,' said Annie. 'He's got a long way to go.'

'He seems very distracted, like he's not there. Don't you think so, Percy?'

'Pardon?' Percy looked up, then at the door which Eddie had gone through. 'Oh, I suppose he's a bit distant. But he's getting better.'

He picked up his glass, sipped it, then stared at the floor.

The silence was so profound, the tension at the table so high that Annie was sure that something must break. The atmosphere was almost unbearable.

She was sure that Alice must say something, but she didn't, she just sipped her lemonade. Annie thought desperately of something that they could talk about that would at least break the oppressive silence. But what? What was safe? Something in the newspapers.

Suddenly something came to mind.

'Is there any news about that young pilot? The one that fought in his pyjamas?'

'Pyjamas?' said Percy, looking puzzled. 'Who was that? He'd be dashed cold.'

'It was that one that Eddie was always talking about?'

'Oh, Ball?' said Percy. 'No, I've not seen anything in the papers. Still, if he's missing and there have been no reports that he is a prisoner then it doesn't sound at all promising.'

'No,' said Alice, the single word delivered in a clipped, abrupt manner. Annie looked at her, puzzled. 'Siggi is still officially listed as missing,' she said.

'Oh but we know...' Annie began to say, before she realised what she was saying.

'We know what? What do you know?'

'She is saying - ' began Percy.

'I was about to say, it's the same with my husband,' said Annie quickly, giving Percy a warning glance. 'That we know really. David is officially missing, but I know, and his family know that he is gone. It's hard but it's the truth.'

'Yes,' said Alice. 'You're right, we know.' She looked towards the house, giving Annie the chance to angrily give a little shake of the head towards Percy. For all the tension it was surely best to keep the secret? 'I wonder where Eddie has got to? Oh, here he is. Where's he going now?'

Annie looked across at Eddie. He was not walking towards them but across the lawn, towards where Nelson was laying in the sun. The spaniel raised his head as Eddie approached, his tail gave a brief wag.

'Eddie, what are you doing?' called Alice.

Annie saw Eddie raise his arm. He held something black in his hand.

'Oh bloody hell!' yelled Percy. The glass in his hand seemed to explode as he leapt from his chair, shards and liquid spraying everywhere as he ran down the steps of the summer house and onto the lawn shouting. 'Eddie, no! Put it down!'

It was happening in slow motion. Annie knew then that Eddie had a gun in his hand. She found that she too was on her feet, though she could not remember rising, but she was unable to move.

She was convinced the report must come at any moment.

*

Five minutes later, she was still shaking. Percy was sat in the chair in front of her and she was attempting to put a bandage on his hand.

'I thought you were a nurse, used to doing this sort of thing?' he said. 'Perhaps you should let Lucy or Alice do it?'

'I'm fine, I can cope,' Annie said, surprised at how irritated she was, forcing herself to just do the job, do what was necessary. Oddly, she found not thinking about it helped, the action of dressing a wound, something she had done a thousand times before, helped still her shaking hands.

'What were you thinking of Eddie?' said Alice, she was stood by the table, by Eddie who was sat at it, looking puzzled. His gun was on the floor next to Percy.

'I was being kind,' he said, as if it were the most obvious thing in the world.

'Kind?' said Alice. 'You were going to shoot Nelson. Why would you want to do that?'

Eddie shrugged. 'Percy was right. He's old. He's got no sort or life. I just thought it would be the kindest thing for him.'

'I didn't mean it like that, old chap,' said Percy. 'I just hadn't seen him in a while, I hadn't realised how old he had got. But he's alright still, just enjoying your retirement aren't you old fellow.'

He reached over with his good hand and scratched the dog's neck. In doing so he pulled the hand that Annie was bandaging out of her hands.

'Keep still,' she said, adding as an afterthought, 'please.'

'Sorry.'

'Nearly done,' said Annie, tying off the loose ends. 'There, you'll do. As I said before, it looks clean but it's a deep cut. I would pop into the local hospital if I were you on Monday and get them to take a look at it.'

'I'm sure it's fine,' said Percy. 'I'm busy on Monday anyway but, to be honest, I've had my fill of hospitals.' Gingerly he tried opening and closing his hand.

'I'm really sorry,' said Eddie. 'I didn't mean any harm.

'None done,' said Percy. 'My own stupid fault for breaking the glass like that. Damn stupid of me. Excuse the language, ladies.'

'Well I think we had better make sure we keep that gun somewhere safe. I don't think you should have it at the moment,' said Alice.

'But it's mine,' protested Eddie. 'It's my service weapon, it was issued to me. I'll get into trouble if I don't have it with me. Percy, you know, you tell them.' Annie could see that there was desperation in his eyes.

'Now, now Eddie, don't worry. You need it on active service or on parade but now it's fine. I don't have mine with me, do I?'

'Oh no, no you don't, of course. Yes, alright, if you could look after it for me?'

'Yes, I will do that for you.'

'Good,' Eddie nodded. 'You understand. I know you understand.'

'It's getting cooler now,' said Alice. 'I'm going to go inside. Shall we play some music on the gramophone?'

'Yes, that's a good idea,' said Percy. 'I could do with some tea, or perhaps something stronger. Father is wanting me to go up to town on Monday to meet someone at his club, though he won't say whom, I might well need something to fortify me.'

'Father?' said Alice. 'It will be some business deal he's doing and needs to trot out his hero son to add some weight. Whatever, feel free to have something stronger. I am getting the impression you need a drink to be in the same room as me. Come on, Eddie.'

Percy was half out of his seat, but stopped, his mouth open at what Alice had just said.

'Alice,' he began. 'I do want to be with you, it's just...'

But Alice and Eddie were already walking across the lawn.

Percy moved to follow her but Annie placed her hand on his arm.

'Don't do it,' she said. 'Please.'

'But I must, I have to.'

Annie saw Alice look back at them as she and Eddie went inside the house.

'What good would it do? What is the point of tearing her apart, tearing the family apart? Because it will you know, it's bound to.'

'But it's wrong not to tell her. She knows there is something wrong by the way that I am with her. I can hardly look at her, I feel so ashamed. I am responsible, I did it, I have to face up to it, to tell her.' Percy turned away from the house and looked out of the garden.

'Percy, please,' said Annie. 'You are facing up to it, I can see that by the way you are. That does not mean that you have to cause more hurt.'

'Why did I do it? Why the hell did I do it?'

'Siggi was your friend. He was family,' said Annie, stepping closer. 'But he was also an enemy soldier, a pilot. He had been trying to kill you a few minutes before.'

'Yes, but he didn't know who I was. He didn't know it was me.'

'No, but don't you think, if you met other Germans, other pilots, face to face you would like them as well? They do the same job, they are drawn from the same class of people as you. You probably do know some of them. That's true, isn't it? You know it is, don't you?'

'Yes, but...'

'Yet that would not stop you killing them because, now, that is what your country needs you to do. If left, they would not hesitate to kill your friends and colleagues.'

Percy said nothing. Annie stepped still closer and whispered.

'I'm sorry, but the truth is that if you had let Siggi go, the chances are he would have flown and killed your comrades. What you did was, extreme, granted. But thinking about it, is it fundamentally any worse than any other act in this war?'

Percy looked like he was going to protest, but then he slowly shook his head.

'She's pregnant though,' he whispered. 'She has Siggi's child inside her.'

'Which means she needs her family more than ever. Particularly, Percy, she needs you. You parents are - well it is not my place to pass comment on them, other than to say they do not seem to be caring and supportive. Eddie is still not well, we've just seen that. He needs you too. Percy, you might feel better to get it off your chest, to tell everyone and then go into some sad little exile where you can wallow in your own misery but, I'm sorry, but that would be selfish thing to do. Alice, her child and Eddie need you.'

'Yes,' he said dully.

'And you have to act normally, put your shame behind you.'

He nodded again.

'Come on then,' she said, and stepped towards the house. She paused and nodded towards the revolver. 'Don't forget that. I'd rather Eddie did not have that with him for the next few weeks.'

She walked away across the lawn. As she reached the house she turned back to look at the summer house.

Percy was still there. He was stood with the gun in his hands, staring down at it. For a moment she felt some alarm, but then he seemed to shake himself and put the gun carefully into his jacket pocket. He walked onto the lawn and followed her inside.

CHAPTER SEVENTEEN

England, Monday May 21st, 1917

Annie woke up on Monday morning feeling better than she had done for weeks.

The tension in the Grenville household seemed to have eased. Sunday had been really pleasant. After Church they had gone for a long walk by the Itchen, taking a picnic with them. It was taken at a gentle pace in light of Alice's pregnancy and had been a delightful day that everyone enjoyed.

Percy had been transformed, he was funny, witty, self-deprecating. Above all, Annie noted, he was quite normal with Alice, chatting to her about everything, not only the past but the future as well. Annie could see the man that Eddie had described for the first time. And, she had to admit to herself, that man was attractive.

The new Percy and the relaxed Alice seemed to have rubbed off on Eddie too. There were times when he was distant still, but at others he was joining in, larking about with Percy in the water at one point, both of them getting as muddy as schoolboys, afterwards reporting to Alice and Annie for a scolding. At one point a flight of aircraft flew over, the boys having a quite animated discussion as to whether they were the new Sopwith scout that everyone had been talking about or were just the old Pups.

Only that evening was a slightly sour note struck, and then from an unexpected quarter. Percy and Eddie had gone for a game of billiards leaving Alice and Annie reading in the library. At least Annie was reading, for she became conscious of Alice staring at her. She put her book down.

'What is it?' she said.

Alice made as if to speak, then seemed to reconsider. 'Nothing,' she said.

'It doesn't look like nothing, what's the matter Alice, my dear?'

'Alright, it's...' she sighed. 'Maybe it is because of my condition, perhaps it has muddled my brain, but, well Percy is definitely different today.'

'Is he?' said Annie, trying to keep her voice light.

'Yes he is, and you know he is. He's back to almost how I remember him, before...well, before the war.'

'Well, that's a good thing isn't it?'

'Yes, yes of course, I much prefer my brother like this. It's just...'

'It's just what?' said Annie, dreading what was coming.

Alice took a deep breath. 'It was after you two spoke in the garden. You can't deny it, I watched you. And it wasn't him that did much of the speaking, it was you. You were telling him something, something that he didn't like to hear, but you made him listen.' Alice frowned, and she stared right at Annie. 'What happened, what did you say to him? I want to know,'

Annie swallowed. This was just what she wanted to avoid. Alice had asked a direct question. She hated lies, hated duplicity but what was she to do here? Percy had done his bit, he had really tried, possibly too well. What could she say?

Time seemed to pass so slowly. Annie was aware that the longer she did not answer the worse she was going to make it, yet her brain refused to provide her with any real solutions. In the end she felt forced to start talking, if only to calm herself down.

'Yes, I did speak to Percy,' she said.

'I saw that. What did you say to him?'

Yes, what. What could she tell her friend? She had to say something.

She would have to lie.

'You were right, Percy had found it difficult, more difficult than he thought in dealing with your being married to a German, whether it was Siggi or not. He had, after all, been fighting against Germans for over a year.'

'But that's silly. He and Siggi were best friends.'

'Yes, that was just what I told him.' Annie was sure that she had gone red, and that Alice could not possibly believe her. 'But many people think the same way.'

'Do you think like that? After all, your David was killed by the Germans.'

Did she think that? At the time of his death she certainly felt hatred for taking the life of such a nice man - though she also hated herself because of the feelings of relief she had that she was now free from the burden of having to make the marriage work. At least, though, she could talk about herself, rather than put untruthful words in Percy's mouth.

'At the time, yes, I probably did,' she said.

Alice nodded. 'Thank you for being so honest.' she said, which made Annie feel worse.

'I don't feel that way now,' she said, though she knew this sounded pathetic.

She was relieved that, straight afterwards, Alice had said she was tired and had gone to bed. Annie had followed soon afterwards.

She had heard some voices downstairs about half-an-hour after she had turned the light off but had thought nothing about it.

The reason for the voices was revealed when she walked into the breakfast room on Monday morning. She could tell that the atmosphere in the house had changed, the staff seemed to be more on edge, Lucy, who was normally always ready for a chat, had scurried by as Annie had walked across the hall with only a very quick 'Good morning'. The reason was sat at the breakfast table, sipping tea.

It was Lady Grenville.

She looked at Annie with some disdain.

'Yes?' she said. 'Do you want something?'

'Er, no,' said Annie. 'I've just come down for breakfast.'

Lady Grenville stared at her.

'The staff do not eat with the family,' she said.

'Mother,' said Percy. 'Annie is not staff.'

'We employ her, don't we?'

'Yes, but she's more...'

'Then she is staff and she eats with them and not with us.'

'Then we will all eat with the servants,' said Alice getting to her feet.

'No,' said Annie. 'Stay where you are, Alice,'

'Annie you don't need-'

'We do not need to hear your opinion, young lady,' said Lady Grenville. 'You do not have a say in...'

'I do, because I am no longer, as you put it, staff.'

'Yes, you are.'

'No, I'm not. I've had enough. I resign. I'll go and pack my things.'

'No, Annie,' said Alice.

'Mother, that will do,' said Percy.

Lady Grenville gave Annie a withering stare. 'You will go when we say you can go and when your duties are complete.'

'With respect, Lady Grenville, I will go when the hell I want to and where I want to,' said Annie. She was pleased to see her recoil at the language. She turned to the Grenville children. 'I'm sorry, I refuse to put up with this, and, frankly, I don't have to, so I am going. Eddie, I'll write to you.'

She turned and was about to walk out when she heard Lady Grenville say, 'Good riddance. That's the problem with letting women be educated and work...'

In an instant she had turned around.

'Yes, it is a problem, isn't it? Because we get ideas, and opinions, and chances in life, we get the chance to choose. Young women and, yes, young men too. It's a problem because we are a threat to your precious little world, Lady Grenville, your world of privilege, and family, and blood ties and wealth that is closed to the masses, whatever talents or qualities they have. That world is going, Lady Grenville, it was going before this war but it's going away even faster now. It's being swept away before your eyes and there is nothing you can do about it.'

Lady Grenville was now on her feet. 'How dare you speak to me like that in my house. Get out! Get out this instant!'

'With great pleasure.'

Annie turned to find Lucy stood in the doorway, a look of shock on her face. Though her insides felt like jelly and she was not sure how her legs were carrying her, she managed to give the maid a little smile.

She started to pack as soon as she reached her room. She was not surprised to hear a knock on her door a few minutes later.

'Come in,' she called.

She had expected it to be Alice. It was Percy.

'Annie, I am really sorry about mother. That was very rude of her.'

'It was.'

'I have told her as such, and that your presence here has really helped Eddie.'

'Thank you.' Annie continued to pack. 'Was there anything else?'

'Well, yes, I was hoping you would stay, at least for now.'

Annie did not stop. 'Are you serious? After that?'

Percy frowned. 'I will talk to mother, persuade her.'

Annie pursed her lips and shook her head. 'No, Percy. As she said, it is her house, well her's and your father's. She has the right to say who comes and goes in it. I have my rights too, my choices. I choose to go.'

She put the last of her things inside and closed the case, pressing down on the top with one palm whilst trying to fasten the clasps.

'Here let me help,' said Percy.

'I can manage,' Annie snapped. Percy stood back, looking abashed. Briefly, Annie felt guilty. 'Percy, there is no use arguing, I have made my mind up. Eddie doesn't really need me anymore, he doesn't need nursing skills and,' she took a deep breath. 'As for anything else, well, he seems to have forgotten about it. I was already wondering just why I was still here. This might be a blessing in disguise.'

'Alice needs you,' Percy muttered.

'I'll leave her a forwarding address. If she needs me she can write to me.'

She picked up her case.

Percy stepped forward again and took hold of both of her forearms in his hands. His face and hers were just a few inches apart. Annie felt a little jolt inside of her, she seemed to be drawn upwards, towards Percy's lips.

'I need you,' he whispered.

It took all her will to resist, just to stay still, not to move yet closer. Annie did not know what would have happened if there had not been another knock on the door. Whatever, Percy immediately let her go and stepped away.

'Can I come in?'

'Yes Alice,' said Annie, finding her voice.

Alice stepped into the room. She seemed surprised to find Percy there already.

'Oh,' she said, momentarily put off her stride. 'Annie, I will have a talk-'

Annie picked up her case. 'It's too late, Alice. I just said the same to Percy. I'll write to you.'

Alice nodded, then stepped forward and embraced her. Annie felt Alice's swollen belly press against her. She had a sudden and unexpected feeling of jealousy, of loss and found herself breaking the embrace rather more abruptly than she had intended. She saw the look of hurt in Alice's face.

'I will get the boy to bring the trap round and run you to the station,' said Percy.

'I don't need it, I'll walk.'

'I insist, in fact I'll come with you.'

'No,' Annie snapped. 'There's no need,' she added, more softly.

'I'm going up to London anyway,' protested Percy.

'Oh very well then,' said Alice 'If you must.'

Percy nodded and left the room, leaving Alice and Annie alone together.

The awkward silence was oppressive. Annie wondered if she should say something, apologise for her brusqueness, for pushing Alice away but she knew that she could not really explain why she had felt that way. It was irrational, childish even. She had not loved David that deeply, so why did she feel the loss of the children they would never have so deeply?

'I...' she began.

'Are you going to say goodbye to Edward?' Alice interrupted.

Annie bit her lip. 'I suppose I should.'

Alice gave a little smile. 'Don't worry, I'll do it.'

There was a call from downstairs. Percy.

Annie put her hand on Alice's arm. 'Thank you,' she said. 'I will write to you, tell you where I am. Look after yourself.'

This time it was her who initiated the embrace, and she was pleased to feel in herself no other feelings than affection.

*

Alice watched the trap pull away from the house, Annie and Percy sat in it together, either side of the driver. At the gate, Annie looked back and raised her hand in farewell. Alice did the same, though she was not certain whether Annie could see her.

'Who's that leaving? Is it Sophie?'

Eddie's voice made her jump. He was stood at the door, the newspaper in his hand.

'Sophie?' she said. 'Who is Sophie.'

Eddie looked confused, he shook his head. 'No, not Sophie, the girl, the one that stayed here.'

'Annie you mean?'

'Yes, of course Annie. Where has she gone?'

'She's left Eddie,' said Annie. 'Mother-'

'Left?' Eddie said. He sighed. 'Damn her! Damn her blasted eyes!' He swung his fist into the door.

'Eddie,' Alice said, stepping towards him and putting her hand on his arm. 'Calm down. What's the matter?'

Eddie pulled himself free. 'Everybody leaves me. Bunny. Bean. Milne. Kerr. They all go. Now her too. Why should I expect anything else?' He held up the newspaper. 'And now Ball has gone too. Dead. He's bloody dead! What's the bloody point, I ask you? What is the bloody point?' He savagely tore the newspaper up and tossed it onto the floor, then stomped out of the room and into the corridor.

The noise of his door slamming could be heard throughout the house.

*

They shared a carriage all the way to London. Annie expected Percy to say something, given his insistence on coming with her, to try to explain his behaviour but he stayed silent all the way, seemingly lost in his thoughts. She wondered if that was the way with the Grenville boys, that they kept things bottled up within them.

That could explain a lot, she thought, including how they were after experiencing war.

She wondered how David would have been if he had come back. Would he have changed too? Would she have loved what had come back?

Then she realised that she had not loved the old David and the guilt returned.

'Percy,' she said.

He answered, 'Yes, Annie,' straight away, so quickly that she was put off her stride and lost what little courage she had to say what she intended.

'Don't tell Alice,' she said. 'Not ever. Not for Eddie's sake but for hers.'

Percy stared at her for a few moments then gave a small, quick nod.

CHAPTER EIGHTEEN

England, Monday May 21st, 1917

Percy rose from the table. The other men rose with him.

'Gentlemen,' Percy said. 'If you'll excuse me, I must go. I have an appointment with the Medical Board at two.'

'A medical board,' said his father. 'What's that for?'

'The Flying Corp. To see if I am fit to return to service,' Percy replied.

'What do you want to do that for? You've done your bit, surely?'

'I'm still a serving officer, father,' said Percy. 'And the war is far from finished.'

Sir Arthur looked like he was going to argue, but the man who Percy had been surprised to find at his father's club, let alone invited to his table, interrupted.

'The boy is keen, Arthur, leave him be,' said Fitzroy. 'It's only natural with his sense of duty. It's admirable. Our country would be in a better position if everyone was like him.'

'Most men are much better than me, and my country does quite well, thank-you,' said Percy, his voice icy cold.

Fitzroy seemed not to detect the hostility.

'Well said, sir. And typically modest.' He extended his hand. 'A pleasure to meet you at last, Captain Grenville.'

'Likewise, I'm sure,' said Percy. 'Lord Hanley,' he added, nodding to the third diner. 'Father, we'll speak later. Waiter, my coat please.' He put his uniform cap on and left the private dining room.

What was that all about? Father with Maxwell Fitzroy? The publisher of that rag that had made up that story about him? Well not made up, but at least distorted the facts so much they were barely recognisable. And Lord Hanley, why was he there? A Tory peer. Percy knew of him but had no idea what he was involved in. He had said so little but Percy had felt like he was being constantly scrutinised by the man throughout the meal.

He shook his head. He must have been imagining things.

Well he had other things to worry about. The Medical Board for one thing.

And Eddie.

And Alice.

And Annie. Especially Annie.

He closed his eyes, he was such a fool. He should forget her, do the honourable thing, never think about seeing her again.

The trouble was he thought about virtually nothing else.

*

Sir Arthur, Fitzroy and Lord Hanley had retired to a quiet corner of the club with brandies.

'Well?' said Fitzroy. 'What do you think?'

'I think he is an ideal candidate. He is just what the party and the country needs,' said Lord Hanley, taking a thoughtful sip.

'Exactly as I said,' said Fitzroy, sitting back. 'A young war hero, fresh from action, from an excellent family.' He raised his glass to Percy's father, who inclined his head slightly in acknowledgement. 'He will make an excellent MP and, in time, be ready for ministerial office when it becomes time to ditch Lloyd George and his damn Liberals. After the war is won, of course,' he added quickly. 'My publication will back him to the hilt, we'll get the country behind him. He'll be carried into office on a wave of popular support.'

'What are your feelings on this, Sir Arthur?' Hanley's face was impassive.

'My feelings are the same as they have ever been. I want Percival to join the family business, as he was always intended to. He, however, seems intent on forging his own way in the world.' He sighed heavily. 'Young people, they think they know best. Always have. Well, perhaps this is a way of getting him to take his responsibilities seriously, but good luck to you in trying to persuade him to stand. Personally I don't think you have a hope in hell. He's as stubborn as a mule.'

'That could be a problem,' said Hanley. 'We do require our candidates to be willing to stand, Fitzroy.'

'I think you are being pessimistic,' said Fitzroy. 'I think young Percival can be persuaded.'

'And I think you are being optimistic, Fitzroy,' said Sir Arthur. 'Do not presume to know my son better than I do.'

'I am not, I assure you, Sir Arthur,' said Fitzroy, his voice as sweet as syrup. 'You will know, to your cost, if I may be so bold to venture, that he has a well-developed sense of duty, does he not?'

'He does.'

'He volunteered for military service immediately in August 1914, didn't he? Even though he had not completed his studies.'

'Yes he did. He was a fool to do so too in my opinion.'

'But it was also a very patriotic thing to do as well, wasn't it? He rose to his country's call without hesitation.'

'Yes, but-'

'So, therefore, all we need to do is to appeal to this. It is a great strength, but, again if you will allow me to speak frankly, it is also his greatest weakness.'

Hanley raised his eyebrows. 'You are saying that if we appeal to that sense of duty, convince him that his country really needs him to help lead it to a better future -'

'- he will be bound to agree, yes.' Fitzroy's eyes were gleaming.

'Sir Arthur?' said Hanley, looking at him.

'Yes, he would,' said Percy's father.

'There,' said Fitzroy, triumphantly. 'That's settled isn't it?'

'Not completely,' said Hanley. 'There is one thing we need to resolve before I go to the party with a recommendation to find Captain Granville a safe seat.'

'What is it?' said Fitzroy, looking puzzled.

'The question of his gallantry award,' said Hanley.

'King and Country have campaigned strongly for a VC,' said Fitzroy. 'The country is behind it.'

'It has not been awarded though, has it?' said Hanley. 'Or even an official application made.'

'My son does not seek honours,' said Sir Arthur.

'Notwithstanding that, having a candidate that would appear on the ballot paper as "Captain PD Granville, VC" would add thousands to his vote,' said the peer.

'Well, we just need to push for the award to be made,' said Fitzroy. 'I'll write another editorial, shame the authorities into action.'

'It's not that simple, Fitzroy,' said Sir Arthur.

'I think you'll find-'

'Sir Arthur is quite right, I'm afraid,' Hanley interrupted. 'The process for awarding a VC is normally quite formal. A recommendation for the VC is normally issued by an officer at regimental level and has to be supported by three witnesses.'

'We have testimony,' protested Fitzroy.

'From an officer?' said Hanley.

'Well, no, from a private from the trench that brought him in, but we a signed account.'

'Not good enough I'm afraid. What about the officer commanding the section?'

Fitzroy shook his head. 'We tried to find him. He was posted missing in February. He did write home to his wife about the affair though.'

'His observer? Was he an officer?'

'Not then but he was promoted before he went back to France.'

'That might help then.'

'I'll see if I can trace him,' said Fitzroy. 'You did say that was the normal process for approval?'

'Indeed.'

'So there are exceptions?'

'The normal process has been waived on occasions, I believe. Where an action has no other survivors, for example.'

'Like has occurred here, for example.'

'I suppose so, yes. But you do need someone to confirm the story.'

'Something that, by the way, Percival has not done,' said Sir Arthur. 'Though that means nothing. He's not the type to blow his own trumpet.'

'So if he did confirm it, to, for example, a senior officer, then, in the circumstances, that might be enough evidence?' said Fitzroy, looking at Lord Hanley.

He nodded. 'It might,' he conceded.

'And if that officer was a member of the General Staff, like, for example, your own brother, Sir Arthur?'

Sir Arthur nodded. 'If he can get Percival to talk about it, of course.'

'There would need to be an independent witness there, another senior officer ideally,' said Hanley.

'I will talk to my brother,' said Sir Arthur.

Fitzroy smiled, drained his glass and sat back in satisfaction.

His plan was falling into place nicely.

And these men thought they were using him and his publication to their own ends, the fools.

CHAPTER NINETEEN

England Wednesday June 6th, 1917

Annie woke.

The curtains were cracked open and the sun was streaming in through the window. She watched the dust motes spiral and twist in the sunbeam, they seemed alive, and, for a moment, she had a notion that they were aircraft, chasing each other, intent on shooting down their opponents. Was this what it was like, she wondered. And was it as inconsequential?

Dust to dust.

She looked away; she was being maudlin.

Her eyes fell on the uniform jacket draped over the arm of the chair by the window. The sun that allowed the motes to display also shone on the wings on the chest. She closed her eyes. This was wrong, so wrong. Yet so right too.

He had rolled away from her in the night. She looked across at his back, smooth and naked, his shoulders, slighter than she had expected, his dark hair tousled by sleep. He seemed so young, innocent even now. It was almost possible to forget what he had done.

She could hear a clock striking in the distance and counted the chimes. Nine, there were nine. Damnation, she had to be at work by ten. Matron would tear a strip off her, again. She had to go, they had to go.

She leant across and shook him by the shoulder.

'Hey, wake up,' she said. 'Percy, come on, I'll be late for work.'

*

Alice eased herself into the chair in the sunroom. She took a deep breath and patted her swollen belly. 'I will be glad once you are out of there, young Siggi,' she murmured. 'You're getting to be a big boy.'

She heard the door open behind her and looked who it was. Eddie, and he was in uniform again. He had started wearing it again a few weeks ago now and was now rarely out of it.

'Has the post come?' he said.

'And good morning to you, too, Eddie,' said Alice.

He stared at her, a look of puzzlement on his face.

'Well?' he said. 'Has it or not?'

She sighed, where had the quiet and polite younger brother she knew gone?

'Never mind,' she said. 'Yes, it came about half an hour ago. It's on the table. There's one for you.'

'Well why didn't anyone damn well say?' said Eddie, striding over to the table. There were half a dozen letters on there, mostly for Percy. Eddie rooted through them until he found his own. He snatched it up with a cry of triumph, in doing so two of Percy's were swept onto the floor. Eddie ignored them and went and sat down, tearing the envelope open as he did.

'At last, these must be my orders,' he said.

'Aren't you going to pick those up?' said Alice.

'Pick what up?' Eddie said. 'Damnation, it's not. Damn their bloody eyes, how much longer do I have to wait?' He screwed the letter up and threw it across the room. The ball of paper bounced off the wall and landed back on the floor near to Alice's chair whilst Eddie sat back, folding his arms across the front of his chest like a petulant child.

She sighed again and pulled herself to her feet. She swayed, lightheaded; she had got up too quickly. She steadied herself against the chair arm. Briefly, she wondered whether she could call the doctor but the dizziness quickly passed.

She waddled over to the table, stooped carefully to pick the letters up, then walked back to her chair, pausing only to pick up the balled-up paper before sitting down again. She should tell Eddie off for his bad temper, but she was exhausted and did not have the energy to get into yet another argument with him. She had to make allowances, she told herself, he'd been through a lot. She had to be patient, though, with the way he was, Eddie would try the patience of a Saint.

'What were you expecting?' she said, smoothing out the paper.

'My orders, of course,' Eddie snapped. 'What else?'

'Orders?'

'Yes orders. To re-join my squadron. Or to get another one.'

'Don't you think it's too soon? Haven't you done your bit?' she said.

'My bit? No, no, not at all. I need to go back, I have to.'

'But Eddie, you were wounded.'

'I was wounded. I'm fine now, aren't I? Look.' He held up his hand and flexed the fingers backwards and forwards. 'And my foot is fine. Well just a bit sore but I flew with it far worse than this.'

'But what about...' Alice began.

'What about what?'

What about your state of mind, Alice thought? You're not right Eddie, not at all right. But she said, 'Nothing.' She did not want an argument.

'This is all so dull. Sitting around here with you, waiting for that bloody baby to come out. I want to damn well do something.'

'I'm sorry we're so boring,' Alice said. Then something in the letter she held in her hand caught her eye. 'Eddie, you've been given a medal. That's what it says in here, didn't you see?'

Eddie scowled. 'I'm not interested in medals. What do they mean? Hell, they are even talking about giving Percy the VC and all he did was let Siggi shoot him down.'

Alice looked up sharply.

'What?'

She briefly locked eyes with Eddie. She saw him look confused for a second, then he seemed to realise what he had said.

'Nothing,' he mumbled. 'What have they given me?'

'Never mind about that. What was that you said about Siggi? Siggi and Percy?'

'Nothing. I didn't say anything.'

'Yes you did,' said Alice. 'Now you're lying. I can tell.'

'I'm not'

'Yes, you are. You always were a shocking liar, Eddie.'

'I'm not lying,' said Eddie, though she could see the tell-tale redness was spreading up his neck. 'I just got confused. You know I've been getting confused lately. Please don't be beastly to me, Alice.'

Alice continued to stare, then sighed and relaxed, at least outwardly. 'Yes. Sorry. Obviously, you were.'

Inside she was still churning. Had Eddie given something away? Was that why Percy had been so different with her, cold at first and then, if anything, overly solicitous? No, she was being silly, reading too much into Eddie's words. He wasn't quite right yet, the family knew that, well her and Percy did at least. She realised she was still holding the letter. She read it again.

'They are giving you the Military Cross,' she said. 'That's quite high isn't it?'

'An MC,' said Eddie, his eyes widening. 'Ball got one of those.'

'Did he?'

'Yes. He was a hero.'

'Well,' said Alice. 'Then I suppose that makes you a hero too.'

'A hero?' Alice could see that his eyes had filled with wonder. 'A hero, yes, I suppose it does. Like Ball. Just like Ball.' He got to his feet. 'I must go.'

'Go? Where to?'

'Back to London. I have got to see the air board. I have to get back to France, I just have to.'

'Eddie!, Eddie, wait,' said Alice but it was too late. Eddie had gone.

*

They shared a taxi back to the private hospital where Annie now worked. He held her hand but they did not exchange a word during the journey. Annie just stared out of the window, seeing everything and nothing. When it reached the hospital and stopped, however, she turned to Percy.

'We can't carry on like this,' she said.

'Yes, I know, I'm sorry,' he said. 'It's not right, I know. I shouldn't put you in this position. We should get engaged at least. If that's what you want.'

She shook her head. 'No. I mean, yes, in time, but now we can't can we?'

Percy looked puzzled. 'Can't we?'

'No we can't. For one thing, I'm still married.'

'Yes but...well, your husband is...'

'Missing Percy. Officially he's missing, not dead. Until that changes there is nothing I can do.'

'We can apply to the authorities. I will go and see my solicitor, see what can be done to declare him dead.'

'Yes but...' she began, then fell silent.

'Yes but what? It's the truth isn't it?'

'Yes, it is. But it's not the only problem we have in seeing each other is it?'

'No,' said Percy quietly.

'There is your family for one thing. Your mother hates me,' she said, then forestalled his interruption. 'But above all there is Eddie.'

'Eddie, yes, yes of course. You still have feelings for him?'

'No. No that was all just...a mistake. It's just that this is unfair on him. We should tell him.'

Percy sat back. He nodded. 'Yes, yes we should. I will go back to Hampshire and see him. It's the right thing to do.'

'No, you can't do that,' she said.

He looked up, puzzled. 'But you just said-'

'He's not in any fit state to get news like that.'

'Eddie? He's fine. He's a lot better. He'll understand.'

'Percy, he's not. He's not right, and you know he's not. Oh hell, I am going to be late, we can't talk about this now, I'm sorry.' She opened the door of the cab.

'Can I see you tonight?' he said.

'Percy, I don't know,' she said.

He put his hand on her arm. 'Please. We need to talk.'

'Very well. I'll meet you at the Lyon's Corner House near the Station after my shift tonight.'

He smiled, that slow, shy smile that had melted her soul and gave her shivers.

'Thank you,' he said. 'Have a good day.'

'Enjoy your lunch with your father,' she said.

He sighed heavily. 'Oh, that, yes. I'd almost forgotten. I have a nasty feeling the old man is plotting something.'

'He's probably just trying to get you back in the family business. Anyway, must fly. Bye, Percy. See you later.'

She heard the cab pull away. She made a conscious effort not to look back.

*

His anticipation about a plot was confirmed almost immediately. Lord Hanley came right out with it over the aperitifs.

'Percival, we would like you to stand for parliament. We want to find you a safe seat as soon as possible.'

'What? Stand for the Conservatives?'

'Who else?' his father said. 'They are the only ones who are standing up for British business. Heaven's knows what a state the country would be in after more years of that Welsh charlatan, Lloyd-George. Why even his name's a fake, did you know that?'

'Who told you that, father? That Fitzroy chap that you've got so chummy with?'

'Never you mind, Percival, let's just say I have it from a reliable source.'

Percy smiled. 'Well I'm sure that if it takes a thief...' he said.

'Whatever, your father is right,' said Hanley. 'Without strong leadership this country is going to go to the dogs. MacDonald and the Socialists are getting stronger by the day. The Liberals will have to give them concessions to stay in power. In the opinion of many we are heading towards anarchy.'

'Revolution possibly,' said Sir Arthur. 'Just like Russia.'

'I don't know,' Percy had replied. 'I don't believe that Britain would ever go so far. I've never been to Russia but I knew a couple of Russians at school. Russia sounded very oppressive, backward even. It was ripe for revolution. Britain is not at all like that.'

'I wouldn't be so sure,' said Sir Arthur. 'Britain is a lot like France, and, with what Hanley has told me -'

'Grenville,' said Hanley sharply.

'I'm sorry. I forgot. But still with my son...'

'It can go no further, Arthur,' said Hanley. 'Percival, if you would please forget what your father just said. Do not mention it to anyone else. Not a word.'

'Of course not,' said Percy, though he was intrigued.

The French, something to do with the French. Had something happened? Something the authorities wanted to keep quiet? He knew things had not gone well on the Aisne, had there been a reaction in the ranks? A mutiny even? Well, Lord Hanley was right, if such talk got to the Germans or even, God forbid, to the British Tommies the result would be awful. The Germans would attack where the line was weakest and sweep the French aside and the British would be helpless to do anything about it, morale would collapse anyway. There would be a rout. Everything that they had fought for, sacrificed, - he had fought so bitterly for -would be lost.

'I can see in your face that you understand,' said Hanley. 'I know as a gentlemen and a patriot that you will say absolutely nothing to anyone, not even the slightest whisper.'

'Yes,' said Percy. He saw his father look abashed.

So his fears were right. Good God.

'But it is one of the reasons why we need men like yourself, Captain Grenville.'

'Maybe so but I'm not sure I really hold the values of your party, Lord Hanley.'

'Don't talk rot, Percival,' said his father. 'Of course you damn well do.'

Lord Hanley sounded more reasoned. 'I think you'd be surprised, the Tory party is a broad church, always has been. It is still the party of Disraeli after all, one nation and all that. It, we, really need men like yourself, young reformers who will manage the country properly. We know there are changes ahead, after the war is won, things will change. Women will want the vote -'

There had been a snort of derision from his father.

'- and women will get the vote,' Hanley had continued. 'But that is not all, the days of the old politics, of the ruling classes are gone. A new Britain will arise. We need people like you to be part of it, Captain Grenville, to lead us through troubled times.'

'But...what about my war service? I'm fit again, I will be bound to be posted back on active duty. How can I be an MP?'

'There are a number of MPs serving at the front, including some in the Flying Corp. Anyway, we would be relying on a by-election. It would take a while to identify a suitable seat for you,' said Hanley. 'You would have time to make suitable arrangements.'

'But, in the meantime, questionable though he might be, we can use Fitzroy and his paper's circulation to keep you in the public eye.'

Percy nodded. It had all fallen into place for him. That was why the newspaper man was there when they had first met.

'I'm not sure I am the man you think I am,' he said quietly.

'What are you talking about?' said Sir Arthur. 'You are a Grenville, we are a good family and you, for all your strange ideas, are a good man.'

Percy stayed silent. He saw Hanley regarding him quizzically.

'Are you being modest or thinking about anything particular?' He had said. 'We can do without any scandal. You're not seeing some married woman, are you?'

'No,' he had said, though he knew that was stretching the truth.

'Something that you did at the front? Well, if it's that you're worried about, put it behind you, it is of no concern. War is war, we all know that, terrible deeds are done every day. It is necessity. You have been doing things in the service of your country. Well, Captain Grenville, Percival, your country needs you to do more service for it. Its need is greater than even you can imagine.' Hanley leant forward and stared intently at Percy. 'We need you. Your country needs you. Will you answer it's call?'

How could he not have said anything but 'yes'?

*

The rest of the lunch had passed in a daze. Percy barely recognised what he'd eaten and had agreed to his father's request come over to the family home in London in the afternoon 'to sign some legal papers' without any argument.

Once he had said yes the misgivings had started. He didn't want to stand for office, he really didn't, yet now he felt obliged. They were right in a way, the country did need good leadership. Was he really the one to give it, though? After what he had done? Perhaps he wasn't in his right mind when he had shot Siggi, he had known long before that final mission that he was under terrible strain, that he needed a rest but, still, there was no excuse for what he had done, despite that there was a terrible, twisted logic to it. And after that, now, what had he done? Started an affair with his wounded brother's girl, even though, in her eyes, she was nothing but a teenage crush for Eddie. It was still not right. Who would want him to represent them if they knew that?

But how could he say no now? How could he back out of all this? There were opportunities too, the Royal Navy and the Army had voices in power - or close to it - arguing their cases. What did the air services have? Just self-serving people like Pemberton-Billing with their own agendas. The result of that was that men like him and his brother had gone to war in aircraft that were obsolete, largely inadequate for the job that they were being asked to do and had, and still were, costing lives.

He could make a difference.

He had all this in mind when he walked through the door of the house so he was unprepared for the first person he saw in the hallway.

'Alice,' he said. 'What on Earth...'

'What is this?' she said, thrusting the paper she was carrying at Percy.

'Pardon?' he said, momentarily stunned. 'What is it? Why are you here?' He took the paper from her hand. 'You shouldn't be travelling, surely? Not in your condition.'

'Never mind about me. Just answer the question, Percy.'

He looked down at the paper for the first time. He recognised it instantly. It was King and Country, an old edition in fact. The edition he recognised only too well.

'Where did you get that from?' he said.

'From me.' came another voice, deep, male.

'Uncle Alfred,' said Percy.

'Good to see you, boy,' said General Grenville, strolling out of the study with his hand outstretched. Percy took it and shook his Uncle's hand warmly. 'It must be, what, two years?'

'At least that, sir. I thought you were in Belgium.'

'I am. Just brought back for a briefing, damned silly if you ask me but that's by-the-by. Do you know Henderson, my adjutant?' A young Captain with the red of staff officer was stood in the doorway. Percy saluted, then took the man's hand.

'These military niceties are wonderful,' said Alice. 'But they don't mean that you can avoid answering me.'

'Now Alice, my dear,' said General Grenville. 'I don't think you should be exciting yourself in your condition.'

'I'm pregnant, not ill,' she snapped.

'Uncle is right thought,' said Percy. 'I think we'd all be better sitting comfortably in the drawing room. Has Lucy brought up some refreshments?'

'She's just doing it,' said Alice. 'But…'

'Shall we go through?' said Percy, his tone quiet and calm. 'I promise I will answer your questions.'

Alice looked as if she was going to argue but then said, 'Very well,' she said, and turned and walked out of the hall.

Percy smiled at his Uncle and indicated that they should follow. The General puffed out his cheeks and leant close to Percy, whispering, 'I think she's getting a bit hysterical. Her condition probably. Have to humour them when they are like this.'

Percy did not reply but followed his uncle and his adjutant into the room. He hoped that he was looking calm but inside he was in turmoil.

Alice was sat on the sofa by the fire.

'Well? she said. 'I'm waiting.' She nodded at the paper that Percy still held.

'Why should what is in here bother you so much? It's just a sensationalist rag embellishing a story with facts that are entirely fabricated,' said Percy, holding up the newspaper.

'But the underlying story is correct, isn't it?' said the General. 'That you were shot down and you carried your observer back over to the British lines, that part is definitely true isn't it?'

Percy glanced at Alice. She was staring coldly back at him.

'Because there's corroboration of that, isn't there?' said Henderson. 'There were witnesses in the trench where you were picked up.'

Percy felt a chill run through him.

'I suppose so, yes. But why do you ask? Why have you brought this with you?' Percy held up the copy of King and Country.

'He wanted to know from me whether it was true or not.' said Alice.

'Really?' Percy looked quizzically at his Uncle. 'Why?'

'Because he wants to confirm your award of the VC, don't you Uncle?' said Alice.

'Now I can't do that, can I, young Alice. I'm a family member, after all.'

'No, but he can witness what you say,' Alice nodded at Henderson, who looked a little awkward. 'But never mind, all that, as you have just said, the story is essentially true, isn't it?'

Percy swallowed. 'Yes. But I don't deserve any award for it, certainly not the Victoria Cross.'

Alice's stare, if anything, intensified.

'What about the German pilot?' she said.

Percy swallowed. 'The pilot?'

'The one you shot, man?' said the General. 'There were definitely witnesses to that.'

'Yes,' said Henderson. 'Apparently the troops were buzzing about it. That's how the reporter picked up on it. How you had picked him off with just one bullet from your service weapon,'

'And that's true as well, isn't it, Percy?' said Alice.

'Well, I suppose essentially it is,' said Percy. 'But…'

'You see the thing is, I wouldn't have been so bothered about it if it wasn't for something that Eddie said to me the other day. Something that I just dismissed at the time, you know how he can get these notions and how sometimes the things he says are confused. But this...this was different.'

'How was it different?' Percy swallowed again, even though he knew that it made him appear guilty. 'What did he say?'

'He said that you didn't deserve the VC because all you had done was get shot down by Siggi.'

'Siggi? What your husband?' said General Grenville.

'Yes, Uncle, Siggi, my Siggi, the man who, yes was a pilot flying for the nation that we are in conflict in but still my husband. He was a good man.'

'He was a good man. One of the best,' said Percy, his voice low.

'Yes, he was. But he disappeared, he was posted missing, on the sixteenth of November last year. The actual day meant nothing to me before now, nothing mattered other than the fact that he was missing. That was the day the light went out of my life, that all joy, all the laughter, all the pleasure left me. When he died...' She stopped speaking.

'Alice,' said Percy, stepping towards her but she turned away from him and put her hand up to stop him. Reluctantly he went back and sat down next to Henderson.

General Grenville stirred uncomfortably. 'Now. Alice my dear, I know you have had a terrible loss but really, in your condition -'

'What day were you shot down on, Percy?' interrupted Alice. 'It will be on record so you might as well tell me.' Her stare was so fierce that Percy felt it almost as a physical assault.

'It was also the 16th of November,' he said.

Neither spoke. The silence became oppressive, like the moments before a storm, the dark clouds billowing, threatening, blocking out the sun. The thunder would follow.

'Oh come on,' said Henderson. He glanced at the General. 'With your permission, sir? This is surely just a coincidence; an unhappy one I admit but sometimes fate works in that way.'

'Yes, I agree with Henderson.,' said the General. 'Total coincidence, isn't it, Percival? That Hun that chased you across no-man's-land, that wasn't young Siegfried was it?'

Still the storm clouds billowed and swelled, the threat still pregnant over Percy.

Pregnant. Think of her condition. He should tell the truth but think of the hurt he would cause. Annie was right, he had already done the deed, he had to live with the consequences of what he had done. He *had* lived with them, every long day and in the nights where Siggi's noble features and trusting face came back to him time-after-time. What had seemed so logical, so obvious on that November day, to mercifully kill someone who was a threat to his friends, his squadron, his service and his country, had become rapidly so obviously wrong and disgusting, immoral, inhuman almost immediately thereafter.

Yet it had to be his burden.

His shame.

His pain.

His alone.

'It is a coincidence,' he said. 'A terrible, unhappy coincidence. I didn't know the German who came after myself and Brown. You were right about Eddie; he is confused. I could not kill Siggi. I loved him as a brother. I don't know how you could think that of me, Alice.'

He instantly saw the relief in her eyes. She stood up, with some difficulty, he did likewise and they embraced in front of the fireplace. He felt the wetness of her tears as her face was pressed against his neck.

'Thank you,' she said, her voice muffled. 'I've been silly. I'm sorry.'

He kissed her head. He felt like Judas kissing Christ. He felt his uncle pat him on the shoulder and murmur 'Good man.'

Good man.

He was not a good man.

*

Later, after his uncle and Henderson had gone, he sat with Alice in the drawing room, sipping tea.

'I'm sorry,' she said again. 'I just saw -'

'Please, Alice, let's this be an end to it,' said Percy. 'We need to concentrate on you now. To that regard, what are you doing here at all? I thought you were staying down in the country. We have had air raids here you know and the journey can't have been good for you. Why did you come? You didn't see that damned article until you arrived, did you?'

'No, I didn't,' she said. 'It was Eddie. I had to come with him.'

'Eddie? What's he done now?'

'He thinks he's recovered enough to go back on active service. He's got a bee in his bonnet about he is the next Ball, that the RFC need him back in action. He insisted on coming back to London to badger the authorities for a posting. I tried to persuade him otherwise but, well, he's got so difficult, hasn't he?'

Percy sighed.

'Yes, he has. Is that where he is now?'

'Yes, I think so. Oh, he also seems to be intent on finding Annie. She's working at a private hospital in London, did you know?'

'Oh, is she?' said Percy, trying to sound non-committal and disinterested.

'Yes, poor girl. Really the last thing she needs is Eddie. I think she realised quite soon that it was a big mistake and that was fine whilst Eddie was virtually ignoring her, acting almost like they had never met. Now though he seems to have remembered and is getting almost as fixated on her as is on flying again.' Alice sighed too. 'That boy, he's not our Eddie, is he?'

'No, I will have a talk with him,' said Percy. He looked at the clock on the mantelpiece. He must go soon to get to Annie on time. 'Alice, you're looking tired. I know it is only the afternoon but would you please humour me and go and try and get some sleep?' He saw she was about to protest but forestalled this by adding; 'Siggi would be annoyed with me if I didn't try and look after you.'

Her smile and nod deepened further his self-loathing.

*

It took several minutes to find a cab, they were in such short supply given the war, and he was running late by the time he entered the Corner House. It was crowded, every table seemed to be occupied and was dominated by khaki with the odd splash of Royal Navy blue for variety amidst the utility colours of the women. It took a full two minutes to spot Annie. She was at a table for two near the left-hand rear corner of the room, the other seat occupied by a man in uniform. Even from a distance, Percy could see she was looking unhappy. He guessed that it was due to his lateness though he did wonder about the officer she was sat with. Had he spotted an opportunity, someone on leave seeing an attractive, apparently unattached nurse sitting alone? Well Percy would soon set him on his way.

Annie saw him coming from about twenty feet away. She glanced up, their eyes made contact. He saw something in them, a warning perhaps? He had a brief notion that the man might even be her husband, back from the dead, a missing man returned, stranger things had happened, but then he dismissed this as fancy and kept on walking. However, something stopped him from greeting her as he wanted to, affectionately and with a caress.

'Hello.' he said as he reached the table. 'Who-'

Then his words died as he saw who she was sat with.

'Hello Percy!' said Eddie smiling and rising to his feet. 'Well this is a stroke of luck, a double stroke in fact, my finding Annie straight off and then you turn up. That's fantastic! Well it's a good old hat-trick because I've been awarded the MC. An MC, me? Who would have believed it, eh? All we need now is to both get back to do our jobs and the world will be perfect again. Waitress, Waitress! Can we have another chair? Excuse me!'

Whilst Eddie was occupied with trying to get another seat, Percy caught Annie's eye again.

Her look was one of utter despair.

CHAPTER TWENTY

England Wednesday June 13th, 1917

Annie walked through the hospital's entrance just after 11am, trying not to catch the eye of the elderly porter behind the desk. Unfortunately he saw her.

'Mrs Ross, wait,' he said.

'Mr Jones, sorry, I can't,' she called over her shoulder. 'My shift...'

'It doesn't start for another half-an hour, Mrs Ross,' Mr Jones smiled. 'You're always here in plenty of time, not like those VAD girls. Well-meaning, I'm sure, but not proper...'

'That may be the case, Mr Jones, but I still have to get ready. What is it?'

'I've got another letter for you. And more flowers.'

She sighed, and walked wearily back.

'Thank you,' she said, taking them.

'I really shouldn't do this you, I've told you before,' said the Porter. 'You know what the hospital policy is about personal correspondence.'

'I do know, Mr Jones.'

'It's only because it's you...'

'I know, Mr Jones.' She was still anxious to get away and her tone was rather sharper than she had intended. 'I promise I'll have a word with him.'

The porter smiled. 'He looks a nice young man. A pilot, eh? Very handsome. You must be very proud of him.'

She did not answer but gave a weak smile.

'I can't keep taking the letters and things, see,' said Jones, looking around him as if expecting the hospital's director to be lurking behind one of the pillars of the hall.

'I understand that, Mr Jones. I'll ask him to stop.'

He smiled. 'Why not give him the address of your rooms?'

Because I don't want him to know, she thought. I don't want him turning up there. I don't want to see him but I can't avoid it, because I am with Percy, yes, but also because, somehow, he scares me. He shouldn't, he is Eddie, he is still the same boy, but somehow he's not; he is changed, there is a part of him I do not know and that part scares me.

But she said nothing of this, she just nodded noncommittally, accepted the flowers and walked away.

She read the letter in the nurses' rest room as she put her uniform on, having passed the flowers onto one of the VADs to brighten up the wards. She had not wanted to read it but, if she hadn't, all the time she would have been on duty she would have felt its presence in her pocket like some alien, unwanted parasite.

It was a boil that had to be lanced.

My Darling Annie,

I only have time for a brief letter today, my love. I have yet another visit to the service's docs to prove that my arm is as good as new and then I am off to badger more of the Red Hats about a posting. I want France, of course I do, that is where the war is to be won or lost (and win we must) but there seems to be more hope about my being posted to a Home Defence squadron. That will mean more training probably and also flying at night but at least that will get me back up in the air and having a proper crack at the Hun. It is so bad how we are allowing the damn Gothas and Zeppelins to come over largely untroubled, heaven knows what our pilots are doing, they must be complete dolts. I saw several of the type over in France, no spine, no ability. Well I am sure I can sort them out and give a much better account.

This waiting though, it is so frustrating! Life is so dull, I am so glad I have got this to occupy me. I can understand how Ball got so frustrated; it must have been terrible for him. I mourn his loss obviously, all the country should, but at least he died doing what he loved and what warrior can ask for anything more? I have not heard the details of his final combats yet (have you?) but I hope that he filled a few Germans full of lead and got at least one flamer on his last day. It would be a great tribute.

I want to fly and fight again to honour his memory. Each kill I make I will dedicate to him - and to you of course.

Annie closed her eyes. She didn't want to read any more. How had Eddie, that gentle boy, got like this? Did he know what he was saying? She almost crumpled the letter up and threw it away but forced herself to carry on.

After I have done my badgering duties I am going to meet up with Percy and that newspaper chap, Fitzroy and one of his reporters. Percy and I have been talking about what aircraft the RFC need in the future, the ones we have been getting have been utter duds, the reporter chap is going to do another story on us, with photographs, to give Percy a leg up in getting to be an MP. Whatever, after I appear in the press, the war office can't refuse me an active posting, can they?

I think the powers-that-be are going to award him the VC you know? That's what Fitzroy says and he seems to be in the know though Percy himself won't even entertain any talk about it, in fact he calls the whole thing nonsense. Perhaps they will award it at the same time as Ball's? His parents are getting it for him. I wonder if his fiancée will be there, they got engaged you know, just before he flew back to France?

Annie swallowed hard at this point. Eddie had brought this up time-after-time in his letters; he was clearly dropping hints.

How are you doing? You seemed so quiet the last time we met, were you tired? Well you should stop doing nursing, you will have no need to soon anyway. I want to see you. It would also be helpful if you could tell me your address, you are an absent-minded old thing, you keep forgetting to put it on your letters -

She screwed the letter up. She had read quite enough.

How on earth had she got herself into this position? She had been so damned stupid, swayed by his sweet nature, his sensitivity, his youth. She should have known better, should have been more on guard, she had been vulnerable, she had known that but when she had met Eddie she was tired, she had allowed her guard to fall. Why hadn't she waited, thought a bit more, not rushed in? Now look at the mess that she was in.

What made it worse was she would have been able to walk away from him when he was ill. She had an excuse, a terrible excuse but one she could have used. The war had taken Eddie's mind, it had changed him, he had apparently forgotten her. It gave her an excuse, though it sickened and shamed her in equal measure. Now he was back, apparently normal, didn't she have an obligation to him?

But she had been there before, with David. Marriage out of obligation, almost pity. Was she doomed to make the same mistake over and over again through her life?

She needed someone to talk to but whom? She was new to this hospital, she hardly knew anyone, all her old friends were back in Nottingham or in Sussex at her old work. There was Alice but she had her own problems and, anyway, she was the sister of the Grenville boys, she could hardly be impartial. Yet, she might understand. Perhaps if she waited until after the baby was born...

She was distracted by a droning noise. What was it? Traffic? Most of the omnibuses had long been transferred to France, as were the heavy lorries. A swarm of bees perhaps? She shuddered, she had been stung badly as a child by a swarm and the memory was one that haunted her nightmares, recurring at times of stress.

She had had the dream again two nights ago.

She looked all around the room, and then out of the window. There was no sign of the throbbing, pulsating mass of insects.

Yet still the droning continued, not continued, rose. What was it?

Percy. She would have to tell Percy. But what would he do?

There were shouts, the crashing of doors, a scream.

Still clutching the letter she went out into the corridor. People were rushing about, their eyes wide with confusion and fear. They did not seem to be heading in anywhere particular but were tripping over each other in their haste to get to wherever they were going.

She turned towards her ward but was sent reeling by a blow that knocked the wind out of her and made her see red briefly as something hard hit her on the head.

Her senses cleared quickly. A VAD girl, flustered, crying was getting up off the floor. The girl's hand went up to her cheek where a red mark was growing.

'Elsie,' Annie shouted, rubbing her own head. 'What on earth do you think you are doing racing along the corridor like that. Don't you know better?'

'I need to get out!' said the girl. 'I must get out. It's the Germans. The Germans are here!'

To Annie's surprise the girl pushed her away and ran wildly away along the corridor, nearly falling again as she did.

Annie went back into the nurse's rest room and went to the window. She undid the catch, pulled the sash window up and leant out. Looking up she saw them straight away. Dark crosses in the sky, a formation of big aircraft, bigger than she had ever seen before, drowning slowly across the sky, passing right overhead.

As she watched something detached from one of the aircraft, then another and another. They did not drop straight down but seemed to accelerate away from the aircraft.

Above the thrum of the engines she could hear a whistling.

*

'Now young sirs, if you don't mind, one final plate?'

Percy let out a deep sigh of frustration. 'Another one?' he said. 'Surely you have enough by now?'

'We can never have enough,' said Fitzroy. 'The public want to see their heroes.'

'We're not heroes,' muttered Percy.

'I beg to differ,' Fitzroy smiled. 'The public can't get enough of you. After the next issue you'll really see what they think.'

Percy fell silent.

'The more we get done now the less you'll have do in the future, Captain Grenville,' said Holloman, his voice quiet, patient. That's how he works, thought Percy. He tries to hit the right note with everyone to put them at their ease. That's how he gets people to talk, how he manipulates people. It was all false. He hated it. 'Now, for this one, if you and Lieutenant Grenville could be holding the plans with you pointing something out to your brother?'

'Like this?' Eddie was eager. Percy was surprised at him, he was lapping this up. He pointed at the plans as if he had spotted some detail.

'That's perfect,' said the photographer. I like the frown , Captain, very good. Ready?' There was a bright flash, the smell of the burnt magnesium powder. Percy's heart skipped. There were too many echoes in the flash and the smell, he knew why it was making him uncomfortable. It was too much like the front, it brought back too many memories.

'That's it I hope,' he said, getting to his feet and trying to blink away the red image of the flash that still danced on his retina.

'Yes, that will suffice for now,' said Fitzroy. 'Holloman here may need to interview you further for his story of course.'

'It would be useful to get a few more quotes,' agreed the reporter, picking up his notebook.

'Oh for goodness sake, is this really necessary?' said Percy.

'Believe me, it is,' said Fitzroy. 'I have seen the way things are done in the US. Politicians in Britain are years behind in their thinking.'

'Britain is not America,' said Percy. 'We do things differently.'

'For now perhaps, for now,' said Fitzroy.

Eddie was still holding the plans, looking at them intently.

'This is an unusual machine,' he said. 'I've not seen this type before. Or heard of…' he looked at the corner of the drawing. 'The Pederson Aircraft Company.'

'They're American,' said Fitzroy. 'Now the States are in the war, I think you'll be seeing a lot more of them.'

'A three-seater triplane scout?' said Percy. 'I hardly think that is going to work well at the front. The Albatros would run rings around it.'

'Yes, it would be totally useless,' said Eddie.

'Mr Pederson begs to differ,' said Fitzroy, moving swiftly to take the plans off them. Percy heard him whisper something to Holloman that sounded like, 'Don't put that in your story, will you?' Holloman smiled and nodded.

'Now, sirs, if you could come with me and -'

There was a huge crack, a percussion that rattled the window panes, the curtains billowing inwards.

'What the blazes?' said Fitzroy.

Percy found that he had involuntarily crouched and had covered his head. He saw that Eddie had done the same. Recovering his senses, he dashed to the window. Before he reached it there was another bang, closer this time and accompanied by a crack and a tinkling of glass. He heard a scream, then another and saw that the windowpane was cracked right across. He quickly undid the catch and pulled the sash up, ignoring Fitzroy's warning to be careful.

Beneath them in the street people were running about in all directions, looking up, dashing into buildings, looking for cover. He looked up himself. He could hear aircraft, but not see them.

'What is it, what can you see?' said Eddie.

Percy did not answer, he turned and ran out of Fitzroy's office, across the newsroom and down the stairs. He could hear at least some of the others following him though he did not look behind him to see who it was. There were a lot of people in the building's entrance, scared, bewildered people, some crying, a child was screaming. He ignored them, pushing past them and headed out onto the street.

Still he could not see enough of the sky to see the aircraft, though he could hear them much better. He had to run as best as he could on his still stiff and painful ankle to the end of the road and the square that lay beyond where he could see better.

Now he could see them. Aircraft, huge aircraft, more than a dozen, possibly at ten thousand feet. They were untroubled, there was no opposition, they just came on and on. He could see the bombs drop from them.

'The station, they're going for the station,' Holloman said, breathing hard.

'The bastards. Where are our fighters? Damn them!' Eddie. Percy had never heard him swear before, he didn't know that he did.

He concentrated on the aircraft. They looked to have twin engines, and were a type he had not seen before. He realised, with a jolt that they were coming from the North-west. The hospital was over there, the one where she worked. It would be right on their flight path, close to their target.

'Annie!' he exclaimed. 'Oh for God's sake, Annie!'

He started to run not caring who was around him or who had been stood next to him. The pain in his ankle became excruciating but he ignored it as best he could. It was like a scene from hell, the end of the world, the familiar London streets once peaceful now filled with panic, and war. Faces, white, anguished, fearful, were all around, seeking cover, running, crying. He ran into someone, the breath was knocked from his body, he was aware of someone cursing, a hand grabbing his uniform jacket but he shrugged them off. All the time, from above there was the sound of engines, then the whistle as bombs fell followed by the heavy crump and crack of an explosion. One fell close by, certainly he did not hear the detonation, at least consciously but felt the hot rush of air and was pelted with stone and brick fragments. Still he ran on.

As he reached the street where the hospital was he saw smoke. He could see that the hospital itself looked intact except that the windows had been shattered. Where was the smoke coming from? He hurried towards where a knot of people had gathered.

As he reached them he could see the source, a bomb had hit the front of one of the houses, had probably bounced off it given the gouge in the roof and upper floor then had exploded in the street just in front. The ground floor wall had been ripped off revealing the rooms behind and scattering stone, bricks, glass and timber out into the road. Some men were venturing inside, even though the first floor, unsupported at one end as it was, was sagging down into the lower floor. One had his arms around a woman, and was guiding her towards the hole and the street. It was hard to tell her age for she was completely covered in white dust, her clothes, her hair, her skin, save for the vivid scarlet trickle that ran from her scalp and spotted her dress.

'A doctor,' the man leading her called. 'She needs a doctor.'

Willing hands reached in from outside, waiting to pull them through.

Percy could see there was enough help for her, he paused only briefly before moving onto the hospital. The crowd moved out of his way. Instantly he saw there were two bundles in the street. They looked just like someone had discarded their clothes prior to some sporting activity, swimming perhaps but, as he passed, he saw the tell-tale dark stains and knew: they were bodies, at least parts of bodies, ripped apart by the explosion and covered by coats and jackets to spare the feelings of bystanders and give the poor creatures some modesty in death. Could one be Annie? No, surely she would be inside, on duty.

Unless she had heard the bombing and had come out to help.

He limped on to the hospital entrance, the pain from his injured ankle almost unbearable. Damn Siggi, why couldn't he have shot the bloody thing better so it could have been taken right off?

Inside there was blood, shouting, chaos and calm all at the same time, the calmness coming from the medical staff, nurses and doctors, as they ministered to the wounded. Some casualties were laid on the floor, some were milling about, often aided by dust-covered able bodied helpers, more followed Percy in through the door. Some were quiet, some crying, one was screaming, a man too, until a nurse slapped him in the face. The screaming abruptly stopped, the man clutching his face in surprise and shock.

'You hit me,' he whined looking at the nurse, who had her back to Percy.

'I did,' said the nurse. 'You were making a damned nuisance of yourself. Now sit over there and we will get to you when we are finished with those hurt more badly than you.'

Meekly, the man did as he was told.

The nurse tuned and Percy saw it was Annie. She saw him straight away, smiled and moved across to him. He took her in her arms.

'Are you alright? I was so -'

'I'm fine,' she said. 'I was inside when the bombs fell. I got showered with glass but I was lucky. But I am rather busy.'

'I can see.' he said, and leant forward and kissed her. As he pulled away he saw her smile, then the smile faded. She was looking at something behind him. Percy turned.

He briefly came face to face with Eddie. He saw the hurt in his brother's eyes before Eddie turned and walked back out of the hospital.

CHAPTER TWENTY-ONE

England Friday July 6th 1917

Percy rubbed his neck where the collar of his new shirt was rubbing. He was sure that the red mark would be visible to all and sundry, particularly under the lights that lit up the stage. It had been a warm day but this evening was stifling and the lights made it much worse. He was sweating profusely, his shirt, stiff with starch, was also soaked at the back and under his arms and was sticking to him. Why on earth he was putting himself through this?

Lord Hanley was on his feet addressing the audience.

'Whilst we are all at one with the Government in the need to pull together to win the war, this does not mean that we will not stay silent when we feel that are certain areas where they are failing our country and our empire,' he said. 'That is one of the strengths of our great democracy, to be free to criticise and hold our elected politicians to account.'

There was a murmuring of agreement and a few cries of 'hear, hear.'

'There have already been debates about the lamentable state that our air services were allowed to get into in the Spring, with our young men being forced to go into battle in machines that were totally inadequate. We have all seen the dreadful casualty lists and read the account of one of the participants in Mr Fitzroy's stirring publication, a very brave participant I would add who is sitting with us on the platform tonight, Lieutenant Grenville.' He opened his hand and extended his arm to his right. Percy watched as Eddie stood and modestly took the applause. Percy noted that he sat down again without glancing in his direction at all.

'The lieutenant was, I would add, awarded the MC for his

bravery during the April battles,' Hanley added. There was another round of applause, with cheering this time. Eddie rose again to acknowledge it.

When the noise had died down, Hanley continued, his face and tone serious.

'That the Government allowed that to happen was shameful yet the recent events in this, the great capital of our Empire is surely even more disgraceful. To allow fleets of enemy aircraft to fly untroubled across London to bring death and destruction to our homes and families, to let the dastardly Hun kill defenceless women, children and babies will forever more be a stain on the Government's record.'

There were cries of 'shame' and one man shout 'Lloyd-George should resign!'

Hanley held up his hands for quiet. It took a full minute for the room to still.

'It is too early to talk about resignation. That is for another time, we do need to be behind our Prime Minister as he tackles his most difficult of jobs. However, something must indeed be done. We need protecting, our wives, property, families need protection from these Aerial armadas.'

There was more applause. Some men in the audience stood up, clapping.

Percy swallowed. His Adam's apple rasped against his collar. His throat was dry. He knew his time to speak was coming.

'I am no expert on what is required; however we are lucky to have a fine young man who is. He is an established leader of men, a flight leader who spent 15 months almost continuous service in France as pilot and flight leader. During that time serving our empire he was involved in the destruction of seven enemy machines. He is a fine man, one who we feel would make an excellent member of parliament and, I think you will agree, one whose constituents would be very lucky to have.'

More 'hear, hears.'

'And so, without further ado, I would like to introduce one of our best and boldest pilots. He is of course, the brother of Lieutenant Grenville, Captain Percival Grenville. Captain Grenville.'

Hanley led the applause then sat down as Percy rose to his feet.

He stared out at the crowd. The audience was looking back at him, staring at him, their faces expectant. His legs felt queer, his foot hurt, he was sure he was going to be sick.

He opened his mouth to speak but nothing came out.

Some members of the audience began to stir uncomfortably. He was losing them. He had to think, do something, say something.

'I...er...thank-you, I...' he began. His mind was blank. He thought back to his notes, about the need for new, better aircraft.

He was aware of the scraping of a chair. Someone on the podium was getting to his feet. He saw the faces move from him and onto whoever it was.

'Please excuse my brother, he is a little bit overcome by events.'

It was Eddie, why was he speaking? Eddie was not looking at him but was focussed on the hall.

'You see, we had a happy event in the family this week. Our sister, a war widow I would add, has just given birth to a son.'

There were sighs and a little smattering of applause.

'Naturally we in the family are delighted but also a little...er... tired!'

Laughter. The audience was laughing.

Eddie's eyes were shining, he was smiling. Percy realised he was enjoying this. His brother continued to surprise him. He was not sure that he recognised him anymore. He sat down.

'There is another reason why my brother may be exhibiting some measure of distraction, some news which he is waiting for but which he is too modest to admit to or, indeed even mention.'

Percy frowned. What on earth was Eddie talking about?

'Well I am delighted that I am the one to give him the news. Before I left our house this evening, our father received a telegram. It confirmed some wonderful news. My brother, Captain Percival Granville, has been given the highest award for gallantry our nation can offer. My brother has been awarded the Victoria Cross.'

The hall erupted in cheers.

*

Maxwell Fitzroy watched in satisfaction as the local bigwigs, sleek, well-fed and self-satisfied circulated and pontificated in the reception. Most of the audience had long since left, it was just the select few that had been favoured with an invitation and they were enjoying the refreshments laid on at the expense of Fitzroy. He did not care much that most of them would be totally oblivious as to who the provider was just if the people with real influence like Lord Hanley did, that was all that mattered.

He looked for Hanley. He found him where he expected, close by his prospective candidate and protege, ostensibly talking to the borough clerk but listening carefully to what Grenville was saying. Fitzroy caught Hanley's eye and indicated that they should meet at the side of the room. He walked across and was pleased to see Hanley making his excuses and heading across to join him.

'Well?' said Fitzroy quietly.

Hanley pursed his lips thoughtfully.

'He's certainly got most of the credentials to go far. Excellent family, his war record and, one-to-one like this he's fine.'

'But he is dreadful in front of an audience,' Fitzroy murmured.

'Yes, indeed,' said Hanley. 'That could be a problem on the hustings.'

'I thought that too,' said Fitzroy. 'However, that does not stop him getting his message across. In the paper we can present the man in whatever way we like to the voters.'

Hanley nodded. 'We can indeed.' Fitzroy saw that he was looking around the room. His gaze settled on Eddie. 'It is a shame that his brother is so young. What is he, 19?'

'I believe so,' said Fitzroy. 'He is quite a performer, isn't he? Perhaps, in time, he himself could be considered as a future candidate.'

'Yes, perhaps.'

'In the meantime I can perhaps ensure that he remains in the public eye?'

Hanley looked back at Fitzroy, smiled and nodded.

'Indeed, Fitzroy, indeed,' he said.

*

Annie was staring into the fire, watching the last of the flames dance and sway as she heard the key turn in the lock. She stood up and walked across the room and out into the hall. He had his back to her as he hung his hat on the stand.

'Hello,' she said. 'How did it go?'

Percy turned and looked across at her. She saw he looked surprised but also that he was weary, he looked suddenly old.

'What's the matter?' she said. 'What's happened?'

'What are you doing here?' he said. 'You've work in the morning. I thought you would be at your rooms.'

He came over and embraced her, though, she noticed that he did not kiss her. She wondered why this should be, was it because he was in the Grenville family house? Was this the way it was always going to be, that she was to be an outsider, someone to be met and enjoyed in secret?

She tried to dismiss these thoughts.

'Alice wrote to me. I wanted to come and see your new nephew.'

Percy smiled, though it looked a little forced. She could see his gaze was hollow. He looked almost like he had in the hospital in Sussex. Haunted, deeply troubled.

'Yes, he's a bonny chap, isn't he? The spitting image of...his mother.'

He turned away from her and went over to the decanters set on the side table. There had been a slight but noticeable hesitation in what he had said. She knew that he had not started that sentence with the intention of finishing it with "mother" and she could guess just what he was going to say. Alice's baby was blonde and blue-eyed, she could guess that was just how his father looked.

'Would you like one?' Percy said.

'No thank you.'

She could see his hands were shaking, in fact so much that he splashed the spirit - brandy or whisky, she wasn't sure which - over the silver tray.

'Here, let me,' she said, walking over and taking the decanter out of his hand. She could now tell from the aroma from the spilled liquid that it was whisky. Meekly he stood aside as she poured him a measure and handed the glass to him. Still his hand trembled.

'What's the matter?' she said.

'They gave me the VC,' he whispered. 'They damn well gave me the Victoria Cross. For...'

'For valour,' she said firmly, taking his free hand and squeezing it. 'For all you did day, after day in France before that day. You deserve it for that alone.'

He shook his head. 'I did no more than any of the other chaps, less in fact, I gave less than most didn't I?' He swallowed the contents of his glass in one go. 'Now I have to face Alice and my nephew, that little boy who looks so like...' He took several deep breaths. 'I have to face him with that medal ribbon on my chest. It's not a badge of honour or courage, it's one of shame, utter, utter shame. I don't think I can do that.'

He shook off her hand and turned towards the decanter again.

'Come on Percy, leave that alone, that's not going to do any good,' she said, stepping towards him.

'Don't damn well tell me what's good for me!' he snapped.

Annie pulled up, startled.

Percy somehow sloshed more whisky into the glass.

'I'm sick of people telling me what's right and what's wrong, what my bloody duty is! Why I listened to people I don't know, to you, to father, to Hanley and that bloody charlatan, Fitzroy. Why have I let them talk me into this stupid idea of standing for parliament? I'm useless at it, even Eddie spoke better than me.'

'Eddie was there?' Annie was shocked. Neither Percy or her had seen or heard from him since the day of the air raid.

'Yes, Eddie was there, on the podium with me. He's a better man than me; his medal was deserved. I'm paraded in front of people, everybody is told that I'm a bloody hero and I'm not, I'm bloody not, I'm just some cowardly rat who killed his best friend in the coldest of cold blood and then steals his brother's girl.'

'I never was Eddie's girl,' Annie stepped closer to him. 'And Percy, please be quiet, people will hear. Alice -'

Without warning, Percy hurled his glass into the fireplace. It burst into a million shards and the fire flared as the remains of the spirit fuelled the flames.

'Don't you tell me what to do, don't ever tell me how to treat my family,' he shouted. 'Not Eddie, not Alice, not anyone, you hear me?'

'No, I...' Annie stammered.

'Excuse me, sir, is everything alright?' Lucy had appeared in door. She looked anxiously at Percy. 'Sir?' she repeated.

Percy turned away without answering.

'Everything is fine, Lucy,' Annie said. 'We have just had a slight disagreement. It's all over now.'

'I should clean up that glass,' said Lucy. 'I'll get a dustpan and brush.'

'Leave it, damn you!' Percy said. 'I'll see to it later.'

'What on earth is all this shouting?' Through the door left open by Lucy, Annie saw Lady Grenville come down the stairs, fastening her dressing gown, her grey hair, normally tightly dressed and up in a loose ponytail. She paused briefly in the hall and looked at Annie with considerable disdain before walking past her and into the room. 'Percival, what is this person doing in my house? I thought I had made my feelings quite clear about her.'

'She came to see, me, Mother,' said Alice from the stairs. She too was fastening her dressing gown and looked pale and tired.

'You had no business doing that, not without my consent, but we will talk about this in the morning. Get back to bed, Alice,' said her mother sharply. 'Your judgement is clearly affected by your condition. You're in no state to be up.'

Alice ignored her mother and continued down the stairs. From above the lusty cries of her son started up. She ignored these too.

'I heard my name,' she said. 'I heard Percy shout my name. What was it all about?'

'Nothing,' Percy muttered. 'It was nothing.'

'Tell me,' said Alice firmly. 'You said something about Siggi too, didn't you? I am sure you did.'

'Don't be so foolish, girl,' said Lady Grenville. 'It was just Percival falling out with this...troublemaker.' She glared at Annie.

'No, it -' began Percy but Annie interrupted.

'Yes,' she said. 'Yes, Lady Grenville, you are quite right. It was Percy and I arguing over something I said. I shouldn't have said what I did, Percy has had a long night and he lost his temper. It was my fault.'

'Really?' said Alice. 'Percy, is that true?'

Annie stared at Percy who was still facing away from everyone. She saw him bring his hand up to his face and quickly wipe his eyes and cheek. He's been crying, she thought, but still she wished him as hard as she could to listen to her and to go along with it. After a long moment he turned to face them all, though he stayed in the darker part of the room.

'Yes, that's quite right,' he said. 'I was tired. I overreacted. It was over something silly too. I lost my temper. It was unforgivable. I'm sorry.' His voice was a flat monotone, lacking any feeling or sense of sincerity.

'Well that might be the case,' said Lady Grenville. 'I am sure you were provoked, however. People like her are always troublemakers. I do not wish to see this person anywhere near my house again, is that understood?'

'But mother...' Alice started.

'But nothing, Alice. I have said my piece and that is the end of it.'

'She is my friend, mother,' said Alice. 'I will not have her spoken to like that. She is also Percy's...friend. Isn't that so, Percy.' She looked expectantly at her brother but he seemed transfixed by the sound of the baby crying.

Annie felt her anger rise. 'Oh for goodness sake, I have had enough. I'm not going to stay here where I am clearly not wanted. Lucy, would you get me my coat?'

'Yes miss,' said Lucy, giving a little curtsey.

Annie pushed past Lady Grenville and went up to Alice, giving her a peck on the cheek. 'Go and look after your boy,' she said softly. 'And get some rest, you need it.'

Alice nodded, then looked at Percy, who had turned his back on them again. Annie gave him a quick glance, then took her coat from Lucy.

'Thank you.' she said, putting it on. 'Lady Grenville, it has been a pleasure as always.'

Percy's mother gave a sniff of derision and turned her head away.

Annie gave one last look in Percy's direction. 'Percy, you know where to find me,' she said and walked out of the hall. Lucy let her out into the night.

*

Holloman was in Fitzroy's office when they heard the raised voices from outside. Holloman could hear Price's voice and someone else, another man.

'What on earth is that?' said Fitzroy, looking up from Holloman's copy, red pencil in hand. 'Go and see what the fuss is about.'

Holloman got to his feet and went through to the general office. Price was stood, attempting to bar the passage of a tall officer, dark haired, slim with a neatly trimmed moustache who was trying to get past him. Price was small, unfit and weedy so the contest was an unequal one.

'And I tell you again, sir, you can't come in,' Price was saying. 'No, stop, I'll call the police.'

The officer, a captain, Holloman noted, pushed Price away.

'Get out of the way, I demand to see your editor,' he said.

'Price,' said Holloman sharply. 'Let the captain past.'

'But...' protested Price.

'Do as I say. Captain, how can I help you?'

The captain stepped by Price into the office and straightened his uniform. 'Who are you, sir?' he demanded. 'Are you the editor of this damned rag?' He waved a copy of King and Country at Holloman who could see it was the latest edition.

'My name is Charles Holloman. I am the senior reporter.'

'Holloman?' The captain looked at the front page of the paper. 'Ah, yes, you are the author of this damned fiction.'

'That story?' said Holloman calmly. 'Yes that is one of mine. Is there a problem?'

'Yes there is a problem. A damned big one. This story about the pilot, Grenville. It's all lies, a complete fabrication. Who the devil are you?' Holloman saw the captain's gaze had moved to the office behind him.

'My name is Maxwell Fitzroy,' said Fitzroy. 'I am the proprietor of this publication. And you are?'

'I am Captain Levy of the First London's and I demand you publish a correction to this story.'

He held up his copy of King and Country. Holloman could see it was the one headlined "The gallant Captain Grenville VC. Full story inside.'

Fitzroy looked puzzled. 'A correction? Why so?' he said.

'Because I was commanding the trench which brought him and his man in from no-man's-land. I saw the man he killed and talked to his observer. This man is not a gentleman. He's nothing short of a cad, an absolute bounder.'

Fitzroy looked at Holloman. 'I think you had better come into my office, Captain Levy. Holloman, if you would join us. Price, please bring some tea.'

*

Annie knew that something was wrong the instant she saw Percy sat in the cafe. He was staring into nothing, his face was set, somehow devoid of colour.

'I'm with my friend,' she said to the waitress and went to the table and sat down. Even then he did not react. She had to lean across and squeeze his hand before he reacted.

'Oh,' he said. 'It's you, I'm sorry, I was miles away.' He gave her a little smile.

'I could tell,' she said. She wanted to know more, to ask what the problem was but, after the incident at the family home, she was reluctant to say something that might upset him. This went against everything that she believed in, she came from a family of talkers who would be open with each other about problems and issues. The Grenvilles seemed to be totally different, they kept things to themselves, bottled things up, kept secrets. It was their way but, to her, it did not seem healthy and was particularly bad for Percy. He was under stress, she was scared that he was changing back into the man she had nursed in Sussex, the bitter, nasty man that she had disliked so much. She spent much of her free time - and too much of her working time too, to be honest - worrying as to what to do to arrest his slide but had come up with no solutions only the fear that if she tried or said anything that he would react angrily again.

'How was your shift?' he said.

'Busy. A lot of new casualties from France. Some of the wounds are very nasty. I had another of the VAD girls faint on me whilst changing a dressing this morning, silly girl.'

'Oh dear,' said Percy, though she could tell that his reply was more automatic than considered and that his thoughts had drifted off elsewhere again. She tried to keep her temper, even though she was almost weary enough to react.

'How's Alice and the young chap?'

'Fine,' said Percy. 'She's chosen the names. Siegfried Arthur Percival.' She saw him swallow after he had said them and knew why. The names of his father, grandfather and uncle, the latter being his father's killer. She kicked herself for straying onto dangerous ground.

'I could really do with some tea,' she said lightly. 'Could you order me some?'

Percy did not reply.

'Percy?' she prompted.

'I've got my orders,' he said. 'I'm to join a new fighter squadron. I'm going back to France.'

*

'Thank you, Captain Levy. We certainly appreciate your taking the time to come to see us to put the record straight. We at King and Country have a watchword: truth. Nothing but the truth is what our readers deserve and what we are honour bound to give them.'

Fitzroy was on his feet and extended his hand to Levy who, without hesitation, shook it warmly.

'Thank you, Mr Fitzroy,' he said. 'I have to admit I had a lot of doubts about what my reception here would be. I am so glad that you have been so willing to listen to what I have said. I am sure you will do the right thing and put the record straight. Mr Holloman.' He nodded at the reporter then turned and walked out of the office.

Fitzroy's smile faded immediately.

'Shut the door,' he said to Holloman, before sitting down at his desk. Holloman resumed his seat. He watched the proprietor who had placed his elbows on the desk, steepled his hands as if in prayer and rested his chin against them. He was clearly deep in thought. Holloman knew better than to interrupt.

At last Fitzroy sighed and sat back. 'Well, my dear Charles, what do you make of what that fucking Jew had to say.'

Holloman, a non-practicing Jew himself, long used to Fitzroy's blatant antisemitism, took a deep breath before replying.

'He is a convincing witness. What he says smacks of the truth, particularly the powder burns on the body of the German.'

Fitzroy nodded. 'And,' he said, 'he was able to talk to the one independent witness, that man Brown, something that you were unable to manage I note.'

Inwardly Holloman bristled at the criticism but said nothing. 'Yes, Brown. That also backs up the Captain's story, how else would he have known the man's name? It was odd though about him. It was almost as if someone had been deliberately trying to hide him from view.'

Fitzroy nodded. 'He went back to France as an officer, didn't he? That does smack of a certain class closing ranks to protect their own, doesn't it? God, these people...'

Yet you are quite willing to use them, Holloman thought.

'So, we have a problem,' Fitzroy went on.

'Well, Grenville has a problem,' said Holloman.

Fitzroy's gaze flicked to the reporter. Holloman felt the full force of the glare.

'If Grenville has a problem, then *we* have a problem,' he said. 'In fact *I* have a problem, don't I? The story appeared in my paper; it is I who suggested Captain Grenville as a suitable candidate to Lord Hanley. If a whiff of scandal arises it will affect me. That is unacceptable. And.' His voice grew even more menacing. 'If I have a problem, Charles, rest assured that you do too.'

'Yes sir,' Holloman said. 'We need to undermine the Captain's story?'

'Indeed, Holloman, indeed.'

'The powder burns, that's not conclusive, the German could have been flinging himself at Grenville, perhaps with a knife or bayonet?'

Fitzroy nodded.

'Good, and what else.'

'What he reported about what the observer, Brown said. Levy admitted that the man was pretty much insensible, that he was rambling. That makes what he said about the German having helped them, that he was some friend of Grenville totally unreliable.'

Fitzroy nodded. 'That is fine if we need to print a rebuttal. I would rather things did not get that far. You get my drift?'

Holloman nodded. 'You want me to investigate Captain Levy. Find something on him?'

Fitzroy smiled. 'That would be useful,' he said.

'What if there isn't anything?'

'Oh I am sure that there will, if you dig deep enough. Or,' he added, meaningfully. 'If you use your imagination.'

Holloman nodded and got to his feet. 'What about Hanley? And the family, will you tell them?'

Fitzroy frowned and it was a few moments before he replied. 'Hanley, I think yes. He's pragmatic, I think it would be useful for him to know. He will appreciate being informed, I'm sure. The family? I think not. I think this information should be distributed around the least number of people, don't you agree?' He looked past Holloman towards the office. 'Speaking of which, pray ensure that Price also keeps his mouth shut as well. If he knows what's good for him.'

Holloman nodded again and left the office.

CHAPTER TWENTY-TWO

England, Friday July 20th 1917

Percy finished tying his tie, straightened his cap and looked at himself in the mirror. Someone he did not recognise stared back.

The pips on his shoulder designated him as a Captain. The wings on his chest above the RFC badge showed him to be a pilot. The purple medal ribbon beneath the wings that Lord Hanley and his parents insisted that be sewn onto his uniform though he had yet to formally receive the medal, proclaimed him to be a hero, the holder of the highest award for gallantry his country could award. It was all false. He couldn't lead anyone, who would follow him? Could he fly anymore? He had not been in an aircraft since October, since that fateful day.

And he was not a hero, he was not brave. Far from it.

It was all fake, a front, an image that was not real. Just like his political career. There was no substance, nothing which showed that he could do the job of representing anyone else, of actually making a difference to his service, his country.

He was just a uniform, a badge and a ribbon. Inside, behind the facade was a frightened little man. He was twenty-six years old but he looked forty and felt sixty.

He almost cried. He had to turn away quickly from the mirror before he did. He had to compose himself before he left his bedroom.

He almost skipped breakfast. His stomach was churning, he did not feel hungry but he decided he had to force himself. He did not want to start feeling faint in the air.

In the breakfast room he had a surprise. It was early, he did not expect anyone else to be up but sitting at the table in full uniform was Eddie. He sat with his back to the door, the paper opened in front of him. He was not absorbed in it, however, he was flicking from page to page.

It took a few moments for Percy to recover his composure. He went to the table, took his cap off and laid it carefully down before sitting.

'Good morning, Eddie,' he said cautiously. Although he had seen his brother at the political meetings, he had not actually spoken to him directly since the day of the air raid.

Eddie looked up from the paper. 'Hello, Percy,' he said brightly. 'Hell, there's a lot of rubbish in this thing, how the hell is a chap to know what is really going on at the front?' He tossed the paper away and sat back in his chair. Unable to sit still, he fidgeted with his hands, and his gaze darting this way and that.

'It's difficult. Reporters are not allowed anywhere near the front,' said Percy, wondering whether he was dreaming this. It was like nothing had passed between the brothers. 'Ah Lucy, may I have some tea?'

The maid had come into the room, carrying a dish of scrambled egg. Eddie immediately jumped to his feet and was spooning it onto his plate almost before she had put it down on the dresser. 'Certainly sir. There are some kippers, sir, it would only take a few minutes to cook them?'

'No, thank you, Lucy. I will just have some toast.'

'I will get you some fresh, sir,' Lucy glanced at Eddie who had sat down and was shovelling egg into his mouth. 'It's so good to have Master Edward back, isn't it, sir?'

'It is indeed, Lucy.' Once the maid had gone, Percy looked straight at his brother. 'Eddie, why are you back?'

Eddie finished his eggs and pushed the plate away. 'Back? This is where I live.' he said.

'I know but...with what happened with Annie...'

'Oh her. That's of no consequence,' Eddie waved his hand in the air dismissively. 'What about this squadron you're joining, tell me about that.' He turned to look at Percy, his face eager.

'I think we should talk about Annie first. We didn't mean it to happen, we were going to tell -'

'Oh yes, yes, yes, I know, I've said, it doesn't matter, you're welcome to her. The squadron, it's got the new Sopwith, hasn't it?'

'Well, yes but -'

'You're off down to it today, aren't you?'

'Well yes.'

'Let me come! Please, I really want to see the machine. It's got twin guns hasn't it?'

'Yes but…' Percy's voice dropped away.

'But what? I'm a pilot, a serving RFC officer aren't I? Why shouldn't I come with you?'

'Well yes, but…'

The brothers were interrupted by Lucy's arrival with the tea and toast. After she had gone, Percy took a deep breath.

'The thing is, old thing, of course you could go, in normal circumstances but, you see, Fitzroy and Hanley want to do a story on me joining the squadron.'

'Oh, I know that,' said Eddie, looking impatient. 'That's how I knew about the Sopwiths. Holloman told me.'

'Oh,' said Percy. 'Did he tell you that they wanted Annie there too? They want pictures of us, both in uniform, at the airfield. War hero goes back into the fray whilst the Angel of Mercy sees him off,' he added, unable to keep the cynicism out of his voice.

'Yes, what of it?' Eddie gave the dismissive wave again.

'Well, doesn't that bother you?'

Eddie looked completely nonplussed. 'Bother me? Why should it bother me? I say, I can come, can't I? Please say that I can?'

Percy just stared at him.

*

The squadron was forming up in Surrey, and the three of them caught the train from Victoria down to Upper Warlingham, sharing a first-class carriage. Annie and Percy sat awkwardly together in virtual silence whilst Eddie sat by the window. Once again Percy was struck by how Eddie could not seem to sit still or concentrate on anything. He had brought a book, had picked up a copy of The Times at the station, yet neither could hold his attention for more than two minutes.

Annie had been shocked to see him but had greeted him warmly. Eddie had smiled briefly and said hello but his nervous energy had been evident even on the station concourse. He was anxious to get his ticket, then wanted to find the platform and seemed more annoyed that the first train to leave was not theirs than over anything to do with Annie.

At Warlingham, Eddie went off in search of a cab to take them to the airfield, giving Annie the first chance to talk to Percy.

'What's he doing here?' she said.

Percy shrugged. 'I don't know. He turned up at the house this morning, demanding to come with me.'

'But...where's he been? And has he said anything about us?'

'He said he's been staying here and there, but lately at the RAC club. He's been badgering the corps to take him back onto active service. As for us, he says it's fine, he does not seem bothered.'

Annie sighed, and shook her head. 'It's not right,' she muttered. 'He's not right.'

'Eddie? He's fine. He's just a little...excited. Excited and frustrated.'

'He's not Percy. I mean, I don't know him that well, I never did, but he's different isn't he, from what he was before?'

'He's a little bit changed, I admit,' said Percy. 'But war does change a man, doesn't it? He's still Eddie, and he's still young. The young are prone to excitement.' Just as the old are prone to weariness, he felt like adding but didn't.

Whatever, he knew that Annie could see it. She put her hand on his arm. 'How are you holding up?' she said, her voice soft and gentle.

'I'm fine,' he said.

He could tell that she did not believe him.

*

It was a short cab ride from the station to the airfield. Annie didn't say a word during it, she was too busy watching Percy and his brother.

Whilst Percy was taciturn, withdrawn, Eddie's nervous energy, if anything, increased. He talked at Percy, asking him questions about what he knew about the other pilots, the aircraft, when they were going to France, most of which Percy replied in the same way: 'I don't know.' This did not stop the flow of questions.

They were greeted at the airfield by the squadron leader, someone that Percy clearly knew, for he grasped the man's hand warmly.

'Paul,' he said, his face lighting up for the first time that day.

'How are you?' he added, then seemed to remember that he was in army, for he let go of his hand, straightened up and saluted, 'Major Proctor. Captain Grenville reporting for duty.'

As he did there was the flash of photographic powder. Annie saw Proctor glance in exasperation to where the photographer and Holloman were standing.

'No need to stand on ceremony, old friend,' said Proctor. Annie could tell he was not British, his accent was colonial, he sounded South African or perhaps Rhodesian. When Percy introduced them, she saw Proctor give Percy a knowing look and smile as he took her hand. Once again there was a flash from the side as the photographer took another shot.

'I wish our ruddy observers were as quick with their cameras,' Proctor muttered. 'I take it this for your benefit, Percy?'

Percy sighed. 'I'm afraid so. I'm sorry about this.'

Proctor shrugged. 'All I can say, Percy old chap, is that you have got friends in some pretty high places. I didn't want them at the field but I was told, in no uncertain terms by the powers-that-be that I had no say in the matter.'

'I'm sorry,' said Percy again,

'If it gets us special treatment from the War office, I don't mind Percy. You must be Eddie, good to meet Percy's brother at last,' Proctor said. 'I see you're in the RFC too.' He stepped closer and looked at Eddie's tunic. 'Is that the MC? Good show, you've done a tour then?'

'Yes, sir. On RE8s though. Love to get a chance with the new Sopwith though, sir. What are they like? Do you think they can best the Albatros?'

'Hellfire, you're keen,' laughed Proctor. 'The Camel is hot stuff but let's have your brother meet the chaps first. Come on, they're over in the mess waiting. May I?' He offered his arm to Annie who took it He led her out of the office and out into the sunshine. Percy and Eddie followed on behind.

'The new aircraft. You called it a Camel,' she said. 'Why so?'

'Because we think it's going to give the Hun the hump,' Proctor grinned. 'Actually you'll see why. It's got a sort of raised cover over the guns that some chaps think make it look a bit like a dromedary.'

'Oh right. I take it you've known Percy for some time?'

'Oh yes, Grenville and I go way back,' said Proctor. 'We both started as sprog pilots late in '15 over Flanders then on the Fee's on the Somme. When I got given this job, I asked for him as one of my flight leaders straight away. At the time, though, the medical board hadn't signed him off as fit.'

Annie saw that an aircraft was being pulled out of one of the hangars just in front of them by the ground crew. To her it seemed incredibly small, squat, snub-nosed and pugnacious and she could see the hump in front of the cockpit. Even though she did not know aircraft very well she just knew this had to be the Camel.

'Who did you get instead?' asked Percy.

'A chap called Carmichael,' said Proctor. 'Scored six kills on the Pup. He was a nice chap.'

'Was?' said Annie. 'What happened to him?'

'I say, that's it,' exclaimed Eddie. 'The new Sopwith.' He dashed past Annie and Proctor and ran over to the machine, almost pushing the ground crew out of the way as he circled the aircraft.

'He *is* keen,' murmured Proctor. 'Has he got a squadron?'

'Not now,' said Percy. 'He went through Arras in April, got wounded during it. Shot a couple of aircraft down though whilst he was there.'

'Did he now? On RE8s? That is impressive. Arras, that was some bloody mess, pardon my French, miss. We could do with someone like him, if he can handle that little B.'

'Little B?' said Annie.

Proctor just smiled. In the meantime Eddie had stood up on the steps to the cockpit and was looking inside. Holloman and the photographer had walked across with him, the latter setting up for another shot.

'What happened to Carmichael?' said Percy.

Proctor pulled a face. Annie saw him glance across the airfield to where there was a dark patch. Burnt grass? Oil? 'He had an accident,' he said. 'The new Sopwith...well, it takes a bit of getting used to. There's a saying going around about it, you know.' He glanced at Annie, then at Percy. 'Ah forget it. Come on, Grenville, let's meet the chaps.'

Proctor turned to lead them inside the mess. Percy though did not move. He was staring at the little aircraft. Annie did not like the look on his face. It was rigid, he was staring at the camel as if it were some dangerous beast that he dare not take his eye off. His right hand, held limply at his side was trembling.

'Percy,' she said. He did not respond so she grasped his hand. He looked at her, uncomprehending at first, then over at Proctor.

'Oh, yes, right,' he said. 'Yes, lead on.'

He limped into the mess.

*

Percy found the ritual of getting ready to fly both familiar and strange. He had done it so many times before, about a year before he had been doing it three or more times a day as his squadron had fought and won the skies over the Somme. Now though, it was like someone else who was putting on the layers and flying coat. It felt like he was recalling a past life not his own recent history.

He wished Annie would go but she seemed determined to stay. Did she want to see him die? No, that was silly, he wasn't going to die. why should he be so afraid of flying now? They were in England, near London for heaven's sake. There were no enemy fighters for hundreds of miles.

He wasn't going to die.

But then he wasn't being silly any more, was he? He hadn't flown anything for months, did he still know how? The last thing he had flown was the old FE. Slow, stable, damn safe. The Sopwith was nothing like that. The pilots he had met, mostly young and inexperienced granted, were clearly afraid of it. It had killed two of them already and put another in hospital, not counting Carmichael.

Hell, Carmichael, he had bags of experience on Pups yet still he crashed and burned. How the hell could he be expected to master the beast? It was hopeless, hopeless.

He would crash and he would die.

He tore off his gloves and was about to throw them across the room but stopped himself. What was up with him? Those men needed a leader, they needed someone to give them confidence. If it wasn't going to be him then it would have to be some other poor bastard. He needed to pull himself together, even though his insides felt like they could take off on their own.

Slowly, he put his flying gloves back on and walked out of his room and out into the brilliant July sunshine.

*

'He looks nervous, God, he looks nervous.'

'Pardon?'

She glanced across at Eddie who was looking at her, puzzled. She realised she had spoken out loud what she had intended to keep to herself.

'Nothing,' she said. 'I was just worried about him.'

Eddie gave a little shrug, as if he didn't care.

She carried on looking at him for a few moments then turned back to look at the aircraft. Now was as good a time as any to broach this.

'Eddie, about Percy and I -'

'I don't care. Believe me I really don't.'

'But...I do love him. I do care. That's why I'm so worried now.'

Eddie gave a little snort. 'He'll be alright. He'd better be, I want to fly it after him. He'd better not prang it before I get the chance.'

Annie looked at him incredulously. From what she could see he was perfectly serious.

'Is that all you care about?' she said. 'Getting a flight in your precious aircraft?'

Eddie smiled. 'Of course. What else?' She saw him give her a little glance, she did not like the look on his face.

'Right,' she said.

Did he really mean all this? He was so different. He'd changed so much.

He spoke again, interrupting her train of thought.

'You know that saying about the Camel? What Proctor started to say then stopped?'

'I'm sure you're going to tell me,' she said.

He smiled again. 'Oh I will. They say flying it will give you three choices; a wooden cross, the Red Cross or the Victoria Cross.' He looked back at the aircraft. 'Percy's got the last one already,' he added.

Annie just stared at him.

*

Percy's stomach churned. He was sat in the tight cockpit of the Camel. It all seemed so small compared with the FE, the breeches of the Vickers guns so close, the Clerget engine and prop just in front. He tried to force himself to listen to what the young pilot who had his foot in the step below the cockpit side was saying into his ear.

'Pump up pressure in the tank up to 2 ½ lbs, sir. In the air you should get above 3 ½ lbs, if it goes higher adjust the air release valve here.'

There was so much to take in. Percy said, 'Right,' just for something to say.

'You want the fine adjustment to be about a quarter of quadrant for take-off with your throttle at about half a quadrant. If you get black smoke that means too much petrol. White smoke means too much oil.'

'Right.'

'Don't run your engine full out on the ground a second longer than it takes to see that you have the right revs per minute, you'll overheat it.'

'Right, not too long.' How much more? He'd never remember all this.

'When you call 'contact' and your man swings the prop, you should usually push forward the throttle lever and then gradually open out fine adjustment until you get mixture and correct rpm.

'Try and taxi out on throttle using the switch as little as possible. Always remember to cut down your fine adjustment when you throttle down. If your engine starts popping it's probably because you have not cut down your fine adjustment sufficiently.'

'Popping. Fine adjustment. Yes.'

'To take off, remember, open up your engine, advance throttle, then fine adjustment. Never take off with a missing engine. Keep it straight and into the wind. You'll need right rudder to do this the moment the tail leaves the ground. Don't turn until you have sufficient height.'

Percy just nodded.

The young pilot smiled in encouragement. 'You'll find it flies nose up. You must consciously push the stick to stop it trying to loop. Watch it when you first get off, a few of the chaps have stalled it doing that and spun straight in. It'll turn right like the devil but left turns are a bit trickier. You ready, sir?'

No, thought Percy.

He looked across at Annie. She looked as scared as he felt. Eddie, well Eddie just looked impatient. He wanted his turn.

Percy nodded at the pilot, who stepped down, and then at the mechanic.

'Switches on,' he called.

Moments later the rotary engine roared into life.

*

Percy unfastened his straps even before the machine had rolled to a stop. He swung his leg out of the cockpit and tried to find the step. He was shaking, his leg included and it just wouldn't go in. He thought he might just fall out but then felt a strong hand on his ankle and his boot being guided into the pocket.

'There you go, sir,' said a voice. 'It's all a bit unfamiliar I suppose, but you'll soon get used to it.'

The chief mechanic, it had to be.

Then he was on the ground but still the shaking continued. It was so bad that he couldn't see straight, it was like he had been dropped into a pool of icy water. His teeth were chattering.

Everyone was crowding around him, all the mechanics, the pilots, patting him on the back, asking him things.

He didn't want to hear, he didn't want to know. He pushed through them, he needed air, he needed to get away.

He really felt like he was going to be sick this time.

And then he was.

As he retched, from behind him he heard someone laugh, it sounded like Eddie's.

Someone else said something about castor oil, how it always got people that way.

He didn't want to listen. He was ashamed.

He knew it wasn't the castor oil.

*

'How are you feeling now? Do you need some more water?' Annie's hand was on his arm.

'I'm alright,' he muttered.

'Yes,' she said, her voice flat and low. 'Of course you are.'

They were watching Eddie being strapped into the Camel. Percy saw the young pilot was doing the briefing again. Eddie was looking keen, far more attentive than he was sure he had looked.

'How bad is it?' she whispered. 'To fly I mean.'

It's a beast, a killer, Percy wanted to shout. It's way beyond my abilities. He had barely completed a circuit. The thing seemed intent on biting its own tail, he was sure it was about to spin in at any moment. Given the choice, he'd never want to even sit in it again.

He didn't have a choice.

'It's quite hard,' he said at last. 'It will take a lot of getting used to.'

The young pilot who had briefed Percy stepped away from the cockpit. The mechanic walked the prop round to suck the fuel in, paused, then swung hard.

The rotary roared into life.

Almost immediately Eddie opened the throttle. The Camel bounded off down the field and rose into the air.

It was only a hundred or so feet up when it banked with its wings at right-angles to the ground and Eddie completed a slow roll, finishing with the Camel's wheels almost brushing the grass.

*

An hour later Annie was sat in the officers' mess, sipping a lemonade. Percy was giving Holloman a last interview. She was only half listening to what was said, instead she was watching Eddie.

She knew next to nothing about flying but even she had been impressed by Eddie's display. Impressed and frightened.

Whilst Percy had looked tentative, even shaky, aloft and his flight had consisted of no more than a few circuits, Eddie had filled the full twenty minutes of his with stunts, rolls, spin turns and stalls. On at least three occasions she was sure he must crash, twice when he pulled out of dives when his wheels were barely a foot above the ground and once when he banked the little machine between two hangars and one of his wingtips had brushed the grass. She had given an involuntary cry of alarm and, as Percy had gripped her arm, he clearly felt the same.

Now Eddie was the focus of attention, surrounded by the young pilots and clearly loving it. His eyes were wide and shining with excitement and he could not sit still. His audience was in awe but also shared his mood, they were chattering noisily and excitedly, laughing loudly and raucously. It was like Eddie was a sporting hero, Annie had seen the same effect after rugby matches, her brother was a keen player and she had been, reluctantly dragged along by her proud parents. The boys would gather round the star player, the man who could do the things they could only dream of, could only aspire to. It seemed in their closeness they were hoping that some of these qualities and skills would somehow be passed to them.

It was the same here. And these pilots were boys. Eighteen, nineteen, no more, all of them.

But then, Eddie was that age. She had to remind herself of that. Somehow, he seemed to be at least a decade older than those who surrounded him.

He was certainly different from the man she had met in February. She had liked that Eddie, his shyness, courtesy. He had a bookish indifference, a total lack of brashness and ego that she had found so appealing.

But now? She did not like this Eddie at all, he was arrogant, boastful, loud, a show-off with a sense of entitlement.

Yet everyone seemed to value those qualities, to appreciate what he had become. Holloman and the photographer clearly thought so. Although they had been there to cover Percy's return to service, they had spent more time with Eddie when he had landed.

She glanced across at Percy. Holloman had just finished the interview; he had stood up and shaken hands. Percy, pale, withdrawn, had released the reporter's hand and put his own behind his back, out of sight. So, the tremor is back, she thought.

Holloman walked away leaving Percy on his own. He looked so lost that her heart went out to him. She saw him look at Eddie, his face rigid, cold. Was there jealousy there? Surely not?

He looked over at her. His face relaxed. He gave her a weak smile then came across to her.

'Mind if join you and Percy, Mrs Ross?' Proctor's voice broke the moment. The truth was she did mind but she did not want to seem rude.

'Of course,' she said. As the two men sat there was a loud burst of laughter from the pilots who surrounded Eddie.

'You'll have to excuse the boys,' said Proctor. 'They're a bit excited. I hope they're not spoiling your visit?'

'Not at all major. I appreciate your allowing me to come and see Percy settle into his new squadron.'

She saw Proctor glance across at Holloman and the photographer who were preparing to leave. 'I wasn't given much of a choice,' he murmured. Then he looked up and her and smiled. 'I'm sorry, didn't mean that to sound the way it did. It really is my pleasure to have you here, and I'm glad to see Percy happy, which he clearly is. I...er...do need to ask you something, Percy old friend.'

Percy looked surprised. 'What's that, Paul?'

Proctor looked over at Eddie and nod his direction. 'That young brother of yours. So he's not attached to a squadron?'

Percy shook his head. 'No. He was discharged from 159 when he was wounded and shipped home. He's been pestering the air board for the last few weeks to get himself passed fit and put back on operations. Apparently, he passed the medical examination last week.'

'Apparently?'

Percy glanced at Annie. 'I haven't seen much of him lately.'

'Well, I'd give my eye-teeth to have him here,' Proctor said, very quietly. Annie realised he did not wish to be overheard and his next sentence explained why. 'I need to clear it with you first, of course. I don't want to make things more difficult for you, having him in the same squadron, all that extra responsibility and all that. How would you feel about it? Be honest now.'

Percy was staring at her. They made eye contact for a few seconds before he said. 'No.'

Proctor frowned. 'No, you don't want him here?'

There was a moment's hesitation, during which time Annie saw Eddie look over at the three of them, before Percy replied. 'No, I meant I didn't have a problem with him being in the squadron.'

Annie was sure that Percy had just changed his mind.

'Excellent!' said Proctor. 'He'll be an asset to us. I'll badger the powers-that-be to get him. Won't put him in your flight, of course, that wouldn't be fair. C-flight is looking a bit light on experience, I'll put him in there – if I get him of course.'

'Yes, of course,' said Percy. 'Though you might have trouble with Eddie himself. On the way down, he was going on about the Gotha raids. I think he'd set his heart on a home defence squadron.'

'He'll get his wish then,' Proctor said. 'Though keep this to yourself, it's unofficial at the moment.'

'What?'

'It seems that HMG are really rattled by these raids and are actually going to do something about it for once. It looks like we're not going to France for a while. We're going to be added to the defences around London.'

'Not going to France,' Percy murmured. 'Oh.'

Annie could see his mood lift.

'Mind you, that will mean extra training.'

'Oh, what for?'

'They want us to fly at night so we can cover the Zeppelin raids too. The crates they've been using for that job are feeble. They need proper fighters.'

'In a Camel? At night?' The colour had drained from Percy's face.

'I'm sure we'll manage it and, between us, we'll get the lads licked into shape,' said Proctor. 'Now, Mrs Ross, we'll have to get a bite to eat organised before we send you back up to London. If you'll excuse me, I'll go and get that organised.'

Annie was shocked when she glanced at Percy. He was staring into the middle distance, unblinking. She had seen a similar look on some of her patients and It chilled her to see it on Percy.

The ones that were on the point of death.

*

Annie had been dreading the trip back to London with Eddie. She had been hoping that he'd stay at the airfield and, indeed, he'd wanted to but Proctor had vetoed the idea, telling him repeatedly that it was not possible until the official posting had come through. Though Eddie had protested loudly, Proctor had dug his heels in. The result was that he was in a deep sulk and had not said a word to her since they had left.

Although she did not particularly want to talk, she found the silence in the train carriage oppressive. She was also aware that if she was going to stay within the Grenville family she would have at least to try to be on speaking terms with Percy's younger sibling. She took a deep breath.

'I'm sorry you couldn't stay. At the squadron I mean,' she said.

She got a snort of derision. 'Why do you care?'

'I know you wanted to stay,' said Annie, trying to stay patient. 'And that you're a good pilot.'

'I'm a bloody good pilot, that's why it's so bloody stupid. Proctor needs me and he knows it. There's no-one there of my quality or experience.'

'Well...apart from Percy, of course,' Annie said, however Eddie didn't seem to be listening.

'Those other flight leaders, I talked to them. What a useless pair they are. Both had been in France for a year on Scouts and do you know how many Huns they've got between them? Well do you?'

'Er, no.'

'Two! Two, I ask you! A whole one each.' Eddie shook his head. 'I laughed, I actually laughed. What a poor show. I spent eleven days at Acq and got two kills on my own on bloody Harry Tates, both confirmed too. I saw the wreckage of the first one, had a look at the bodies. One of them had jumped, he'd burst like a pig. I saw him.'

'Oh really.' Annie was sickened, now she wished she had not bothered, wished that he'd stop talking.

'Mind you, Percy is probably worse than that pair,' Eddie said.

'What do you mean by that?'

She had not meant to lose her cool but could not help it. It did not help that he had a smug smile on his face.

'Oh nothing,' he said, and sat back, his arms folded.

He's deliberately goading me, she thought, he's just trying to upset me. She decided she was not going to rise to it, not going to give him the satisfaction. She would be mature, reasonable. So, she should start properly, grasp the nettle.

'Eddie,' she said. 'We should talk, it's important. About Percy and I. Neither of us meant it to happen. We didn't mean – '

'Oh that,' Eddie waved his hand dismissively. 'I thought you said it was important. It's not. He's welcome to you.'

'Oh, right. I thought you might have felt hurt.'

'Hurt? Why should I be hurt?'

'I...just thought you might be, that's all.'

He wrinkled his nose. 'Hurt because some strumpet of a nurse switches her talons from me to him? I think not.'

'Strumpet?'

He smiled. 'That's what mother calls you. And far worse, believe me.'

She stared at him. 'Oh, I do believe you, don't worry,' she murmured.

'And, anyway, with these,' he stroked his wings and medal ribbon on his tunic, 'I can get any nurse I want. Younger and prettier ones than you.'

She stared at him for a few moments. 'Well done, Eddie,' she said at last. 'That was so beautifully put. I'm sure your mother would be proud of you.'

'Oh, she is, Annie, she is.'

'But thank you for the information, Eddie. I'll be sure to warn – to tell, sorry, my colleagues and the VAD girls at the hospital so they can avail themselves of this opportunity. I'm sure they'll rush to do so.' She turned to look out of the carriage window. 'We're not far from the station,' she added, not able to keep the relief out of her voice.

She had tried, she really had, for Percy's sake more than her own. Well, Eddie could go to hell, he was simply horrible now. What had she ever seen in him? At least she could concentrate on Percy now with her conscience clear. She would need to, he was doing too much, heading towards a breaking point, back to the state he was in when she had first met him. He was horrible then, she had hated him but now –

'I hate hospitals,' said Eddie.

'Pardon?'

'I hate hospitals. I always have.'

'Right,' said Annie.

'I bombed one once. A German field hospital, at least I think it was German. Dropped my eggs right into the middle of it. Boom, boom, boom!'

Then he laughed.

He was still chuckling as they pulled into the station.

CHAPTER TWENTY-THREE

England, Wednesday July 25th 1917

Percy was in agony.

His shoulders were burning with the tension, he had a sharp, slicing pain right across his back and down his spine. His injured ankle, shattered by Siggi's bullet eight months before, was hurting like he had been shot again but, this time, just from the pressure he had to keep on the rudder bar to keep the thing flying straight.

He was shaking, locked in fear, his eyes fixed on the horizon, the faint line of the coastline his one fixed point of reference. The gloom was suffocating.

It wasn't the dark itself that was the problem, nor flying at night, he had done that many times. It was the aircraft, the Camel. It was terrifying.

He had gained some experience of the aircraft over the previous week but had not by any means mastered it. Although he had led his flight on several training exercises and had sought to encourage his young pilots to appreciate the new fighter, the truth was he detested it. Certainly, it was manoeuvrable, but he found its handling vicious and the fact it needed constant attention wearing on the nerves.

The issues were of his creation though. He was reacting to problems, not anticipating the aircraft's needs. His instincts had gone.

He had spun it once, accidentally when he had been caught in the wake of one of his pilots' machines and had struggled to recover it. The near collision was his fault and, what made it worse, it had occurred in front of his entire flight. He was sure they were talking about him behind his back, that doubts about his ability were starting to be raised in his young pilots' minds.

This was one of the reasons why he had taken on this flight. It was his responsibility; he could not ask anyone else to do it. They had to know what the Camel was like to fly in and, above all, to fight in at night. They had been tasked with night defence, at least in the short term, and they needed to know whether it was possible.

Percy was not sure it was. The Camel with its tail-heaviness and constant desire to loop, twist and turn were magnified in darkness. It was hard enough to maintain a level flight when you could see but at night ... He felt like he was standing on one leg on tiptoes with his eyes closed trying not to fall over. That was why he was so high, over 10,000 feet. Even so, if he lost control, he would struggle to recover the aircraft.

He feared for his young pilots, alone, in the darkness, perhaps flying into the disorientating turbulence of cloud. Some of them would die, he had no doubt, and probably for no good purpose because they'd never find the enemy anyway.

He could die too, probably tonight. It would be easy to crash. He still had to find the airfield. He still had to land. Neither were guaranteed.

And yet there was still one more thing he needed to do. Something that was even more terrifying than flying.

He had to fire the guns. That was the point of this exercise. That was what really scared him.

His fingers kept moving to the firing lever but then moved away. He was shaking. He knew what would happen, that was the problem. The twin Vickers machine guns were right in front of him, in his line of sight. As soon as he fired the flashes would take away his night vision.

He couldn't see much now. He would be totally blind after he pulled the trigger.

He needed to do it. He owed it to his pilots to do it. They needed to know how long the blindness would last.

Could he make himself fire? He was taken back to his boyhood, the rock at the swimming hole at the river, him stood at the top gathering the courage to jump in. The jeers of his friends when he couldn't.

Coward. That's what they had called him. Coward. Yellow.

That's what he was. A coward. He was afraid. Him, who was about to get the VC. For an act of shame, of pure disloyalty and cowardice.

He had to prove to himself that he was wrong, that he had changed. He had to face up to his demons.

He moved his hand to the trigger and fired.

*

Annie checked the clock as she hurried into the station. She was late, late and flustered, just what she had wanted to avoid.

But she had not had a choice. Matron needed her to supervise the VAD girls, make sure that they had completed all the tasks they had been assigned to them. They were keen enough, most of them at least, and they were volunteers but that did not make them competent. The Scottish girl, Fiona, had made a hash of redressing a leg wound. Annie had had to redo it, demonstrating the right way as she did. It would not have been so bad if it had happened earlier in the evening but, no, it had to be right at the end of her shift.

She'd rushed to get changed, had no time to do her make-up or her hair as she had planned. Then all the taxis were busy, she'd walked halfway to the station before she could find one. This was not what she had wanted, her aim was to make Percy's life easier, not to cause him more problems.

He was already taking on too much, the squadron, his flight commanders' job was enough but he also had the added pressure of the election campaign and the publicity that Maxwell Fitzroy and the rest of his cronies were placing on him.

And there was the VC. The investiture was coming up. That, she knew, was troubling him more than anything.

When she had first known him she'd hated him for his anger, for his self-loathing. Then she'd found out, through Eddie, what he had done, and, at first, that had made things worse because she was disgusted with him. It was only when she had come to know him that she'd understood; he'd taken responsibility for it. He had discounted his mental state at the time, his tiredness, his near mental collapse due to the strain of months of combat, that did not matter to him, what did was the need to live with his guilt.

He was such an honest person. He needed to own up, to tell all, to admit his guilt. Yet he couldn't. Circumstances meant that he had to stay silent.

And now there was the VC. She could guess what this must

feel like to him, an award for his ultimate shame and guilt.

It was too much. It was far too much.

And now she was adding to it by making him late for this dinner. A War Bonds drive, at least on the surface. In fact it was a Maxwell Fitzroy event to promote his pet candidate and war hero and, by connection, himself. Percy was expected to shine, to make small talk and then, even worse, make a speech. It was too much. It was far too much.

Had he gone already? She would not have blamed him if he had, she was at least 15 minutes late.

At first she thought he had, but then she saw him. He was sat on a bench by the ticket office, in his dress uniform, his arms crossed, his head lolling forward. Was he asleep?

'Percy?' she said.

*

It was silent.

Why was it so quiet? The engine was still running - wasn't it? He couldn't see it, he was blind.

Blind, he couldn't see. He was spinning, yes, yes, he was spinning, crashing, he had to pull out. Where was the horizon? Where was up?

It was going to break up, there would be a crack and the whole thing would collapse.

He saw Siggi. His face. The look of surprise, disgust. The neat hole in his head.

Alice. Her face. Smiling.

They were ganging up on him, he needed to get away.

Someone was calling him.

'Percy! Percy, are you all right?'

He screamed.

'Leave me alone! Go away! All of you!'

*

She had the presence of mind to jerk back so she was only caught by the tip of his fingers. Even so the blow came as a sharp shock.

'Annie!'

She had turned away and closed her eyes as the sting peaked and then receded. She felt his hand around her.

'I'm alright,' she said. 'I just wasn't expecting it.'

She straightened up and blinked the tears from her eyes. A few people had gathered around them, curious but with the usual reserve of Londoners.

'I'm alright,' she said again but this time more loudly. 'It was an accident.'

The people started to move away, most of them satisfied, though Annie noticed that some of the men were looking askance at Percy.

'I'll find help, get someone to look at it,' he said, looking around.

'It's all right, I don't need anything. It's nothing, really.'

'But-'

She looked at Percy appealingly. 'Please can we go?' She just wanted to get away from the attention.

'Of course,' he said. He took her arm and led her off the concourse. 'I'm so sorry, I don't know what happened. I can't believe I hit you.'

'It was nothing. You were asleep. I woke you'

He shook his head. 'It's inexcusable. What was I doing falling asleep in public like that anyway?'

'That's obvious,' she said. 'You look all in.'

He sighed. 'I'm fine,' he said.

'You're not fine. You're exhausted -'

'Oh for goodness sake, mind your own business will you? What right do you have to tell me what to do?'

They were outside the station now, on the forecourt. He was wide-eyed, his face distorted with anger, his voice was raised. Once again, they were the centre of attention, but this was not what most disturbed her. Annie was scared. The man who could do terrible things, go to war, kill his brother-in-law was back. Still, she stood her ground.

'I thought,' she said, her voice even and, to her mind, surprisingly calm, 'I had every right to care. If that's not true then I might as well just go.'

She turned and walked away.

'Annie! Please, wait, I'm sorry.'

He was with her in a moment and the old Percy was back, soft, caring, deeply troubled. 'I'm sorry, I shouldn't have spoken like that. I don't know...' his voice trailed off. 'Actually, of course, I do. You're right, I'm all in.'

She caressed his face. 'It's all right, I know.'

'It's unforgivable though. I...I...should let you go, I'm not worth being with.'

'Of course you are,' she said softly stepping up close so her face was rested against his. 'You just scare me when you get like that because you are not the man that I know you are.'

'Maybe you are seeing the real me when I am like this,' he said softly.

'No. I know the real you. I didn't when we first met but I see him most of the time now.' She let her head drop. 'Until recently. Until you took all of this on.'

'But...what choice do I have? It's my duty. I have to do my duty.'

'Duty as others see it. Duty as others impose on you. You don't have to go along with this. Like tonight, this dinner. It's not necessary is it? Not with everything else you've got to do.'

'The dinner?' he said. 'Oh hell, yes, look at the time. We'll be late. We need to find a taxi'

Immediately he was flustered again, nearly overwhelmed, and seemingly forgotten what they had been talking about. He looked up and down the street, frantically waving at passing cabs, until at last he saw her face. Once again the switch was sudden, from the unreasonable to the reasonable man. He dropped his arms, slumped visibly. 'That's what you mean, isn't it?' he said.

Before she could reply, a cab drew up next to them

'Where to, guv?' said the driver.

'Where...? Er...' said Percy.

'The Grand Hotel, Mayfair,' said Annie opening the door.

Percy looked at her, puzzled. 'But you said...'

'We can talk on the way,' she said. 'We're here now and you've told them you'd do this. It will only eat at you if you don't go. Come on.'

He nodded and got in behind her.

As the cab moved off, he said. 'What do you think I should do?'

She grasped his hand. 'I think you should stop driving yourself so hard. It's going to kill you if you're not careful.'

'But, the squadron...I'm a serving officer.'

'Yes, I know. I think you've done enough but I do understand why you feel you need to go back. I wish to God that you weren't, that you were doing anything else but, as you are, you've got to give yourself the best chance of survival.

She paused, took a deep breath.

'The problem is that you're taking on far too much. You've got to give up politics.'

'I can't, I've given my word.'

'What good is your word if you're dead?'

'Oh, come on, it's not that -'

'Of course it's that bad. Are you seriously going to tell me it's not? Do you know what it's like, watching as you come to pieces in front of my eyes, seeing you change from the wonderful softness, the caring, considerate man that I've come to love to...'

She stopped and looked out of the cab window.

'Into what?' he said. 'Changed into what? Tell me.'

She turned back to him. She had come this far, there was no point in stopping.

'Into the man who can shoot his own brother-in-law,' she said.

She saw the words hit home as if she, herself, had returned his slap with interest. She regretted it instantly.

'That means I owe my country more. I'm committed to this, it's too late to back out now, surely?'

The time to step back, to apologise had passed, as much as he she wished she could. Now she had to press home her advantage. 'It's never too late...'

'But the squadron, the investiture, I have to do those.'

'Yes, you probably do, but this MP business, you don't have to do that do you?'

Percy looked deeply troubled. 'I've said I'll do it.'

'But you've every reason to give it up now. You've said yourself; you have a duty to serve your country. Your duty is first and foremost with your squadron. You are the senior flight commander, the second in command with the responsibility of introducing the new aircraft into service. The political appointments are interfering with that, aren't they? You can't commit as much time as you need to it, can you?'

'No,' he said, staring at her. 'No, I can't.'

'Then the answer is clear. You have a reason, a good reason.'

He shook his head. 'I'm just making excuses though, aren't I?

No, I have to keep my word.'

'But...'

'No, and that's an end to it.'

Annie turned away and stared unseeing at the street.

*

Lord Hanley glared across the table at the woman sitting alongside his candidate. He wasn't sure who she was but he knew she was doing one thing that irritated him immensely; she was dominating the attention of Captain Grenville when he should be doing his best to meet the other notables at this event. Bloody nuisance that it was, it was still important and he didn't want to see the chance wasted like this. Not when Grenville was so bad on the hustings. Couldn't he see it? He needed to use his skills to impress but what was he doing? Talking to some floozy. A cheap floozy at that by the look of her. Didn't she know how to dress for something like this? Clearly not. He was no expert in women's fashions but her outfit looked well-worn and second-hand, and she had not even bothered to do her hair.

It seemed he was not alone in regarding the woman with some disdain. He noticed that Sir Grenville was also glaring at her. He leant across to his table companion.

'Arthur,' he whispered, 'Who's that damned woman with your son?'

Lord Grenville's look darkened further.

'She's nobody,' he said.

'Where did she come from?'

'She's a nurse, she used to work for us, looking after young Edward. Until we sacked her that is.'

'Sacked her? What for?' Maxwell Fitzroy had obviously been listening in to the men's conversation.

'For being bloody rude and having ideas above her station. She took it on herself to have airs and graces and talk back to Lady Grenville. Her ladyship thinks she's probably a Bolshevik. Anyway, she's got her claws into Percival now. Stupid oaf, never had any sense.' Grenville suddenly looked abashed. He grimaced at Hanley. 'Sorry, he's a bright enough boy, he'll be good for the party but...' he sighed. 'Youngsters, eh? Think they know everything.'

'Indeed, indeed,' said Hanley. 'I'm worried about Percival, She could be a bad influence. We should do something.' He glanced across at Fitzroy.

Fitzroy nodded. 'Don't worry, Gentlemen, I am sure that I can sort out this situation. Leave it with me.'

'We're in your hands, Fitzroy,' said Hanley. 'Are you alright with this, Grenville?'

'Absolutely,' said Sir Grenville. 'Do whatever you need to do.'

*

'I think they are talking about us,' Annie whispered in Percy's ear.

'Let them talk,' said Percy. 'I don't care. There's nothing they can do.'

Annie caught Maxwell Fitzroy's look as Percy leant back to allow one of the waitresses to refill his coffee cup. It was so self-satisfied, malevolent, confident that it chilled her.

She hoped Percy was right.

*

'Captain Grenville, may I have a word in private before you leave? The manager has kindly let me use his office.' Fitzroy was at his oily best. 'You don't mind do you, Mrs Ross? I will only keep your... er...companion for a few minutes.'

'Yes, of course,' said Annie, ignoring the barb. 'That's no problem. I'll wait in the lobby. It's perfectly comfortable.'

'Thank you, Mrs Ross.' Fitzroy nodded to Annie and led Percy through a side door marked as being private.

She found herself alone amongst the finery as the last of the guests in their evening wear left. She couldn't help but notice that they largely ignored her.

She hoped that Percy would soon be back. She was missing him already.

*

Fitzroy had taken ownership of the manager's office, settling in behind the mahogany desk as if it were his.

'Take a seat, Grenville,' he said.

Percy stayed standing. 'This won't take long,' he replied. 'There's no need to sit.'

'Really? Well, suit yourself.'

There was something different about Fitzroy's manner, something that Percy found disturbing, but he dismissed it. He had decided to say his piece, go part way to address what Annie had asked him to do. He had to tell them to ease off a little, to let him prioritise the squadron.

'Look Fitzroy, there's something I need to speak to you about. You see -'

'Yes, you said. And we – Lord Hanley and I - need to talk to you. About Mrs Ross.'

Percy looked up. 'Annie? What about her?'

Fitzroy just smiled.

*

'Excuse me, madam, are you Mrs Ross?'

She looked up into the eyes of an elderly man in the faded uniform of the assembly rooms staff.

'Yes, I am.'

'Ah good,' said the man. 'I have a cab waiting for you. I'll take you to it now.' He swung his hand towards the exit.

She stayed where she was. 'I'm waiting for my friend,' she said. 'He's still inside.'

'Oh yes, madam, I know that. They said most definitely that I was to take you to the cab though. Please, it's this way.'

'Oh, all right,' she said. This time she rose and followed the attendant. Percy must have been thinking about her, not wanting her to feel awkward. He could be so sweet at times.

There was, indeed, a cab right outside the entrance.

'Here we are, madam,' said the attendant opening the door. She stepped inside and sat down and he closed it behind her. The cab immediately pulled off.

'Hey!' Annie yelled. 'Wait, stop! I'm waiting for my friend.' The driver ignored her, so she banged on the screen. She saw him glance back at her looking puzzled, but kept on driving. Annie banged harder and repeatedly. 'Stop! Stop, I tell you! Where are you taking me? Stop or I'll call the police.' She hit the glass so hard that her hands stung and she was afraid that she might crack the glass. The driver must have thought the same because he pulled over to the kerb and pulled the screen down.

'Stop that!' he said. 'Madam, control yourself. You may be drunk but there's no call to damage my vehicle.'

'Drunk, I'm not drunk! I'm perfectly sober. Where are you taking me?'

'Well, home of course. That's where I was told to take you. Cavendish Street, isn't it?'

'Yes, it is but –'

'Well, there you go then, madam. Now if you sit back –'

'Who told you to take me there? Who was it?'

The cab driver frowned. He turned to the front and rummaged under the dashboard, pulling out a piece of paper. He squinted at it, holding it up to the streetlights. 'It was a Captain Grenville, that's what it says here. He came out and gave me the address and a ten-bob note.'

Annie's mouth dropped open. 'But...why would he do that? No, wait, he couldn't, he was still inside.' She looked back at the Assembly Rooms, now a hundred yards or so back down the street and was just in time to see Percy come out onto the street and look agitatedly up and down. Even in the gaslight she could see he was flustered, angry and confused.

'Wait here,' she said to the cabby and stepped out. 'Percy!' she called. 'Percy, I'm here!'

He saw her straight away and half ran, half limped down the street to her.

'Annie, what's the matter?' he said. 'Why were you leaving? Why didn't you wait? Have I done something wrong?'

He was so obviously upset that she embraced him. 'Of course not, but why did you send me home without you?'

Percy stepped away. 'Send you home? I did no such thing.'

'The driver said you did.'

They both turned to look at the man who was standing by his car looking back at them.

'Driver, this is Captain Grenville,' she said.

'Beggin' your pardon, madam, this wasn't the officer who talked to me.' He looked at Percy. 'I'm very sorry, sir, I was just doing what I was told.'

'Hanley, damn him!' Percy yelled. 'Hanley and Fitzroy! What a nerve, what a damned nerve, how dare he? I'm going to have it out with him once and for all!' He made to set off back down the street but Annie caught him by the arm.

'Percy, please, don't,' she said. 'It's late and I'm tired. Take me home and you can tell me what just happened on the way. Please.' She leant forward and kissed him.

Percy continued to bristle for a few seconds but then his shoulders sagged.

'Yes,' he said. 'Yes, yes, you're right, of course.' He looked at Annie. 'I'd rather take you to my home though,' he added quietly. 'If that's all right with you?'

She nodded. 'Yes,' she said. 'That's fine.'

Percy turned to the driver. 'Would you take us to Berkeley Square?' he said.

'Yes, sir, of course, sir.'

In the cab, it was obvious to Annie that Percy was furious. He sat away from her, leaning against the window, his balled fist thumping into the seat next to him. She watched for a while then reached across and put her hand on the fist, holding it down.

'Calm yourself, my love,' she said. 'Getting yourself worked up is not going to help anyone. Don't bottle it up, talk to me.'

'It's Hanley. Hanley and Fitzroy. How dare they? It's intolerable.'

'I don't understand, what is? Tell me, Percy, please.'

Percy took a deep breath before replying. 'That quiet word he wanted with me? Do you know what it was?' She shook her head. 'Well he had the nerve to say that you were, what was the word? Oh yes, unsuitable. You were an unsuitable companion for a candidate.' He tried to thump the seat again and she struggled to hold onto his hand to stop him. He was rigid, tense like an over-wound spring, one that might break at any moment. 'He said I had to stop seeing you.'

The words were like being drenched in ice water but, although she was seething, she kept her voice soft. She had to avoid winding the spring yet further. 'So, what did you say?'

'What do you think I said? Of course, Mr Fitzroy, whatever you say, Mr Fitzroy.'

His raised voice caused the driver to glance at them through his mirror. She squeezed his hand.

'I told them it was none of their business, that they could go to hell.'

Annie leant across and kissed him. 'Thank you,' she said. She looked at the driver. 'So sending the car was them trying to force things, to make it looked like I'd walked out on you without saying a word.'

'Yes, damn them!' The spring wound a little more. 'How dare they? Do they think they damn well own me?'

'Apparently they think they do,' she said. 'But that shows they don't know you very well, do they? You're more of a man than that.' The cab pulled up to the kerb. 'We're here. Come on,' she said, gently. 'Let's get inside and talk.'

*

Inside Percy's flat she had to be patient. He spent the first ten minutes pacing backwards and forwards, cursing Lord Hanley and Fitzroy. All Annie could do was to talk softly, keep herself calm, keep her movements slow and easy, effectively talking him down. Eventually, she got him to sit on the sofa next to her and was able to get a glass of brandy into his hand.

'I'm sorry,' he said at last. 'I've been behaving like a child, a complete idiot. It's unforgiveable.'

'No, it isn't. You were provoked.' She attempted to judge his mood. He was calmer, his voice was much more normal. If she was going to say anything it should be now. 'You're already on edge. This is what I was trying to say before. You're taking on too much. You've not fully recovered.'

'Don't talk rot. I'm fine.'

'No, Percy,' she said firmly. 'You're far from fine. No, listen to me, please,' she added because he was trying to rise, trying to interrupt. 'Remember, I know what I'm talking about. I've had three years of cases like yours, I know.'

'Are you saying I'm crazy? Is that what you really think because –'

'No, you're not crazy, you're ill. It's not weakness, it's not a lack of character or a failing on your part, it's an illness. Your temper is erratic, your concentration is shockingly poor, your tremor is back and I can tell from your eyes you're not sleeping. Your being on active service, even though you're not in action, has brought back all the memories of what you went through last year, consciously or not, it's true.' She squeezed his hand. 'You know I'm right, don't you?'

The tension grew but then, abruptly, eased.

'Yes,' he whispered, and a tear appeared in his right eye and flowed down his cheek. 'But what would you have me do? Admit I'm a coward?'

'You're not a coward, far from it. Everyone has their limits. You've just been pushed to the edge of yours.'

Percy nodded, but then shook his head. 'No. I have to do my duty. I have to keep flying.'

Annie stroked his hair. 'If you do, you'll die.'

He shrugged. 'Tens of thousands already have. Why should I be different?'

'You're different because I love you,' she said.

He looked at her in astonishment.

'Pardon?' he said.

'I think you heard me.'

'Yes, but really? How can you, after what I did?'

She kissed him. 'Quite easily, as a matter of fact. I know that what you did wasn't you. I've met the real man now. He's pretty fine.'

Percy smiled. 'Thank you,' he said. 'I cannot agree with you, but thank-you. I cannot and will not ever forget what I did. Whatever the circumstances I am responsible for my actions.' His face hardened again. 'I am afraid that your love for me, and mine for you, makes no difference –'

'Of course it does, it has to.'

He shook his head. 'No, it doesn't. I'm a soldier, my country is at war. I must do my duty. I can't let everyone down.'

Annie nodded. 'You might already be doing that.'

'What do you mean?'

She took a deep breath. 'It's what I said before. Your standing for parliament is distracting you. You should just concentrate on your service, that's your real duty. Forget the politics, You're not suited to it anyway and it's just something else to burden you with when you are already overloaded.'

Percy looked astonished. 'But...I have to give the Flying Corp a voice.'

'That's how they sold it to you? You don't really believe that's true, do you?'

'Yes, I –'

'Hanley and Fitzroy are using you, using your fame for their own ends. They are moulding you, manufacturing an image of you. Why do you think they are doing that? For your benefit? Or theirs?'

'I'm my own man.' Percy's protest was weakly delivered.

'Yes, of course you are but in your own way. You're not bombastic or an orator like Lloyd-George or Churchill. You're quiet, shy even. You'd rather listen than talk.' She stroked his face. 'You know I'm right, don't you?'

'Yes,' he said quietly.

She decided to play her trump card. 'Surely tonight was the final straw. They showed their true colours. They want to control you, tell you where you can go, what to do, what to say.' She paused. 'They also want to say who you can see and who you can be with. You are your own man, you are not someone to be ordered around and used. Give it up, Percy, please. Give yourself a chance, give us a chance to be together.'

Percy nodded, she was pleased to see how determined he looked. 'Yes, you're quite right. I'm not due back at the squadron until after noon. Hanley will be at his club tomorrow morning. I will go and see him and tell him to go to hell.'

Annie had to resist sighing with relief. 'Thank you, my love.'

They kissed again but when they parted he looked rueful.

'It's a shame Eddie isn't older.' He said. 'He'd be an ideal candidate for them if he was.'

'Yes, but Eddie's not –' she began but then stopped herself.

Percy looked puzzled. 'Eddie's not what?' he said.

'Nothing, forget it.'

'No, go on, Eddie's not what?'

There was no way out, she had to say something. 'He's not right. He's unstable, unbalanced even.'

Percy shook his head. He looked puzzled. 'No, not Eddie. He's just keen, that's all. He's settled into the squadron really well and he loves the new Sopwith. All the other boys look on him in some awe. He's itching to get back into action.'

'Do you really think that's normal, after what he went through? He's not the same man I first met.'

'Oh, he is.'

'He isn't. You should hear the things he said to me on the train.'

Percy shook his head. 'You must have misunderstood. Eddie is fine.'

'He's not fine. He's dangerous. He's going to kill himself and take other people with him, most like.'

Abruptly Percy got to his feet, pushing her away. 'How dare you? I won't have talk like that, d'ya hear? I will not have my brother called crazy by you.' He was shaking. 'I think you should go.'

Annie also stood and found that she, too, was shaking. What had she done? She'd messed up, been careless. 'I'm sorry,' she said. 'I truly am. I'm tired, I didn't mean anything.'

Percy turned away from her and leant his hand on the mantelpiece, staring into the empty fire grate. She waited a few moments then walked up and placed her hand on his arm. 'You're right, it wasn't my place to say anything. Please don't send me away. Not now, not tonight.'

She waited. He did not seem to be yielding. She was at the point of giving up when he suddenly turned around, embraced and kissed her. Afterwards she pressed his face against his chest. She felt safe there, this felt so right.

She knew that she could not push him too far. He was as fragile as fine bone china, the slightest piece of rough handling could break him.

She could not help Eddie. He had to be someone else's responsibility. She had to concentrate on the Grenville brother she loved.

CHAPTER TWENTY-FOUR

England, Thursday July 26th, 1917

'So, gentlemen, there it is. I am very honoured to be asked but I feel I have no choice. I must withdraw as candidate.'

Percy sat back and looked at the two men sitting opposite him. He had not expected to find Fitzroy here with Hanley and he would have much preferred to have things out, man-to-man with the peer but the newspaperman's presence at least killed two birds with one stone. It was a relief to get the deed done.

But something wasn't right. The men's reaction was not what he had expected. He had anticipated surprise, perhaps a degree of restrained anger – or at least restrained on Hanley's part, he, at least being a gentleman – but he could see neither. All he had seen as he had spoken was the two men exchange glances, a slight raise of an eyebrow. They were calm and confident. It was disturbing, as if they had expected this to happen.

Well, what if they had expected it? Perhaps they had wanted it, Percy knew he had not performed well, that they were not happy with him, maybe they wanted him to step aside? It did not make any difference. He had made the decision, there was no going back.

The two men exchanged glances again. Hanley gave his companion a little nod. They had agreed something, Percy knew that for sure now.

'You are right in one respect, Grenville,' said Fitzroy. 'You do have no choice.'

'I beg your pardon. What do you mean by that?'

'He means that what happens is not up to you,' said Hanley.

'We will decide whether you withdraw or not and we will not let you.'

'Not let…what?' said Percy. 'I will not do it and that's an end to it.'

'No,' said Fitzroy. 'It's not. We've invested far too much time and money promoting you, building you up as a war hero just to have you change your mind. You will damn well do as you're told.'

'I will not. How dare you speak to me like that?' He got to his feet. 'Gentlemen, I cannot say it's been a pleasure but I am due back at my squadron so –'

'Sit down, Grenville,' said Hanley, his voice low and menacing.

'I will not sit.'

'You will if you know what's good for you.' Hanley stared coldly at him. 'I assure you, you will regret it if you don't.'

Although the club's lounge was quiet, Percy was away that he was now the focus of attention of the half a dozen mostly elderly men whose soporific morning had been interrupted by the raised voices. More out of his desire to avoid a scene, he took his seat again.

'Very well,' he said. 'I'm listening.'

'Good,' said Hanley. 'Now, Maxwell, would you be so kind as to explain to Captain Grenville about the information we have received about him?'

'Certainly, Lord Hanley.'

'What information? What are you talking about?' said Percy, though he suddenly felt lightheaded.

'Information that, if revealed, would drag the Grenville name through the mud.'

'I…I don't follow.'

'Don't insult our intelligence, Grenville,' said Hanley. 'Of course you damn well do.'

'Did you think we wouldn't check your story?' said Fitzroy. 'I'm a newspaper man. My paper investigates the facts, seeks out and prints the truth.'

'The truth? Your rag?' said Percy. 'Your printing the truth would be a first.'

'As would your speaking the truth, Captain. After all, it's you that have fraudulently claimed the highest award for gallantry that your country can award. Isn't it, Captain Grenville?'

Percy did not reply.

'You see, we know that the real hero of that affair was not you was it?' said Hanley

Percy shook his head.

'It was, in fact, your brother-in-law, an officer who put his own life at risk to get you and your badly wounded observer back to the British lines.'

'Yes,' whispered Percy. 'How...'

'We talked to the infantry Captain who brought you in,' said Fitzroy. 'And then to the family of your gunner, Brown. He told his father what you'd done.'

'So we know that you rewarded your brother-in-law's selfless act by putting a bullet in his brain,' said Hanley. 'Hun or not, that was a disgraceful, inhumane thing to do, wasn't it?'

Percy nodded.

'But then, to cap it all, you have made it worse by accepting the Victoria Cross. A medal that you are due to receive from your King, I would add.' Fitzroy's voice was low but there was a sneer in his tone that was deafening.

'That wasn't my idea, was it?' Percy snapped. 'I didn't claim to have done anything brave or honourable. That was you, Fitzroy. You and that damned rag of yours, peddling its usual lies, half and quarter truths, rabble rousing just to sell more copies.'

Fitzroy went red and looked as if he would forget himself and where he was. Hanley obviously thought the same because he put his hand up and leant closer to Percy.

'Whatever the circumstances, Grenville, you chose not to deny the story, did you?'

'No,' said Percy. 'I couldn't. I tried but with Alice in her condition –'

'Oh, don't you give me the sob story about your poor, pregnant sister,' snarled Fitzroy. 'You didn't think about her feelings when you consigned her to widowhood, did you?'

'Nor did you protest when you allowed us to put you forward as one of our candidates,' said Hanley. 'To appear on our platform, to have us promoting you. No, you let the lie persist, didn't you?'

'Yes,' said Percy. 'Yes, I did. But this has gone too far now. That's why I will do now what I should have done in the first place. I will tell the truth, resign my commission, face the consequences like a gentleman and an officer should.'

'No, you will not,' said Hanley. 'If you do that you will drag us into the mire with you. That is not going to happen.'

'But...what about the truth?' said Percy.

'Bugger the truth,' said Hanley.

'The public are not interested in the truth,' said Fitzroy. 'I know them, I know what they want. They want to be told that everything is going well, that we are winning. They want to be told that God and right is on our side, that atrocities are committed by the other side and not by us.' He stared into Percy's eyes. 'They want heroes they can believe in. Real ones or fake, it doesn't matter.'

'It's too late anyway,' said Hanley. 'The misrepresentation has already taken place.'

'That's why I must –' began Percy, but Hanley continued.

'If you think facing the consequences is the best option, think again. Think of the effect it will have on your family, your father's business, your mother's standing in society and, of course, your poor sister who now has a young son but no father. It must be hard enough for her as it is but does she have to have her family name dragged through the mud and lose its support too?'

'But what else can I do?'

Hanley smiled grimly. 'You will carry on. You will accept the VC. You will play the hero. You will stay on as our candidate and do exactly what we say.'

Percy nodded but then a though struck him. 'The witness, the captain? Won't he speak out?'

'Not when I've finished with him,' said Fitzroy. 'I'll find something in his past. Believe me, he won't even dare talk to his mother when I've finished with him.'

'I do believe you,' said Percy quietly. 'May I go now?'

'In a moment,' said Hanley. 'There is one more thing. We need to talk about Mrs Ross.'

Percy just stared at them.

*

Annie was instructing one of the VAD girls when she heard her name being called.

'I'm in here, Mabel,' she called. 'What is it? I'm rather busy.'

The junior nurse put her head around the door.

'I know sister but Albert in the lodge says it's urgent,' she said. 'You've got a visitor.'

'A visitor? You know we're not allowed visitors during our shifts. I can't see anyone right now.'

'Oh yes, I know that but Albert said it was all right because it was you and because he's an officer, and that I had to come to tell you but to make certain no-one else knew.' Mabel looked at the VAD girl and began to redden. 'Oh, I forgot, sorry.'

'I'm sure Edith won't say anything,' said Annie. 'Will you?'

'No sister,' said the girl.

'He's ever so handsome,' said Mabel, her face dreamy. 'He's a pilot, I think.'

Percy? It had to be, but he should be on his way back to his squadron now, shouldn't he?

'Oh, very well,' she said. 'Mabel, make yourself useful and help Edith here. Make sure she finishes the dressing properly and clears up afterwards. I'll check when I come back.'

Mabel looked crestfallen. 'Yes, sister,' she said. Annie guessed that she'd been hoping to come back with her to eavesdrop.

On the way over to the lodge the doubts started. Surely it couldn't be Percy, she had only seen him this morning. A chill struck her, what if he had not been able to see Hanley, gone back early and there had been an accident? Was this someone coming to find her to break the news?

No, no, she was being silly, there wouldn't have been time. So who else could it be. She only knew one other pilot – Eddie. She did not want to see him.

It *was* Percy. He was sat outside the Porter's office looking, if anything, even more haggard than he had on the station the previous evening. He got to his feet as soon as he saw her but there was no pleasure or greeting in his stance, he was not smiling, his eyes were dull and cold.

'Percy,' she said. 'What are you doing here?'

She moved to kiss him but he stepped away.

'Annie, I've got something to tell you,' he said.

*

She stayed in the hallway outside the porter's station for a full five minutes after Percy left. There was a dull, sick feeling in her stomach, like she'd been punched. It had all happened so quickly, he had been so abrupt, so definite, that she had no time to even say a word, to protest.

'Excuse me, Mrs Ross – Annie, are you all right? Would you like a cuppa? You can sit in our break room, no one can see you there.'

She looked at Albert, the porter, unseeing for a few moments.

'No,' she said at last. 'I'm fine. Thanks though, Albert.'

She turned and walked back to the ward, though, light-headed, was not sure how her legs were keeping her up. Her shift passed in a daze.

By the time it was over she had started to think more clearly. By the time she got home she had worked out what must have happened and was extremely angry.

*

Fitzroy took a sip of the club's best brandy. It had been a good lunch.

'Do you think he will toe the line now?' he said.

'Oh I think so,' said Hanley. 'He's not stupid. He knows he has to protect the family name.'

'And will continue to do so once he's elected,' said Fitzroy, nodding and taking another sip of the fiery liquid.

'It's a shame that brother of his isn't older,' said Hanley. 'He's really got something about him. He looks and sounds like a hero. He's coming to the investiture, isn't he?'

'I think so but I can send my man, Holloman down to make sure that he does, if you like?'

'Yes, pray do so,' said Hanley. 'That young man may be useful to us in the future. If he survives the war that is.'

Fitzroy smiled and nodded.

CHAPTER TWENTY-FIVE

England, Sunday July 29th, 1917

'No, I'm not going to the investiture. Why should I want to?'

Holloman took a deep breath.

'I would have thought seeing your brother get the VC from the King would have been reason enough,' he said.

Eddie pulled a face. 'That's Percy's medal, not mine. Why should I be bothered about it? Anyway, the squadron might not be in France, but we are operational. We'll already be one pilot down with Percy gallivanting off to the palace. I've a job to do here.'

'I know that,' said Holloman, using all the patience he had developed in the years of working for Fitzroy. 'But Major Proctor is happy to release you from your duties for a few hours. Surely you can see that it's important.'

'So is the defence of London. I'm the best pilot in the squadron, you know.'

Holloman wanted to scream. The young Grenville's inflated opinion of himself was the polar opposite of his brother. He wanted to slap him, tell him some home truths but knew that was not an option.

'I do understand that, lieutenant, so does Major Proctor but he has deemed this event important enough to sacrifice your presence for a few hours. He understands that it is not enough to be the best, you also have to be seen and known as that.'

'Why?' said Eddie. 'That doesn't make any sense.'

'Yes it does. Yes, you are the best and, yes, you are the one actually fighting for your country but you can't do it on your own can you?'

'Of course I can.'

'No, I'm afraid you can't. You need the support of everyone in the country to do what you do.'

'Do I?'

'Yes. Think about it. Firstly, you need your mechanics to prepare your machine, don't you? Before that you need people to build it in the first place, all the woodworkers in the factory, the metalworkers, the linen workers who weave the fabric, the women who sew it all together. You need the munition workers to make the bullets for the guns and the guns themselves will be made by thousands of others. All those workers need to be fed, they need the farmers and the land workers to put in the hours to get the crops sown, tended and harvested. You need the merchant seamen to risk the U-boats and the Atlantic storms to bring grain from Canada and beef from South America. You need all of those people behind you, lieutenant, simply to get you into the air to do your job.'

'I suppose so,' said Eddie sullenly. 'I still don't see why I have to attend this stupid, pointless ceremony.'

'It may seem stupid and pointless to you but it's not to those thousands who stand behind you. Those people will only continue to give their best if they believe we are right and that we are winning. They need that belief, it needs reinforcing, because this war has already been long yet there is no end in sight and the cost has been dreadfully high. Do you know what gives them that belief, lieutenant Grenville?'

Eddie shook his head.

'It's newspapers like the one I work for. We report the news, certainly but we also report on those men that are doing extraordinary things on their behalf, ones that inspire those thousands of workers to keep going, to keep trying. Men like your brother, like Ball, like you, in fact. These ordinary people need and want heroes they can look up to, they want to read about them, see pictures of them.'

Eddie nodded. 'Heroes like Ball, yes, I see that.'

'Yes, like Ball. Shame about him. His father's going to be collecting his VC from the King at the same ceremony as your brother. That's what is going to make this such a huge event,' said Holloman. 'That's why we need you there, so the public can see that there are live heroes out there ready to take over from the Ball's of this world.'

'Yes, yes, I can see that. Heroes, yes.'

'So you will be there?' Holloman thought he'd won but needed to check.

'Yes, of course I'll be there.' Eddie's eyes were now gleaming. 'The country needs it's heroes.'

Thank the Lord for that, thought Holloman.

*

Annie stood under the shade of an Elm, listening to the leaves whispering in the light breeze. She was watching the street and the entrance to the small park in the centre of the square. It felt like everyone was watching her, that it was obvious that she didn't belong. Of course, what she was doing was not illegal but it was alien to her. It felt more than a little underhand.

This was the third time she had been here this week. She wondered how many other spies had to fit their watching around their shifts. Two days before she had only been able to stay an hour before she had had to return to the hospital. Today, though, she was not on duty until the evening and, this time, she was determined to succeed.

In fact she only had to wait about thirty minutes. The small procession she spotted was just what she expected, two women, one in a smart black uniform pushing a pram, the other also in black, walking alongside carrying a parasol to shield herself from the hot July sun.

Alice, her son and his nanny heading for the park. This was just the scenario she had hoped for. As they reached the entrance to the park, Annie stepped out from behind the tree.

'Hello,' she said.

'Why, Annie!' exclaimed Alice. 'What on earth are you doing here? How simply wonderful to see you.'

Annie leant over the pram. The boy was plump, blonde and pink cheeked and was sleeping soundly. 'He's gorgeous. Is he a good boy?'

'He's wonderful. Even at 2am when he's demanding a feed,' said Alice.

'I thought you'd have a wet nurse for that,' Annie said automatically, and immediately regretted it, particularly the way she'd delivered the words. Fortunately, Alice seemed not to have noticed.

'Mother say's I should, of course. She says it's beneath me and that I'm ruining my figure but,' she paused and caressed the sleeping infant's cheek. 'I just can't trust him to anyone else, he's all I have left of Siggi. Well, I trust him with Spence, of course,' she smiled at the nanny who was gently rocking the pram. 'She's a jewel.' She looked up at Annie. 'So where have you been? Why have you been such a stranger? You were waiting for us here, weren't you?'

Annie nodded.

'Why didn't you come to the house? I wrote and told you I was coming up to London for the investiture, didn't you get the letter?'

'Yes, I got it,' said Annie. 'I just didn't want to come to the house.'

'But why? Ah, mother.'

'Exactly. She and I don't exactly see eye-to-eye,' said Annie.

'Sorry about that, I didn't think. Though we would have seen each other tomorrow of course.'

That confirmed it, Annie thought, she doesn't know.

'I'm not coming,' she said.

'Why not? Percy must have invited you, surely?'

'He did but we're no longer seeing each other.'

Alice looked aghast. 'Oh no! What on earth happened? You were the best thing to happen to him in years. Was it your choice or his?'

'His.'

'Well he's a bloody fool then.' Alice glanced at the nanny. 'You never heard me swear, did you Spence?'

'No, Mrs Von Leittner,' said Spence.

'Good girl. So what got into him?' Alice frowned.

'When did you last see him?'

'Not for a while. Perhaps six or seven weeks. I've been stuck down in Hampshire and he doesn't seem too keen on babies.'

'Then you haven't seen what a state he's got into.' Annie looked around. 'Is there somewhere less public we can talk?'

'Of course. Mother is in town today so we can go back to the house. Spence can give young Siggi his promenade on her own today. Follow me.'

*

Alice sighed. 'I hadn't realised things had got so bad,' she said. She had listened in silence whilst Annie had explained her worries about Percy, though, of course, omitting one key fact.

'It was as soon as he was put under pressure. It brought back the problems he'd had when he came back from France.'

'I'd been so focussed on my boy I never even thought about Percy – or Eddie for that matter. I mean, I know flying is dangerous but I thought whilst they were in England they were alright.'

'You weren't to know. And you certainly had enough on your plate.'

'He won't give up flying, he's said that, it's his duty,' said Alice. 'But that stupid politicking. That's a damned fool idea. Why doesn't he stop that?'

'That was what he'd agreed to do,' said Annie. 'But then he went back on it.'

'Is that what you argued about?'

Annie shook her head. 'No. In fact, the truth is we never argued at all.'

'Pardon? So why…?'

'It doesn't matter,' said Annie quickly. 'I don't care about us. I care about him. You're my last hope. Can you talk to him?'

'Me? Why would he listen to me? You said yourself that you'd talked to him and he'd agreed. Why did he change his mind?'

'I don't know,' said Annie.

Alice stared at her. 'You're a terrible liar, Annie Ross,' she said. 'You do know, don't you?'

'What does it matter if I do?' said Annie. 'All that's important is that you get him to change his mind.'

Alice continued to stare. 'You're not together. Why do you care?'

Annie gave a mirthless laugh. 'Why do you think?'

Alice nodded. 'I know,' she said. 'But I still don't see what I can do if you won't tell me why he did it.'

'I'm sorry, I just can't.'

'Did he take a long time deciding?'

'No. At breakfast he was going to give it up. After lunch he wasn't.'

Alice frowned. 'Was this the same point when he ended things with you?'

'Yes,' said Annie.

'Did he see someone? He did, didn't he, I can see it in your face. Who was it? Tell me, Annie, I know that there has to be someone else involved, who was it? You might as well tell me, I'll find out one way or another.'

Annie swallowed. This was going wrong, she was losing control of this. She should have expected it, Alice was astute, strong-minded and intelligent, she was bound to ask questions, why hadn't she known that this would go this way? She only wanted Alice to talk to him, in the hope that the family relationship would overcome what Hanley and Fitzroy had on him. The last thing she wanted was to shatter the world of her friend, and this felt like this was where it was heading. She was committed to this now though.

'Hanley,' she said. 'He met with Lord Hanley.'

'Hanley?' Alice scowled. 'I might have known. Even so, Percy is stubborn. Once he's made his mind up on something there's normally no shifting him. You must have seen that?'

'Yes, of course.'

'I mean, you're a case in point,' Alice went on. 'You should have heard the arguments he had with mother over you.' Alice gave a little smile. 'She was furious but Percy just dug his heels in and said he was old enough to make his own decisions. That's what makes all of this so strange, giving you up so abruptly particularly, let alone changing his mind on the politics. That's not like him at all.'

'As I said, he's not himself,' said Annie. 'He's not thinking straight.'

Alice shook her head. 'There has to be more to it than that,' she said.

'No, I don't think –'

'Hanley must have been able to put pressure on Percy for some reason. So what is it?' She stared at Annie. 'What does Hanley know about Percy?'

Annie opened her mouth, then closed it again. She couldn't risk saying anything.

Alice continued to stare. And then, to Annie's horror, she saw the truth dawn.

'Oh God. Oh my God! That thing that Eddie said. Percy denied it but it's true, isn't it? Oh God, no, no, no!'

She got to her feet, clearly distraught. Annie rose herself.

'Percy wasn't well, he wasn't in his right mind,' she said. 'You have to see that.' She put her arm around Alice but she angrily through it off.

'Don't defend him!' Alice screamed. 'Don't you dare! And you, you knew, didn't you? You damn well knew.'

'Yes, I did.'

'How long? How long have you known?'

'A long time. Before I met you. I'm sorry, I'm so sorry.'

'I don't believe it! How could you? He killed my husband, didn't he?'

Annie nodded.

'In cold blood. He murdered my husband, didn't he?'

'Yes, but…'

'That's why he's so strange around me, why he can't bear to even look at his nephew?'

Annie nodded again.

'And you love him? How can you, he's sick. How can you bear to be with him?' Alice was crying now. 'Get out! Get out of this house. I never, ever want to see you again.'

Crying herself, Annie dashed out of the room and into the street.

CHAPTER TWENTY-SIX

England, Sunday July 29th, 1917

Percy sat in his study, staring at his service revolver on the table in front of him. It was a weapon he had fired just once.

He would never forget that moment, the report, the red flash that lit up Siggi's face, Siggi's expression – shock, disbelief, betrayal – were all indelibly printed on his memory. The images came back to him time and time again, both awake and in sleep. Siggi, blonde-haired, blue-eyed, honest, innocent, trusting, loyal.

His friend.

He sighed and reached for it. Everything had to look at its best for the King. It needed to be cleaned.

It was fitting that he'd be carrying his gun when he received the medal. Both would be a reminder of his shame.

His thoughts were interrupted by the door opening.

'Is your room all right, Eddie?' he said without looking up. 'Has Mrs Mackenzie given you everything you need?'

'Yes,' Eddie muttered, slumping into one of the chairs. 'I still don't see why I had to come here tonight. The morning would have done. What if the Zeppelins come over? I'll damn well miss the chance to have a crack at one then.'

Percy sighed. 'I thought we'd gone over this. Proctor thinks it's unlikely they will come over until the nights get a bit longer and, with the war on, there's no guarantee that the trains will run on time. It's best if you're here already.'

Eddie just grunted a reply. He picked up the newspaper and

flicked noisily through it.

Percy was too weary to say anything more. Eddie was so awkward these days, very different, always on edge, a bad-tempered bundle of nervous energy, quick to fly off the handle. He was not the brother he recognised, the boy he had known pre-war. Annie said he wasn't right and she was spot on, he could see that now. It was too late now, too late to listen to her, too late to have a future with her.

He went back to cleaning his gun.

There was a knock on the front door. It continued, loud and insistent.

'Who the devil's that?' said Eddie. 'I'm trying to damn well read here.'

'Calm down, Eddie,' said Percy. 'Mrs Mackenzie will see who it is.'

'Yes, and send them packing.'

He heard the door open, muffled voices and then Mrs Mackenzie say, 'No, wait, where do you think you're going?' before the study door was flung open.

It was Annie.

'Percy, I need to speak to you, please!' she said. She looked distraught, her eyes red, hair astray.

'I'm sorry, sir,' said the housekeeper. 'She pushed me out of the way. Shall I call the police?'

Percy stood up. 'No, Mrs Mackenzie, there's no need for that. Annie, would you like some tea?'

'No, no, I don't want anything. Oh, Percy, I'm sorry, I've done something awful. I need to speak to you. Please don't send me away.'

'Of course I won't,' said Percy. 'That will be all for this evening, Mrs Mackenzie.'

'Very well, sir,' said the housekeeper, giving Annie a cold stare before leaving, closing the door behind her.

'Now Annie, what is it? Come and sit down. I've never seen you in a state like this.' He led her to the chair he had just vacated. 'You look like you could do with a drink? Brandy?'

'No, I don't want anything. I've just got to tell you what I've done. It wasn't on purpose, I thought I was doing right, I thought I could help.' He saw her look across the room at Eddie. 'I'd prefer to talk with you alone though,' she added.

'I've got more right to be in my brother's flat than you have,' Eddie said, without looking up from his paper.

'Eddie, please,' said Percy.

'Why should I?'

'Oh never mind,' said Annie. 'He knows anyway, after all, he told me. About Siggi I mean.' She took a deep breath. 'Percy, I'm sorry, Alice knows now as well. I wasn't going to tell her, I didn't mean to, I was just trying to get her to talk to you, to convince you to give up politics but she guessed. Oh God, Percy, she guessed what Hanley had on you and, once she had, I couldn't lie to her. I'm sorry, my love, I'm so sorry.'

Percy had dreaded this moment. It was the one that had haunted him but, now it had happened, he was surprised at his reaction. It was actually a relief, like a great weight had been lifted off his shoulders.

He pulled Annie to her feet and took her in his arms.

'It's all right,' he said, kissing the top of her head. 'It's for the best, I'm glad she knows at last. How is she?'

'How do you think she is?' Annie's voice was muffled. 'She's very upset and angry, very angry. It's horrible, totally horrible and it's all my fault.'

'Of course it's not your fault, how could it be? All this is my doing. It was me who shot Siggi.'

'But...'

'But nothing. This is for the best. I wish I could have spared Alice this but, now she knows, I can do the right thing.'

Annie pulled away from the embrace. 'What do you mean?' He saw her look at the gun on the table.

He smiled and shook his head. 'Not that,' he said. 'I'd never do that, that's the coward's way. No, I'm going to do what I should have done from the start, tell the truth. I'll go to the authorities, admit my guilt, refuse the medal and resign my commission.'

Suddenly, Eddie was on his feet. 'No!' he yelled. 'No, you can't! That's all wrong.'

'Eddie, it's not,' said Percy. 'It's the only way.'

'No!' yelled Eddie again. He walked aggressively over to Annie. 'This is your doing! Yours, you interfering bitch, look what you've done now.'

Percy grabbed hold of Eddie's arm and pulled him away. 'That's enough,' he said. 'Don't talk to Annie like that.'

'Why shouldn't I? She's a nothing, a nobody.'

'She's the woman I'm going to spend my life with – if she'll have me.'

Annie looked surprised. 'Of course I'll have you, but I thought...'

'There's no reason to give you up now. I only did it because of

Hanley.'

'I know,' she said.

Eddie shook his head furiously. 'No, no, no, you're a bloody idiot, Percy. This can't happen, it can't.' He stomped out of the room, slamming the door behind him.

Annie put her arms around Percy. 'Oh, my love, I'm sorry. I didn't want to come between you two.'

'You haven't. He'll calm down, you'll see,' said Percy. 'You really want to be with me? Life is going to be very hard from now on.'

'I love you,' she said. 'I don't care.'

'As long as you're sure.'

'I am.'

He kissed her. 'Can you stay tonight?'

'I'd love to,' she said. 'I'm on duty though. I really shouldn't let them down. Still...'

'No, you're right. Duty comes first. I'll be all right. I've got a big day tomorrow, I'll go and see the authorities first thing. First though, I'll go and see Alice. I owe her that. I'll do it tonight.'

Annie nodded.

'This is as bad as it's going to get,' she said. 'Things will only get better from now on.'

Percy nodded and kissed her.

'Yes, this is as bad as it's going to get,' he said.

EPILOGUE

He hears the woman leave. Good, that's what he needs.

When he hears Percy come up to his room he goes out of his. He only has a few minutes.

To win a war you need to be ruthless, he knows that. You need to do the right thing. Siggi was a good man but he was the enemy. Percy did the right thing; if he had let Siggi escape he would have killed more of our pilots.

Percy had done the right thing. Now he was doing the wrong thing. Yes, he didn't deserve the VC, he wasn't a real hero like Ball but, to the man in the street, stuck in the trenches, working in the fields or in the factories, he was, they didn't know any better. To them Percy was a hero.

This country needs heroes.

Percy was going to hurt his country, he could not allow that to happen.

There was an alternative. If he suffered an accident, a tragic, careless accident, witnessed by a close family member, then his reputation would be intact. He would stay a hero.

He hears Percy come out of his room, he'll be going out, starting the sequence of events that will lead to disaster and disgrace.

He picks up the service revolver from the table, puts a bullet into the magazine, rotates it into the chamber and walks out into the hallway with it in his hand.

He does his duty.

Made in the USA
Columbia, SC
19 April 2025

56853064R00269